KILLERS UPON HULL

A TALE OF SECRETS, LOVE AND MURDER IN THE 1890s

KILLERS UPON HULL

A TALE OF SECRETS, LOVE AND MURDER IN THE 1890s

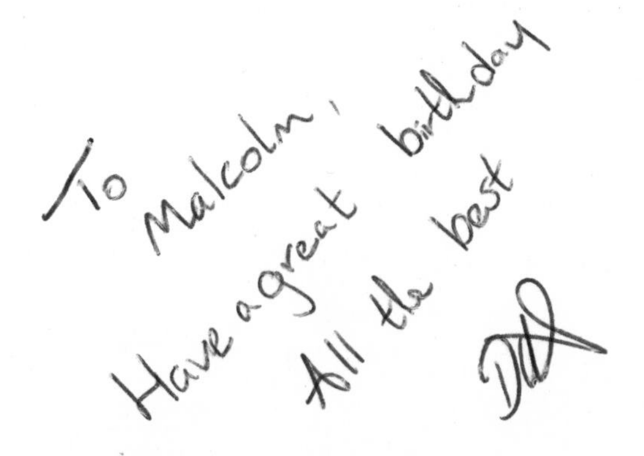

DANNY RADFORD

Published in paperback in 2021 by Sixth Element Publishing
on behalf of Danny Radford

Sixth Element Publishing
Arthur Robinson House
13-14 The Green
Billingham TS23 1EU
www.6epublishing.net

ISBN 978-1-914170-11-9

British Library Cataloguing in Publication Data. A catalogue record for this book is available from the British Library.

Printed in Great Britain.

"We are each our own devil,
and we make this world our hell..."

"No man is rich enough to buy back his past..."

Oscar Fingal O'Flahertie Wills Wilde

CHAPTER 1

Beethoven was a genius.

It's simply inconceivable to think of him in any other way.

The opportunity must be made at any given time to embrace his melodic tunes.

If I were to make a recommendation to any player on which he was to try and recite the deliciousness of audio set by Ludwig himself I would suggest Piano Sonata No. 8 in C minor, Op 13 'Pathetique'.

From the beginning of the score to the end, I close my eyes every time, visualising flowing fluid, no faster than an idling cloud. With the higher keys as droplets in a dream, making waves only to be disturbed by the next note creating a sense of symmetry perfectly matched.

Then as you are led to believe the whole picture is set, a change and the whole idea becomes something anew. Another type of divine. Albeit a more sinister sound with darker hidden depths but gorgeousness incarnate. You are taken to layers you never knew were there. Mixtures you had no idea existed. Then settled once again with the original melodic flow.

I myself am not a genius but when the stage has been laid and the actors all in place, then I make 'murder' my Piano Sonata.

First comes the unstoppable flow, the droplets that each individually disturb the next, then the change in pace with a sinister note and finally the calm when all is reassuringly back to how it previously was, however with a residual sense of completion, knowing you heard the angels themselves during the course of the tunes and tribulations.

The police are not a fan of my music so I must often change

my tune. I relish in the scores that I leave for them. Strewn across the rooms that are transformed into demonic canvases.

It is not purposely so they can obtain my whereabouts and cease my dedication to the attempt of making angels sing and tulips hum. No, this is simply not the case.

I leave with a glowing sensation behind me that they can appreciate what I do and know it is I that made these wonders.

I am not so careless as the much talked about 'Jack the Ripper'. If only they knew the truth, but that is neither here nor there.

His work to me simply reeks of mess. Of vulgar rush that you would expect in a dimly-lit backstreet tavern. No class, style or subtlety in its plebeian simplicity. The work of an overzealous abattoir worker unsatisfied with the cuts of his day's work so he decides to take it to the whores of foggy London or perhaps a sign left by a Masonic madman sending warnings via internal organs. Either way, the artistry remains commonly uncouth.

So far, my music has not been made totally public. It is still well within its infancy. My hand becomes steadier with each given opportunity but I feel one day I shall have my masterpieces admired for all to see. In awe of my achievements, people will see my name, not knowing how this kind of chaotic collide can create such wonder yet be envied with the vision I possess.

I now tally six works of art, seven if you count the unborn child inside the woman I laid bare with my blade as she sang so beautifully, but I however do not.

An 'unborn' has no knowledge or appreciation of the depth of my chores. My undivided dedication to the details.

I have secured myself with the greats already but my work is far from complete and until the universe is satisfied with my achievements, then I shall continue to do great things.

CHAPTER 2

Some people dream of flying. Not him.

Always falling.

From a height that it would be impossible to survive.

As he falls, he falls past ledges with people's faces, all chalk white, ghostly and judgmental. A stark contrast to the grey rocks littered with moss.

They are faces he knows all too well.

Faces that visit him late in the lost hours of the morning.

Faces that once knew his own, as it was the last beguiling malevolence they ever saw of the world.

He had made sure of it. As their dying breath was taken, he stared right into their eyes. So that they would recognise him in the circles of Hell when his own time came.

Although Hell seemed an exaggerated concept, he wanted to hedge his bets. He also wanted them to realise the pleasure he had from ending their sick and unjustified existence.

One and all, they were the faces of people that morally deserved to burn for a long time. But it had never stopped them from haunting his dreams as he fell.

Somewhere near the bottom, empty ledges on the cliffs were stacked.

Missing faces that he knew he would put there before his time to eject from this mortal coil.

He didn't know 'who' they were or why they would qualify but he knew he had more work to complete.

It was however different this time. The dream was the same, but something was seemed unfamiliar.

This time upon landing, he fell into water.

In his ears, he heard the rush but then a stop of silence as the abyss of fluid rose around him and sucked him under. He wasn't scared. He longed for it. It felt right. His mouth flooded. He could feel the cool refreshing intoxication as it filled him with the much-needed spirit of life but inevitably bringing death.

•

His eyes shot open and he didn't feel refreshed at all.

The roof of his mouth felt like a worn piece of rug that had lost its tread a few decades ago. It was his body's way of telling him that he needed liquid.

The room spun. The previous night had clearly warranted this feeling. The feeling like his head had been put on a stretching rack and pulled until 'alcohol' had decided he had suffered enough and that he couldn't take any more punishment.

Details were translucent and sketchy. He knew a worn-down tavern and a half-undignified wench were involved but how much was in excess? He didn't know. It would probably come back to him later in small gut churning, fleeting visions.

He sat up in his dirty sheets, surveying and amazed he'd made it back to his lodgings, but here he was.

A stumble and shaky line made for the sink and his head was under the tap, guzzling greedily, trying to make up for lost fluids.

It was a surprise the tap worked as running water had only recently been fitted to these areas of the slum in the new-forming 'city to be'.

He opened his eyes as the water began to rasp through the brass tap and he noticed the colour. Distinctly brown with a smell worse than his 'morning after' breath of tobacco and cheap spirits.

Instantly he pulled back. It was too late to bring the rancid substance back up and in any case, the fluid was essential if his headache was to be cleared.

He doubled over coughing, trying to rid the atrocious taste. Next to the sink, his slop bucket was full of a collection of bodily excretions he could not remember depositing. Smart thinking not to have vomited in to the sink as the drainage system was never as guaranteed as the bucket.

Standing up straight, his back cracked. For a man of a relatively young age, the noise sounded worrying. The air in the room was stale and dust floated freely with no direction. His nose was congested, which made his breathing laboured, even more so from an old injury of a broken nose.

He opened the window, secretly hoping for a blissful Babylon of bright blue skies, beaches filled with joyous masses and a view only obscured by palm trees bustling in the breeze blown in from the crystal-clear ocean.

'No such luck this time,' he thought, just dirt, dung and houses which stood too close together to achieve a view of any kind.

No, the view was only a vertical one below to see horses clatter down the old road, led by men in tattered clothes with sullen eyes, rich in unemployment.

An attempt at a deep breathe did little to refresh him. He picked up the slop bucket and emptied it out of the window.

Directly below a horse reared as the slop landed a foot or two away. He allowed himself a wry smile as he sat on the edge of his bed, taking in the flash of memories from last night. He decided the best thing he could do would be to light a cigarette and gather himself as carefully as chunks of broken glass pieced back together.

As he lit it with a couple of sulphur-tipped matches, taking two drags and instantly exhaling, he assumed this would probably be about the sum of what he would achieve this day so finally he took a long drag.

As the burn reached the back of his throat, a loud knock forced him to cough repeatedly in his startled agitation.

He wasn't expecting company and it was as welcome as another gulp of the questionable unhygienic tap water.

CHAPTER 3

He dashed out the freshly-lit cigarette and staggered his way to the door, wearing only his trousers and tattered off-white vest from the previous evening's antics, braces flapping.

He opened the door to a smartly-dressed gentleman sporting a top hat so immaculate that you could shave in it under the glossy gleam in the right kind of light, the suit he was wearing suggesting an obvious mass of accumulated wealth.

"Good afternoon, sir," the gentleman said. "Do I have the pleasure of addressing a Mr Stephen Howes?"

The two men on the opposite sides of the threshold could not have been further apart in social standing or dignified manner.

Stephen was giving off the impression that death's own touch could not do much more damage, yet still managed to maintain a look of handsome features if not a little worn. His eyes hazel and curious, however, in an obscure contrast they were blood-shot through squalor and ill-living. His frame was solid but, perhaps again like his hair, slightly unkept.

It took Stephen a few seconds to take in the contrast of damp walls that smelled of wood left out in the rain for too long, rotting door frames and worn floor in comparison to the appearance of the gentleman that stood before him as he swung the door wide, breaking the silence with unattended hinges.

A variation of scenarios and probabilities ran through Stephen's mind as to 'why' this gentleman would be here. Although the man was dressed for the occasion, Stephen doubted the vision of refined upper class had gotten lost on the way to the theatre and stopped at his door for directions.

Even though his attire was impeccable, his face showed

signs of a deep sadness. Doom had followed this well-dressed individual for a long time and the closest of shaves or the finest trim of whiskers could not hide the obvious.

Stephen recognised those dark rings under the gloomy grey eyes. The slight redness of the whites, the sunken shoulders attempting to appear rigid for the occasion. This man had suffered loss on a grand scale.

Stephen could have registered this, not only through the appearance, but also because it was the reason why most people like this 'well to do' darkened the entrance to his abode.

Clearing his throat, and in a tone that must have seemed mocking, due to his physical appearance, had it not been a natural way of speech for him, Stephen replied, "You do indeed. How may I be of assistance to you, sir?"

"Ah, my name is Craven Wilkinson and I was wondering if I may come in?"

"By all means. Please excuse the mess. I was unaware I would be expecting a visitor or I might have made the room a little more… accommodating."

"Not to worry, Mr Howes. Judging by the mixture in the bucket that you recently emptied out of the window that caused the horse of my carriage to rear, I doubt your activities last night were that of a 'spring clean'?"

"Indeed… please take a seat. I would offer a beverage but it would appear I am scarce of resources."

"Thank you all the same."

Craven Wilkinson shifted across the room, heavily dependent on the cane he leaned upon. The light coming through the window caught his hat and made a brilliant white stripe vertically, as Stephen took in his details. Wilkinson was once a tall man. Without the stoop on the cane he would have stood a good six feet. His suit was new but it was doubtful that it had been bought for this meeting. The wedding ring on his finger was old and worn, fitting tightly. Howes guessed it had not been expanded because of some former memories tied to the band, as if adding any width to it would dissolve some of the ring's relevant symbolism.

Stephen knew already that this was where the sadness came from and where his next pay check may come in.

"Am I to presume you are Stephen Howes, the Private Investigator?"

"You presume correctly."

"Then I am also to presume that you are currently not occupied in any investigations?"

"With presumptions like that, Mr Wilkinson, you should be an investigator yourself."

Craven Wilkinson chuckled. "Oh no, Mr Howes, I am afraid I would never have the stomach for it. It would seem after asking around, your talents suit the kind of job that I need doing perfectly. Talents, I hear, that are total dedication, results and the ability to cross lines if the price is right..."

"I see you have done your homework, but I don't like to commit with any surprises that may occur, Mr Wilkinson, so why don't you explain what it is you need from a man with 'my talents' as you so put it."

As Stephen struck another couple of matches to light a new cigarette, the room seemed to take a sudden chill, a drop of temperature that could be contributed to the sun shifting behind the rapid moving clouds dimming Craven Wilkinson's hat a little. Or it could also have been contributed to the unknown course Stephen Howes' life would take from that very moment onwards.

CHAPTER 4

Stephen stepped from the train with only the slightest hesitation at the journey he was about to embark upon. He had spent four days in a small village just outside of Kingston-upon-Hull, close to the East coast.

The reasons being to prepare himself for this job in an essential way and the much-needed chore of sobering and cleaning himself up. His arrival up to this point was a blur and for that he was grateful.

Whilst residing in a small inn with a friendly landlady overflowing with mothering abilities, he had made the decision to procure an arrangement of respectable clothes. Everything made to measure and of a high quality. These would be needed for the very first elements of the 'deception'.

At a little over six feet tall and broad shoulders, Stephen Howes could be one to stand out in a crowd but the extra expense charged by the tailor based on the size of the suits mattered little to him. Craven Wilkinson had set him up with more than enough currency to see him living very well for the assignment. Deciding not to capitalise on this and spoil himself with luxury, Stephen purchased a local Hull newspaper dated 15th of October 1890. He hadn't realised that he'd missed his birthday only days before, but it was certainly the last thing on his mind of late. Right now, he needed to seek lodgings of a moderate standard. The hotel attached to the train station took his fancy but his experience told him that a constantly manned lobby entrance was not always a good thing. Not for Stephen in any case.

The streets bustled and the contrast in people was from one extreme to the next. In the distance, to his right he saw signs for the dockyard, with a clearly audible bell from time to time coming from the ships. He noticed the hats of the men seemed to grow increasingly tattered the closer the people were to the dock area. To his left, the theatres stood proudly.

He'd left his baggage at the station, deciding he would send for it as soon as lodgings had been acquired.

A hansom idled close by and, not knowing the area in detail, he approached and enquired as to its hire.

"Notta problem, pal," the driver said. "Jump in an' I'll get ya there."

At such an early hour of the morning, the smell of alcohol that lingered in the carriage was an unwelcome sensation, but it was a thing he would have to become used to.

He knew Hull was known for fish, fighting, ale, blood and crime. Elements he was no stranger to, except for perhaps the fish, but it was part of the culture more than any of the other aspects.

Ambling down the busy, clattering streets, loud with the hum of trade, he tried to lean out of the window, not only for fresh air but also to take in the area. Market stalls with vocal tradesman gave contrast and colour to the curbed, slim streets. Tattered men stumbled to or from work whilst keeping their hats low, unwilling to make conversation. Women stood in groups of two or three, talking enough for everyone, and a solitary policeman kept an eye over all occurring.

In no time at all, Stephen reached his destination, which was a blessing as it had given him no time to work up his nerves. To think too much about what could go wrong.

Stepping out on the narrow cobbled road of Parliament Street, he took one last deep breath before well and truly diving in at the deep end and entering the solid, looming building sporting thick slabbed bricks, barred windows and a dauntingly heavy wooden door that gave all the impressions of a prison.

CHAPTER 5

Approaching the front desk, he smiled and said cheerfully, "Good morning, my name is Stephen Howes. I was wondering if you could point me in the direction of Chief Inspector Rudyard."

"Yes certainly, sir," the desk clerk said. "May I ask what it is concerning and if it is worth me disturbing the CI? We are very busy and I doubt he would take to time wasters." The clerk gave Stephen a look up and down as if to say 'that is exactly what you are' whilst leaning forward on one arm, keeping his pen poised in the other hand.

The small in height but wide in diameter desk clerk had been quite clearly left as a desk clerk for a reason. At face value, he seemed wholeheartedly to believe in his own self-importance. But Stephen recognised authoritative figures with ease and this man was clearly barrelled up on behalf of visitors, with an air of cocksure arrogance that was annoying and slightly within the realms of the comical.

Turning as if to try and shift his over-exaggerated mass, giving a huff as though Stephen had disturbed his entire morning, the desk clerk was halted mid-turn by a tall but thick set elderly man with glasses who appeared from behind swing doors, holding his hand out to shake Stephen's.

The man spoke in a refined but jovial manner for his appearance, a type who would be easy to warm to, but one not to cross. "Detective Howes? We have been expecting you, young man. I've just arrived myself. May I be the first in the offices to welcome you to our debatably glorious, ever-growing town of Hull. Kingston-upon-Hull, if we are splitting hairs." The look of joviality didn't leave his face. "My name is Chief Inspector

Rudyard and if you should have any troubles, you come to me first. Your papers arrived on my desk two days ago, with an element of mystery, and considering these are the Police Head Quarters of this area, mystery is usually an unwelcome visitor. However, the accompanying letter explaining that you were to assist in any local crimes of brutality, or worse, will be nothing but welcomed by our fair squadron. Here, let me take you through and introduce you to them. Have you any questions before we do?"

Without giving Stephen time to answer, the desk clerk had a question of his own that took priority over everyone. "Ah, sir? I was not made aware that we were to be expecting another detective. Should I not have been informed?"

CI Rudyard looked at the desk clerk with annoyance, tilted his head forward and moved his small, round glasses forward so he could get a look without the barrier of spectacle lens, before he could say anything, he seemed to change his mind as if to give up on a lost cause. Turning to Stephen, he said, "Don't mind Desk Sergeant Alan. He seems to have illusions of grandeur that may one day come to fruition if he can learn to deflate himself during any kind of conversation. We keep him out here because it's the only desk that can support his ego."

Stephen had seen a thousand 'Sergeant Alans' before and, in positions of power or authority, they were dangers to themselves and others.

The comments were instantly justified as Desk Sergeant Alan turned back to his notes and said, "Right you are, as you were, gentlemen."

Almost synchronised, Stephen Howes and CI Rudyard shook their heads and, without any further comment, walked through the waist-high double swing doors with Rudyard leading the way.

Walking into a busy squad room, Rudyard wasted no time in announcing, "Gentlemen, this is Detective Stephen Howes who I told you about. He will be joining us from a special nationwide unit put together to try and capture a killer that is believed to be in and around our area, someone so cunning who we may not have even picked up on yet. Please give any assistance to Detective

Howes. I'm sure with his knowledge and expertise, he may even be able to clear up a few of our own mysteries."

And that was it…

The complete fabrication and forgery that Craven Wilkinson had suggested and set up, claiming that Stephen was part of an 'out of town' special branch had taken less than fifteen minutes to become gospel. The self-belief pep talks and 'quick practised answers' in case anything had turned sour quickly, were not needed, neither were the cold sweats or sleepless nights.

He had been welcomed and had to stifle a thought… no wonder the killer had evaded detection if this was how easy it was to infiltrate the police force under false pretences.

Stephen had fabricated the documentation that had been sent to the East Yorkshire branch. He had to admit after replicating emblems and forging names, it looked genuine enough but a simple return address meant any correspondence would be replied to every time by a preset-up source and no further requests or actions were needed.

When the job was over, he had half a mind to continue the charade and even see about claiming pay but, as Craven had told him, if he completed the grim request that was required, he would have no need to work again. With what Stephen had been through to get to this point, he didn't want to have to ever live through such high risks again and only wealth could ensure that.

He would become a higher member of society with all the gold promised. Although it was a high amount indeed, it came at a cost, namely personal danger and the manner of the job. 'Danger money' of the greatest stakes and that was even before he had got to this moment.

Craven had insisted Stephen be paid with gold and if he was to travel and needed any expenses, he would also use the same currency. It was a time-honoured trade value and no matter where you were, it was accepted.

"Detective Howes?" Rudyard said. "Would you like to say a few words…?"

CHAPTER 6

"Right... thank you, Chief Inspector." Stephen was taken aback, unaware that an opening speech would be required but he knew he had to say something.

Cautious eyes stared blankly at this newcomer who was now halted in a very rare moment of nerves. He looked around the room, trying not to focus on anyone. Instead he saw the discoloured walls, not unlike the river Humber, murky brown, the careless filing systems scattered here, there and everywhere, the small handguns in their holsters near each detective's desk as though they were kids' toys left out due to laziness.

What was he doing? Was he utterly insane? How did he ever agree to any of this situation?

Stephen had to make this look convincing and, being practically assaulted by the stale smoke hanging in the work area air, he cleared his throat and began. "My main objective here, gentleman, is to find a killer that my HQ believes is now operating in your area. He is as dangerous as they come and, before anyone questions it, he is not Jack the Ripper. The Ripper had a way he liked to kill and his crimes were easily recognisable due to their brutality."

With the response of silence and confused look from his audience, he continued. "Our killer, however, does not relish in leaving clues to goad the police so he can eventually gloat in his murders like more of his kind. He believes he has a purpose so he will want to remain at large for quite some time, so we are led to believe."

His next statement would certainly arouse some form of response as it asked them to do the exact opposite of what they were doing now.

"Now I would like to ask you all… I know I have only just arrived but this killer might have been operating for a few months, maybe years… so I ask that if you have unsolved murders that seem extreme in how they were carried out, or something particularly gruesome over the last few weeks, I'd like to hear about them. In return, if any of you have any cases that you require assistance with, I will do what I can to help you."

Although Stephen had heard scoffs at his request for assistance, his offer to help the others out in return seemed to sway his newfound work colleagues back into his favour.

No longer did they stare in contempt.

Looking round the room, he saw five detectives of all shapes and sizes. He'd worked with all of their types before.

A half-dozing detective at his desk with feet up and hands behind his head.

A tall fellow with his hands in cabinet, browsing through files which Howes was guessing only happened when a supervisor was present.

A thin gentleman with trimmed facial hair and glasses that made him look as bright eyed and bushy tailed as a spring rabbit on the moors.

A short bulk of a man with menacing features, both rock-sized hands clasped in front of him on the desk obviously 'sizing' Stephen up. And the final of the elite, sitting behind a spotless desk with no clutter save for an origami swan and the shell of a tortoise.

Stephen would surely find out if they were capable as a collective or to help assist in the catching of his murderer.

It seemed before he could even begin his own search, Stephen would be tested for his commitment, effective immediately.

No sooner had he begun his short and unprepared speech, CI Rudyard had slipped away to a sectioned off back office. His own office was all that Stephen could guess.

Returning with a piece of paper in his hand, Rudyard walked

directly to the tall detective with his hands in the filing cabinet, who had once again began rummaging intently as he noticed the Chief Inspector making a bee line for him.

"Flint, early start for you it seems. Shooting down at The Old Bush pub. If he is as good as his word, take Detective Howes with you. It will give you both chance to get acquainted and help Howes familiarise himself with the town."

Flint looked deflated. As if his appearance to look busy had been well and truly rumbled.

He took the report from Rudyard with a muttered word and taking his coat from the stand, looked back at Stephen with the face of a scolded child and said as gloomily as he could muster, "Guess we better make a start then?"

CHAPTER 7

"No need for a carriage. The pub's only a short walk."

Stephen nodded and fell into step with Detective Flint. "I guess you'll have to improve your 'looking busy' skills?"

Flint looked with a side glance, seemingly cheered now he was out under the cloud-filled sky and laughed as he stopped to let a horse and cart pass in front of them.

As the cart rolled past, heavily and cumbersome, Stephen was surrounded by the overpowering smell of coal. A group of young scruffs were picking lumps of coal one at a time from the back of the cart, attempting to stuff as much as they could into their filthy pockets.

Flint let out an, "Oi!" as he made a half-hearted kick towards the nearest of the bunch without even taking his hands out of his pockets.

The delinquent had caught sight of Flint before he had made his move and managed to dodge the offending policeman's boot. The coal carriage robbers knew the game was up and scattered in different directions.

"Much obliged, mate," was heard from the flyblown man that led the carriage, and Flint resumed his course.

"Do you know much about round here then, errrrr…?" Flint asked casually.

"Stephen, no need to bother with the Mr Howes stuff when we are out of office, is there?"

"Okay, seems fair enough, Stephen."

"No, it's all fairly new to me. How long have you been here?"

"Me? Born and bred 'ere, mate, originally from the west of Hull. My old man was a fisherman and after eating that much fish,

I realised I had to do something different. I didn't fancy getting shouted at much so that was the army ruled out, something about the force seemed appealing so after a few years on the beat, I got my promotion about a year ago. Watch the shit."

Stephen had taken to the habit of watching people closely as they spoke. A lot can be derived from a person's facial expressions, however this did run the extra risk of trotting through waste in the dung-strewn streets. With Flint's warning, he managed to avoid an unpleasant shoe massacre.

They exited Parliament Street to the right and could see a busy dockside.

With only a scattering of boats anchored, a few temporary stalls had been set up by crew members on leave, attempting to offload foreign goods. This was a polar opposite to the permanancy of the buildings, businesses and boats all in need of vast repair.

"Well, as for a guided tour," Flint said, "this is the Queen's dock although as the rumour goes, not for much longer... big changes happening. It's like they're trying to make it cultured or summut. Word is that it's due to be closed and some sort of garden built, if you can believe it? Traders buy from the crew then transport it from here to the stalls so the rich don't have to risk coming away reeking of haddock if they want to do a bit of jewellery shopping. With boats from all over the world, the rich totty go mad for the trinkets."

Stephen stopped, took out his cigarette case, picked one and lit it.

Looking over the stalls and customers surrounding them, with an educated eye, he could already spot two pickpockets but he figured from their appearance that the people being lightened of their riches could deal with the financial loss more than the thief could deal with the starvation.

He had to keep in mind that this was not his area to protect from petty thieves. He wasn't even obliged to be helping with this 'shooting' that he and Flint were about to investigate, but he knew it was a 'necessity' to gain assistance at a later date and also to grasp a sense of how the local detectives operated. Also, this early on, he did not want to begin by refusing the promise he had just made.

Flint had kept walking and asked over his shoulder, "That's an odd baccy. What is it?"

Stephen had to think quickly. "Do you want to try one? It's from back home."

Flint dismissed the offer with a hand gesture. "Nah, might have to give chase in a bit and all that stuff will make me want to do is have a drink and a nice sit down in the pub."

They both shared a chuckle as they walked past another public house that advertised hotel lodgings above, and ahead was a steel bridge with a spider's web of framework.

The instant Stephen's foot touched the bridge, an overwhelming aroma offended his nostrils. It was the unmistakable smell of yeast.

Stephen held back a choke from the stench. It didn't seem to affect Flint.

Detective Flint's manner was that of a very laid back man and Stephen could not tell if he had at all smelled the same thing as himself.

"Detective Flint, can you not smell that?"

"What? Oh yeah, the yeast. It's from the Hovis factory. No, I can hardly smell anything. Keep meaning to go to the doctors about it but never get round to it."

As if to give credence to the issue, he gave a snort with his nose.

"Right, this is the place."

The high-sided building had modern brickwork, solid-looking features, arched windows for eyes and a door in between as the mouth that made the side entrance seem like the house was yawning, almost rousing itself for the day.

In big bold letters the hanging advertisement board read 'The Waterloo Tavern'. This raised the very first line of questioning and gave Stephen his very first mystery to solve of the day.

"I thought the chief said the place we were going to was The Old Bush?"

"I'll be honest…" began Flint as he stopped in front of two uniformed officers standing sentinel, obviously waiting for the detectives to show up and take over. "I haven't a clue about the name difference, something to do with weeds that grow here or something… just always been like that. It's been open a fair few years now and opens early for the dockers. Some people say it never shuts but if it keeps the trouble in here and not on the street, then it can stay open come rain or shine for me. The owner used to be a docker, rough as they come and known to be a bit heavy handed if the customers step out of line, so we'll keep the questions to the point for the time being."

Stephen gave a nod in understanding as the younger of the uniforms stepped forward and straightened himself out. Tall and thin, the young man seemed eager to impress. "Good morning, sirs."

"Morning, son. What we got here?"

"Well, as far as we can see, sir, one of the fishermen, local man, been in since the night before, went to the lavvy for a slash… I mean, err… to urinate and moments later, a shot was 'eard. Four other people in the pub at the time as well as the owner… a Mr Clive Mackie who says 'e came up from the cellar after 'e 'eard the shot, never 'eard the main door go so whoever did it, must still be in the pub. The other four all swear on the bible they never saw a thing. We've made a search of the building and can't find a weapon. Thought it best to keep 'em 'ere till you arrived, sir. They have all still been drinking since it happened so they are a little more forthcoming but still nothing to indicate who shot the victim."

Flint suddenly adopted a vocal authority especially for the 'uniforms', his career path from local bobby to detective was a big step and he intended to make the most of the rank. "Right, you lads better hang around in case it gets out of hand but let me and Detective Howes here do our job."

They pushed open the heavy oak door with frosted glass

panelling and were met by a cloud of tobacco smoke. Although it obstructed his visual assessment of the public house, Stephen was glad for the drowning out of the yeast smell.

A slight, bald man with a solid look from years of hard toil stood behind the bar with his arms folded, tattoos on his hands and scarred knuckles from a life of disagreements. He looked flustered, but what landlord would not be if his regular patrons had been scared away from entering by the sight of two uniformed police officers standing by?

Four other men sat scattered on different tables, each looking as worried as the next. With a variation of fingernail biting and hair scratching, they all looked like they may have pulled the trigger if they could only see straight and focus.

With the expertise expected, Detective Mick Flint passed the bulk of the work over to Stephen.

"You have a look at the scene, Detective Howes. I'll start taking details from this mob."

It appeared Flint's job at shirking duties did not stop with the filing cabinet in the office at the police station. The main assessment would be the difficult part of any police work, but Flint had made the task of taking notes seem singularly relevant at this moment in time.

Stephen looked around the pub. It was decorated with darkened wood which was heavily varnished and the walls were covered with a murky green paint which gave a gloomy, dank feel to the place. Small gold-framed paintings of ships and busy docks were here and there on the walls, as if to cover over holes. Although the decorative features looked as though they would crumble with the slightest touch, the surrounding walls looked like they could withstand a boulder crashing into them.

Scattered around a bookshelf on the far right wall, a few maritime books had been torn from the shelves. This appeared to have occurred in the search for the weapon, either that or the patrons did not care much for reading and had no regard for books. Either explanation seemed likely.

The space was not large, the bar spanning the length of the room. The hatch of the bar was open on rusted hinges.

Only a single door to the right was visible, Stephen guessed this led to the lavatorial area next to the bookshelf. To the left was a tall window set at an awkward angle. Nothing of substance grabbed his attention on this side of the room so he made his way to the door.

He opened it and stepped in to find a urinal running along the left wall and a solitary toilet trap to the right.

The trap's door was wide open and jammed that way by the victim's crumpled body. The smell of the room made it seem like the body was well into a state of decay rather than only being a few hours old.

The victim was an old gentleman with a brown suit that looked like it had been varnished as much as the bar. His scruffy grey hair and unkempt beard painted a picture more vivid to Stephen then any gold-framed snapshot into the dead man's life. A hole the size of a watch face with pieces of bone and skin that looked as though they would flap easily in a breeze decorated his chest, his chin resting near the wound, and, if it was not for the hole or the concoction of 'death colours', he would look like any other drunk that had passed out in the lavatory.

Blood had collected on the floor and most damage would surely be where the bullet had exited. The lips and skin of the man had the beginnings of the cornflower colour that haunted Stephen's dreams. For once he was gazing on a corpse that he wouldn't have to see in his dreams when he had passed out drunk.

Taking in the surroundings, Stephen closed the door to the toilet behind him and stood a couple of seconds, looking high and low and breathing deeply, almost trying to mentally picture the moment it had happened… where all the players had taken position. The stains on the walls ranged from brown to yellow, missing every colour of the rainbow in between. The red spray almost seemed to decorate and blend well with the theme of the rest room.

Stepping over to the body, Stephen reached into the man's

left trouser pocket. The victim was dressed like almost every other onshore dock worker, wearing the tatters of a three-piece suit with a pocket watch chain, although the watch was missing, probably pawned long ago or stolen but the chain remained.

Stephen took out the pocket's contents… the stone-dead sailor's leave papers which confirmed the name and address of the recently deceased.

As he stood taking in each detail only a trained eye would notice, he then felt satisfied, dropped the pieces he did not need onto the man's chest and made his way back to the bar.

Detective Flint was seated at the far end of the room, speaking to an elderly man who was informing the detective in a less then polite manner that he "dint see a fing mate," shaking his head and making the jowls of his chin swing like a pendulum.

Even with the air of suspicion hanging over them, Stephen deducted that this would be the reaction from all the customers.

He stepped outside to see the uniformed officers leaning against the wall. Seeing the detective return, the younger stood to attention as if in some army roll call.

"What's your name, Officer?"

"Brent, sir, Officer Brent."

"Well, keep alert if you will, my lad. You might be needed shortly."

Receiving an enthusiastic nod from the bobby, Stephen walked around the back of the building.

After a quick search, moving rubbish here and there with his foot, Stephen made his way back in, asking the uniforms to join him. They stood by the door, this time on the inside, as once more Stephen opened the toilet door, something not sitting right in his mind, like he had forgotten something but instinctively he knew he had left something unchecked, whilst internally cursing himself for not having noticed a certain significance the first time inside the toilet. He found the wallet of the victim on his body. Coming back out of the room, he pointed to the owner of the pub.

“Officers, arrest that man.”

Perched behind the bar, the owner unfolded his arms and, knowing this to be his only chance at making a run for it, he sprinted for the exit, ramming his left elbow into the face of the first unsuspecting uniform and then with a left hook he sent the younger bobby sprawling.

Flint made for the owner, again taken aback by the urgency that had materialised from previous calm but as the owner swung the door open, it provided an oak blockade between the two and a forcefully blunt facial rest for Detective Flint, although he should have been lucky the glass had not connected. Stephen knew Flint would not feel lucky for some time.

Stephen was out the door quickly… after the owner and gaining sharply.

Behind, he could hear the now pursuing officers blowing their police whistles.

Within a striding distance to the pub landlord, Stephen swept his leg across the back of the lead suspect’s churning legs, sending him sprawling and rolling, coming to a halt face down before trying to get back up. Stephen dropped a knee into his back, alleviating any hope of making a further run for it.

By now the two uniforms had caught up and proceeded to ‘subdue’ the guilty party with their billy clubs. The younger had forgotten to remove his whistle from his mouth and with each strike to the body and head, he gave a short comical toot. After eight or nine, Stephen told them to make sure they left something to prosecute.

Panting heavily, he walked back into the pub and, catching his breath, he took out his notebook and, with a few choice questions to the remaining occupants inside, he confirmed all that he had suspected whilst the uniforms cuffed the cursing and irate pub owner and led him with arms pulled painfully up his back on the short walk back to the station.

The entire arrest, from leaving the office to arresting the landlord had taken about an hour or so. Record timing in solving a crime with no witnesses coming forward.

On their own now, walking back to the station after finishing up the remaining statements, Stephen smoked his cigarette and Flint held his head back, under the instruction of Stephen, to stop the bleeding from his nose. A full explanation was needed for Flint as to what had occurred whilst he had been taking down statements.

Firstly, Stephen explained that he noticed the pub customers were not sitting around the same table, which suggested they were not of close acquaintance, so would therefore have no reason to provide false alibis for each other, which made none of these men seem likely suspects.

This only left one other option… to find out who was relatively simple. To find out 'why and how' was more of a conundrum.

Clive Mackie used to be a fisherman from Grimsby. This became apparent with the Grimsby-based maritime books strewn around the room and the tattoos of 'GY FOREVER' on show for all to see.

It was not uncommon for sailors to collect money and make the most of it by purchasing into the public house business to leave the life at sea behind but at the same time, keep in contact with old friends when they returned from voyages, ready to spend their hard-earned cash.

Although an unanswered question arose as to why not buy somewhere across in his own side of the Humber?

Only legal trouble or similar could be assumed.

When Stephen spoke to the pub occupants after the arrest, they confirmed the victim and the landlord had had a few heated arguments and the cause had been the divide of the fishing trade upon each side of the Humber.

With tattoos of 'Hull till I die' on the recently deceased man's arms, it was clear they were both equally passionate about their heritage.

When Stephen had entered the lavatory, he could not smell the gunpowder from a recently fired weapon. This could only mean the gun was not fired from inside the enclosed room. If it had been, then the lingering smell would have been noticeable from an acrid taste in the air. The only other place it could have been fired from was through the large vent, leading to the outside alley adjacent to the trap.

When he looked round the back of the building, the grill of the vent could only be unscrewed from inside, this meant the kill was premeditated.

Whilst searching around at the back of the pub, Stephen located the cellar entrance, laid behind one of the empty barrels, a gun was found.

Finding the barrel still relatively warm and the fresh smell of powder argued that the gun had been recently fired.

As Stephen had the uniforms follow him back in, Mr Mackie had not moved, as if covering something. At an angle from the lavatory door, Stephen had clear sight of a gun box of perfect size for the handgun. The uniforms could not be blamed for missing this small clue as they were concentrating on finding a weapon, not where a weapon should be sitting.

That Mackie had fled only further confirmed his guilt.

All in all, the episode had taken them to around midday, and the early morning mist that was inevitable for this time of year had burned away. The air still cold and feeling damp, it was a welcome return to the office, not only for the heat but for the reception from the newly-acquired work acquaintances.

His explanation to Flint ended as they entered the police station. Clapping and taunts were given as Flint looked dishevelled at his blood-spattered handkerchief.

"Get sick of him and clock him already, Detective Howes?" shouted the detective with his feet still up, through almost insane-like laughter.

Stephen thought Flint's humiliation had played a bigger part in the joviality rather than being accepted as part of the camaraderie. But he was happy to not have to make any more front and centre speeches.

CI Rudyard walked up to Stephen with an almost deliberate saunter. "The uniforms told us all about what happened and

I think, Detective Howes, if you need 'our' help to catch your killer, we'd better get started right away."

CHAPTER 8

By the end of the first shift, the taunts for Flint had died down and his nose had eventually stopped bleeding. The entire station seemed abuzz about the new recruit who had broken an all-time record within one morning of being there.

In turn, each occupant of the office, save one detective who seemed to have a clear disdain for everything and everyone, introduced themselves to Detective Howes with a polite and welcoming manner.

Detective Raffle paid hardly any mind to the introduction but the likes of Detective O'Connell, Detective Napier and Detective Ford could not have been more pleasant.

The room had all the usual markings of a police station with the heavy wood, the spaced-out tables, the high ceilings and creaking chairs, yet the only difference was that the place held a distinct smell of cigarette smoke and Scotch.

Save the papers scattered here and there, this could quite easily have been a gentleman's club.

Flint, at certain points of the day, tried to claim some of the glory for the arrest, but this was only met by more taunts as to his incompetence.

Stephen was given a work-space to the right of the swinging doors against the wall, where he could sift through cases handed to him that may be important or relevant to his own case.

The desk seemed an ideal spot until at around two o'clock when the light shone through the high window, practically blinding him.

Stephen stood and heaved the desk around with a solo effort, creating a loud screech as the table legs struggled to move.

Placing his chair so his back felt the heat of the sun instead, he was content that another obstacle had been overcome, albeit a minor one.

No sooner had he settled in and passed a few hours with general chit chat as to things to 'see and do' during recreational time, mainly public drinking houses to visit, Chief Inspector Rudyard called Stephen into his back office. Sitting down, he poured them both a brandy from his 'special occasion' drawer.

"I must admit, Detective Howes, I am very rarely impressed but it seems today you have that honour."

"Thank you, Chief Inspector. Just doing what I am sure any of your other detectives would have done."

"Ah well, I appreciate your modesty but 'congratulations' all the same. The boys will no doubt be asking you to join them for a drink but I have after work errands to run so I wanted to wish you much more success whilst I have the chance."

They raised their glasses in unison and through whiskered cheeks Rudyard muttered a toast regarding King and Country.

The brandy burned Stephen's tongue, even more as he felt it sliding down his throat. Feeling the liquid eventually reach his stomach, Stephen took another drink and already it burned less.

Rudyard asked Stephen about his task and his time in the police force.

Merely repeating what the papers said that had arrived before Stephen had, the Chief Inspector seemed happy enough.

When done, Stephen stood and placed his glass on the Chief's desk and took his leave. Sure enough when he returned to the main office area, a detective introducing himself as, "Russell Ford, no need for the detective now we are out of hours," asked if Stephen wanted to join him and a few of the others for a drink.

He agreed and asked where they were all planning to drink, a joke was made about "one more spirit being added today but a lot less by tomorrow morning." Stephen gave a chuckle with the rest of the work force, although it wasn't until they made their way across the bridge, past the factory that smelt of yeast for the second time in one day, that he realised what they meant.

There was, however, one detective less at this point. As the men had left the station, Raffle left at the same time but after exiting, bid them all happy evening with a, "Right, gentlemen, I'm vacating," and with his hat pulled low, he walked in the opposite direction to the remaining officers wishing their farewells.

No further comment was made to the situation and Stephen didn't think it his business to ask any questions.

CHAPTER 9

Stephen watched as Detective Flint removed the pub's keys from inside his jacket and unlocked the door to The Old Bush. The inside was blanketed in darkness due to the early setting of the winter sun.

The external gas lamps of the public house did little to light the features that had previously been seen by the newly welcomed detective.

After a few minutes of searching and expert team work, the rest of Stephen's fellow law upholders had the candles lit throughout the main bar area.

Stephen, curious as to the whereabouts of the body, asked Detective Napier, who was in the process of putting on a barman's apron, which he had discovered in the candlelit gloom. Napier informed Stephen that the corpse had been moved to the morgue earlier in the day.

A poor choice of words of a comical morose selection had Napier behind the bar and asking, "Choose your weapons, gentleman." There were a few laughs and each placed their order with the stand-in, self-appointed barman.

There was a distinctive nature to Detective Napier. Something that was obvious with only a few minutes of exposure. Stephen knew that within the office Napier was the type to rarely take things seriously. He always had a light-hearted manner to the grimmest of situations. As apparently insane as the inadequate joke may be, it was often required to keep the sanity.

Everyone made themselves comfortable by removing hats and coats, apart from Ford who only removed his hat. When the glasses were full, Stephen had a few more questions. "Is this normal conduct?"

It was Flint who answered. "What? Drinking in a bar? It is for tonight, mate. Someone needs to look after the place or all sorts of criminals could be skulking to get their hands on the unguarded booze. It just so happens we are having a few drinks to keep us from being parched."

A few shouts of "ere, ere" were given from the other detectives and Stephen decided to lighten the mood as his line of questioning could have clearly being misconstrued as 'do gooding'. "Good enough for me," he said, and for the second time in a day Stephen raised his glass in unison.

"Remember the good and forget the bad," boomed O'Connell, which came as a shock as it was the first time he had spoken since they had all entered the deserted establishment.

They all knocked back drinks that were instantly refilled.

Ford spoke, but it was more to Stephen then the rest of the drinkers. "I can't stay for long, fellas. I've got to help my daughter with a recital for her up and coming play at the theatre, but just wanted to share a drink with our newest recruit and welcome you to the team. I can see you'll be nothing short of a very valuable asset."

Stephen collided glasses with Ford and the rest of his helpers. "Thank you, one and all, for the warm welcome, gentlemen."

Ford put the glass down and said, "Cheers, much obliged," then excused himself, braced himself for the outside chill and bade everyone a good night.

The remaining occupants were all drinking whisky, so the decision was made to retire with the bottle to the comfort of the lounge-style chairs.

A recap of the day's events, with Flint becoming animated in his explanations, was held for Napier and O'Connell as they were the only two of the four remaining who had not witnessed Stephen's detective work.

O'Connell asked detailed questions and it was Flint who

offered answers, possibly with the attempt to highlight his own significance, but this was fine by Stephen. He had very little enthusiasm for recognition.

His main task was to dispatch a specific murderer… as instructed by Craven Wilkinson, and for which he would be paid handsomely. Anything else was a bonus along the way.

The drinking continued and as the group made their way onto the second bottle of whisky, O'Connell made his way to the door.

Napier's eyes followed him with a grin in the expectation that O'Connell was about to vomit but instead he announced it was time for him to head home as his wife would certainly be worried.

Flint called out, "John? Are you not forgetting something?"

O'Connell looked back, radiantly ashamed at his own error. He was drunk. It was not until he had stood up that this became blatantly obvious and, in his drunkenness, he had forgotten his coat and hat. Something unheard of in any decent society.

He clumsily put on the two whilst making apologies. "Sorry, fellas. You'll have to excuse me. I can't keep up with you lads, eh?"

Howes noticed that now O'Connell was drunk he seemed to let his natural accent slip. He was possibly Liverpudlian in origin, around early 50s with a ragged bristle of hair upon his upper lip. He was friendly to the core.

As he left, the obvious was stated by Flint. "And then there were three…"

All three did their very utmost to fumigate the long bar area with smoke, and, on production of a pack of cards, the idea was given that due to Stephens' distinct lack of card game knowledge, a simple game of American black jack should be played.

Cigarettes were exchanged for winnings but it made very little difference as when it was noticed the collective amount had begun to dwindle, the winnings that seemed well within Flint's favour were taken and smoked regardless.

"You must play this quite an amount, Flint, to be winning so much," Stephen slurred, not realising how tipsy he was until now.

"Only when when I am round the dock area with the Chinese. They loiter around the same places, so I join in with them from time to time."

Napier pulled a face of mischief that showed he was waiting for Flint to divulge further information, information Napier was privy to, but wanted to see if Flint was drunk enough to share.

"What…?" Flint asked in a mock annoyance whilst swaying backwards a little and inadvertently blinking one eye that would have looked like a wink had his other eye not been so lazy.

Napier began to laugh hysterically. The joke was lost on Stephen and when he enquired, Detective Napier said that if Flint wanted to cavort around them areas then it was not for him to judge or pry.

Stephen read between the lines… Flint must have either a weakness for 'women of the night' around that area or opium, the Chinese were renowned for both.

Flint slurred a "ffffffuck off" and they laughed before playing a few more rounds of black jack.

"Anyway, enough of prying into my private life… what's your story, Detective Howes? You've joined the group but we don't know anything about you. Rudyard… burp, sorry… Chief Inspector said we were getting some sort of travelling policeman?"

At this moment in time, Stephen knew it was a blessing that his drinking was more than just a pastime. Although the effects of alcohol were immoderately felt by him, he had enough of a clear mind about him to stick to the pre-planned story of his previous employment.

His integration into the police force was essential, and to do this he knew he would have to become colleagues and even friendly with some of the men, but he wanted and very much needed his past to remain hidden. This was mainly because his job was not only to catch his killer but to do much worse to him when he had done so. When he eventually caught sight of his target and he claimed his reward, he had no intention of allowing a group of detectives to have insight as to where he might be or where he might travel after the deed was done.

Until that time came, his story would remain simple.

"Well, Flint, there's not a lot to tell. About five, was it? Yeah… about five years ago, I was taken on by Scotland Yard for a special unit. There are a few of us known as 'the set'. The name, I think, came from the term 'a fresh set of eyes' as when sometimes working on cases, that's what it takes to see things others might have missed, right? We answer to one authoritative figure and if I get results, I am left to my own devices."

A slug of whisky gave Stephen the chance to let his story sink in to his drunken colleagues.

"Every now and again, a case will come up that requires special attention and this killer I am trying to find is one of those cases. I'm here to do what I can with the help of you fine bunch of young fellows."

It was delivered flawlessly. An actor couldn't have recited it better. Even in his drunken haze, Stephen did not miss a word. This would hopefully hold off much discussion as to his past or authority in and around the station. He only had his mind set on one objective but any good investigator knows that to stand alone in such circumstances often leaves stones unturned and, for the offered reward, Stephen was willing to crawl along the seabed.

His drinking companions seemed wholeheartedly satisfied with his explanation and the only thing he got in any kind of response was from Detective Napier who was now looking through one squinted eye to obtain full focus on his cards. He leaned back a little and then slowly began to lean forward, as if to get a closer look. Finally his forehead touched his cards and then his cards carried on the momentum with his head. Together they reached the large table and it was not until his head rested on the wood and ceased to move that Flint and Stephen, who had been watching the whole affair, waiting for him to continue the game by either requesting another card or to hold on the hand he had been dealt, realised that he had fallen asleep. They laughed aloud but this did not wake Detective Napier.

They decided to discontinue their card playing as some of the cards required for a full deck now lay beneath Detective Napier's head, serving as a paper-thin pillow.

"You know today, Stephen? I have to admit I wuz impressed. I knew it were bound to be one of the people in there, iinnnnnnn 'ere, I mean, but with 'ow you put it all together, swas brilliant."

Flint's hands had become animated whilst talking, almost to make up for the poor quality of speech due to his broken nose.

"Thank you, thank you, Detective"

"I'mmmm going to go. I 'ave someone to meet."

Stephen drunkenly chuckled. "A dragon… a dragon to catch by any chance?"

Stephen said it with a smile, but as Flint's head swayed, he seemed surprised at the bluntness.

"Issssssit that obvious?"

"Not at all, Detective Flint, but I am after all… a detective. But don't you worry, your secret is safe with me."

Flint attempted to nod his head in appreciation but it seemed to be more of a flop forward. As he stood to leave, he asked Stephen if he was good to stay until the morning.

"Of course I will, Detective Flint. Does Napier have nobody to go home to?"

Flint simply shook his head in a solemn, drunken motion.

"Well, I have no digs and it's too late to start looking now, not to mention this remaining whisky…"

Holding the bottle aloft a moment as if it was a trophy won, Stephen poured himself another glassful and Flint wished him a good night.

"I might be able to 'elp you with lodgings tomorrow. Make sure you remind me. All the best."

He left staggering.

The lonely silence after Flint had gone filled the establishment, along with the residue of a corpse's sadness from the murder that had occurred.

Sipping at his glass, the newly accredited detective allowed himself a smile at such an activity filled day and how it had all gone so well. The candles burned low and the last thing Stephen remembered was how nice it felt to be accepted.

When he woke, he had been lying on his side for quite some time judging by the pain in his neck.

Once again it had been his usual dream of falling, only this time he landed on the roof of the Waterloo Tavern but at the moment of impact, he startled himself awake.

At first, he had no idea where he was but then the gentle snoring of his drinking companion reminded him of the night. As he raised his head, he did not need to view the bottle of whisky to know it was empty.

The room was beginning to fill with the gloom of grey morning light and it had been the noise of a tram passing by outside that had woken him from his restless slumber.

He was grateful for his first night's lodgings but he had no intention of making a habit of such accommodation. He would assess the work situation and then from there, find somewhere he could live while he hunted.

A flash of memory from the previous evening crept back and something Flint had said jogged his memory with regards to a future possible abode.

He walked to the restroom, hoping to fill his mouth with water to try to dilute some of the cheap whisky that had been taken in excessive consumption.

When he opened the door, a putrid smell forced him back. He had forgotten that a murder had occurred here, and in his haze, the coppery tang of coagulated blood mixed with fragments of human innards and flesh that still lined the toilet walls… not to mention a gathering of festering flies.

He closed the door and stumbled behind the bar for some sort of substitute, confident in the knowledge that if he had to sit in the stink of a corpse whilst he felt this tedious, he may potentially empty what little lined his stomach around the discarded crime scene.

After finding what could only be found in such a public house, whose customers were of the excessive drinking kind, he located a half empty box of eggs. He filled a pint glass with the pub's ale and cracked a raw egg into the glass.

In a painfully long attempt and after spilling a quarter of the glass's contents on himself, he finished the concoction.

If he felt better or not, he could not tell.

He rested his hand on the bar and lowered his head forward whilst he tried to let the liquid settle his stomach.

It was Napier calling a woman's name as he woke that brought Stephen's concentration back to the room. He didn't quite hear it but when he looked up he couldn't stifle the laugh at the ruffled hair of Detective Napier and a playing card stuck in place on his forehead.

As the recently roused detective surveyed the room, attempting to relocate himself, Stephen poured another pint of ale and cracked an egg for his accomplice.

"Good morning, detective."

Napier groaned and held his head like it was attempting to implode, as if holding it steady might avoid the disaster. The playing card fell and the agony of a hangover had never seemed more evident. He looked every inch of how Stephen felt.

"What time is it?"

Stephen looked at the large clock that hung behind the bar, ticking with a slow pendulum motion.

"Eight thirty."

"Fuck! We better head to the station. Won't do to be late. I'm bad enough for turning up as it is."

As they left and put on their jackets and hats, Stephen smiled at the empty glass that had been drained without a second thought by Napier.

He could tell he was going to like working alongside this group of professionals, even if he was here to murder a murderer.

CHAPTER 10

Tonight was not of my usual taste.

However, the urge crept upon me like a slow, malevolent snake.

In my hands, I felt the warm familiar rush, not constricting my skin but entering it. Boiling it from inside out.

Taking over it.

The heat of the bodies in the theatre rising to my balcony. Like a fire of burning souls, letting me feel their sins scorching me. As I looked over them, the first movement of Beethoven's Symphony No. 5 bellowed out on stage. I could never miss an opportunity to listen to the god-like touch, no matter how unpractised several members of the string group may have been.

The notes complemented themselves and each other and when the rest of the orchestra held its own, the violinist raised a determined agitation within me. I became aware of my jealousy towards them that they could perform to an audience, yet I never could.

I could leave my work behind in all its glory but only in the rarest of circumstances would I be permitted watchful eyes.

My sinister crawling urges needed to scrape out the distraction, my hands, resting on the soft yet worn, hard-backed chair, began to become restless, my nails wanting to peel back from the tips, knowing what damage they could do when pressed firmly into flesh.

Then a contagious feeling for destruction began a slow methodical crawl into my fingers, aware what damage they could do to a thorax if compressed in the exact correct area, to my arms reminding them that they should be at work, dragging a body into the River Humber, knowing the tide would soon sweep it along.

As an artist, I know the need for practice. However, I would not bring myself into the applause and halo'd light of the crowds, if I did not believe my work was at a standard that could only be admired.

With small, petty and impulsive kills, I simply act out desires, spur of the moment thrills but in this case, I knew what was lurking.

The creature that is 'Demise'.

Not my own.

Maybe not even anyone here, but an end to an existence, that was what was needed. A luminescence needing to be extinguished.

I had been pressing the binoculars to my face with my other hand so hard with the rage of the cool and satisfying but essentially controlled impulse, that the pain of the sharp edge brought me back to rational thoughts.

Part of me wanted the theatre on fire with all of them trapped.

With the orchestra still playing as the heat melted the varnish from the instruments. I wanted the screams from the percussionist to drown out the drums.

It would be too messy. Too out of control.

As I sat back, releasing my grip from the chair arm, allowing the blood to extend back to my fingertips, I looked directly across from my own balcony to see a gentleman and a lady in the throes of cavorting.

The man was dressed in a suit made long ago and it had evidently been well used.

He appeared to be of middle class, trying to appear to be higher than his born right, which is a common practice in these areas. The girl in a fluster, clearly practised for this type of customer. Older men in the sham of social class were, I believe, good for this type of woman's business.

Dressed to impress for all those who cared to pay him attention, he would attempt to dine the lady, allowing him a small insight to what he was missing at the top of the ladders that were possessed by the elite.

This man was a counterfeit and, if his balcony had not been sheltered to all but mine, his coarse actions would inform the entire theatre to this effect.

I knew what I had to do. I arose from my seat, almost mechanically and exited the balcony. I walked around the rear of the theatre, arching a semi-circle of the outer walkway that passed the main entrance of the building, each step a rush to my back pushing me for the excitement as I reached the high wooden door in the darkened theatre corridor.

The connecting walkways were tight, almost enclosed and with the gas lamps dimmed they gave off a smell that one had the impression of suffocation.

Upon reaching the final door to the couple in question, I gave a knock to the charismatic charlatan.

The pipes of the musical performance were high now and the chances of being heard were slim.

With no reply, I eased the door open and at that moment the drums gave four sharp beats and then a stop.

The music seemed to be from another planet, yet in perfect synchronisation with my actions. I took out the knife hidden in my walking cane and dropped the cane cover as I shut the door behind me, giving complete privacy to my 'soon to be sketch pad artwork'. This was to be an improvised piece, yet one still worthy of a stroke of genius.

With two steps, I was at the side of the mock gentleman's chair. The whore raised her head from his lap like a violin player gazing at the beauty of musical notes upon page and with mouth still open in shock at the unexpected intrusion, I made a slash across her throat. If she had still been carrying out the act of oral, I believe the cut was so deep it would have made her customer a eunuch.

Her eyes were wide with shock. Her arms shot out as she tried to stand, perhaps to flee. I grasped her hair, pulling her forward so she fell onto her soon to be previous employer. The chair fell back and her twitching dead weight pinned him. He didn't make a sound.

Even before I placed the blade into his wide, shocked mouth, he couldn't comprehend what was happening.

He registered what I had done only moments later and appeared to attempt to talk but his teeth chattered on the wet blade.

By this time the orchestra bellowed its grand final death throws, I pushed the blade so far forward the blade handle rested on the inside of his mouth and stifled the gurgling. If the blade had not cut into the nerve at the nape of his neck, killing him instantly, his own blood would have surely drowned him.

On my knees, I lifted to stand as the orchestra reached its musical climax and raising and spinning in one smooth motion the crowd began to cheer.

I gave a bow to my followers.

Finally, I felt the wave of an audience's appreciation.

From that moment, I knew.

Now the time for the beginning of 'the final solo' begins.

The apocalyptic rain of my hand began.

Blood at my feet and the cheer of the crowds, I became aware that this was the beginning of my rise.

CHAPTER 11

The days that followed were nothing short of intriguing to see how the office was run in such a dismal manner. Each detective would be given a case file and they would try and 'plod' through the details and if nothing seemed to jump out as obvious then very little was done.

Another folder would be passed and nonchalantly they would cover the previous with the new.

Crimes in themselves appeared open and shut with the street officers taking most of the details and noting down whatever they found of interest. Witnesses were very forthcoming and nine times out of ten the crime was financially or jealousy based. In which case, it was an employee, relative or a partner in whichever form they may have taken.

Stephen's days had been long but he had taken the time to try and learn the names and ways of his newly acquired work colleagues.

As he got to know the town, he made sure to make time for himself to visit Duncan's Gun Shop to purchase a gun of his own, and also managed to acquire a length of lead pipe that fit nicely into the sleeve of his jacket. He wanted to be prepared.

His nights, on the other hand, were exactly how he normally spent them, drinking to oblivion in the company of strangers, each one of them reluctant to begin conversation. These were the establishments he frequented often, but he could not say he enjoyed them.

Wearing old tattered clothes purchased from here and there, he fit into the crowd and was just another face. He needed this therapeutic release to help him sleep. His dreams were not nightmares but he wished he could forget the cliffs for just one night. He'd been tempted by opiates to release him from his normal state of mind but was terrified at the prospect that it was his normal state of mind that had managed to keep the demons of his doings at bay.

One night Stephen became fantastically drunk. He befriended an old woman who looked more like furniture than bar staff and, as the hours whittled away, he began to tell her of his past life. In his infancy he had hardly known his parents. A distant mother and a father in the forces, and as he grew, the regimented morals he had learnt kept him upon the straight and narrow. That was until he had found his calling of tracking people. His old accomplice had taught him many things about how to 'locate' and up until the day he had died, Stephen saw him as a father figure, a brother and a moral compass for guidance.

Leaning on a bar a million miles from the life he knew, Stephen cried for the path his life had taken him on, but knew it shaped him for the better.

When he woke the next day, he vowed never to return to that particular pub for fear of what he may have 'let slip'. A sin that would never be forgiven.

Flint had indeed been true to his word when he had mentioned somewhere for Stephen to stay, as he knew a lady who was recently letting out the top floor in her house.

Mrs Pritchard, as she insisted being called, as first name terms were very ungentlemanly, was a widow and had decided to rent the rooms of her upstairs to trustworthy occupants. She had the demeanour of a woman who held a short fuse for any nonsense and routine was top of her agenda.

With stout warnings of 'no unruly behaviour' for Stephen, he tried to make her feel at ease with his assurance, but she seemed a little more comforted that he was recently made a member of the Hull police force.

She had two spare rooms upon a top floor of a three-storey house. The room that Stephen took was large and furnished with left overs from past tenants. Running water and a boiling kettle for tea and cleaning was all he would ever need so anything else seemed a luxury in its own right. The only hindrance was the sloped ceiling/wall that followed the external roof. For a man of Stephen's stature, walking upon the left side of the room had to be completed at a peculiar angle.

More than once he had forgotten and rose from his bed, quite literally 'on the wrong side' and jolted himself suddenly with potential concussion.

The sharp pain thankfully had never produced blood but the dizziness caused him to stagger and seat himself. Each time hungover and each time vowing that he needed to stifle his drinking habits. Always refusing to call it a 'problem' but secretly knowing others may see it that way.

'If they had seen some things I've seen,' he thought, 'they would have a bottle of whisky or two with me.'

Sorrowfully, lonely and still ringing from the clump of the ceiling, it wasn't long before he was back on his way to the police station and, in an almost routinely fashion, supping from his hip flask. His ability to focus in a crime scene was the only thing that saved him or made him anything that resembled a good detective.

Within a week, he was beginning to think that Craven Wilkinson had sent him on a fool's errand of a grand scale as very little crossed his desk with regards to his killer and he began to lose sight of his intended target.

Thankfully, upon his sixth day of work, that changed. He felt fresher than normal from his strongly brewed tea, and walked past officer Alan and into the office that, although it was small, with only a few people present, seemed charged with chatter and conversation.

Before Stephen could seat himself, Rudyard came out of the back office and motioned for Stephen to join him.

Little time was made for chit chat.

"It seems we might have something for you, Detective Howes," Rudyard said. "Last night in the theatre, a man and woman were killed. Somewhat brutally, to say the least. The bodies were not found until much later after the show and it appears there were no witnesses. The crime scene is a mess but we have taken all the details we could. Ford is already down there if you would like to meet him and see what you can find."

After hailing a passing carriage from close by the police station, once again taking the trip through the town centre, and noticing a few public houses for future reference, Stephen quickly arrived outside the theatre not far from the train station.

With columns crawling up the front of the main entrance, the building did not seem big enough to hold an orchestra, let alone theatre attendees. However, a glance down the side of the building revealed it to be very long and narrow.

He entered through the smaller side doors, as the impressively immaculate front entrance seemed to be locked. This was more than likely to keep out any press or curious public after the night's horror. A uniformed officer met him in the red and gold gloom of the reception and offered to show him the way.

"That's quite okay, officer," Stephen said. "If you just direct me, I'd rather make my own way."

"Very well, sir. Take the stairs up to your left through the doors, keeping to your left and it's the very last viewing box to your right."

With a 'thank you and good day', Stephen followed the officer's instructions exactly.

As he stood at the foot of the stairs for a moment, he surveyed the area.

Two officers were milling around and Stephen enquired as to who would normally be here on the night of a show.

"Sorry, sir?" one of them asked.

"When a show is in progress, who mans the door and reception to ensure no persons may sneak in?"

"That would be the ticket man, sir. He would stand in that booth."

"Has he been questioned?"

"Yes, detective. Doesn't seem to remember anything out of the ordinary and as the show 'ad finished, 'e left. About an hour later, the cleaning staff entered and that was when the bodies were found."

"I see, and do you have a name and address for the ticket man?"

The officer ripped a page from his note book and handed it to Stephen.

He thanked the officer and continued the assessment of the area.

The stairs were well worn but only in the middle as the audience who were seated in the boxes would have descended the stairs after the crime, he was safe in betting that no evidence would be found on the darkened stairwell.

He climbed slowly, carefully placing one foot in front of the other, knowing that hours before, his target, his ultimate kill, may have walked this very same route up with murder on his mind and back down with blood on his hands.

A narrow corridor with dark red walls led to where he could see Detective Ford with his notepad open but not paying it any mind, using it as a time-wasting device, something to stare at but not focus on. He seemed reluctant to enter the room which undoubtedly paved the way to the crime scene.

Along the right of the corridor were doors leading to the other viewing boxes, which were closed, all dark brown adding to the foreboding sombreness.

Apparently with attendance at full capacity the previous night, if no commotion was heard then Stephen was to assume that the deaths had happened during the performance to drown out the noise of the murder. The end of the hallway was the only visible light. Walking to the open door was surreal.

Like a beacon for him, informing Stephen it was 'his' murderer, the air was stuffy with candles, still yet to be converted to gas, and seemed to be rushing towards this vortex to pull him closer. He didn't believe in signs or signals, not being religious, but his instinct told him this was the work of his target for sure.

If not his instinct, then the scene that greeted him vanquished any form of doubt.

In a chair in the centre of the box but close to the balcony, the male victim's face was towards the door. His body however was not. His head had been forcefully twisted 180 degrees away from the stage. His eyes had been removed, leaving only the coagulated stems. His ears were also missing.

On the back of the chair dangled a note but it was too far away for the detective to read. He only noticed the bloodstained collar of the man, in contrast to his starched white shirt.

In a place so dark, the shirt stood out as the only bright thing where it was not covered in claret-coloured life blood.

He stayed in the entrance at the door, surveying the room, exactly how the killer intended for the finders to observe his 'work'.

The female lay slumped in the corner against the balcony. An empty lifeless face, it seemed she was merely an annoyance to the scene. A discarded puppet whose strings had been cut. Both victims were not meant to be watching the show. Her throat had been cut deeply but her blood had been 'used'.

On the right wall, which would be angled towards the stage, written in four inch letters with dried blood that would mostly flake to the touch, read:

my work mIrrors tHe gEnius of the music

And on the left wall that would be visible to the audience if their attention was not drawn by the performance on stage, it read:

soon you will AdmiRe My art, UnderStand Its CreatIoN

Detective Ford stood next to Stephen, still motionless, and when he talked, it broke the overpowering silence. "I think it's safe to say that this is who you are looking for...?"

"Undoubtedly," was all he could think to reply, taking a

deep swallow before he stepped inside the copper-tasting toxic room.

Leaning down, he read the note on the back of the chair, bringing his face close to the skull-like victim. He was not fazed by the ghostly features, more annoyed that amongst the chaos of the scene, it all still seemed so delectably fashioned. Even the eye stems, that dangled from the sockets, were at an equal length.

The note was in a very eccentric style of writing, it simply read:

dead And unwoRthy to behold the delighTs of beethoven.
now it begins

It was not a challenge. It was a starting pistol, a way to inform all interested that more was to come and more than likely on a grander scale.

Stephen asked for the room to be cleared. His mentor had once told him that people will mull around death like ants to food that has been dropped and discarded. Each taking a piece away that could have been useful.

With everyone gone, he could look at everything in an individual light.

He wanted no distractions as he surveyed further but he found nothing. For all the drama that had been created, there was not a helpful piece of evidence to collect. Everything had been purposely placed. A painting with attention to detail.

He left the theatre with a very heavy heart.

The game had begun and Stephen had nothing to begin the chase with. He was frustrated.

A sharp blade, an artistic nature and an unparalleled determination.

He had been hired for many alike cases but he knew this was different.

This murder was not planned. It appeared the act had been carried out on a whim. Yet it was pulled off gracefully. There would be no real way to predict the privacy that the killer would have required, the unsuspecting couple, also the time he would have needed to arrange his victims, yet he was as careful as the most demonic of characters.

Stephen wandered towards the town centre with his mind racing and headed to his new lodgings. He agreed with Detective Ford's assumptions that this was indeed a killer who would develop.

Notes were not usually left behind for people to find after such grotesque acts unless the killer enjoyed the anticipation of the shock they were to cause. If the killer enjoyed the shock this time, he would increase it the next.

CHAPTER 12

Arriving home to his rented abode and hanging his jacket and hat, Stephen sat on the bed with a large exhale of air. There was no holding back on a firm slug of whisky.

The beginning of most investigations like this were hard for him. He knew he needed a mistake to be made by the killer and for that to happen more people would inevitably have to die. It was an injustice common throughout all walks of nature, the equal reaction to an evil act was for justice… however that evil action still must occur in the first place.

Two more days had passed and since the killing, he had taken as much detail in and around the theatre as he could. No witnesses, no clues, no apparent motive or conviction apart from to send a message.

In his almost morose pondering, it was obvious a lot more files were passed onto his desk from his work colleagues. The stack now arched, threatening an immediate collapse, be it psychological or actual. It did not seem to decrease no matter how he rifled through them.

He noticed that during times after his break, the stack seemed to loom higher and after a tally count one morning and then again by the end of the day, he was getting the response he'd thought might occur.

During his wanderings the other detectives, although he could not be certain who exactly, were adding to his pile of suspected murders and other violent crimes with any unsolved cases that came their way.

He had requested only the most gruesome, out of the ordinary, most irregular or flamboyant murders.

It was an easy 'get out' for the team, as when questioned about cases they should have been chasing up by Chief Inspector Rudyard, the simple retort was becoming, "They are currently with Detective Howes, sir."

He didn't mind being a scapegoat for the others, as his job was not an official one and essentially, he did not live by the code of the law to the degree that everyone had to. He wanted one criminal. One he knew little about, apart from his face, but one he intended to condemn to total damnation when he could get his hands on him or around his throat more specifically.

Stephen had strangled only a few men previously and each time it was a matter of self defence. People he had gotten too close to during his investigations, who had read his intentions and attacked him.

His hand-to-hand training had paid off, fortunately for him.

When the tussles came in close and it was a matter that he knew the right places to press his thumbs to ensure his opponent 'joined the cliff faces' before he did.

When he had listened to Craven Wilkinson describe why he wanted Stephen to pursue this killer, he hoped it would come down to his hands around the target's throat.

He wanted to grasp around the windpipe in an old-fashioned grip, not one of a swift death, one that would let the killer know how at least one of his victims must have felt as the blood rushed to the head, as the throat constricted, like a large chunk of meat lodged in the only path to the lungs. Forcing the veins on his forehead to palpitate alongside the beetroot red colour encapsulating the face, bringing an instinctive struggle to 'the judged'.

When the eyes bulged, his victim would hear nothing but that all-consuming roar of over-pressured vessel and veins being overridden by the blockage of non-circulating blood.

Stephen imagined that at this point he would release the vice-like hold and sit back to make a clean slice with a razor blade across the throat.

As the blood rushed in a fury of panic back to the heart, instead it would stream out of the gaping wound.

He would feel the spray cover him and it would be like a plasmic shower of victory.

After his kill, Stephen would return to where he came from a wealthy man, free to live how he had always wanted. In luxurious and drunken peace.

The thought of catching the killer momentarily suppressed his ever-increasing gloom. He needed a kill to ease his conscience, although what he was feeling guilty about, he could not say. Perhaps if he could not stop his target then other potential victims could be saved by him slaying another killer…

Possibilities of different scenarios ran back and forth in his mind. Sometimes not even that of the self-proclaimed artistic-like killer. Random acts of making wrong do'ers pay for deathly deeds.

"What are you so happy about, lad?"

Subconsciously, Stephen had leant back on his chair, closed his eyes, imagined the reality of how that situation would feel and began to smile. It must have looked odd to anyone passing by, even odder if anyone knew the real intent that lay within.

"Detective O'Connell… nothing, just thinking about the good old days, you know how it is," said Stephen.

O'Connell gave a smile that seemed to suggest he knew what he meant, blissfully unaware that he could not be further from the truth.

"That was an impressive murder case with Flint, lad. Christ, everyone keeps talking about it. Must be a branch record. It's just a shame it had to be spoilt with the theatre murders. Poor souls."

O'Connell stood with his head hung a little, paying silent respect to the deceased.

Stephen knew O'Connell had something else he wanted to ask and thought he would wait it out until he found the courage.

"Thing is, lad, I know you are busy, but I was wondering if you might be able to help me out with something. If you're not on with something regarding the theatre murders… I'd totally understand if you are, my mate."

Stephen looked at the stack and motioned to it to give O'Connell the clear message that his time seemed slightly taken up at the minute.

"I know you're busy, but this is a dinner hour assignment this, me old mate. I'm only asking for an opinion. Don't worry, no hands-on stuff. Plus, after one week of being here, I think you stand more of a chance detecting anything than the majority of this lot in here."

Stephen leaned back again in the worn chair he had been given and surveyed Detective O'Connell, a very pleasant man, never had a negative word for anyone or anything. With his built-in survival instinct, Stephen assessed just how O'Connell could be 'of use' to him.

He knew things about his own killer. But he kept this level of knowledge to himself, as any information sharing may have resulted in the capture of his murderer.

Stephen wanted assistance, but the 'collar' was his own. For obvious reasons, he did not want his artistic killer in custody. But he knew that his target was a well-spoken and gentlemanly kind of chap, potentially mixing with the same ilk and if worse came to worse, Stephen may need help.

If it be surveillance or back up, he needed all he could until he could reach his target.

From 'weighing up' the rest of detectives littering the office, Detective O'Connell was the only occupant of the room that had the mannerisms and grace to pass as a gentleman besides Rudyard or Ford.

Although his ragged trousers and his worn shirt did not suggest so, in a three-piece suit and dicky bow tie he was every bit the 'well to do' Stephen might need at a top tier get together to act as a look out.

"Okay, Detective O'Connell, but on two conditions. Firstly, we stop with this 'Detective' formality during non-working hours as we both have first names… and secondly, you're buying lunch."

Although slightly hurt over the potential loss of finance during his lunch break, O'Connell smiled, raising his whiskered top lip, and offered his hand to Stephen. "Fair enough me, old mate. It's a deal."

The weather was as it always seemed in Hull, the so called King's town, and it had begun to dawn on the detective that 'overcast' was a bonus, as it meant people's umbrella's were getting a rest for the time being.

Stephen had been trying to take his free time and use it to the best of his ability by walking around the town centre and surrounding areas of the docks or markets for a lay of the land. Granted, he normally headed from public house to public house but walking was thirsty work and he had the coin and time to spend.

He was beginning to get a good bearing for the centre and was now expanding. The town seemed a constant hive of energy with ships arriving, unloading and overzealous bargaining and other trades littering the streets along with the scores of children running to and fro, more than likely to or from trouble.

O'Connell led Stephen out of the main door and was seemingly the only person to give courtesy to Officer Alan, bidding him a 'good afternoon' and informing him that they would be taking an early lunch break.

Officer Alan seemed to note something down as the two men left but Stephen did not even hear the scribble of pencil on paper, suspecting Alan was carrying out the act more for show.

The sun was trying its hardest to melt through the clouds but to no avail. The two men made their way north to the end of the cobbled street then turned left along the once again busy market at the docks.

Children ran in and out of the legs of the upper class and the down-trodden alike, each keeping a respectful distance from the other with the kids as a dirty barrier. There were children wearing expensive cloths keeping close to their parents, their malnourished counterparts free to run and play games in an ocean of colours and smells. Those children were free to let their youthful imaginations take hold of the world and make it a playground for all to share. With only a hungry belly to slow their mischief, it begged the question of who were the richer class?

Stephen's stride fell in with O'Connell's and he began with the foremost burning question. "What is it you want me to take a look at, John? What's so important you don't mind buying me lunch over?"

"Well, if you look at what I have noticed these last two weeks then we could be stopping a robbery and maybe even a young man from the Hedon Road hangman's trap door."

"The what?" asked Stephen.

"Sorry, lad. Hedon Road is where they hang criminals. Right there in the prison."

O'Connell was evidently a well-placed soul. With a vision that the world could one day be free of sin and suffering, he reminded Stephen of a priest. Some form of true believer, he admired this outlook but had seen enough in his own time to know that some people are born bad, the devil is in the roots of mankind and it is fear that keeps most in check. Be it of the law, or of the gallows and ultimately judgment itself.

Crimes remain uncommitted because of fear.

When a person is no longer concerned with the consequences, then he or she is free to do as they like.

"That sounds awfully intriguing, John, but why would you need me to have a look?"

"Lots of reasons, lad. You know your stuff, that's for sure, you're a fresh set of eyes, just like you said, and I have been working on this for a while. You look like you can handle things if it gets a little hairy. Not only that but that stack of paper on your desk in the office looks like it might fall on you any minute and you needn't be there when it happens."

John O'Connell's whiskers tilted up, showing a smile which made Stephen laugh, almost out of character.

"It does seem to be growing with no end in sight, doesn't it?"

"Not my doing, lad. Seems to me like you want to be catching this fella you're after pretty sharp so I will only come to you with worthwhile things… after this, of course."

They reached the main buildings of the dock offices and took a moment to become familiar with the streets. Stephen was unsure as to the building's purpose apart from the name, as although it was labelled Dock Offices, there were many other variety of shops, but he felt it was a question for another day.

They continued and reached the collection of buildings where O'Connell slowed his pace and began to explain the reason for this excursion.

"About three weeks ago, I came here for a bit of fresh air, something to eat and watch the people pass by. It's a relief getting out the office even if it is to see different faces. So here I am leaning over there…" He pointed to a curved wall that belonged to a building that separated two streets with the most prominent part of the curve pointing directly at a church. "At about lunchtime, it's a good place to catch the sun… when it makes an appearance, that is. Anyway, I'm just about to bite into a savaloy when I spots a carriage. Nothing new in that, but this was one of a bit of real class. A lot of businessmen use them. It pulled up outside of the Jewish jewellers. That one there with the gold writing."

Although O'Connell was pointing, Stephen felt it a waste of indication because five shops to the right of them a shop could clearly be seen with the word 'Jewellers', in more of an off yellow than gold, was boldly spanning the front.

"This big fella gets out, posh-looking suit, only he didn't look like the type to be wearing one. He was carrying a suitcase and walks in. Nothing odd with that, you might think, but as I look beyond the scene, there's a young lad about eighteen years of age sat on the bench a little further down. Again, nothing odd you might think but he is very obviously angry or anxious about something. All the time, he never takes his eye from the man entering the shop and never once takes his right hand from his pocket in his jacket."

Stephen, looking up and down the street, made a mental note that this small, cobbled road would be an ideal place for a robbery. Secluded unless you were standing either side of the street, then when you were free from the street itself there were endless possible escape routes unless you headed to the dock in which case the screams of robbery would almost certainly bring a policeman or a watchman from their station.

O'Connell had fallen silent as he waited for Stephen, who had finished looking around and casually took a cigarette from his pack nestled in his inside pocket. "Okay, so what happened next?"

"Well, the man walked out. Got in his carriage and left. So, nothing really."

Stephen waited. He knew Detective O'Connell was building up to something and he didn't want to steal his thunder.

"But then, the following week, same time, same scene played out. This time the young man seemed more anxious and even made a small rise to get up as the big fella leaves the shop. As I drew my pistol, expecting a robbery, the young lad sits back down in a heap of sweat. He never saw me, so exactly why he just sat back down, I couldn't tell you."

"Okay, so he's building up the courage. When do you think the next scene will play out?"

"Well, here is the thing, mate, that's the carriage passing the young man on the bench as we speak."

Stephen could see what O'Connell meant… the carriage was that of a wealthy hire. The driver was smartly dressed and the horse finely groomed. It stopped a few paces past the jewellers and the door furthest from the shop door opened.

If the occupant was to enter the shop, why would he exit through the carriage door in the opposite direction to where the shop was?

However, as soon as the man made his appearance, Stephen could see why.

Like a male peacock displaying its feathers for all to witness, which is exactly what it reminded Stephen of, the bulk of a man stepped out and breathed in. More of a statement to potential onlookers as a 'look at me' but nobody seemed to want to meet the Peacock's attempt to catch attention.

That is of course except for the young man sat on the bench at the opposite end of the street from the two detectives.

The day was cold, but his glare seemed to radiate heat enough to burn the cobbles off the ground and bricks from the buildings.

For a moment, the man holding the briefcase and the youth locked eyes in direct assessment of one another, but the Peacock simply gave a shake of his head and began to walk around the rear of the carriage towards the jewellers.

This act seemed to infuriate the youth and his face burned crimson. He rose and the Peacock stopped and looked at the young man as if mentally willing it to happen, but the youth sat back down, all the while his right arm stuck rigid in his jacket pocket. From a distance, it was hard to tell but he appeared to be shaking. It seemed rage had gotten him to his feet, yet fear had failed his legs.

Stephen was watching the would-be attacker when he heard the shop door ring out with a bell to alert the owners of entering customers. Through the glass, he could see the owner's demeanour deflate at the sight of the peculiar well-dressed oaf making his entrance.

The exchange had taken no more than ten seconds but the atmosphere had seemed to bend time to the almost boiling conflict.

Stephen was processing scenarios when O'Connell's voice interrupted his train of thought.

"See what I mean, lad? What do you reckon?"

Stephen had seen this before. He knew exactly what was going on. He was about to wrap up another case in record time and it would be one he would take pleasure in.

O'Connell had the potential of a detective, that was for sure, but his compass was in the wrong direction.

"John, why don't you go talk to the lad? See what he says. Try and get information from him. If we both go, it might seem a little intimidating to him, so I'll wait right here and cover you."

"If you think so, lad. Keep an eye on him in case he pulls any shenanigans."

Stephen waited until O'Connell had reached around ten paces away and begun, in his usual friendly manner, to question the youth as to his reasoning for loitering, then he made for the shop door.

With jewellery either side and a desk towards the back, the confines were not substantial in space, but it was an Aladdin's cave with a worn wooden floor that rested solid under the feet of the three occupants. The owner and the Peacock both drew their attention to the doorbell announcing Stephen's entry.

In the most civil manner Stephen could muster, he bid both men a good afternoon, the short and obviously nervous shop owner perspiring far too much for the cloudy day and attempting a smile. His eyes darted rapidly between Stephen and the Peacock through his small circular glasses.

The Peacock nodded in a curt enough way, but was clearly disgruntled by the interruption.

"Do excuse me, gentlemen," Stephen said, "I hope I am not interrupting anything."

The shop owner began to say something in a flustered way but was cut short.

"Actually, you are." The Peacock's voice was deep, intimidating but only because of practice. He seemed to have a slightly southern accent but in his attempt to unnerve Howes it sounded an almost gruff monotone. "Come back inna bit."

Stephen was a couple of paces from the man. He focused all his attention now on the shop owner, practically looking beyond the Peacock as if he was not even present.

"Tell me, my good man, why would you be handing so many coins over to a customer? Surely he should be paying you?"

Stephen was referring to the stacks of coins that were previously being gathered by the bulk in a suit, who was now adopting a more menacing manner.

"You see, I should have introduced myself, gentlemen. I am Detective Howes and I have reason to believe something illegal may be happening here."

The now clearly aggressive, suited man lowered his briefcase to the floor. He didn't return to standing tall instead arching a couple of inches shorter, as if in a stance to pounce at Stephen. He lowered his brow and said, "I'd suggest you fuck off, copper, before things get nasty. My boss won't be best pleased about this."

Stephen, standing with his arms clasped behind his back, remained in the composure of a gentleman having a friendly afternoon chat. He met the eyes of the Peacock.

"My counter suggestion to you would be that you do not act as I suspect you are about to."

With an obvious waver of the 'suggestion', the Peacock reached into the inside pocket of his jacket and withdrew a small six-inch knife, waiting for a second or two to let his target acquire a full view of the weapon in an attempt to scare.

However, in this exact instant, out of sight, Stephen dropped down the piece of lead pipe concealed in his jacket sleeve for just such an occasion, and the Peacock's lunging arm holding the knife was, in a flash, broken.

Stephen was fast. It's what had saved his life time and time again.

The man's stance had shown he would lunge. He was telegraphing his intentions and with a small side step, an arching swing of the pipe connected with the satisfying crack of bone.

Still in the momentum of the lunge, the large man dropped the knife as he dropped to his knees, clutching his wrist in the process of exhaling a howl that was cut short by Stephen pivoting on his right foot and smashing his left knee into the Peacock's face.

If indeed he had been a Peacock, his feathered display was well and truly ruffled for the future. At least a cheek and nose had been broken as he took the blow then slumped forward heavily. He lay face down motionless and the air seemed to have been taken from the room.

Stephen looked to the shop owner. "I take it he was demanding money for protection or else he'd put the shop out of business?"

The small Jewish man nodded, clearly ashamed, not noticing the drop of gentlemanly manner from Stephen's speech.

"The young man on the bench outside? Your son?"

Again, the shop owner nodded. "It eats William up paying these people for nothing. He works here most days but when I know it's collection day, I send him out on errands. It's been going up recently and we can't afford to pay. We are moving to London to be with my wife's family. This was our last payment but he didn't know that."

The owner took off his circular wire-framed glasses to clean them on the lower part of his off-white shirt, although they were already crystal clear. Stephen saw he had a tear in his eye and thought it was probably best they were getting out of town.

The Peacock was nothing more than a debt collector to higher authorities, the people who run the machine without getting their hands dirty. The top brass.

Stephen motioned for the shop owner to approach where the unconscious collector lay and handed him the lead pipe.

"If he moves, hit him with this. Don't worry, I will report that I did this for my protection and yours. I'll be back in a moment."

The detective picked up the knife and made his way out of the door. Looking to his right, he saw O'Connell still speaking to the young man on the bench, in front slightly to the left of the horse and carriage which was where it had been all along. Stephen leapt up the diver's mount, catching the driver off guard. Almost face to face, he pressed the knife to the driver's neck.

"Your Peacock friend is a little worse for wear right now. I'd like to report that to his master. Who would that be?"

Without a hesitation, the driver told all. The collections were finished for the day, regardless of what had taken place and they were to return to the office of a Mr Sören.

As Stephen stepped down after finding out all he needed to know, he told the driver to wait. He would return with the collector's briefcase and he was to deliver it to this Mr Sören.

Upon walking to the entrance, he was met by O'Connell.

"That lad's not going to rob that fella, his dad owns the bloody place. How wrong was I, eh, mate?"

"Wrong? You've made a great arrest today, Detective

O'Connell," Stephen said and motioned for him to enter the shop.

They both did, even though O'Connell could not make head nor tail as to what Stephen had meant. The owner was still standing perched over the dormant debt collector, holding the lead pipe in a white knuckled grip.

"Hey! Hold on there, me mate, what's going on here?"

It was all a new sight to O'Connell.

Stephen rested his hand on his shoulder. "This man has for weeks been paying protection money under duress to the now apprehended collector. He attacked me after you asked me to investigate, Detective. Now, thanks to you, I believe the man is under your arrest. We can wait till he comes around and walk him to the station or you can summon a paddy wagon to take him away while I wait here with the owner."

O'Connell knew he was being thrown a bone for this arrest, even if he didn't know why, and decided to capitalise on it. He looked at Stephen as if in total appreciation.

"You wait here, mate. I'll arrange the pick-up," he said and with that, he swiftly left.

Stephen turned to the shop owner after taking the lead pipe from his almost vice-like clammy nervous grip.

"How many days till you are out of Hull?"

"We'd planned to be away from here in a few days. We've already packed most things," he answered, pushing his glasses back up to the bridge of his nose.

"I think after what has happened here, you should make that sooner rather then later. Hand me the briefcase."

He did so and Stephen opened it on the counter. A collection of money lay strewn in the case, probably from the other 'collections'. He took a handful and placed it in his pocket. A hefty wedge but still leaving more than enough in the case.

"Get me a bag."

Hurriedly, the shop owner obeyed.

Stephen opened it and the remaining money was emptied into the bag.

He closed the briefcase and walked outside to the still-waiting carriage. Opening the carriage door, he left the case solitary and centred on the carpeted floor and said, "Take that where it needs to be."

With a whip and a holler, the driver was off as fast as manageable on the cobbles.

Returning to the shop, Stephen addressed the owner. "Take this money. He never came in with it and nobody needs to know anything else. It should help where you are going, but go now. The man who was expecting his payments will begin asking questions very quickly, but that's a policeman's job to deal with and it will go a lot easier if we don't have your safety to worry about."

With that, the shop owner's boy returned and saw the extortionist lying face down.

"Father… what…?" The confusion was evident.

"Do not ask questions, my boy. Get upstairs and tell your mother to hurry the preparations for leaving."

With so many questions, the boy reluctantly agreed and made for the back of the shop, going to the stairs leading above, never taking his eyes from Stephen.

When he left, the shop owner looked to Stephen.

"I cannot thank you enough, my boy. My heart lay heavy this day before you came and took the burden from me."

Before any more could be said, the door bell chimed.

"That's him, lads. Cuff him and take him away." O'Connell had returned with a beaming grin raising his facial hair to all new levels and watched as the crook was picked up and carted off.

Stephen patted O'Connell on the shoulder whilst giving the shop owner a wink.

"Well done, Detective O'Connell. You helped this old chap out a lot today. Shall we head back and tell the fellas about your big catch?"

O'Connell led the way back to the station, but before they entered the main doors, he stopped and turned to Stephen.

"Anything at all you need, lad, with your killer, you let me know. I'm not sure why you let me have this one but I needed it, that's for sure. I'd have looked a fool if you'd let me rush in like I was going to."

Entering the station, Detective O'Connell was the all worthy hero. He'd obviously spilled the beans to everyone in ear shot when he had previously returned for the bobbies and the paddy wagon.

It was not a regular recognition for him judging by his reaction, and he almost seemed emotional.

He answered the other detectives' questions with a prideful manner, even attempting to be modest. After a while, as the banter died down, Stephen returned to his mountain of paper work.

He opened another folder that he was positive had not been there before his lunch break. Just as he started the title, he was interrupted by O'Connell.

"Listen, lad, I just want to say once again tha…"

"Detective O'Connell, can I just stop you there?" Stephen's voice sounded stern. "It's obvious to see that I am busy, so please…"

Deflated and losing his recently-acquired vigorous stature, O'Connell pursed his lips nodded and began to skulk away from Stephen.

With a grin as he said it, Stephen called out after the him. "And Detective? You still owe me lunch."

O'Connell didn't turn, but the shoulders picked up and Stephen swore he could see the protruding whiskers raise in a smile from behind as he walked away.

CHAPTER 13

First movement.

It was Bach. Orchestral Suite No 3. In D major. Air.

That is the delightful melody that filled the inner sanctum of my mind. The dark and cobbled roads on the edge of the town centre makes this place a perfect expanse to create music.

I know on occasion I must change venue, but for my first real effort, I want it to be somewhere close to my heart. Close to where I was reborn in my current form.

Moisture hangs in the air like the anticipation of the audience becoming seated to bear witness to the delights of the evening.

I closed my eyes and pressed my back hard against the solid door.

There was barely room to stand with my equipment in the dark with me.

A musician, an artist needs tools and instruments to create and tonight these where my own instruments of demise. Three four foot lengths of metal wire. Just over a half inch thick. Easy to bend when heated up but hard, near impossible, with just bare hands.

I had tried and tested this theory just in case.

Until my very own portable burner was applied, the wire would remain stationary.

Perfect for the perfection I had in mind.

My subject: Harry Keen.

A local butcher.

I had attempted to acquire meat from him not two days ago, I had developed a taste for slabs of red meat since my theatre 'sketch'.

As he slammed the food I had intention of purchasing from him on the counter, he saw my disgust in his manners, or lack thereof. So, uncouth.

"What's up, mate? Not good 'nough for ya or summut?"

The question he asked, which positively sounded more of an accusation, I had decided not to dignify with an answer. I spun upon my heals and, without a second glance, walked out.

As I did, a loud grunt of amusement followed, not to mention more slights as to my character and attire. I did not hear them however.

By this time, I had decided it would be Harry who would assist me in my next work of art and I was already formulating a picture.

Such an honour, I doubt, he had an appreciation for, but an honour all the same.

He would aid in my aim to achieve a showing of genius to the masses.

Tonight, his footsteps echoed loudly before he was anywhere near where I waited with bated breath. As no other footsteps from anyone else could be heard, it was safe to assume we were alone.

He was not a rich man by any means. He had taken to sleeping his drunken nights in his shop recently… where he slept, when not slumming, surrounded by hunks of meat, I did not know, nor care to find out.

I had watched him lock up the premises earlier that evening from undercover as I took the disguise of a street sleeper. The wretched clothing I had acquired from a recently disposed 'practice piece'.

He even kicked at my blanket as he passed. A shot of pain ran through my leg but I knew he was heading to a public house nearby, and also that he would pay for that slight along with all his error-filled ways later the very same night.

When he returned, I had abandoned the idea of using the same disguise. In his intoxication, he might take to attacking a homeless person, which I had found out was extremely common, so I donned black yet again and waited in the dark. Feeling at home in the shadows. The snake that urged my killing and masterpiece simmered, eagerly awaiting to have its meal, rather than rush in anticipation.

He staggered by me, only feet from where I stood, however I was invisible in my perch.

He shifted from one side of the street and around the back of the shop, down the alley, clumsily fumbling for his keys. I heard the key find its mark and he unlocked the gate.

I glided slow and steady, my shoes hardly making a noise. The only noise present to me was still Bach, soothingly reassuring me with his notes of pleasure. I wanted Harry to turn when I rendered him docile for my own satisfaction, rather than require positioning. As a way of pleasantries and by way of rousing his attention, I spoke.

"Good evening, Harry."

He spun with his chin almost on his chest as the slouching subcategory of a human being without the decency to compose himself to an unknown passer-by greeting him civilly.

It made no difference.

The club I used caught his collar bone and sent him to the floor instantly. He let out a groan and another blow to the head ensured unconsciousness. I took a moment to compose myself once more.

The key was still in the latch and, after looking around to make sure no passer-by had seen the ruckus, I opened the door and dragged him inside. He was not a heavy fellow and delightfully easy to shift.

The gate led into the backyard of the shop, a set of wooden stairs leading to a top floor apartment, which had neither light nor life present and a back door to the shop itself, nothing else present but a putrid outside lavatory.

Taking the keys and finding a suitable fit, as silent as death himself, I eased open the shop's back door. My excitement barely containable, I saw a cutting table of around five feet long and three feet wide that I had already assumed would be present.

After some manoeuvring, I had Harry inside of the building

and lying flat on his back on the thick slab designed for displaying meat in a desired formation. How fitting.

I exited but did not close the door.

Reaching my previous point of camouflage, picking up my tools for the evening, the night felt more electric. I gleefully traced back to the shop and closing the external door, I cast a survey over the shop itself to ensure total privacy for our forthcoming event. Walking back to the cutting room once more, I paused at the entrance. Looking around the room, an effort was made to make a mental image of a dull and simplistic blank canvas.

Its filthy appearance to others may have been sickening to most senses, a dismal viewing and an old meat taste hung in the air, but to me it was a sheet of white that requires the attention to detail only someone with a mind such as mine could pay attention to.

Using a collection of sturdy rope, I set about securing Harry's body to the carving table. Although he was just a bit longer than the table itself, it was reasonable that his feet could have as much movement as they liked. With his upper legs wrapped in place, they were not going to be of use to him.

Also, his left arm was free for movement.

Of course, it would have to be…

Taking his filthy and bloodstained working apron, the very same he had worn whilst he insulted me, I put it in his mouth. If he was to wake abruptly, it would be needed to stifle his screams.

Taking off my jacket, waistcoat and hat, it was a sheer struggle to control my glee as I hung them on a meat hook. What a poor piece of meat Harry would make? I pondered as I rolled up my sleeves.

Picking the first metal rod, Bach began once more as my art began to take form. The rod felt almost light in my hands, the adrenaline rushing and making me feel as strong as a hundred men. Practically god-like in what was to be achieved. As if God himself were guiding my hand.

I did not need the heavy gloves for this task but I slipped them on before handling the metal all the same. A tight grip would be required and I did not wish to be left with blisters on my hands as they are a sign of the lower classes.

Lining up my aim, placing the rod on Harry's left shoulder, taking in the details, I noticed the indent the weight of the rod made on his filthy beer-stained shirt. Metal made an indent on his flesh.

In an instant, Harry Keen became one and the same with my piece of metal. Using my grip and body weight, I forced the rod down heavily. I couldn't hear anything. The music in my cranium amassed to a peak. Keen opened his eyes as the rod found bone to push against. Blood quickly stained his shirt around the shoulder where the rod had entered. Leaping upon the table I leant down and picked up the pre-laid lump hammer and struck the top to bypass the obstacle of solid bone.

My hands were no longer sophisticated organs of touch, they were something different. Something malevolent in their construction.

With three strikes I heard the rod hit wood and knew it had fully made its way through Harry's now writhing body.

Long loud howls muffled into the butcher's apron, filling the air as it blended with the violins that so eloquently smothered the room.

Although his arm was free, it was now more or less disabled. Dismounting the table and basking in the fits of delightful song he made, I began, or should I say I tried to ignite the homemade burning device with the protective gloves, I made a quite a clumsy attempt and stifled a chuckle at my own idiocy.

It was quite lucky no one was around to see my mistake, as it may have looked quite foolish, almost amateur, however I was nervous for my first solo inspirational performance. Who wouldn't be? I wanted it to be so delightfully perfect, like some actors' first tread of the boards, I would shake and forget elements but soon enough I would become an experienced thespian in my own right.

The burner sparked a huge concentrated flame and turning to Keen, the notion crossed my mind that his eyes were practically bulging from his head upon seeing my instrument.

"Now do not fret, my good man... No doubt this may horrify your every thought... Try to rest easy and know dignity in the fact you are the sole witness to my greatness of this very night... However, the shame in itself, is that you cannot tell others of how unique the masterpiece will be, the finished product will speak volumes." For a second, I envisaged burning his eyes with the flame I held in my hand, but I had a plan. One that I was to stick to.

Applying the burner to the lower end of the rod inches away from Keen's shoulder, it quickly began to glow. The heat conducted down and burnt Keen's skin.

It was quite a smell, only rivalled by steak prepared and cooked on hot coal or rock. This created and odd mixture of senses. A raw meat smell lingered on every aspect throughout the room yet here close to the source of blistering flesh, it seemed to blend a taste to the palate that I became curious about.

When I was convinced the heat had made it possible to bend the rod, and with the assistance of the protective glove, holding the base as close to the shoulder as could be managed, I began to bend the rod over his shoulder but also down his outstretched arm.

The slow business of curling the rod down, then under, around then over and again around seemed to take an eternity, but one hardly noticed. They do say that time flies when one is having fun.

Every now and again, heating the rod caused burns to his wound. When reaching the end of the rod, I was very happy with the appearance it produced.

Keen's arm was forcefully held in place by the rod, like a metallic spring enclosing his limb that now, sufficiently cooled, would be near impossible for him to free himself. Held out in front of him it gave the appearance of a half 'hugging' structured arm.

There was enough room to fit a body between his chest and hand, which also faced inwards due to the forced positioning of the tip of the rod.

Harry had been passing in and out of consciousness, more than likely due to the shock and pain as every time I attempted to bend the rod, inevitably it pulled and tugged at the part penetrating his shoulder. As I freed his other arm, he was awake enough to try and resist but his diminishing hope of freedom soon became apparent when I inserted the second rod this time in his right shoulder.

With only two strikes of the hammer this time, I was happy that so quickly 'efficiency' had been learnt and achieved with the hammer.

The same process repeated to his right arm, Harry Keen lay on the table mumbling through the cloth still wedged in his mouth in a splendid stupor.

His eyes lulling, he was ready for his final part in our joint accomplishment.

With his arms held in a full hug but holding nothing, it was time for the third and final rod.

Arriving at the head of the table, I pulled his head back via his thick grease-like hair, my hands feeling dirty even with the recently and richly scorched gloves.

Placing the rod into his mouth I spoke the last words he would hear on this planet. As if to a fellow actor forgetting his lines, the words were delivered in little more than a whisper.

"Good manners cost nothing, my friend, but this, Harry, this will straighten you out..."

Using as much force that could be mustered, leaning in so my body weight was fully upon the rod, it followed Harry's body horizontally via his mouth internally. No doubt becoming interrupted by organs, but keeping its aim true, the pushing continued until grip would not allow me to push further.

A rush of blood, mixed with pieces of body parts torn by the intrusive rod from his gaping retched mouth along with the disfigurement of his windpipe and I knew he would not last long. The act itself had taken mere moments.

The rod had punctured several of the major elements needed to live. An array of noises from his rotten mouth spilled forth, certainly no match for any musical instrument of the time but just as reactive to the ear, he twitched and thrashed. He looked more like a doomed fish than ever and I had no choice but to stand back and admire the splendour of the man's final attempts at breathing. My own panting seeming as laboured as Mr Keen's. I bent to observe his eyes and couldn't help but smile at my perspiration. Creating art was indeed frightfully exhausting work.

At last he lay dormant.

Some type of device to capture the visuals would have been a god's gift but fortunately or unfortunately, I shared that sight with no one and once more, much delight was taken watching the light and life fade from another misguided heathen.

Before my work was done, the message had to be left which was the cause of all this bloodshed, to let all know that this was indeed my work and not that of an imposter. Using several of Mr Keen's implements around the shop and after approximately an hour, I took my leave, not before turning in the doorway, visually devouring my work as it would shortly be appreciated by other persons to find.

In awe of the beauty, whilst bowing, a simple word passed my lips…

"Masterpiece."

CHAPTER 14

"Detective Howes?"

"Russell, you don't have to refer to me as 'Detective' in conversation."

"Sorry, Stephen. You asked for extreme cases of murder? This one shocked us all a while back but we never found the culprit. I have daughters myself, sir, and this one sprang to mind instantly. It's nothing short of disgusting. If he could do this, then who knows what he is capable of?"

Stephen had only been given a few cases of any real gore or significance since the theatre killing. Sparse with a potential as to lead anywhere but with few details taken at most crime scenes, almost nothing could be gleaned.

As he read the report to Russell's case, Stephen knew that this particular case was nothing in the slightest to do with his target, but it certainly touched the core of his humanity. He had to act all the same.

The following information was collected through eye witness accounts and previously kept police files:

Martin Slick of West Hull, eighteen years of age, was still at large on the suspected murder of his own child.

His long-term girlfriend, Beth Hauge, and her younger brother, both recount that on March 30th 1890. Martin, after returning from a Wakefield house of correction for a third time, was told of the birth of his daughter.

He was noticed to be agitated upon hearing the news.

During the following week, Martin's unemployment clearly had tension rising in the house, directly centred around the child.

Beth, for the courtesy of her brother, had taken to changing in another room (not that of the main living room) to keep a common decency.

Whilst she did so one morning, she heard the muffled wail of her child. Returning to where she had laid the infant in her cot, she saw her brother waking, as he had been asleep in the living room chair.

Martin Slick stood in the middle of the room, holding the baby to his chest with the child's face firmly grasped by the back of the head. Martin appeared to be attempting to stifle further cries from his daughter.

Beth rushed to the aid of the child and pulling the unfortunate from Mr Slick's arms, she noticed a discolouration in the child's lips.

She instantly called her brother to fetch the surgeon who lived two doors down the street.

During the panic, Martin Slick made his exit and has not been seen since.

The child did not survive the injuries and the surgeon recognised the cause of death as asphyxiation due to a crushing of the wind pipe which was later confirmed by the police surgeon.

By the time he had finished reading the report, Stephen had unknowingly started to clench his jaw at the callousness of the crime.

The shear disgust at the thought had caused him to be momentarily absent from his surroundings. He was not even focused on anything accept rage when Detective Ford's voice brought him back into the room.

"How someone could do that to a poor child is beyond me? We interviewed the mother, Beth, but could not get a lot of sense from her. As you can imagine, she was distraught to say the least."

Stephen informed Ford that he would be away from the office for a while. Although ultimately focused on his actual task of finding the Artistic Killer, he had an unrelenting urge to act upon this new case.

Unfortunately for a certain Mr Slick, Stephen's humanity and moral compass matched his anger. As any case would start, he would interview all those who saw the incident and those who knew the culprit best. How it would end however would be very different to normal police cases.

He had noted the address of Beth Hauge and, making his way towards the Queen's Dock, he hailed a passing carriage and told the driver to head for Charles Street.

He had the driver pull to a halt at the top, and, stepping out, he took in the road.

He could almost picture the young Martin running from the scene of his crime. Along past the shops and away to who knows where? That adrenaline pushing him forward. Away from the guilt. Or had he felt any guilt at all? With a crime such as this, a justification was needed.

A motive.

He needed a reason to even attempt to kill his own flesh and blood.

Stephen walked on the busy road and made his way to the address further along, away from the town centre.

Finally, he arrived. The path was unkempt and weeds sprang from between the cracks in the floor, like a disease encompassing, consuming, intent on devouring the suburbs that had grotesquely begun to plough over the great green land.

Stephen's rule as an investigator was that nobody just 'vanishes'.

Arriving at the small house of Beth Hauge, his hunt would start.

A young man of around thirteen answered the door with a sullen look and dirt covering his hands and arms, ruffled hair and more dirt around his features.

"Wot do you want?"

The tone was not that of arrogance, more of disdain.

"I'm Detective Howes of a special branch in Hull's police force. I was wondering if I may speak to a Miss Hauge?"

The young man appeared annoyed at the very idea that this detective might even slightly impede on his time.

"I know you're a copper an' I don't give a toss 'bout where you're from. You're dressed fancy, but none of you lot are smart enough to catch that murdering bastard, are ya?"

Stephen kept his composure that of a pleasant nature. Just reading the report, he had been incensed, so to be present at the crime being committed and not have prevented it, must have left an ocean of bitterness within the young man.

As reassuring as he could muster, he answered the youth in a manner of certainty and without grace.

"Not as yet, but I will be changing that soon enough. Am to take it you are Miss Hauge's younger brother, Billy?"

"That's right. I want to see that bastard swing for what 'e did but we've 'eard nowt from you lot."

The two stood for a while until finally Billy moved back but made no other gesture. Stephen took the youth's meaning and stepped inside. Though the day had been overcast, the look of cold and foreboding decline inside made Stephen wish he could conduct his business anywhere else but here.

Even in the cramped, almost claustrophobic hallway, the house had a sombre tone. The smell of damp wood rot seemed to seep into his clothes like cigarette smoke in a hansom, as he stood waiting for Billy to close the front entrance. The colour of the walls was indistinguishable due to the lack of natural light.

From the living room, he could hear the faint sound of humming. Other than that, the place vibrated silence.

The humming was a familiar child's lullaby.

The next situation for him was going to be a difficult one, but essential.

In such moments, Stephen had a unique gift of fact finding.

He could turn off the part of his brain that would become clouded with judgements, emotions and misleading thoughts.

To be able to distance himself allowed him to digest the facts and accurately assume possible and actual events within the compounds of his mind.

He had once heard a saying: "Even as a tiger leaps to attack you, you can still admire its beauty." With this unique talent he could investigate to the best of his ability because stepping back from emotions allowed the clearest vision of all.

It was a crude gloomy walk with only a single door to his left dividing the hallway from what he could guess was the kitchen at the end.

The door frame, yellow and stained with years of neglect, gave way to a dark room with shards of light from outside faintly illuminating the bare surroundings. All the room held was a fireplace, a chair and an empty, childless cot.

A young woman haunted the crypt-like room, dressed in a scruffy and unkempt black mourning dress. A ghostly apparition in flesh.

Her face was turned away from Stephen as she knelt by the cot.

He waited in the doorway as he expected the young man to announce his entrance to the lady, but instead he simple walked past Stephen and into the kitchen.

Although he needed to speak to Billy, he knew it would most likely be a better option to ask his questions when Billy and his sister were apart.

With a silence, save for the gentle humming, Stephen took a breath and entered the room.

"Excuse me, ma'am, am I to assume you are Miss Beth Hauge?"

She turned her head at breakneck speed as if she had not been aware of his presence until that very instant. She was not a woman of beauty and nor would she ever be. Her hair was frayed, unkempt and tied back, her features simply not of a complementing manner with her pale face, sunken eyes and gaunt cheeks.

The sadness was evident but there seemed a hint of something else. Like she was angered at Stephen for making such a noise.

She rose from the cot and walked towards him.

Like an apparition in a crow black gown, she carefully walked closely and, in a hushed tone as if not to disturb someone, asked what he wanted in an extremely annoyed manner.

Subconsciously, Stephen adopted the same hushed tone to

answer her. "Miss Hauge, I was wondering if I might ask you a few questions?"

He looked at the cot and realised this woman was extremely and understandably traumatised.

A doll lay in the place where a child should be, a tatty porcelain doll with its face broken slightly below its ice cold blue eyes.

The irony of the broken mother and the doll's face made Stephen aware that his 'typical' line of questioning may not be as direct as he was used to, but this was not a 'typical' case.

Something very terrible had happened here, unspeakable and unmanageable for Beth.

As soon as this had registered, he immediately adjusted his mode of enquiry.

"If you don't mind, Miss Hauge, I was wondering if you could tell me if you know a Martin Slick?"

Almost appreciative of his hushed question, she relaxed her tensed shoulders and answered in a less agitated, reasoned voice. Although she spoke softly, the noise disturbed the silence of the room like an earthquake. Resonating from floor to ceiling. The house was so quiet, every person in the abode appeared to be trespassing on the muteness.

"Of course, we were walking out fer years but I aint seen 'im in ages, not since 'e upt an' left us."

At this, she turned towards the cot as if to indicate Martin had abandoned mother and child.

"I understand, but can you think of where Martin may have absconded?"

She looked perplexed and her face wrinkled in obvious confusion. "You mean where 'e's gone? No, I told the men who came looking for 'im before that I didn't know where 'e was… 'e's always in trouble, an' a wrong un but I fell for 'im, plenny said I shunt but I've ad nuff of 'im now… 'e's not good for any of us."

Again, with her head down, a little more sombre this time, she looked towards the cot.

"When he was here previously, did he have any associates or 'friends', I mean?"

She gave a gasp that in other circumstances could be interpreted as a sarcastic laugh but this was probably all she could manage in the form of any gesture not of a glum, laborious nature.

"You've not met 'im before, mister, 'ave you? Martin dunt really mix well. 'E's a bit of a charmer with women but 'e's not really one fur friends. All 'e would do was go out first thing, then 'e'd come 'ome after looking for work with a bit of cut meat and fall to sleep before waking all grumps and groans with me, an' the young un."

She looked again at the cot, taking two steps closer and, standing on her toes, she peeked in.

She was clearly looking at the doll but Stephen knew what she saw lying there.

He wanted to leave right there and then, but as a saving grace in the worst type of way, she craned her neck and then as if seeing the doll for the first time and not her deceased infant, like a puppet cut from its string, she gasped, raised her hands to her mouth and then Beth fell to her knees. She hardly made a sound as she slumped.

Stephen stepped to her and rested a hand on her shoulder.

She was sobbing and with a whisper he heard her brother from the doorway.

"Best leaving 'er alone for a while, mate."

Stephen didn't know what to do. Wanting to make the situation better, he knew her mind was as fragile as trust among thieves, it needed to go through its own process of fixture and rebuilding.

He nodded and stepped solemnly from the room.

Billy nodded towards the kitchen and closed the door to the living area. Following Stephen, he placed a dirty, damaged kettle to boil.

"See the dints in this? That bastard bounced it off my head more than once."

Knowing Billy would be able to recount the murder, Stephen suspected that the young man was of a delicate temperament of rage rather than sorrow.

"Have you lived here long?"

"Since I was born."

"Who else lives here?"

"Just me an' Beth. We 'ad a couple living upstairs but after what 'appened, they didn't stay about much longer… can't really blame um, can ya? It was me dad's 'ouse and 'e left it to us when 'e died."

"Do you have their names? The tenants upstairs, that is."

"Yeah, Mr and Mrs Harris. They won't be able to tell you much though. They wernt in when it 'appened."

"Do you know where they moved to?"

"Yeah, I have a forwardin' address for letters. Seems daft as non of um cud read."

Billy opened a drawer with half-rotted handles and handed Stephen a poorly scribbled address.

He copied the street name and house number in a notebook that he kept in his jacket and resumed asking questions. All the while Billy waited with his arms folded, leaning against the side and his legs folded too, watching the detective write.

"How would you describe Martin?"

At the mention of the name, Billy spat into the hard-wooden flooring. " 'Opefully dead, but 'scum' or 'bastard' usually sums 'im up."

The disdain was simmering but it did not get Stephen any closer to finding his culprit.

"Physically, what does he look like?"

He had to remember to simplify questioning as some words might not be within reach of the young man's vocabulary.

As Billy Hauge gave a description, often interrupted by outbursts of varying vulgarity that were certainly within reach of his vocabulary, Stephen noted the particulars into his notebook.

When he was satisfied that he would be able to pick the guilty man from a crowd, he asked Billy if he might have any idea where Martin might be or even if, when Billy had gone to fetch the surgeon, which way he had gone? Anything that could be of use.

"I 'ope 'e's fucking rotting in hell! That's which way 'e's going."

His voice was raised significantly and he was clenching his fists… Stephen needed to calm the young man.

"Billy? I understand your hatred, trust me, I do. I lost someone very close to me. The only way I coped with such a tragedy was by helping others around me, those who also felt the loss, and by remaining calm."

This statement was not entirely true, Stephen had lost a friend a long time ago but as for having to help others with the loss… that was a fabrication.

He lied simply because if people thought he understood their grief, they opened up more. It was a basic of questioning.

If the agitated didn't feel the need to make people realise how they felt then they could put that emotion aside, the need of empathy. The need of understanding.

Billy's posture seemed to alter. He collected himself and answered in a calmer tone. "I don't know where 'e used to go. 'E didn't 'ave any mates that I know ov. Jus' used to leave the 'ouse early on and come back 'bout four with a few pieces of grub, and fall asleep, waking up all arsey if the meat wernt done. Other than that I don't know much else. If I did, I'd tell ya. I want him shaking 'ands with the 'angman for what 'e done."

Stephen thanked the young man for the information. Billy also indicated which way Martin had fled on the day of the crime. It was the way Stephen had approached the house, towards the town centre, and he told Billy that if he was to hear or see anything that might help the police catch Martin Slick, he was to tell only Stephen and that he could be found at the central police station on Parliament Street.

The detective saw himself out of the house. As he passed the living room door, he could once again hear the humming of the same lullaby that had greeted him. He hoped he wouldn't have to come back to this place, for his own selfish reasons.

The horrors contained within its walls… he believed nothing could equal the killing of a child. The desperation of the damned that was on a spiral of decay seemed to reach out and try to take him back into its embrace as he closed the front door behind him.

Madness at that moment seemed contagious and he wanted to be upon his heels, sooner rather than later.

Taking the address, he started to walk towards the new residence of Mr and Mrs Harris, the previous upstairs tenants of the crime scene, a little down the road to Waterloo Street.

When he arrived, it was evident the couple were not of wealth. The house they now resided in was not unlike their previous abode apart from the distinction of sorrow surrounding the bricks and mortar.

Mr Harris answered the door, a frail-looking man with bushy eyebrows and hair that reminded Stephen of a feral animal, and after a brief introduction he showed the detective to the back half of the terraced house which he and his wife were renting. The owners of the house were not home and neither was Mr Harris's wife.

He offered Stephen a cup of tea and asked him to sit whilst he prepared the brew.

The accommodation was not welcoming or homely but a bed in the corner and a table in the centre, although taking up most the room, were made to a tidy fashion.

Poverty was rife in the town. Although Stephen had been fortunate to receive a large down payment for his assignment and had taken to suitably lodgings, he was seeing more of the bleak conditions than most people with his promised wealth were used to.

The investigation he was hired to complete by Craven Wilkinson was of a sinister nature in its outcome, but Stephen knew he would be seeing far worse conditions before his task was complete.

Mr Harris placed a cup of hot black tea in front of Stephen and he thanked him accordingly.

"You will 'ave to beg my pardon, sir. I wuz workin' late shift. I took the odd hours to ern a bit more… as you can see we're not sackly rollin in it."

Mr Harris let out a long rasping cough, clearly a heavy smoker.

Stephen offered him his handkerchief and Harris took it and looked at it, as he wheezed the last of the cough, as if he had never in his day seen the likes of it.

Without making any use of it, he handed it back with a distinct lack of understanding as to why it had been given to him in the first place.

Not wanting to embarrass the man as to what a handkerchief was used for and explain that 'using the back of the hand to shield only some projectiles of phlegm was not the done thing', Stephen thought better and proceeded with why he had come to visit in the first place.

"Mr Harris, I understand you were not present during the incident at the Hauge residence, I am however interested as to if you know anything that might help me locate the whereabouts of Mr Slick."

Harris pulled the opposite chair without lifting it and the wooden chair legs on wooden flooring made a scraping noise that made Stephen want to thrash manners into the man, but he had a feeling that Harris's lungs would give out before a drop of decency could be achieved.

"If you wud 'ave been 'ere when Isyet was 'ere…"

"Isyet?" said Stephen.

"Dat's me wife, Isyet. She's Polish. If she were 'ere, I wud not be able to say a fing. but since she aint I can share somefing I cunt wiv the coppers before… sorry… police."

Detective Howes gave a dismissive wave of his hand as to let Mr Harris know that manners and formalities were a thing not to be present in this room.

"I've a problem. Can't 'elp puttin money on 'orses, I love me wife but I need to 'ave a bet now an' again. Keeps me yun, dunnit?"

The coughing started again and he took a sip from his cup to calm his throat.

Stephen hoped it would not be a long story, because he didn't think Mr Harris would survive it at this rate.

"I finish about two frum wurk an' 'ed to the bookies. I usually quit an hour or two later, I don't want 'er knowing I spend me wages in there. Well, a few times I've sin that little toe rag walkin' from the alley not far from where the bookies are. First time, I tried sayin' ' 'ello' but he straight ignored me, so after that I never so much as paid 'im the time a day. 'E tret them in that 'ouse like shite but rent was cheap, so me and Isyet just kept ourselves out ov it. When 'e did what 'e dun, we left an' got this place. Every day I used to see 'im, seemed odd though cuz it don't lead to nowhere that alley 'e'ed come from. Just a back bit to the shops."

Stephen waited for the next batch of splutters and fits of chesty coughs to finish, as he did a large piece of phlegm made its way over the table at high velocity and into Stephen's cup of tea which he subtly pushed to one side and made a mental note to not touch it again.

Finally, when the wave of a potential rib cage collapsing rasps had passed, Stephen asked where his bookies were located and in his simplistic yet directionally inadequate answer, Mr. Harris had not only landed phlegm in front of Detective Howes, but possibly the biggest piece of the puzzle yet.

As soon as soon as he gave a description of where the alley was, suddenly it all came together where Martin may be.

"Just down the road, on Charles Street… you can't miss it."

Mr Harris pointed down the street as he launched into a fresh batch of coughs. As heartless as it seemed, the detective quickly made his exit as he was too busy catching a killer to be pumping Harris's chest to keep him alive after he could potentially collapse at any minute.

The rest of Stephen's day was spent in a small tea shop just a bit further down from where the alley was located.

Around a quarter to three, and four cups of tea later, Stephen noticed the curtains to the upstairs of the suspected abode of Martin Slick move slightly on one side and then the other.

Someone was peering out cautiously.

A few minutes later, a man walked from the alley in a long

jacket with the collar up and a flat cap pulled down. He couldn't have looked more suspicious if he'd tried.

If fortune favoured the brave, it was not favouring the cautious because the poorly disguised chap was walking straight to the café in which Stephen was situated. If it was who Stephen thought it was, then this was a perfect chance for him to get a good look.

Slightly lifting his head to view the occupants of the cafe, Martin Slick unwittingly revealed himself to Stephen. With the ginger hair, long beard and slight scar on his eyebrow exactly where Billy Hauge had described it, he glanced over to Stephen, who looked nonchalantly back to his paper that had been on the same page since he had first sat in the cafe.

Satisfied under the misconception that nobody knew who he was, Martin Slick made his way to the counter with an uneasy speed which radiated that of 'a man in a hurry'.

Even if Stephen had not been looking for Martin, after seeing the man's actions he would have been suspicious of him being 'up to something'.

In a voice barely broken with age, Martin ordered a cup of tea and a sandwich.

Stephen had gotten everything he needed and stood to exit the café. At the scrape of his chair, Martin jumped and would have bolted had it not been for the fact that Stephen purposely paid him no mind as he left.

He took a position down the road and after a few minutes he saw Martin cautiously peer from the doorway, looking both sides of the street, and, satisfied the coast was clear, make his way back to the alley.

Stephen returned to the police station. He now knew where his prey resided.

He felt pity for Beth Hauge, that the truth would never come to light, but given her current state of mind, it was probably all round a better situation for the young lady.

In a court, any good solicitor would pick apart her story due to her duress. Stephen did not want Martin to pass through the legal system… he wanted a primal sense of justice to be served. He could not risk that the judge may or may not don the black cap as he passed sentence on the wicked Martin Slick.

Being mid-afternoon, only Detective Raffle and Detective Ford were present in the office.

Desk Sergeant Alan busied himself with non-existent tasks at the front desk but even in the short time of assisting the branch Stephen had learnt to ignore him.

He bid a good afternoon to both detectives and received pleasantries in return.

Ford asked if any progress had been made and Stephen felt a twinge of guilt towards his work colleague, as he lied and said, "Nothing more than the report had depicted."

Ford, by what Stephen had seen so far, was a competent policeman and seemed like he wanted to make an honest difference in the world.

Stephen enquired to the whereabouts of the Chief Inspector and as he had expected and hoped, CI Rudyard was not in the office.

Mumbling about having to collect a file, he went into Rudyard's office and, opening the bottom draw of the desk, he found exactly what he had been looking for.

During one afternoon, the collection of detectives had decided to congratulate O'Connell down the local pub, leaving the place empty. Stephen had searched the police station for something like this that he could use in such an occasion.

A gun that could be mistaken for a hand cannon. Big and menacing, Stephen wouldn't even need ammunition but it would be accompanying him on his 'wrapping up' of the latest case. He needed it for the shock factor, to ensure Martin Slick would not make a run for it.

Wrestling the lump into the back of his trousers, he picked up a few loose sheets of paper from the desk and, strolling back into the main office, held the paper up as evidence. "Got them," he said but the words were wasted.

Ford was writing and Detective Raffle had left in the space of time Stephen had been in the office.

He slipped from the police station with gun in belt and made his way by foot to his previous destination, to make sure Martin Slick did not abscond, to lie in wait.

Clutching his coat against the wind that had built suddenly and securing the gun still in the back of his trousers, he waited with the alley in plain view.

As the dark of the day crept in and the wind brought a chill, people hurried home to the comfort of their households.

He focused on the task at hand, picturing all scenarios and possible outcomes. He knew Martin would be there, but more than likely when Stephen arrived, Martin would suspect that he was being taken into custody.

The gun would shock enough to make Martin not want to lunge or dart for an exit.

If someone else was unexpectedly present, then that would have to be dealt with accordingly.

In the café, Stephen overheard that Martin had only ordered food for one person, which was in itself was reassuring.

Martin Slick was a thief, a leech of life and a baby killer. He ranked extremely low on Stephen's list of people who deserved to exist and after tonight, he would no longer be part of that list.

Just another face added to Stephen's sleepless dreams and reminders.

When darkness had completely fallen and he was satisfied that Martin's sandwich would be digesting by now, and hoping to catch him dozing, Stephen made his way to the alley. Like so many hundreds of them in and around the area, it was damp and putrid to the senses. Locally known as 'ten foots' due to their width, a maze of them could be found around the entire network of streets. Stepping into the mouth of it, Stephen gave himself a minute to adjust his vision.

Seeing the layout assured him that passers-by would not be able to see in clearly because of the poor gas street lighting in the area.

Unless of course extra attention was paid and he hoped not to be spending enough time in the alley to give anyone that chance.

Stephen walked along the building, down the cobbled side street and reached the back gate with his heart pounding in the familiar feeling of stepping into an unknown danger.

The latch lifted on the wooden gate but it was locked. He had thought as much on seeing the heavy gate, but this was not an issue for Stephen. A quick jump and grasp of the wall to the side of the gate and he was hoisting himself up and over, dropping down with much less effort and noise. Peering around into the back, he saw a crooked stairway that looked unable to hold any type of load, led to the upstairs flat where Martin was residing. There was also an outside toilet at the back but as there was no noise coming from it, he could safely assume Martin was not present in a dark dank little WC.

Stephen crept up the stairs as quite as nightshade itself and reaching the top, he placed his ear close to the dishevelled, neglected door.

Although on the run, it seemed Martin was not as cautious as he should have been.

No scampering could be heard from the inside so Stephen retrieved his lockpick kit from his jacket pocket and began on the small obstacle separating Martin Slick from his fate.

This particular lock was poorly developed. His practise on much harder locks was not put to waste, as it only took seconds to unsecure the door.

Stephen took a deep breath.

He steadied his footing, although unable to stop the nervous shake that plagued all in high intensity situations. Not fear. Rather a sense of not knowing. He let the cold air sit in his lungs.

The wind kicked up as if to push him into his task.

With a swift smooth motion, he was in the room and covering all points with his pistol. He saw Martin rising from a worn chair in confusion at the disturbance to his dozing. The room was lit by only two candles but Stephen was used to the dark by now.

In an authoritative voice, he spoke to the waste of blood and oxygen for the first time. "Martin Slick, you're under arrest. I have a gun pointed at your chest and if you attempt to flee, I will shoot you where you stand."

Stephen stepped forward purposely and Martin's eyes widened at the enormous pistol, stopping his half attempt to stand in a wave of better thought.

Before the fight had even gotten into Martin, it had diminished.

'Coward,' thought Stephen, but he was also glad of the lack of effort needed.

"Do you know why I am here, Martin?"

Martin's drowsiness cleared through the severity of his situation and suddenly he turned into the arrogant taker of life that Stephen had mentally built for him. Suppressing a yawn, he said, "Has that fat pig downstairs tol' the coppers?"

"The shop owner? What makes you say that?"

"Cus for long nuff I've bin milking the fat idiot."

Martin made to reach for his pocket but stopped as Stephen stepped closer to emphasise his intention of using the pistol, the barrel seeming bigger than them both at this moment in time.

"Calm down. Am gettin in a cig."

Stephen's blood boiled whilst the cocksure killer reached in and lit his tatty self-rolled cigarette. The smell was putrid, even to a fellow occasional smoker. Martin was making himself comfortable. Stephen let him relax, seeing no reason to rush what was coming. He knew the despicable creature had a story to tell.

"I wor with his son in Wakey nick. Carl 'is name was, nowt but a little cry baby. I 'eard his accent and pretended to be all pally cus we wer both from 'ull."

Martin took a long drag from his rancid tobacco filled rolly. He blew the smoke out directly towards Stephen's face. This was not the best of actions on Martin's behalf, but up until now he was still unaware of the gravity of the situation he was in.

"Few weeks before I got out, 'e tells me 'bout 'is old man 'avin' a shop, so I ask why 'e didn't get me a job lined up for when I got out? Says something about 'is old man mebey not liking me and I never took kindly to it. Told 'im 'e better write to 'is dad and tell 'im to look after me on the outside when I got released. I told 'im if 'e dint, I would give a few of the lads the nod in Wakey and they would take care of 'im good and proper. Told 'im if 'e warned 'is dad, I would make things even worse for 'is dad than I would for 'im. 'E did as 'e was told and when I got out, 'is old man couldn't give me work but sum things, meat off cuts to get me by if I needed it. A bit ago I needed somewhere to stay so 'e gave me the room as 'e was waiting for Carl to get out n then it would be 'is place."

"Another reference to your character, Martin, but try again… why else would a policeman come to arrest you?"

Stephen found it near impossible to keep from squeezing the trigger. Martin grinned, a sly grin, barely recognisable in the low light but it was there and enough to make Stephen's face flush with anger.

"Probably cus I killed that baby."

"Your baby?" The words were spoken through gritted teeth.

"Says uw? Nowt to do with me, mate. I went to Wakey nick for seven months and when I came out, the tart 'ad got knocked up and pushed that thing out."

Stephen, before this day, had been in many rooms with many killers.

Men who had taken the lives of other people's loved ones.

On many occasions he had been paid to end their life.

It was exactly what his 'needed' specialty had been when someone would hire him.

He may have only been a competent investigator, but when someone needed finding and then 'losing' forever, he was the first person on people's list. And for very good reason.

To do this, he needed nerves of steel, vision of crystal clarity, awareness to cover all situations and to be able to deal with potentially negative outcomes but on this occasion his nerves frayed.

He lost his crystal-clear vision.

The sound of Martin's voice and uneducated mind as to the complexities of child birth were leading factors in his next actions.

Not to mention the damning of such a poor helpless child, whose end was met by such low-level sub-human scum.

He pictured the baby being picked up, expecting kindness and nurture. Almost excited at the unfamiliar face, then the terror at this man's next actions as the infant would cry out in pain and misunderstanding.

Stephen was across the room in an instant and brought the butt of the gun down on Martin's head.

A clunk of metal on bone and Stephen stepped back to witness Martin howl and clutch his head where an arc of blood had first spurted and then started to pour.

Stephen felt that he was a little more in control of himself but was still struggling with his detestation.

He threw Martin a dirty rag that lay on the floor and resumed his previous position of standing a few feet away and pointing the gun square at Martin, who at this point was on his knees. His eyes rolled a little and blood oozed its way down his face which contorted in pain, his breathing heavy through crooked teeth.

"Aaaaaa what the fuck? Ya dirty cunt! Fuck!"

"I think we better get you to the station, Martin. That looks a nasty cut and the officers waiting downstairs are eager to have you in the cells."

Stephen had lied because he didn't want Martin running as soon as he made it through the door. Martin stumbled up, unsteady on his feet and cursing. Stephen waved the gun towards the exit in a hint of direction to the youth.

"Der better be someone to stitch me up, you fucking pig!"

He feebly attempted to sound demanding as he staggered towards the door. When he was a couple of steps from the front door, Stephen called Martin's name.

"Here, you'll need your jacket, it's cold outside"

As Martin turned, one arm up to his head holding the cloth to stifle the bleeding, Stephen thrust his hand out.

His fingers locked straight in a downward facing salute instead of a clenched fist.

The finger tips collided into Martin's windpipe and immediately visibly dented above the thorax.

A splutter, along with a gurgle, forced through Martin's gritted teeth as he stumbled back, confused. He held the bloody rag to his throat, forgetting to drop it in utter confusion as he switched from the deep cut that was still heavily bleeding, to the fatal indent, instantly struggling for breath and coughing as air could not take its natural route to his lungs.

Stephen stepped forward, close enough to see the bloodshot veins now bursting in Martins eyes.

In an emotionless voice, he spoke one final time to Martin Slick. "This, you piece of filth, is what your daughter would have felt like."

He pushed Martin without any real effort needed. The youth stumbled back out of the door that had been left open and, whilst still feebly clutching his neck, he toppled over the old wooden handrail of the stairs.

The crack of body on ground, although it was only one storey up, was still satisfying for Stephen.

He lowered the gun and placed it into the back of his trousers. He controlled his breathing as he walked to look over the handrail, glad he didn't have to test whether this wooden staircase would hold two people.

Martin was motionless. His body lay prone with his head to his shoulder.

Lighting a cigarette and inhaling to combat the cold in his lungs and to steady his hands, Stephen took his time in descending the stairs.

Satisfaction filled his thoughts that it had been a good day of detective work and also that he was the hand of the earthly laws of justice.

He stood over Martin's body and, taking a large drag of the cigarette, he knelt down and forcefully pressed his knee against Martin's neck. Using his own body weight, he pressed further and slowly until he heard the pop-crack that he knew confirmed Martin's demise.

Standing, he exhaled the cigarette smoke, then turned the lump of body over and it was evident it was no longer a living organism. Decay was soon to be his only task and Stephen revelled in being the instrument of his demise, so to speak, watching as the death twitches rattled Martin's body until finally, it rattled no more. The world already seemed a better place without him.

It was slightly disappointing that Martin had died so quickly. Due to his crimes, Stephen could have gladly taken his time.

He folded Martin's arms over, both wrists meeting just on his stomach and hooked his own hands under the armpits. Making him more carryable in this position. The very much 'off duty' detective then dragged Martin into the alley after unlocking the gate from the inside, waddling backwards to the large metal rubbish bins lined up side by side a little further down the darker side.

Taking off the large lip and removing a few of the contents, he hoisted Martin up and in. With a forceful correction to his limbs here and there, Martin lay in the bin, crumpled and now covered by the previously removed stinking tatters of various rubbish.

It was a fitting place for the vulgar filth that he was.

The corpse would be found in a few days but hopefully not before the rats had had a few mouthfuls of him.

Locking the gate again from the inside and vaulting the wall so to not raise any suspicion if the shop owner wondered as to Martin's whereabouts, Stephen walked to the edge of the alley and the street, staying in the darkness before satisfied that the street was as desolate as it could be, he calmly walked away, deciding to circle the town to find a pub to be just another 'face in the crowd'.

He would need a drink tonight. Something strong. Something to help him not worry about the falling in his dreams. Also about the new face of Martin Slick that would surely accompany the others on the cliff edges as he fell.

CHAPTER 15

The night air felt as though it almost wanted to envelop him with a fine mist of the inevitable rain that somehow managed to hold off, yet all the while seemed imminent.

Stephen didn't feel cold as the adrenaline still frantically reminded him of the god-like feeling of justice served.

Each breath was a refreshing moist intake, as if it were his first ever. Replenishing him to the core.

He felt good.

As he walked longer and longer, he could feel the adrenaline dump, knowing fatigue would soon follow, so a drinking establishment was required with haste.

Walking past the Waterloo Tavern, which was still closed to the public since it had no landlord, he followed a long road with tram lines running as far as he could see, away from the town centre. It did not take long before glancing sideways on his right, he spotted the all too familiar lights of somewhere worthy of intoxication.

He exited the main street down a narrow side street, not feeling like he needed to use the footpath.

The streets were empty and, after the kill, it was almost like everyone knew to avoid him and the potential he had.

Another sharp intake of breath that was held before breathing out, he let the steam dance in front of him, the freshness of the night seeming to dwindle a little, so he took out another cigarette.

Searching for matches, he heard a grunt that could have only been human, from around the corner of the pub. Curiosity won him over and he decided to hold off on igniting his nicotine rush.

As he rounded the street to the left, a trio of drunken men

stood over a blanket laughing and each throwing an insult followed by a kick or two.

There was an entrance to the pub at this side of the building also, so Stephen made for it as if not noticing the three, determined for a closer glance at what could be so amusing in the abuse of an old rug.

It was as he suspected. It was a drunk or a tramp that they were mercilessly abusing, as if it was nothing more than a street dog, and tonight was not a night to be spied by Stephen in such a callous act. There were clearly no Watch Committee present, so the job was left to Stephen to intervene.

He stopped around four feet from the attackers although they were too engaged with their 'plaything' to notice.

With an air of drama, he struck his match and lit his cigarette. One of the three noticed him, the tallest of everyone present in the street. Puff-chested with a smug look and wit to match, the biggest of the three brought the others' attention to Stephen with a nudge and an aggressive gesture.

"What du fuck you want, mate?"

Half a threat, half a question.

Stephen answered but not before blowing his first smoke plume and letting it hang in the air. "I was wondering what might be so amusing at this hour."

The youth laughed but it was his second in command, a ratty-looking fellow, that answered. "Nowt to do wi' you, now fuck off, ya moocher."

Stephen inhaled again but this time not taking it back but blowing it from the side of his mouth almost immediately. "No problem, but I was wondering if I could get a light for my cigarette?" He held out the already lit smoking tobacco.

The furrowed brows matched on all the three youths and as the tallest stepped forward to enquire and no doubt reiterate his threat, his manner became quite hostile.

"Look…"

But he was cut short.

In the ruse as to how a lighted cigarette would become lit,

Stephen had drawn the pistol, the barrel pointing towards himself. He raised it and before any counter reaction could be given and for the second time of the evening, he cracked the head of the largest of the three.

Unlike Martin, the ringleader did not remain conscious. Like a brick from a height on a frosty evening, he dropped to the floor, out cold.

The satisfied detective placed the gun back into his trousers and looked coldly at the gang's 'ratty number two'.

"You can either pick your rather silly friend up and have him taken care of or you can all be found by the Watch Committee in relatively the same condition. This is a choice I am completely leaving up to you, gentleman."

The number two stooped and, always keeping his eye on Stephen, he reached for his friend. The number three of the gang, for the first time in his life actually being any use to anyone, assisted as they lumbered their dreaming companion away.

Stephen thought about the three maybe returning later to take out their revenge, but he also knew those type of people were cowards. Three against any man was low, but if they paid enough attention to the weapon Stephen carried, he thought they may have had more sense and simply called it a 'battle lost'.

When they were out of sight, he bent down to see their victim.

An older man but by no means old, although his homeless dress would have him placed late forties.

He looked up from behind the hands that had been protecting his face.

As they lowered, shaking, he looked a pitiful sight, his face worn and dirty.

"It's okay, my good man. They won't be bothering you again. Are you okay?"

The man smiled as best he could as he tried to sit. "God bless you, young man. Now why on earth would you help an old fool like me, sir?"

For a while Stephen seemed perplexed at the question. "Why

wouldn't I? There's not a bully that does not require a 'squaring into shape' occasionally, eh?"

"God bless you, sir, a thousand times for you're surely a saint? God bless you."

The man stood, helped by Stephen but seeming to be in some pain with his back. Maybe from the beating he'd been receiving but more than likely from sleeping on hard floors for far too long.

"Are you okay to stand? What happened?"

The street sleeper tried to redeem the centre parting in his ruffled greying hair after removing his cap, coughing slightly, more to clear his throat for the purpose of appearing respectful. "I sometimes find myself without a doss, sir, and round here is cover from the bitter winds, sir. They must have had a bit too much ale and took offence, sir, and that's when you arrived, God bless you."

Stephen could see the man was not of an unpleasant sort and right there and then decided that, if what he had done with Martin Slick could be perceived as a bad deed, he was now about to offer a hand to the needy as a good one.

"Tell me, what's your name?"

"George, sir, God bless you."

Stephen smiled and took George's hand to shake it.

"Well, George, I am Stephen and if you have no other plans I was wondering if you would do me the honour of having a drink with me?"

George was bewildered. He could hardly get the words out. "M-me, sir?"

The question was asked to Stephen, as if there maybe another man named George in the immediate vicinity.

"Yes, George, you. There is one thing worse in this world than a man having to suffer the injustice of sleeping on the streets and that is a man who is forced to drink alone. Cigarette?"

Offering one to George, Stephen was convinced he could see tears well in his eyes.

"God bless you, sir, God bless you a hundred times, mother

Mary and Jesus bless you, sir. You are too kind. An angel, sir. Why, I would never be believed, sir. God bless you."

He continued along the same manner as Stephen led him into the pub.

With only two other people present in the establishment who may have quite easily have been mistaken for part of the furniture, the barman saw George and without reserve pointed. "Oi you, out! You know you're not allowed in 'ere bothering patrons."

Stephen stepped to the side of George and, as officially as he could muster, he addressed the bar man. "I'm a detective of the local police force and this man is assisting me in an investigation into a recent assault. He is under my scrutiny and will certainly not be bothering anyone in your establishment this evening. Now if you would be so kind, he insists on assisting whilst being plied with ale so we will have two beers and two drams of whisky or gin, whichever is closer to hand."

Before the barman could provide any further objection, Stephen placed a handful of coins on the bar.

"Better still, we will take the bottle and any bread or meat you have, we may be a while."

As George seemed to grow ten inches taller under the protective wing of his new-found angel, Stephen sat down on the farthest solid seat away from the bar.

This was irregular behaviour for Stephen. Even though he had been in Hull for some time, he had had not yet enjoyed the company of someone unrelated to work.

It was true that he was under the pretence of a detective for a specific reason but he was no closer to solving his case than he was when he started. This frustrated him more than anything but he knew he had been doing good by helping others.

He needed a release from the pressures of a hunt, as all hunters do, and tonight the circumstances had offered him a friend.

Cautiously the street wallower pulled a stool and, leaning in close to Stephen in a low yet cautious voice, he asked, "Is that true, sir? Are you indeed a man of the law? If so, am I in trouble? If this is about me street sleeping, sir, I swear on the one true

Bible itself I shall do it no more, sir. To you I swear that on my own two eyes, God bless you."

Stephen smiled, as he too leant closer so to not spoil the pretence that George was helping further and investigation. "I am indeed, George, but you have not the slightest worry. I am off duty and, even if I was working, I would have very little concern as to where you choose to lay your head to rest. I suspect it's been a long night for both of us and I am in need of some well-deserved recuperation in the form of alcohol."

As Stephen lit another cigarette, his company clearly relaxed a little and cheered up instantly when a bottle of whisky reached the table.

It was not a particularly fine brand to say the very least, but it did not stop both men throwing back the contents of half-filled glasses almost in synchronisation.

George, it transpired, was golden-hearted in streets of squalor and his gratitude almost seemed to extend him as an entertainer.

He told Stephen how he came to be on the streets and although it was a story of the loss of his wife at a young age whilst he was working away at sea, he was undoubtedly a man of the church and believed there was a reason for it all.

He told Stephen that he had worked the fishing boats for a lot of his youth.

Starting early, it was all he knew but when his wife was trampled by a horse in an unfortunate accident, he had decided to leave the vessels behind.

He told Stephen how he thought that Jesus himself was giving him a sign. Apparently, Jesus had foretold that 'only drowning men would see him' and after the loss, he wanted to drown himself in desperation. Seeing as how the sea had not swallowed him up, he truly needed the words of the Bible to carry him through his life.

He'd translated the Bible in the strangest manner and gave up all he knew to try his hand on the shores. "I was away at sea when The Almighty called my Mary back, so's I didn't want to be there when The Lord came for me too."

Hull being predominantly based around fishing and trading

town, his attempts to find work elsewhere turned out, quite obviously, unsuccessful.

His living allowance dropped by the week until he was reduced to walking the streets by day and trying to collect what he could to afford a night's rest in a leaner or a doss. Preferably a doss, as a 'leaner' was simply a bench filled with people held upright by a thick rope. Depending on who you were seated next to, you could either sleep well or should keep your wits about you, as those places attracted the worst kinds of hungry.

Few places offered salvation during daylight hours. One of them being a church not far from their current drinking abode.

The priest, as most did, took people in for confession, to hear the ceremonies throughout the day and the people who remained at the end, rather than taking early leave, received tea and sometimes small amounts of food that could be spared.

It seemed that the priest was one of the few people George would ever confide in as he did not like to associate himself with other 'tramps' because he did not brand himself with that title. He was merely a man out of work, searching for a trade and a sign from The Almighty.

Although religion was not a practised pastime for Stephen, he had to admire his new-found friend for keeping his faith and dignity when he had quite literally been 'kicked whilst he was down'.

As the night wore on, the detective listened eagerly. George was indeed a man knowledgeable about the place he lived in and loved. Growing eccentric in his explanations and descriptions he was a vibrant one-man show, turning a previously thought glum arena for fish trade into a maze of streets with life, friendliness and character. Stephen decided he would accompany George whenever possible to find out more about the town he now resided in.

The time rolled by and the two shared laughs and the entire bottle of single Scottish malt.

George's words began to slur and Stephen's head would sway as he joined in with the joviality of the stories.

At one point, he ordered another bottle for the two of them and glanced at the time. It was well past one. The barman, thankful for the custom but perhaps not for the customers, remained open and obliged the trade.

When Stephen paid for the bottle, he sat back down and resumed the merriment.

Moments later, the landlord approached the table and asked if the detective thought that "a drop of something a little stronger for the chap 'assisting' his investigation may hurry it along?"

Stephen had an idea what he meant and even though he was not keen on the landlord's tone, he ordered one for each of them.

Stephen swayed as he and George looked towards the bar to see the barman take a dark green bottle from beneath the counter. The bottle almost made the liquid appear black apart from when the light caught at a certain angle, and it was clearly intended to be out of sight for a reason. They watched as the barman poured two healthy measures of the apparent lime green liquid into a glass then taking a tiny metal civ he placed it atop of the glass. Balancing a lump of sugar and adding a drop more of the liquor on top, he lit the sugar with a match.

The majestic blue flame seemed to entrance Stephen and George alike as they were served the potent absinthe on a tray.

They watched as the last of the sugar dissolved and the barman stood by. He gave a final stir of the concoction and resumed his perch behind his bar as the two new acquaintances toasted.

More followed as George gave Stephen a run down on the comings and goings in Hull, infamous names of local thugs and places to avoid.

"Don't even get me started on The Barge," George slurred at one point. "Avoid him, yer hear me… God bless you that you never run into that…"

There was more but Stephen was starting to lose track.

"To forgetting the bad and remembering the good," was George's heartfelt final comment.

Stephen placed the glass to his lips and tilted his head back. Mentally he saw an ocean rolling, dark green waters as though finally he had fallen from the cliffs and landed in a thick, almost treacle-like ocean.

Slamming the glass back down, it seemed an age had passed as if he had drifted off into a deep dreaming sleep as he could no longer hear George's voice.

He craned his neck to glance at the clock across the room which had taken a darker, blue shading all around, but before he could focus and make out the time, the door to the pub opened.

With a limp neck, a bloody face and a gurgling noise, the wanting patron slowly came into view.

It was Martin Slick.

Deathly white, cornflower blue lips and his body broken, he turned his head with great effort towards Stephen.

Martin's jaw was wide open, almost loose, his tongue lolling in his mouth. He began to drag himself toward Stephen, who now sat pinned to his chair.

Trying to reach behind into the inside of his jacket for the gun, Stephen realised that he could not move. It was like two anchors were dragging his arms down.

Slowly and deliberately, Martin drew closer.

Panic, more at his paralysis than the vision of Martin, made Stephen want to shout out, but he couldn't.

He internally began to struggle when he noticed behind Martin, another person had entered the room.

Craven Wilkinson's frame seemed spider-like in movement, his limbs over extended. He moved towards Stephen quicker than Martin and was soon face to face with Stephen, and in a deep voice, he said, "This is not what you are here for. You are here to do a job, now do it!"

CHAPTER 16

Suddenly he could move. He reached for his pistol but he was no longer in the tavern.

He was in his lodgings. His sheets were drenched with sweat and he thrashed around the room in confusion.

It had been a dream.

His heart was pounding as he stumbled to the window to let in some air.

As he struggled with the latch, a voice from behind him:

"You're awake then, sir?"

Stephen spun around on his heels but his head was in such a hungover state that his brain seemed to take its time and when it caught up it kept on spinning. In the dim lit room he hadn't even noticed this figure sitting in the chair by the door.

It was George with a blanket wrapped round him for warmth.

"Forgive me for startling you, sir. You were a little worse for wear the early hours of the morning when we left, just after the absinthe hit, sir, God bless you, so I had to carry you most of the way. You wouldn't hear of leaving me to sleep on a doorstep, God bless your heart, sir, so I slept here on this chair here, sir. Your shouting woke me. I do apologise, Mr Howes. You have already been kind enough, God bless you. I'll gather my things and take my leave."

Still trying to take in the situation, Stephen asked George to sit.

"Thank you, George. I doubt in my state, I would have been able to find my way back. I will boil some water. Would you like tea?"

"I couldn't be so bold, sir. I appreciate it, sir, but you have already been so kind, God bless you."

Stumbling around and trying to regain some slight coordination,

Stephen insisted, "Don't worry, George. I couldn't think of anything worse than starting a day without tea. Especially when the night was so full of absinthe."

Stephen took water from the receptor and began to heat it, and as they waited, the two men talked.

George, mostly with "sir" and "God bless you", but Stephen had asked George if it would be possible to now and again hire his services as tour guide for the town.

George could not be more obliging and told Stephen to find him around the same area that they met last night any time that he wished to know anything, and that he'd either be at the church hearing the word of The Lord or making money for his night's lodgings through the donations of people.

They shared tea and a few barely manageable half-hearted laughs before George took his leave. After seeing him exit, Stephen returned to his wash bowl and washed his face.

He fell back upon his bed and closed his eyes. Moments later, there was a knock on the door.

He had expected it to be George once more, perhaps to ask for an outlay of coins.

Instead, a young officer in uniform stood at the door, holding his hat in his hands.

"Detective Howes, sir?"

"I am. And what can I do for you this early, officer?"

"Chief Inspector Rudyard wants to see you, sir. A brutal murder on Charles Street and he thinks it might be the man you're looking for."

This disappointed Stephen as he now knew he had to take a false interest in a murder he had committed himself on Charles Street only hours previously.

He had not expected for Martin Slick to be so swiftly discovered, if not purely for the wishful thinking that Martin would have been found for his decaying smell alone.

"I'll be there shortly, lad. Let me gather my things."

By 'things' he meant another facial wash in the hope it would clear the throbbing in his cranium left by the ungodly Absinthe.

Twenty minutes later and unable to get rid the rancid taste from his mouth, no matter how much tea he could stomach, Stephen stepped into the damp air.

Hull reminded him of cold soil, not altogether negatively. Wet, dirty and riddled with filth but somehow required for some form of function. Like growing flowers.

His heels seemed to announce his arrival as he'd walked the entire distance back to the alley where Martin's body was now more than likely strewn out so any possible clues could be more easily spotted.

Through the bustle of a nosey crowd eager to glimpse the fresh visit of the grim reaper, Stephen pushed through, but was truly taken aback to see the alley untouched.

The police were guarding the shop below Martin Slick's hideout.

Vomit was on the pavement and one or two policemen were visibly shaken, faces white or green.

A priest with his back to Stephen stood talking to one of the policemen so that the officer's face was in plain view… he was almost lime with what he had seen and was trembling uncontrollably.

At that moment, as if to rouse Stephen from his confusion, Chief Inspector Rudyard approached him. "I hope you didn't have too much breakfast, Detective Howes, as I am afraid the pavement cannot take much more stomach contents."

Rudyard offered Stephen a cigarette and kept his back to the shop below Martin's hideout.

Harry Keen's butcher's shop.

With the hangover in full progress and Stephen's general confusion, details were laborious to digest.

He entered the butcher's shop and heard conversation.

It was not until Detective Ford began to repeat Stephen's name that he realised the conversation was directed towards him.

"Hmm? Sorry, Detective Ford, this is… this is not what I was expecting."

"I don't think any of us were expecting anything like this, Detective Howes."

A crude curtain towards the back of the shop draped, partitioning the front of the business from a storage and meat preparation area at the back.

Although he had seen the back door externally when he had ascended and descended the stairs the previous night, Stephen had paid it no mind.

His assumption was that at such a late hour, the shop would be closed and therefore unoccupied.

Little did he realise that below his own work, hours after or before, his target killer had been present.

Not only present but working. Killing. Creating.

Detective John O'Connell came from behind the curtain at a pace and spluttered.

Retching, and foregoing any form of greeting, he made for the street. Stephen watched as O'Connell had his hands on his knees, bent double but avoiding vomiting, only producing large amounts of mucus.

Stephen's head was now devoid of the effects of last night's drinking.

Something terrible lay behind the curtain and he was unable to resist the urge to witness it, but at the same time never wanting to see the sight as long as he lived.

When he pulled the curtain back with his right hand, his left raised to his mouth. The copper-like blood taste in the air hit the back of his throat as it seemed to flood into the shop front. A vapoured mist of diminished life that should have been internal to a human.

The gleam from the morning shone into the back room and although a thin strip of sunlight entered the space, it soon shone red with the wall, floor and ceiling's colour.

It was impossible to tell if the room had previously been this colour due to it being a butcher's cutting and storage area.

If it had or had not, the body hanging from the meat hook at the back was certainly a new feature.

If a silhouette had been drawn of Harry Keen's body, it would resemble that perfectly of a ballerina.

His arms were elevated above his body in arches, held in place by some form of metal rod curled around his bicep and forearms, his head tilted backwards by a similar type of rod inserted into his mouth vertically.

If the rods were of equal size then the one in his mouth skewered him.

His body had been elevated onto a meat hook, presumably impaled between the shoulder blades and his left leg was held up and bent via a long blade inserted through his left foot into his right knee and out the other side.

It was to all intents and purposes a 'perfectly postured ballerina's pirouette'.

On the wall, another message, to leave no one in any doubt as to the who the murderer may be. It was written in blood but how much was written in Harry's blood and how much may have been 'borrowed' from choice meat was anyone's guess.

wIth my CREATion evEn the most disGraceful beings
becOme beautiful in my DesIgN of DEATH

No sooner had Stephen read the writing on the wall, he heard a constable calling for Chief Inspector Rudyard who was standing behind Stephen with his head bowed so as to not have to look at the 'creation'.

"Chief Inspector? You better take a look at this. In the alley."

Stephen knew exactly what had been found but at least he did not have to pretend to be surprised for at least one murder of the day.

Martin Slick's body was removed from its cramped condition and the general assumption had been made by others that he was an unfortunate witness to the murder and disposed of as a result by the killer.

That was until Detective Ford recognised him as the currently wanted but now deceased Martin Slick. Upon realising, he turned to Stephen. Not a word was said, but if something had become apparent to Ford, he kept it to himself.

Due to the known details of Martin's own crime, little attention was paid to his murder but much concern was raised about the death of the butcher.

In the theatre killing, the press had been held off to an extent. The murder had been written about and any specific details were not made public.

However, with the butcher's gruesome discovery, it appeared more journalists littered the street than police officers and questions were constantly asked of the 'green featured' policemen returning from the back of the butchered butcher, Mr. Keen.

For Stephen, it remained as much of a mystery as it did to everyone else. The style of murder was different, the choice in victim, the place in which it occurred, the cause of death and near enough every detail was totally dissimilar to the first discovered theatre killing.

With no pattern besides the writing on the walls, it would be hard to try and assess the next potential victim.

Detective Flint lasted the shortest amount of time in the scene than any other detective.

Even before he entered and peeked behind the curtain, he looked how Stephen had felt.

Slightly panting, he made his apologies for being late to the party. When he exited the shop, he looked like he wished he had not arrived at all. Stephen remained inside and only managed to hear what followed as his gaze was well and truly fixed on the grim surroundings.

Doubled over like O'Connell before him, Flint made to vomit. Nothing but bile managed to make it onto the pavement but as he did the local priest patted him on the shoulder with some form of explanation as to 'sheep being called back to a flock'.

Flint stood in annoyance at the church leader and in a more roused state than he had ever been seen since entering the police force, he pushed the priest back, and shared his opinion. "Fucking God? Your God is mentioned on the walls in there. I don't think you'd call that massacre a merciful God-like act!"

He made to push the priest again whilst journalists scribbled frantically. Rudyard stopped him however with a heavy hand on his shoulder. "That's quite enough, detective!"

His tone showed annoyance, agitation, calm… and bellowed authoritatively all at once and it certainly did the trick.

Flint ceased his aggressive actions and made for the town centre but nobody followed.

Reports were written, conversations were had with anyone who might have seen anything but the crime scene gave no indication as to who had committed the crime, other than the Artistic Killer.

His identity was still far from being discovered so all that was left for the day was to wallow in a collective silence. Stephen stayed until most had left. He was determined to find something that may help but when he was finally satisfied that no more could be found, he left.

CHAPTER 17

He did not return to the police station however. Once again, he took to the shelter of a public house. It was a familiar one a little south of his lodgings and when he entered, the barman already knew what drink he would be ordering. Stephen asked for an extra dram of whisky to follow. After barely taking the time to breathe, and wanting to drown out his feeling of incompetence, he finished his dram and pint and made for the street.

It was late into the afternoon and the time of year meant that the dark had already crept in.

He walked towards the town centre and after making a few enquiries, located George and asked if he would accompany him for a stroll and a drink.

This was alien for Stephen. Never before had he sought company or solace in others, but from the friendship he and George had struck up, he found himself needing someone oblivious or ignorant to the murders.

They strolled the town centre and George pointed out main areas. The Station Hotel bustled with high class visitors and, around the dock areas, ropes, boxes, horses and varieties of young and old from far and wide came together.

Purely by accident, George led Stephen in a complete square from the hotel to the theatre towards the main town market and then turned back towards the hotel. Stephen pointed out that most tours lasted a little longer and didn't finish where they had started. George seemed slightly embarrassed as to his wandering and admitted not noticing that they had come full circle and it not being much of a tour at all.

Stephen joked about the street sleeper not earning many drinks in payment at all with such poor tourist information as that. They decided to head nearer the River Humber, as drinking abodes were plentyful towards that end of the town.

As they entered another public house, its cramped enclosure huddled workers fresh from the day's turmoil. Stephen shifted to the bar under the watchful eyes of most patrons.

George talked to a few of them in turn, who seemed to know him from a time long ago and soon enough, they eyed Stephen less suspiciously.

They both found a place to sit and Stephen began to ask George of the main candidates for the town's monopoly.

He knew it was no uncommon thing for the main elements of business to be controlled by a select few and once again he heard the name of Victor Sören, first from the Peacock's cab driver and now here.

Sören was a Dutchman who had not been in and around the place for long but had certainly come with an intention to branch out his reach in all forms of business.

If money was not an issue, then the trade that followed soon became even less of an issue. Sören had turned up with a daughter but no wife and since then, he held the company of most people with high stakes in and around the area.

It was even rumoured that the mayor of Hull had had him over for dinner and for a town such as this, that was a highly sought-after invitation indeed.

Stephen and George set aside little restraint from the intake of alcohol and when a smartly dressed young man sat himself next to Stephen, he hardly noticed. It was not until the stranger interrupted conversation with a wry smile that the detective paid him any mind.

"Detective Howes? It's a pleasure to meet you."

He had offered no form of introduction as to his own title, which sparked Stephen's intrigue. Stephen felt that something was clearly amiss with this ratty looking fellow.

"Horrible business with these murders, eh? Anyone suspected yet?"

Stephen was up on his feet, grabbing the young man by the collar, and as he roughly ejected him from the door, the act was met with cheers for the patrons.

The young man was quite obviously a journalist and to investigations like this, Stephen regarded them as worse than bottom feeders.

Never had he been on a manhunt where the cooperation of the press had assisted in the capture of a criminal.

The fact that the journalist had tried a deceitful entrance to Stephen's company had exasperated his great disgust, although the alcohol, by this time, couldn't have helped the situation.

Stephen returned to his seat with jovial clapping from the pub full of his new friends and resumed his boozing.

By the time he left the Whittington and Cat, the hour was not very far from midnight. He had left George drinking merrily in the bar and even left coin to aid his night along.

Poor lighting and a walk past a graveyard added even further to Stephen's sombre mood and when he reached his lodgings, he found himself deep in thought.

Retiring to bed did little good as he knew he would not sleep. Even if he did, the nightmares were sure to wake him in a sheet of cold sweat.

He drank whisky from the bottle with his seat facing the wide open window, as he once again regurgitated the facts as to where the killer might be and who he may target next?

Craven Wilkinson had told him that quite literally anyone of higher class could be the killer. The Artist was certainly not the type to reside in a sub-class or even humble abode. Something extravagant would be more suited.

Being well educated and of a higher level of intelligence made this killer elusive prey. He may have been in and around the Hull area for longer than Stephen had first thought, which further elongated his suspect list, as ghostly as that was at present. His hope of the Killer making a mistake had, so far, been futile.

For the first time in a long time he dwelled upon his past. No good would come of such thoughts, but he remembered the early days of military training. The things he had seen in the poor excuse for conflict.

He had never gotten close to anyone in his squadron, because soon enough they were taken away cruelly in the blink of an eye. He had counted himself fortunate to not have been killed himself, but as he drank himself potentially to death more each evening, he was not sure that such a thing as luck was on his side. Time changed men, but what of the men that always looked backwards or forwards in time?

The next day he awoke and the view through the window showed threats of a hard rain and darkened clouds.

After a night of mental strife and many slugs from the bottle of malt, Stephen decided he would not make an appearance at the station until later in the day.

Instead he decided to perform a good deed.

Finance was not a problem for him in the slightest. With this in mind, he made to seek out his landlady, Mrs Pritchard, and after making his enquiries with her, he set out to find his street dwelling friend, with his jacket collar pulled high and his hat pulled low.

Stephen did not need to look for long, as he entered the Whittington and Cat once again he could see that George had not moved and had apparently been kept well intoxicated with ale by his old fishing companions.

Stephen drank with him once more but after telling George he had something for him, George replied, "For me, sir? God bless you, sir, you've already given me enough, sir. God bless you, I couldn't. Not after you've done so much, sir. Why I haven't drunk this well in years, sir. Not since… well, not since I was upon the seas, sir. God bless you."

Eventually and after fond farewells to the old shipmates, Stephen led George through the streets and, arriving at his lodgings, they were met by the landlady.

Her agitation was apparent, but was perhaps partly for show.

She spoke to George directly and unbeknown to Stephen, she had known the him for some years, again offering an insight to just how connected local people were with one another in and around this town.

"You listen 'ere, mister," she said. "When detective 'owes 'ere tells me 'e's paying for the lodgings of a fella uw sleeps on the streets, I tells 'im 'not a chance'. 'E tells me it's you and I tells 'im 'e's mad to do it, but 'e's paid a month upfront so I'll allow it but any messing and yer back on the cobbles, understand?"

George for a moment seemed unable to answer. It was as if someone had replaced him with a statue that looked extremely life-like.

When Mrs Pritchard pushed George to see if he was not asleep standing upright, he shook from his daze

"Are you listening to me, George, you silly old sod?"

George made to speak and all the while was completely unable to utter a word.

In frustration Mrs Pritchard handed the keys to Stephen and with warning words and a pointing finger that any misbehaving and he would have to answer to her, she left.

In another life, Mrs Pritchard and George would have been the ideal married couple, with his total and utter obedience and her word being final, they would somehow work.

Stephen walked through the door and motioned for George to follow.

The room was on the top floor, the stairs were loud and the pathway claustrophobic, and with each step, the walls seemed to close in more and more until they reached the top landing which gave way to two doors. The first and nearest was the new abode of Stephen's friend, tour guide and drinking colleague, the furthest away was Stephen's own.

Stephen opened the door for George. All during the ascent of the stairs, the man had still not spoken. Stephen was slightly grateful for this, as he did not wish for any thanks or praise. His reasoning was that he could well afford to pay for his friend's lodgings and somewhere within the darkest recess of his mind, he knew he was committing a good deed.

One man from the cobbled street would not make an adjustment to the grand scheme of Roundtree's poverty tally, but to the man himself, no longer having to collect money for a place to sleep, it certainly made a world of difference.

Stephen expressed things in a matter of fact way and hoped that although George had not spoken, he was taking in what was being said.

"George, I want you to understand that this is a temporary arrangement whilst I am present in Hull. I wish to know the streets and ways of the town. I need to be aware of any news and happenings that people may not pass onto a policeman but will certainly gossip to others including yourself. I need to know people of a suspicious nature because I need to catch this killer before others get hurt. Remember the killer I told you about? I will be back later with provisions. In the meantime, make yourself comfortable and when you have settled, I would appreciate if you could make a start on finding out anything you can. If I am not back and something of importance comes along, then post a note under my door and I will receive it when I return."

George remained unmoving whilst situated in the centre of the room.

Although it was not a big room, George's stance made it all seem giant compared to his almost 'deflated' frame. For once, the usually vocal vagrant was so overcome with emotion, he was speechless.

CHAPTER 18

Stephen made his exit and as he closed the door, he paused, pondering whether George could read or write, if a noted needed to be left.

He made to open the door to enquire, but stopped when he heard a quiet sobbing from inside. It made Stephen extremely uncomfortable so he decided against it.

He would return later and hopefully the emotions would have worn off for his new neighbour.

Once again, he returned to the butcher's shop. Knowing that his target had walked the room below as he committed his own murder upstairs made Stephen feel closer to the killer somehow. Like he had shared the same sights with similar intentions.

The butcher's body had been removed from the shop, but much of the surrounding area and walls were still as they had been found.

A constable guarded the door and Stephen introduced himself. Little else was said as the horror that had taken place inside the shop seemed to darken any form of pleasantries.

The smell was a little more disturbing and, even without the presence of Harry Keen's corpse, the walls seemed to hang with death.

There was very little motive in the madness by the looks of things and no known connection was obvious. Stephen was all too aware of Slick's threat to Keen's son inside of Wakefield prison, that if his father did not 'help out', he would make his father pay but with Slick's body also located, his son would hopefully know that Slick played no part.

To everyone but Stephen, Martin was simply an unfortunate who happened to stumble upon the act and paid with his life.

After a while, it became clear that no matter how long Stephen spent at the crime scene, nothing new would come from it.

He returned to the station in the latter part of the day and the sun was already making its descent, after only just making its appearance after the morning's rain clouds. It did little to warm the bones of the sullen stand-in police detective.

His footsteps were heavy and he was unsure if this was due to a lack of progress or an equal lack of sleep. Either way he needed a remedy for both and not acting at all was the only thing worse than acting and not making progress.

When he entered the office, the atmosphere seemed to mirror his own feelings. Quiet and introverted.

Raffle, Ford, Napier and O'Connell were each at their desks in various forms of work. Flint was missing but by the way he had left the crime scene, this was not a surprise.

What did surprise him however was that looking back, it had been the first time he had not heard John passing out pieces of information which may or may not be useful at a later date or seen Napier in a state of relaxation.

He could only assume that the Artistic Killer's killings were spurring people to work and help Stephen catch him or they were appearing to be busy so as not to get involved in confronting such a sadistic madman. Either way he had little time to contemplate as Chief Inspector Rudyard entered the room and beckoned Stephen to join him in the back office in a none too friendly manner.

CI Rudyard remained standing as he took position behind his desk and looked ready to lash Stephen with fire and brimstone.

"Detective Howes, I will be blunt, the men haven't had to deal with anything like this in the past and quite rightly, they are concerned. We have a working machine here in Hull. Bad people are caught and then hanged, newspapers report it and we are all the better for a job well done. Yesterday an incident occurred that did our public image very little good and to make things worse..."

Whilst still talking, Rudyard threw a copy of the morning's tabloid onto his desk in front of Stephen.

"You hurl a journalist through the door of a public house, in which you are seemingly drinking the merry night away, when you are supposed to be out catching this 'Artistic Killer'...?"

He left the statement in the air as if expecting an explanation, his hands now on his hips and his face a warm glow of red. The headline read: 'Another grisly murder as police do nothing'. The press was a pet hate for Stephen and he hadn't the slightest interest in what they had to say.

He did however have to catch himself in that he was indeed impersonating a detective, an upholder of the law.

He decided to play along and play as nicely as he could muster.

"Chief Inspector," he said, "I can assure you my intentions were to indeed catch the killer, however, I need assistance in doing so... and not that of a police nature."

He stepped closer to the desk as he had only made it a single step inside the office before the Chief had unleashed his questioning.

"We could have a million constables on the street and it would still not be anywhere near as informative as one man who has the trust of the locals. That is what I was doing in the Whittington and Cat. I was working with a man who has an abundance of trust with the locals and I was trying to find out if anything had been heard with regards the murder. Rumours always contain an element of truth and considering we have not a single speck of evidence, I am exploring every avenue. The journalist was impeding my investigation with his attempt at deceiving me and I decided, quite rightly, that he should be made to leave."

Rudyard leant down and took a bottle of whisky from the bottom drawer of his desk. He took two glasses and filled them with three fingers' worth.

Offering courtesy, Stephen sipped and let the liquid burn his mouth and throat, enjoying the almost pain-like feeling.

The CI however took the whole drink in one.

Seeing this as a time to imitate, Stephen did the same with the rest of his drink.

When fixing the glasses for another round, Rudyard spoke in a sullen manner, shaking his head and avoiding eye contact with Stephen. "I have to apologise… I have been getting pressure from the top since the first murder. Apparently, this town cannot tolerate 'culture and murder in the same household'. With our lack of progress being made so public, it helps my situation very little." He took a sip of his whisky before he continued, "I should not have taken it out on you, I'm sorry. You're a very capable young man, Detective Howes. It's a shame your stay isn't extended beyond this one killer, but we need to catch this one and have him up on a rope as quickly as possible."

This time the drinks were savoured. They sat in silence for a while, Rudyard looking like an old oak tree, another adaption to the room's decor. His hair white and strongly built frame due to years of harsh conditions made him appeared 'weathered' and Stephen was apparently ageing the same way but only within the last few weeks of his time spent in the area.

He now felt the lack of sleep creeping in. His eyelids felt heavy and the mixture of the darkened room and fine whisky made his body yearn for a warm bed and a cloud-like comfort.

He wanted to sleep and not see the faces of the people he had killed. He could not say to himself that he had 'murdered' them because to Stephen 'murder' was a word that implied wrong doing.

He had killed because it's what every moralistic human being would have done in the same situation had they been so inclined.

Martin Slick had been his last victim, but the dream Stephen had had when he drank the absinthe had altered his usual 'falling' dream. He didn't fall, Martin made to attack him and for the very first time in a long time, he felt helpless.

Perhaps Martin's form in the dream had truly been that of the killer, because unbeknown to Stephen they had been carrying out a murder in unison and the victims were in some way related to each other.

When he thought more about it, he shook the notion from his head because he'd had no idea that the butcher hung dead hours either side of Martin's own death.

But he now knew something inside of himself had shifted. He wasn't plummeting towards a solid object, he was being taunted whilst he could do nothing about it.

He finished his drink and assured the Chief Inspector that he would do all he could in the capture of the Artistic Killer and sooner or later the murderer would surely shake the hand of the hangman.

Stephen left the station and the dark winds that had seen the day washed with rain then gleam in sunlight now offered nothing but a cold wintery night.

He left his long coat to flow loose as the wind seemed to remind him that he should not deserve comfort until his task was complete. The honour of warmth should not be his while his target's heart still beat so bold.

When he returned to his lodgings, George was sitting upon the step outside, waiting. He saw Stephen approach and stood, holding his cap in his hand.

"Mr Howes, God bless the very ground you tread upon, sir, but I cannot accept this kindness, sir, God bless you..."

Stephen held his hand up. The gesture was rude but he was in no mood for politeness.

"George, let's not discuss this now. I need a drink and the hour is still early. Will you join me?"

Before a retort could be made, Stephen carried on past his newly-found neighbour and made haste to his apparently now 'local' public house.

George followed, keeping silent and falling into step with his friend as they made their way to The Dram Shop.

Something hung heavy upon Stephen's shoulders and when a man's heart feels empty, often the only solace is ale. When the two entered the public house, Stephen was shocked to see O'Connell and Napier drinking at the bar.

Stephen had frequented this place on many occasions and had never once seen either of them here.

O'Connell saw Stephen first and from a glum stare, which he had been lost in only moments before, he now beamed with joy at seeing his colleague.

"Alright mate! Come here, lad, and get yourselves a seat. What you drinking, fellas?"

George was over and seated before he could finish his request of a pint of ale, but Stephen still felt a twinge of suspicion as to the present and unexpected company.

O'Connell ordered with the enthusiasm of a long-lost companion reunited and then struck up conversation about the weather and other trivial matters.

His mood never seemed to alter from a friendly nature and this was a relief to Stephen, but sitting on the other side of O'Connell, Detective Napier appeared to have something he wanted to talk about.

They all finished their first drinks and whilst Stephen ordered the next round, John excused himself to use the toilet stalls. Instantly, the mood took a sombre tone once again and George, seeing what was plainly obvious, excused himself to speak to an old acquaintance who was perched in the corner of the public house.

As soon as he was gone, Stephen thought it best to broach the subject head on.

"Is something the matter, Detective Napier?"

Dave Napier took a breath. He looked as worn out as Chief Inspector Rudyard, as if the grief was infectious.

"Yeah… you see, the thing is, I heard the Chief start at you today when you were in the office and I felt guilty. I couldn't hang around so I asked O'Connell if he fancied a pint. I knew you'd get here eventually."

His spoke as if he were a little child admitting a sin.

"You've helped the lads out so much already and I feel like I haven't lifted a finger to help you."

Stephen unintentionally raised an eyebrow but it clearly showed his thoughts.

"Okay, okay, I admit I haven't lifted a finger at all, because in all truth I thought you would be gone by now. Fleeting visit and all that, but after seeing the butcher, I know I need to help out a lot more and I came here to tell you that."

Napier took a drink from his freshly stacked pint and motioned towards the lavatory door.

"O'Connell came because he thinks the sun shines out your arse and we both came because we wanted to get very intoxicated with it being the weekend tomorrow."

As if he had been stood waiting for his cue, O'Connell returned and Napier continued, "So, what do you say? Do you feel like having a good drinking session with the likes of us slackers?"

Stephen raised his glass and in a cheerful tone replied, "With an offer like that, gentleman, how could I refuse?"

Finally, the group were complete when George promised his friend he'd share a drink with him soon. Stephen ordered four drams and the night continued from there.

Soon enough they were seated in a booth with the glasses stacking higher as they chatted and laughed and told ungentlemanly jokes.

At one point, O'Connell stopped the good cheer and asked if the detectives had heard about the man coming into the office with a concern a few days ago.

Looks of confusion followed as this neither narrowed the enquiry down or seemed relevant to the present conversation.

"Well, it turns out, right," he continued, "that this fella wanted to speak to a man that had broken into his house. He was told he could do it when it all went to court, so this fella turns round and he says, 'It can't wait, I want to know how he snuck in without waking the missus up. I've been trying to do that for years…' "

A moment of silence passed until they realised it was a joke and fits of laughter followed whilst O'Connell sat upright, grinning with satisfaction that he had made everyone laugh rather than being laughed at for a change.

George shook his head with a smirk, saying, "Oh Lord, forgive me," as though it were the work of the devil to listen to the profanities.

This made the group laugh more and from the morose morning and afternoon, the night cheered the group up no end.

CHAPTER 19

Hours later, the clock struck midnight and conversation had lulled as much as Detective O'Connell's head in his drunken state.

He was the first to excuse himself and as he made to leave, George insisted on seeing him home safe in a hansom and reluctantly admitted that the lack of sleep from the previous night and constant alcohol consumption throughout had taken its toll upon him.

He stood unsteadily and, with an arm around Stephen, slurred his way through the story of a man with a heart of gold who had taken him in from the squalor and put a roof over his head.

Up until that point, the other two detectives were unaware that Stephen had made a neighbour of George and all agreed it was a testament to his good nature. The foolishness of friendship never seemed more apparent in the gang than under the heavy blanket of whisky and ale.

They hugged like brothers, wishing farewells and safe journeys to O'Connell and George as the two made their exit.

Napier and Stephen remained the only two remaining patrons of the entire public house and ordered more drinks from the endlessly patient bartender.

"That… that's a good thing you done there, Stephen." Napier struggled with his wording as he hiccoughed his sentence, raising his eyebrows but not opening his eyes, his body swaying although he remained seated.

"I know we haven't… we haven't known each other long but I can… I can tell you're a good sort."

Stephen, although drunk, was not in the same state of drunkenness as Napier.

"You know... you know... you never talk about where you're from. The lads all wondered but none of um... none of um will ask... you."

It was at this point Stephen realised that the explanation he had given the very first day of solving a case had obviously been forgotten. He once again glazed over his past with as little explanation as possible. Purely because he didn't want anyone knowing his past and also because no doubt it would be forgotten by Napier in his drunken state by the morning. Not that anyone would believe him anyway.

"I'm not from as far away as you'd think, Napier. I just like to forget where I'm from and dive into what I am doing."

Detective Napier let out another hiccough and swayed a little more whilst nodding his head as if he knew exactly what Stephen was referring to. Stephen continued as the room spun and he took another slug of malt.

"Anyw... Ooooo, that's rough!"

Attempting to speak had kept a little of the liquid at the back of his throat burning with that familiar fire that just would not quench.

"Anyway, what about you? I know Flint goes off and gets up to who knows what, Raffle is as much of a mystery, O'Connell is married and Ford is a dedicated family man. What's your story, Napier? How do you spend your nights?"

As he looked at Napier, his sight dropped out of focus. When his vision came back into clarity, Napier looked at Stephen with an immense depth of sadness. Through a hiccough and a sip of whisky it was clear to see something troubled the normally nonchalant detective.

Napier looked at his glass. For the first time ever, Stephen saw him not as a 'half full' man, but his glass was half empty and as he made to give something in the way of an explanation, the words were interrupted with what can only be described as 'projectile vomit'.

The next few minutes were full of apologies to the landlord and offerings of money, as a cloth that had seen better days was used to clear the contents of Detective Napier's stomach from the table and floor.

For the liquid that had reached the floor, a healthy helping of sawdust was applied and the two detectives exited the public house, barely able to walk.

Outside, Napier leant against the wall and inexplicably began to laugh. As he continued to do so, Stephen burst into laughter and the two laughed uncontrollably, before staggering in the direction of Napier's home and the opposite to Stephen's, Napier with tears in his eyes from laughter or crying, Stephen could not tell as Napier called out, "For another time, Detective Howes. Good night and safe journey."

Stephen stood until the detective was almost out of sight and whispered to himself in Napier's direction, "Be lucky," and made his own way home.

Eventually when he arrived at his lodgings, he climbed the stairs and upon reaching the top, searched for his room key.

As he did so, he heard the almighty snore of his new neighbour and laughed to himself as he entered his own room, falling upon the bed into a deep sleep for as long as his dreams would let him.

CHAPTER 20

Stephen couldn't remember opening his eyes but he could see that his feet were perched over the unsteady ground that gave way to an almighty drop.

White cliffs and water were the only things visible in his line of sight. The breeze shifted his body forward and his reaction to try and step away was fruitless in its attempt.

He could see people on different levels below peering up at him. They were too far down to be able to make out their faces, but he knew exactly who they were.

His body arched forward but before the fall, he heard voices from behind him.

Calling and shouting his name.

He could still not move his feet but he could twist his head to see the employees of Hull's detective police squad calling for him and beckoning him away from the edge.

Once again, he attempted to turn but just as before, he fell.

Past the ghost-like faces of his previous assignments and the judged souls he had sentenced to death by his own hands, closer and closer to the water until something happened.

The water was no longer water at all.

It became solid.

Like a thatched roof.

Milliseconds before impact, his eyes shut tight and when they opened, he was bolt upright in his bed.

His head pounded which let him know it was to be another day of strongly brewed tea and fighting a hangover.

His dream had changed again, but before he had time to contemplate what it meant, he needed water.

CHAPTER 21

George must have heard Stephen clambering around the room, as half an hour later, he knocked on the door. Stephen answered to an annoyingly happy face in comparison to how he felt.

"Good morning, sir. God bless you and the day. Do you fancy a trip out today, Mr Howes, sir?"

"Trip? Where did you have in mind, George?"

"Well, a fella I know, God bless him, plays for the All Blacks. Mostly plumbers and the such making up the squad but always worth a trip out to see the All Blacks, sir. Rumour is they are looking for a merge and to take off to better things. What better a time to pay a visit when folk be in their infancy as it were, sir, God bless you."

"Are you talking about 'rugby', George?"

"Indeed, I am, sir. Rugby league, God bless them and yourself, sir."

The need for fresh air and a brisk walk would certainly make Stephen feel much better so he agreed. "Why not? It will certainly be a first. Sort of. Give me a minute."

Stephen closed the door and made his way to his wash bowl. A splash of water then he drank the remains of his tea. He finished dressing and was ready for the day. As ready as his present condition would allow anyway.

He followed George onto the cobbled path and proceeded east of the town. When they arrived at the field in which the game was to take place, a collection of finely-dressed men were present for observing the morning of rugby league and to Stephen's inquisition, George informed him that a new man about town often visited the games, so the collection of 'well to do's', as George referred to them, would attend the match on the off chance they might bend the ear of said gentleman with regards to business.

"Men with lots of money to spend and nowhere to spend it, will often attract the greedy guttersnipes."

"Who is it these men are waiting for, George?"

"Why Mr Sören, of course, sir."

Stephen had to admit, he was more than a little curious to see this man.

He was relatively surprised upon hearing that Sören had only been in Hull for around two years, yet already had so much sway as to force businessmen into the dull and damp grass of a Saturday morning rugby match.

The game kicked off and it was an easy win for the All Blacks. Stephen never even thought to enquire as to the opposition's name but he was not paying the game any mind.

Instead, he kept a watchful eye upon the vultures of economics, thankful to be in the cool breeze that for once did not sweep rain across his brow.

It appeared Victor Sören had not made an appearance at the game but it was interesting to observe the persistency of the financial followers who had waited in the hope that he would arrive.

"Is there anywhere else you wish to see, Mr Howes? Or would it be to another public house?"

George asked the question with the look of a dog awaiting a treat. He would probably have gladly taken Stephen on a tour through the town and back several times over, but it was abundantly clear what George's preferred answer was.

As determined as he was to avoid another morning's hangover, Stephen was all too much aware that the only cure for such a poor state of health was another pint or two of ale, possibly with a raw egg in the mixture for good measure. He told his dipsomaniac tour guide to take him somewhere quiet, as any form of loud noise could not be suitably managed or tolerated in his present state.

CHAPTER 22

Stephen decided to call it an early night whilst he was still able to make the decision. George remained in the public house that they had been in for a few hours, as once more he was known to the patrons who were happy to slide a drink in George's direction due to his good nature and company.

Stephen arrived at his abode and, removing his hat, jacket and shirt, pulled the solitary chair to the window. He poured himself a whisky into a well-used glass and sat with effort. Taking a sip, he looked out of the window and watched the night sky mix with the glow of the gas lamps.

His mind drifted. His thoughts were fragmented to say the least. He was frustrated at his lack of progress but happy at the impact he had made in the Hull crime fraternity.

He felt frustrated that he had not been born into the existence that he was pretending to be part of, but was happy all the same... even if his immersion was a fallacy, it was one he could savour.

He thought about his past. It was rare for him to do so. It never left him in a good mind afterwards, but, of late, he couldn't help it.

He'd been introduced to detective work by a rock of a man called Melton Johnson.

Melton had been a kindly man with a stern way with words but also a manner of acceptance.

He had led Stephen away from his previous vocation of the army and into the delicate nature of tracking people who did not want to be tracked.

Up until that point it had not been anything more than an opportunity to earn some money. Money that was indeed for old rope.

Together they accomplished the capture of several villains and vagabonds all the same.

That all changed one fate-filled night when Stephen was checking one floor of a house whilst Melton checked the other.

Stephen was armed and as he burst through a locked door, he observed their next pay check in an unspeakable act upon a recently deceased woman who had the contorted face of someone who had not died 'well'.

Something burst inside him. Like a dam instantly removed from waters held back. His eyes filled with rage, he had little control over himself as he raised his gun and fired twice into the head of their target.

Melton bolted into the room and saw that the 'murder' had been impulsive on Stephen's behalf and from that moment on, their alliance altered.

Melton would not look at Stephen the same way and Stephen would no longer treat wrong doers in the same manner. He began taking on extra cases and when he thought the circumstance were right, to the paying customer, he would hint at the notion of making the 'target' truly pay for the crimes they were wanted for.

Not once was this refused by them and when Melton, in a true detective fashion, figured this out, it was decided that they should part professional company.

Six months later, Melton was stabbed in an abode whilst he tracked a target.

Stephen was overcome with guilt, but for all the wrong reasons. He told himself that if he had taken the case, the perpetrator who had slayed Melton would have been dead instead of on the run.

Stephen found Melton's killer and satisfied his 'natural law' urges. Another face to the cliffs and a solemn promise that only cases with a 'final' solution were to be taken from that moment on.

A promise that he had kept, but somehow here he was… arresting people.

A bittersweet attitude could be argued that they were not actually his targets, so he applied his 'devil may care' mentality to these. However, soon enough the nightmares started and the drink became needed, rather than optional.

He drifted in these thoughts and before he was aware, the night had slipped into the small hours of the morning and the glass had slipped from his hands as he fell asleep, thankfully without smashing.

Stephen jolted awake and thought it had been the glass landing that had woken him but moments later there was a knock on the door.

He had his gun to hand, as always, and decided in a situation like this, it was better to be safe rather than sorry. He took the gun and pointed the barrel at an estimated head height on the door. He inched the old but solid door open and in the dim light, he could make out Officer Brent, who he had met at the Waterloo Tavern.

"Detective Howes, I'm very sorry to bother you, sir, but it's Chief Inspector Rudyard's orders. I'm to find who I can at this hour and ask you to join 'im on the Waterhouse Lane, sir. There's bin a murder."

Stephen did not feel drunk, merely tired. More to the point, he felt himself capable and told Brent to wait downstairs and he would come presently.

A cab was waiting for the men in the street below and the constable said to the driver, "Take us back."

A crack of the reins and the carriage set off, leaving Stephen's hope of a night's sleep far behind.

CHAPTER 23

Stephen recognised the route the cab was taking. George had walked him around this area but with an air of caution. He also knew that Flint frequented the streets that made up the Waterhouse Lane. It was well renowned for prostitution and the lodgings of drug distributors that had arrived from the trading ships. When he had asked why the area was not raided more often, the reply was simple, "If all the hoodlums are in one area, when something goes wrong, we know where to find um."

The constable had little to say as the carriage rattled along the cobbles. The smell of the docks seemed to wrap the night in a blanket of the day's labour and smother the senses.

The whisky had settled upon Stephen's tongue.

At the moment, he was about to ask Brent what it was exactly that was so important about this murder that made it of interest to him, but he thought better of it. Mainly for two reasons. Firstly, that speaking would cause a smell of whisky probably causing concern with the constable as to the detective's judgment. Secondly, he had almost forgotten himself – not just tonight but recently – he had to keep in mind that he was not an actual detective of Hull.

He had been hired to catch a killer and, in all likeliness, he hoped, the place that they were heading could be linked to his target. The rest of the journey was spent in deep pondering and a stern self-reminder that he had to get himself back on track with regard to his case.

As they stopped, the rain had been spraying the streets. It had not so much been falling, but floating in the form of a heavy mist.

Rudyard stood at the entrance of an alley, wearing a long thick coat, a bowler hat pulled low, gleaming in the street lights, almost silhouetting his form against the tall building that shadowed the crime scene, made clearly evident by the policeman standing sentry a little way down to a door that glowed with a candle-lit brightness from inside.

Smoking his customary pipe, the extra illumination made the strain on the Chief Inspector's face evident.

Stephen stepped down and held the door for the young constable.

Brent declined the offer as he made Detective Howes aware that he had to try and locate the other detectives, if they were available.

Stephen walked alone to the Chief Inspector and wished him a good morning.

"Is it Detective Howes…?" replied Rudyard. "We have another murder. Can you tell us if it's your man or just another brass cut down in her prime?"

Stephen was unsure, but for a moment in the overwhelming smell of his own whisky and Rudyard's pipe, he was almost certain he had caught the scent of brandy.

It had not occurred to him that Rudyard himself may be in the throws of actually taking time away from work.

Stephen shifted his thoughts into a manhunting mindset. There was nothing in the street that may offer up as a clue. The rain had made sure of that.

He stepped into the alley and, lighting a collection of matches, held them up to both walls to check for any messages.

The alley had only one entrance and if a message was to be left external to the room, then it would certainly be here.

Nothing showed. No words of what a demented mind felt an unequalled urge to share.

He stepped inside the room and saw what was in itself, in some unfathomable and ungodly way, a relief.

This was not his killer.

Across a bed, a young girl of around fifteen lay strewn in

the supine position, sheets half covering her body, the possible reason of modesty could have been given as it was her entire lower half that was covered.

There seemed to be a number of stab wounds evident on her torso and neck.

Blood had sprayed high up to the ceiling to the right of the room and along the back wall at which the bed was located.

Stephen stepped out and back towards the street.

The room had been extremely hot compared to the night air and this could be due to the amount of candles that had created such a bright light to throw on the darkened damp stone walls and floor.

Rudyard had not moved. Only the match he used to light his pipe had increased in length. He'd started anew and had chain smoked. The discovery of another murder on his streets clearly anchored Rudyard's mind, especially of a girl so young.

A cab sat in wait in the street across the road and the horse that dragged it shifted from hoof to hoof, creating the only noise in the night air. The driver was cloaked heavily and his hat pulled low against the elements.

Stephen hunched his shoulders and raised his collar to protect him from the chill.

"It's not the Artistic Killer," he said.

"Are you sure, detective?"

"Yes, there is no message and it does not fit his style. Looking briefly, I would say the young girl worked the streets using the abode as a 'head quarters'. Higher end of the market in customers and probably looked after. There is no furniture or home comforts, the excess lighting would more than likely be so she could get a good look at her client in case they left without paying. The neck wound caused the death as it lay directly over the artery and was more than likely sliced in the middle of the room, judging by the spray."

Stephen took a breath. He was aware that his speech was faster and perhaps erratic but he was describing the exact nature of his inner workings.

"She was then stabbed in a frenzy which means there was an argument beforehand as her 'after attention' showed signs of an aggressive nature. If she was 'protected' by perhaps a pimp or such and no one comes forward to check on her, I'd wager it was her 'protection' that caused this poor girl's demise."

"You can tell all that by walking in for thirty seconds and walking back out?"

"It's unfortunately not the first murder I've seen in this manner, Chief, or as the Yankee's say, 'It is not my first rodeo,' and as it stands, it is merely an uneducated guess."

The CI gave a short huff. He looked towards the cab, seemingly making a decision.

"Care to join me for a drink, Detective Howes? The guard will keep watch till the others arrive. They can do their job for a change."

Without waiting for an answer, Rudyard made for the carriage that would take them. He ordered the driver to an address that was west of the town, the side of the town that had been much ignored so far due to George's knowledge being predominately on the east side of the centre. Without so much as a second thought, Stephen joined his temporary superior. After seeing the girl, he needed a drink and unless he found a better offer in the next minute, he was convinced to follow Rudyard.

As the coach pulled away with both passengers firmly seated, the Chief Inspector broke the silence that so far had only been filled with the clatter of horse shoes upon cobbles.

"Two things bother me, Detective Howes. Firstly, that you can't be a permanent fixture to our squad, as I see great potential in you, and secondly, that we are lacking in results with your killer. Not simply because I want him caught and strung up, no! But because you have helped us all so much already, yet as for progression we have given you nothing."

Stephen was shocked. He hadn't expected this sort of honesty from the Chief. He had imagined that no matter the company or situation he would always be the solemn spectre overseeing everything and everyone.

He didn't know if it was the whisky from earlier or the effects of seeing a girl so young needlessly killed but Stephen's head swam a little.

He took a breath and watched the streets clatter past.

"I'm sure soon enough we'll have our man, Chief Inspector. This one will be no Ripper. He'll make a mistake and when he does, we'll catch him. People like him give us a distinct disadvantage."

The CI looked a little puzzled. "Oh? And what's that?"

"They want to be caught. As absurd as that sounds, the studies have proven it many times… they seek recognition for what crimes they commit. It's all a show and shows have an ending. He will want his ending to be spectacular. Not just to fade into the night, no, he'll want music playing and an audience."

"Well, let us hope you are right, Stephen, and his audience is our smiling selves as he tightens the thirteen twists of a hanging rope with his neck."

The rest of the journey was filled with the smoke from Rudyard's pipe and the silence of unease. Nothing further was required.

They turned along a long road, a street drowning with desolation and darkness.

Rudyard leaned forward and spoke into the cab's squawk box. "Here is fine, driver."

CHAPTER 24

Stephen followed Rudyard as he stepped out and handed the driver some coins. The horses took off with haste.

The Chief Inspector looked around and seeing no prying eyes were peeping, he made for the door of a large terraced house.

Only a single candle illuminated the upstairs window towards which Rudyard gave a solitary gruff. Stephen was becoming increasingly uneasy. Something felt wrong about this situation.

Taking a large key and swinging open the front door, Rudyard motioned Stephen to lead the way. His curiosity reached an all-time high when closing the door behind them, the CI left them both in crypt-like cold darkness.

His head still feeling light from the murder and malt, Stephen realised he was in a strange place in total darkness and only the sound of Rudyard shifting around on the heavy wooden floor broke the silence, yet elevated the eery tension-filled noiseless hollow. A scraping noise, first of metal and then something drew close to him.

His fight or flight response now well into overdrive, he cursed himself for being led into such a situation so willingly. Where was he? What had Rudyard led him into?

The sudden light from the match struck before him was a shock to his senses. Stephen jumped back, hitting his back against the wall, every nerve tight, his body waiting to react to what was about to happen.

The room lit along with Rudyard's disgruntled features. Almost menacing.

"Bloody fools!" Rudyard made to reach towards Stephen, his

hand appearing like a tomb door shutting out the light towards Stephen's face.

Stephen stepped quickly to one side, not knowing what was happening and fraught with fear at being caught so off guard. His heart pounded and he was in such close proximity that any counter attack to what he now thought was an actual attack would be difficult.

But the Chief Inspector didn't make to grab the detective at all. Instead, he reached for the candle holder upon the wall over Stephen's left shoulder.

"Every time I tell them to leave the candle on the ledge by the door but do they listen?"

He lit the candle and began to walk up the stairs, seemingly unaware as to the sudden distress caused to Stephen whose nerves were screeching like a violin.

Before the candle's light totally faded out of sight along with the CI, he followed Rudyard up the stairs, trying to compose himself.

The Chief entered a room to the back of the house on top of the landing. What lay within was yet another surprise to the already curious night.

Two men sat in the high ceilinged, large, open and brightly lit room which had a dark oak and well made self-serving bar across the back.

Scattered here and there were several comfortable-looking single chairs arranged around small tables, which upon them sat chess sets and domino pieces.

From the bleak abandoned appearance that floated around the rest of the house, this room gave all impressions of a gentleman's club in the night air of Africa after a hard day's hunting with several decorations to suite.

One of the men, who seemed the younger of the two but in no way, shape or form was he young, raised his glass of healthy measure.

"Montgomery! A surprise and a pleasure. Who's your guest?"

The other who was sitting with his back to Stephen and the

door, now turned to gain full view. His whiskered eyebrows and thick white beard stained with yellow from God only knew where, seemed to give signs of a disapproving manner towards Stephen, yet he said nothing.

"Gentleman, this is Detective Howes. He's helping catch the Artistic Killer and as an outsider, he's more than welcome to our club for now. Temporary membership and all that."

The older man in the chair turned back to his game of chess and began to mumble of 'letting anyone in' and 'the French will be in next' as he then fell into contemplation in the age old game of kings, queens and pawns.

"Stephen, what would you like to drink?"

He turned towards Rudyard who was removing his coat and hat whilst walking to the bar.

"A whisky would be pleasant, if you have it. What is this place?"

He heard scoffs from both seated fellows. As if the answer should be quite obvious, but with maps of places he did not recognise on the walls to animal furs on the floor, it was still all a little too much to be taken in.

"This is a quiet little place we keep for us old war vets."

"Which war?"

Rudyard let out a guffuffing laugh that echoed around the room. "You cheeky devil, Howes. We are not that old. The Crimean, of course." The CI poured drinks as he continued. "This place came up for sale after a bit of nasty business downstairs, which fortunately or unfortunately meant no one wanted to live here. I suggested myself and a few of the old boys put together on the cheap rates and have a little place we can call our own. Be with our own kind and all that. The candle in the front window means someone is present so as not to give any of these old buggers the fright of their lives when they come up."

"Cheeky swine! I may be old but my heart is young, I'll have you know, Montgomery," said the younger of the seated.

It also occurred to Stephen that he'd had no idea that Chief Inspector Rudyard's first name was 'Montgomery' up until now.

"Shall we?" said the Chief, motioning to two chairs that surrounded a table with dominos scattered upon it.

As they sat, the chief began to mix and then divide the pieces.

"This is nothing to do with being involved with the detectives, but you are ex-army, are you not, Mr Howes?"

Stephen was in mid-drink and the question caught him off guard. Spluttering a cough, he replied, "What gives you that idea, Montgomery?" The name sounded almost foreign on his tongue.

"I've spent enough time in the army to learn how a fellow conducts himself. Regardless of regiment or region, an ex-officer knows a troop when he sees one."

Stephen was shocked to say the least. Rudyard had guessed correctly, but as for details, Stephen certainly had no intention of sharing them. He needed a subject shift as quickly as possible.

"I was indeed enlisted, sir. How long were you in the forces?"

"Well, believe it or not, I was young once and quite the horse rider. I was in the lights charge and well decorated, I can tell you that for nothing."

Rudyard laid his first domino before he had asked Stephen if he cared to play or knew how.

The piece was a double 5.

"Unfortunately, I caught a nasty injury to the leg for my efforts and had to take up lighter duties."

Stephen took his turn. A 5 and a blank to the left.

"I came out of the army and like most fellows, I joined the police force. Bit of a limp but like I say I was a hell of a rider. Not a lot of men can outrun one of those beasts, haw haw."

Rudyard. A 5 and a 3 to the right.

"Few years later I was promoted and climbed the ladder accordingly."

Stephen. A double blank to the left.

"I got the title 'Chief Inspector' and realised that was as far as I wanted to go."

Rudyard. A double 3 to the right.

"I could hold my own little band of men there, you see."

Stephen. A blank and a 1 to the left.

"I promoted in turn the men you see around you in the office, with the best type of qualities."

Rudyard. A 1 and a 2 also to the left.

Stephen was puzzled at this because although the men were likeable and competent enough, they hardly seemed the cream of any crop with the exception of a small percentage. Of course he decided against mentioning this.

Stephen laid a 2 and a 6 to the left and after Rudyard placed a 6 and a 4 to Stephen's previous, this left Stephen with nothing to play so he had to knock and pick up an overturned piece.

But it was as if the CI had read the Stephen's mind as Rudyard said, "Don't get me wrong, Stephen, they may not be the brightest tools in the tool shed but they are unbendable to bribery. Corruption is like a virus. I learnt that coming up the ladder and when I knew I could select my own group, I wanted a set of fellows that wouldn't take 'extra earnings' to look the other way. As for constables, I can do very little about those because they are a law unto themselves, but my team are honest and open and what more can a man ask for?"

Stephen laid his final piece, making him the victorious and with a slight element of gloat, he answered, "Another drink?"

"Guffaw, cheeky devil! Watch out for this one, lads, his a shark with the domino."

Rudyard poured himself and Stephen another drink each and two for the older seated gentleman still locked mentally in chess.

"What's your outlet then, Stephen?"

Unsure of what the Chief was referring to, Stephen asked what he meant.

"What we talk about in this club remains here. It's a place of sanctuary and I am sure you'll be abiding by the same rules."

Stephen nodded but altogether unsure as to where the conversation was leading as Rudyard continued, "We see death and desperation on a daily basis, detective. Drink is here nor there so we all need something to keep our minds elsewhere. Now this is between me and you, but I have a young lady on the side. People may damn me for such, but my wife and I have been together a very long time. Habits get formed and life turns to grey around the edges. Throw in a mixture of what we do for a living and believe you and me, you need an outlet. Do you have a young lady in your life?"

On a night that seemed teaming with surprises, Stephen was shocked once again. The Chief Inspector seemed so straightlaced and dancing closer to seventy… for him to have a mistress was barely believable.

From entering the previous crime scene to his next words, a lot of what he thought he knew about the Chief Inspector had been completely upturned. He was more than happy for the element of trust that had been bestowed upon him, yet surprised all the same.

He explained to Rudyard that with his job he had had neither the time nor chance to meet a lady as of yet, but that he was sure once the Artistic Killer had been caught, he would be taking a well-earned rest and make the correct efforts.

After agreeing nods followed his explanation, Stephen began to think about past female encounters. There was never anything of value with the women he had known. He had always been somewhere involved in work and never there very long.

He certainly yearned for the comfort of a relationship and as he had told Rudyard, the capture of the killer would ensure his life could be nothing short of leisurely.

It all seemed to connect at once. Everything he had done, every hardship he had endured would no longer be an issue after this case. It was clear that at the end of the Artistic Killer's life, Stephen's would truly begin.

He drank until daylight shone through the curtains and decided he needed to bid the gentlemen good day and also to a thoroughly surprising night.

It was now Sunday morning and the masses prepared for church, to pray to a God that had so recently allowed the murder of a girl cut down so early in life.

Stephen made his way home and to his bed.

He slept and by the time he woke again from a fitful rest, the day was well on its way.

CHAPTER 25

"I know who it is!"

Detective Flint burst into the room at breakneck speed, almost knocking over officer Alan, who had taken to standing just behind the swinging doors, which, as it turned out, was a poor attempt at trying to gleam information from idle chit chat but only succeeded in getting in people's way.

Stephen had noticed that Flint had bypassed several detectives' desks and headed straight to his. He took this in the form of a compliment as to the confidence that the collective office now had in his work.

"The stabbing of this young girl! You said we were to keep an eye out for any crimes that seemed excessively violent and random, well as I was… errrr…" Flint shifted uncomfortably, knowing he would have to verbally 'place' himself somewhere that an enforcer of the law should not be seen when not on official police business. "…as I was leaving the Waterhouse Lane area by the docks on Saturday, I saw a man walking quite briskly away, not far from where this 'appened. I thought it odd, as most people from that area are never brisk. They are either reeling from the drugs or… serviced by a lady of the red gas lamp. I caught a glimpse of who it was an' I knew he would be up to no good. I just saw the paper and it all clicked."

"What where you doing round there, Flint?" asked Detective Napier with a Cheshire Cat-like grin.

"Does it really matter, Napier? I'm talking about a potential lead for Detective Howes here, an' all you're hung up on is why I was round Prossy Lane?"

"Sorry, Prossy what?" asked Stephen, evidently oblivious to the nickname.

Napier explained, still beaming with a grin, that the area was known for prostitution or 'Prossy's' and opium dens.

"What difference does it make about the area? I'm trying explain who it was I saw and all you keep going on about is me enjoying myself." Detective Flint had said it before he realised that he wasn't in the company of just friends but in the eye of judgemental work colleagues.

Hanging his head and truly losing all the excitement he had just built with his dramatic entrance, Flint tried to continue in as dignified a manner as he could muster. Taking a deep breath, he said, "I'm sure it was him, but you won't like it when I tell you." Another pause and he seemed to stop breathing. Knowing the impact the very name he was about to utter would have, he looked towards Detective Napier as he said the words… barely audibly…

"Say that again?" said Napier, losing his grin and leaning forward from his chair, elbows on his desk and his head slightly tilting to assist with hearing Flint's next words.

This time Flint looked Napier straight in the eye, "Armeen…"

The atmosphere in the room chilled in an instant and everyone seemed to understand why, apart from Stephen.

"Okay, gentleman, I'm going to have to say I'm a little in the dark here. I'm a detective, not a mind reader so would someone like to explain to me who or what an 'Armeen' is?"

Detective Napier didn't say a word, only collected his jacket as he left.

Several room regulars pretended to be busying themselves with pieces of paper or looking for something non-existent in or around their personal space, avoiding Stephen's look of confusion as well as his request for an explanation.

Flint headed for the door and motioned Stephen to do the same. "I'll explain on the way."

They were soon outside and Flint cleared Stephen's confusion.

"You know 'ow you see them couples who go out strolling in the park and seem to have a glow about um?"

Flint and Stephen's steps, although rapid, matched in rhythm. They had set off quick-footed after Napier, who was some distance in front of them.

"Well, that was Napier 'n Ms Marie. Together they were like those couples on a postcard or something. Umbrellas, doves flying, sun shining, the lot. But what Napier didn't know is that whilst he was out earning the crust, Ms Marie was getting visits from the bread man. Fella called Armeen. As you can tell by the name, he is not from round 'ere but fits in quite well. 'Angs out with the very worst of them, and that is no exaggeration. Even drinks with 'The Barge'."

Detective Flint said the name in an almost cautious manner… the same name that had been mentioned by George during Stephen's absinthe-fuelled drinking binge, as a fella to avoid.

Unable to fathom if two people could share the same nickname, Stephen had to assume it belonged to the same man.

A name such as 'The Barge' in a fishing town? A label like that was hardly thrown around easily. It had to be well chosen for a reason.

By now they had circled east of the Queen's Dock and were heading toward the smaller River Hull that led into the Humber.

Taking a swift right, crossing a cobbled road and avoiding a tram, then taking a left, they now followed the embankment.

In the distance they could see Napier with his stern walk, fists clenched and eyes fixed on the road.

Stephen had heard enough from Flint and realised why all the drama had caused Detective Napier to be so brash in the first place.

An anchor, no matter how heavy, could not weigh more on a man's heart than when dealing with the betrayal of a woman he loves.

The only question that remained was to 'where' exactly they were heading?

Detective Flint told Stephen that Armeen and his bunch of "cut throats and tattoo'd thugs", not to mention The Barge regularly hung around at the Bay Horse Public House.

"An 'out of the way' hole that held the majority of a gang 'owned' by a someone you've probably already heard about?"

Within two sentences, a second name was brought up that seemed undoubtedly to cause some form of collision in the near future with the newly-formed member of the Hull Police Force and a certain Victor Sören.

Stephen despised bullying figures and in a town in which destitution seemed to thrive, it was as if Hull needed another financial drain like the streets of Amsterdam needed one more canal.

The well-known figure that had been mentioned to Stephen had sprung already from a very recent case.

The Peacock's driver had blubbered Victor Sören's name and no retribution had yet to surface on the missing money that had disappeared into the 'not so law abiding' detective and the jeweller's deep pockets.

Stephen suspected it was only a matter of time before he would eventually meet the fellow. Not only because he was sometimes spending Victor Sören's money that he had pocketed from the Peacock's briefcase, but because it now seemed that although Victor Sören was portraying himself as a businessman, he was also a dab hand at being a crime lord.

The detectives caught up with Napier, both men knowing the actions taken in the next few minutes could result in either conflict or comfort, so they approached cautiously.

Each side of the cobbled path loomed high with industrial buildings dripping with steaming labour. Even the endless onslaught of drizzle seemed to do very little to the stench of manual self described 'graft'.

Each step took Stephen and Flint closer to the now deflated Detective Napier.

David Napier stood to one side of a large door that looked

more like a barn door than an entrance to a pub. He was bent doubled over with his hands on his knees, breathing heavily.

"David?" Flint said, trying to appear calming in tone. "Are you alright? Let's just head back to the station and decide what to do from there."

This, Stephen suspected, was not from a practised form of negotiation but more than likely from hours spent on his side, reaching for an opium pipe, as comforting as a mother's cradle to let the world flow by in its own chaotic melody.

Stephen had only tried opiates once, but they only suppressed so much of his true nature at the time. He was a man full of rage on a grand scale after what had happened to his former mentor and when the high had subsided, his former mental state returned, probably the same as Detective Napier felt now.

"Nah! Fuck off, Flint."

Napier pushed Flint aside as he stood as tall as he could muster with water-filled eyes, taking a breath. He paced two steps right and then one left.

Stephen knew this moment.

Napier was facing the confrontation within oneself before the storm.

It made Stephen think of how many times he had been in this situation.

His life, before now, was one of mayhem. But like a boxer adopting the Queensbury rules stance or a warrior on a battlefield, it had made him ready and aware of the best action to take in these situations.

He cooled his blood and prepared himself for what was to come.

'When a situation becomes heated, the one with the blood of fire triumphs, waste that fire before you need it and all you're left with is smoky embers…'

His father had told him that, and he had never forgotten the words or stern look from his military-minded dad.

Stephen heard footsteps and looked behind him, almost

registering the oncoming sound as an ambush, but it was the cavalry from the office.

Forced by guilt, or more than likely Detective Raffle, they were here in support for their colleague. All but O'Connell were present.

"What's happening?" came Raffle's voice in a deep tone that resonated malice. He even cracked his knuckles.

Stephen thought at that moment that they perhaps were cut from the same cloth, he and Raffle. No chance was given for a reply however as Napier had entered the public house via the dark and sturdy wooden door.

Stephen shrugged nonchalantly and turned to follow, with a 'poised for combat' Detective Raffle and a battle reluctant Flint and Ford.

The usual plume of smoke from the pub drew the men inside.

It took a moment for his vision to adjust from the daylight to the darkened interior but when it did, the public house was not unlike many of the surrounding area.

An open fireplace blaring heat to their right, a bar to the left just big enough for the owner, a few barrels of ale and almost nothing more.

A group of men were sitting toward the back of the room but due to the cramped confines, they rested merely feet from Detective Napier.

"Armeen! You're wanted for questions."

Stephen could not see Napier's face, but he knew the words were spoken through gritted teeth.

A dark-skinned man sitting with his back to the wall stood up slowly and uncertainly, giving glancing looks from his comrades to Detective Napier.

"What fur?"

"You fucking…" Napier did not even attempt to finish the sentence. He made a lunge for the man, who Stephen could only assume was Armeen, but was instantly held back by two men who jumped up between them.

A small fracas took place and an almighty bellow sounded.

"Oiiiiii!"

The noise stopped everyone. A life-worn old man stood behind the bar and for a second time made his voice heard. "Coppers or not, I've paid my fees. If you lot wanna piss about, do it in the stable out back."

Before Stephen could contemplate what 'fees' he was referring to, it was obvious everyone knew the day's outcome.

The rest of Armeen's band of merry followers stood from their previous seated positions and Stephen caught full view of The Barge for the first time.

He was under no doubt this was indeed who he had heard about.

At least six feet six inches tall with a frame to rival a large vessel, the bald head and bulking body stood and walked towards a back door, close to the bar.

As he did so, he had not once taken his eyes from Stephen.

Whether it was because he was a new face or due to the Peacocks' arrest, The Barge kept a furrowed brow towards Stephen.

After the gang had exited, the policemen soon followed, Napier first, although now seeming a little deflated after seeing The Barge stand up and make his presence known.

Stephen was next and then Raffle.

The other two followed.

Behind him, Stephen heard Flint say something to the owner in a hissed tone but the conversation was lost.

The daylight streamed down and the line of thugs, like an unkempt tribe, stood in and around the horse dung and straw of the stables, shovels and bridles hanging on the walls, buckets strewn on the floor. The area was isolated and out of sight of any members of the public.

Outnumbered by one or maybe two, Stephen and the rest of his men lined up with around ten feet between the opposing sides. Stephen found himself standing opposite The Barge. He almost seemed to block out the sunlight.

Daunting in appearance and obviously menacing in nature, The

Barge spoke, looking at Stephen but clearly addressing Napier. "What's all this about, David?" His voice was gravel and dust. "We've paid our money." His eyes gave a quick flicker towards Flint.

Stephen had begun to formulate a picture of exactly who might be on the 'take' within the police unit even though Rudyard had seemed confident in his men to avoid such temptations.

"You don't come bouncing into our place like this unless you'll be wanting bother, am I right?"

"No problem with you, Barge. We have some questions for Armeen. Just him. That's all we came here for."

Detective Napier was visibly nervous in his manner with Barge.

Stephen didn't need to look at Napier to pick up on this. Instead, he was now trapped in a battle of willpower with the oaf of a man. They had not deviated their stare now for what seemed like an age. This situation was heading one way, that much was evident, and the slightest flicker of weakness or complacency could well and truly cost him his life.

"Well, here is how I see it… you want him? You have to come through all of us."

Slowly and deliberately, he removed his unkept working jacket, handing it to another of his followers and Stephen did the same of his own suit jacket, using this calm before the storm to formulate his plan of attack.

He had fought men of all shapes and sizes, more times than he could count.

In bulk, The Barge rivalled the biggest of them but he reminded himself once again that all men bleed, hurt and die. It was only a matter of finding out how to take The Barge through this process.

Stephen spat on the ground in between the two rows. Although nearly a dozen men littered the outdoor stable in confrontation, the main event focused on Stephen and The Barge. Previously upholding the air of a common decent man, he no longer had this luxury.

For what was to come, Stephen could do nothing but survive and no deception could be upheld to achieve this.

Not a word was spoken between them, but a primeval knowing and understanding surged and the pair moved forward in the same moment. In a matter of steps they would collide, steel and solid rock clashing in unison, however in that moment of pre-conflict, Raffle rushed forward to the two men to the right of The Barge.

The first, he dropped in a heartbeat with a straight right to the jaw.

The thud of the body hitting the ground forced everyone else forward if they wanted to or not and also signalled the beginning of Stephen's own fight.

Raffle waded into the second of his personally picked opponents.

In that moment, The Barge grabbed Stephen's right shoulder by the shirt and began the workings of a slow yet obviously powerful punch. Stephen lifted his right arm up, inside and then around. The motion was instantaneous, twisting The Barge's arm and bringing them both too close for the right-handed curved blow to glance from Stephen's left shoulder.

Locked close, too close to throw anything that might be effective, Stephen brought his left hand up and planted it square in The Barge's eye. Soft and delicate tissue mushed beneath his thumb.

He spanned his hand so any attempt to pull back by The Barge would not disrupt the gouging, and using this leverage, Stephen leant forward and sank his teeth into The Barge's nose, all too aware he had to stand on tiptoes to reach. It would almost seem comical if not so malicious.

In the adrenaline of the moment Stephen didn't know if he had bitten into his own thumb or The Barge's nose. The pain would be dampened until it was agonising.

All he knew was that he needed to hurt his opponent and he may not get a chance like this in the future.

He bit down a solid, 'tough meat' devouring bite and thankfully felt cartilage, not bone, locked in his teeth.

He heard a low growl from The Barge as he released Stephen's shoulder and pushed him back, throwing a punch that connected but was nowhere near its full potential. Merely glancing but damaging all the same.

The punch was more thrown from panic, but Stephen knew he would not want to be receiving a fully intended impact as he felt the chances of keeping his teeth or relatively handsome looks would be slim.

Hurt and angry, The Barge would now be acting on rage and not instinct.

It was a chance Stephen would have to take, but he honoured the shove and staggered back a couple of feet. Righting himself for the next wave of attack from the man mountain, he knew his cards would have to be played expertly and correct.

The Barge rubbed his eye and looked at the palm of his hand as if to expect to see blood or some other discharge.

The rush of the fight running through his ears, Stephen saw The Barge say something but could not hear the words.

Gritting his teeth, the man moved forward, looking all the more of an unstoppable force than ever. Stephen backed away slightly and ducked under another punch thrown by the attacker, again a big right hand. Stephen was back up and throwing his own fast left hook.

He connected with The Barge's jaw but if the punch was felt, it was not made evident by the recipient.

Stephen threw another. This time as hard a left hook as could be mustered and this time, rocking his opponent.

Following with a right hook, he made The Barge stagger. His hands lightning fast and his instinct finely honed, Stephen was backing away on his toes as The Barge made for a second grab, yet only slightly moving forwards, like an oversized child taking its first steps.

The fighting around them paled into insignificance and nobody disturbed the two.

Stephen glanced side to side and spotted a shovel within reach.

Now was as perfect a time to use a weapon as any.

He picked up the shovel that had perhaps once been used to

muck horse manure from the floor and swung it as hard as he could, consciously not using the bladed edge but instead the flat surface area to connect. His intention was not to kill The Barge, although with a sliced impact he could have quite easily done so, instead he wanted him out of action.

The prang of metal connecting with the giant's cheek and temple sounded like something used in a theatre show for laughs.

The Barge staggered to his right and dropped to one knee. The fact that anyone could take that sort of abuse and still be able to function surpassed all of Stephen's expectations and in a moment he had a resounding respect for his temporary enemy, who was now clearly dazed yet appeared to be attempting to regain his footing.

Stephen took his opportunity, and dropping the shovel, he pivoted on his right foot, dipped his left shoulder and brought his right fist back. With every ounce of strength he had, he struck The Barge with his fist in the same place the shovel had landed. The motion took Stephen through and off his feet. Hearing bone crack, he didn't know if this was his hand or The Barge's face.

He twisted and landed on his back at the same time The Barge landed, now well and truly out for the count on his front.

The scuffs of feet sounded all around Stephen's ears and he was about to rise to assist any of his work colleagues that may have needed it, when to his left in his line of sight, he saw over the sleeping head of The Barge the legs of someone else standing held in a headlock, then Armeen falling on his back, coughing blood.

His face was contorted in rage.

Almost instantly the contortion turned to take on a different face altogether.

Stephen knew that face.

Napier stood above him with a horse mucking pronged fork buried deep into Armeen's chest.

Pushing heavily on the fork, Detective Napier's features were locked in an insane grin of revenge.

He seemed to be trying to push the fork forward, even though it had reached its full capacity upon the cobbles beneath Armeen's body.

He grinned more as he realised Armeen was well and truly dead. He simply coughed no more as his eyes lolled inside of his head and stared at nothing but eternity.

The intensity of the sight was disturbing for Stephen, when someone tripped over his legs, as he was still lying upon the ground bearing witness to the murder.

Sound seemed to muddle together as he staggered to his feet and saw Raffle grip Napier's shoulder and forcefully push him towards the small half-open exit of the stables.

Most followed as the fight had clearly gone one way.

It was only now he could register the situation. After the initial injuries to The Barge had been inflicted, the majority of his gang of thugs had made for the exit as swiftly as possible. It was now time for the battling blue brigade to do the same.

In a truly disturbing manner, Stephen realised the policemen were now fleeing a murder scene they themselves had created.

CHAPTER 26

Calmness, equanimity, serenity, tranquillity and as still as a bobbing boat upon the midnight windless waters.

There is simply not a feeling in the world that rivals this intoxicating state of mind.

My only regret is a little ruthlessness with my clothing to a point of forgetfulness on my own behalf.

As much as I may scold myself for such actions, the sedate mood which washes over my person, currently overrides my shabby appearance.

I have not changed my clothes since the act itself.

A part of me still longs to savour the image, the dampness upon my attire, the smell of crude muddied water in my nostrils and the sudden silence of stifled screams upon the tiny bones located in my ear.

Recounting from the beginning of this particular endeavour will no doubt bring me joy.

Her name, I never chose to locate, as it made very little difference.

To misquote Shakespeare, 'A cyprian with any other name can still cut as deep'.

For the girl may well and truly have been a Rose to some, but it was certainly a shared Rose without the knowledge of the men who held her dear.

Her admittance was quite blunt in the cove of a tea shop.

She and her friend had no idea of my attendance, so they spoke freely.

Holding the heart of one man, it appeared she desired the pockets of another. And also another that had caught her eye as she caught his wanting.

Alas, such a plan she could not wait to engage, so she had taken up with all three unsuspecting fellows at once.

Her callous manner touched something within the core of my being. Strange you may think as my very own nature is that of deceit and pain.

However, the financial gain and joviality in the act is uncouth and base of devious instinct. I felt I had neglected certain targets in my selections and perhaps it was time to choose a deserving victim.

As she exited the tea room, she became aware of my presence, that much was clear, but my illusion of being distracted in the local newspapers seemed to quell her fear of discovery.

She turned and walked along the outside pathway, allowing me a clear view of her appearance. She was a thing of divinity. Her soft and delicate features, although angelic, radiated an innocence.

A very well disguised predator indeed. But then again, so am I.

I followed her to her abode, which lay not far from our original passing.

She bid farewell to her female companion who seemed equally as joyful to the frantic telling of deceit, although she would be spared as 'the ears that the words lay upon, do not carry out the original sin'.

After two days of watching my heartless harlot, I bear witness to the act of betrayals personified. A gentleman of name and nature stepped from a carriage, held out his hand and she took that of his affections.

She glided from the inside of the hansom with the grace of a lady in every sense of the word.

From my home of shadows, I saw him oh so hopefully lean down to kiss the lips of his beloved and upon reeling back his elation was evident. With a courteous bow and a snap of his heels, he bid her farewell and climbed back inside of his ride, waving from the window as the horse carried him away.

She took a final wave and went inside after unbolting her front door.

The change of gentlemanly company had been so swift that if it had been cut much closer, I doubt that one of my blades could have rivalled the timing.

The clicking of heels upon cobbles approached from the opposite direction of the now vanished horse and carriage. A man much further along in his years than the previous enraptured rival approached the house of the desired little lady.

After a rapping upon the door and several moments of waiting, she answered herself. If she had servants, it had been my guess that they had been previously dismissed to avoid arousal of her deceit.

From my location, even I could have been fooled by her look of innocence but I have the mind of a man that believes that 'evil knows evil' and clearly she deceived her current visitor better than she could me.

She bade him entrance.

I needed no more to witness and took a slow walk home, my mind awash with possibilities regarding the angelic devil's demise, I took pleasure in the options that lay ahead.

By the time I had reached my very own destination my mind was well and truly settled.

It's a rare occasion that I get to use chloroform. Indeed, in my masterpiece creation, it would serve many great purposes if I were slightly more amateurish. It is with a blush however that I admit, even with spontaneity, I can create worthy works of art without it and therefore have little chance to call upon its uses.

In this case, it was very much needed as time and tide did not assist my work. Ha ha. You will realise my pun soon enough if you are to read this diary. Her abduction required very little in the stages of planning.

Her younger accompanying gentleman, once again with a flutter in his heart, bid her farewell under my concealed gaze once more. As she watched his carriage disappear with a glorious air of dissimulation, I pulled my own hansom alongside her.

Unhanding the reins and bending over to lavishly splash the

liquid upon the cloth, ensuring my actions were concealed in the dark, I stepped down from the helm of my own carriage and made to hand the young lady a note. With sure of foot, I placed the cloth over her mouth and within seconds she lay limp in my arms.

Without a moment to lose and the ease due to her slight frame, she was in the back of the comfortable carriage and away we rode.

Upon waking, she appeared quite clueless to her new situation. The shock and realisation as to her grim and unfamiliar surroundings could almost be seen as amusing, I chose not to mock her plea in its vision of horrific protest.

For the first time in a very long time, this incarnate of false hope muffled a cry through the cloth secured in her mouth. I could almost imagine it harboured the most honest thing to pass from her lips in many years gone by.

She thrashed only slightly but soon stopped, evidently her bounds causing her more pain than she had accounted for. When one is shackled to a wall in a dark and damp room, the fight or flight is extinguished surprisingly quickly.

I had remained dormant in the dark recess of the room. Silent, statuesque and watching.

My aim had been to gauge how long the chloroform would render her unconscious. With my experiment complete, I exited the room to the sound of more muffled cries. I felt nothing for my captive. I simply remained indifferent.

Her callousness had rendered her in this predicament. Although she would not be aware of this fact, I would have plenty of time to explain much later.

When the time was right, I returned to my fallen angel of disgrace.

She huddled to the wall when I entered the room. In my hand, the cloth soaked in the intoxicating essence of a sweet and almost nut-like aroma.

When applying the chloroform once more, it seemed a

welcome smell, as opposed to the damp mould soaked into the surrounding walls. Almost forgetting the effects of too much inhalation, I sharply gathered my thoughts. For the next part of my creativity, I needed a clear head and wits about myself.

Her words were incoherent and, bending closer towards her, I reassured her that she would soon feel sweet freedom once more. Her beauty had not faded as she drifted into darkness.

A mask camouflaging her ill intent so well.

In turn with her demise, I would be ridding the world of an illusion, hurting the very souls of the men she deceived and again creating a magnificent message in its true artform for my feeble, 'would be' captors.

When dormant, her relocation from the 'holding area' to the canvas of my work was easily achievable.

She fit comfortably into a potato sack. I did, however, feel ashamed to be placing her in such a filthy confinement when she was clearly used to much more 'refined attire' but I could not let this dampen my joyous night.

When hoisted, she delightfully posed no problem in reaching my pre-prepared and awaiting hansom.

The journey was not an unpleasant one. The cloudless sky gave a sting to the air in bitter cold fresh reminder that Hull, and indeed England itself, was capable of seeing unhindered stars much to the common misconception that cloud and smog were forever present.

Bellowing music played in my mind's ear... Beethoven's Overture to Egmont... dramatic then soothing as I passed from the town north along the river.

Bidding a fine evening to anyone who may have witnessed me in my journey, only sniffs and grunts were returned. Indeed, it was evident that only I myself felt the occasion's appreciation and importance as to what was about to occur.

The frequency of passers-by soon began to die away, although unfortunately not literally, and the night took on a familiar embracing grim silence.

A lamp barely lit my path, and once or twice the horse had to be steadied as a soft river verge gave under its hooves.

It was almost impossible to say how much time had passed but no longer could any dim glow of the towns be seen.

I had prepared for this and when I stopped the horse, I made no delay upon lighting the candles that I had gathered for the work in which I was about to partake.

She did not wake when I moved her from the carriage. Nor did she stir when I bent and manoeuvred her over my shoulder. Her body being delightfully light, I was also able to carry a lamp to avoid stumbling as I neared the edge of the river to where the other candles had been arranged.

It was a cautious event to descend the metal ladders with her upon my shoulder and looking back, it was a miscalculation on my behalf, but nonetheless the act was achieved.

When the tide was at its lowest, the ladders that were usually submerged in water were currently a slippery obstacle that came to a halt at the level of the mud banks, the brown sinking mud that was usually under water.

The distinctive wet banks of the River Hull vigorously attempted to drag my ankles further below its deathly gripping and relentless waste.

Remaining steady footed, the devilish angel's hands were bound and firmly secured to the pre-descended ladder and I was able to ascend to the damp higher bank and my own safety, leaving her in a sitting position but sound asleep, her hands just over her shoulder.

The carriage had not only been the transporting method of my latest piece of art, but also that of a spare pair of shoes to replace the muddy pair on my feet, and a new pair of trousers to replace the tattered ruined pair that had also become splattered with clay like mud.

As I changed my clothing in the quite deathly silent night which held only the noise of the passing river in its embrace, I began to hear its gloriousness.

Peer Gynt Suite No.1 Op. 46; In The Hall Of The Mountain King.

The rising strings in perfect symmetry with her waking confusion.

A mumble and the music building. A low, woeful moan and more strings added to the music. A shallow call and now the trombones added gently to the ever-increasing sound of the current, yet one day classical song.

By the time she had reached full screech, the symbols were crashing and enthralling. It was almost perfect but I needed visualisation to complete this artistry.

A small container of bottled wine and a fresh cold meat sandwich were the only items I arrived back at the riverside with, and to my surprise the water had already began to rise with the tide.

Licking at her ankles she had taken a step up the first rung of the ladder having to bend slightly due to her bound wrists restricting her ascent any further.

She ceased her yelling at the sight of me and began to ask for help.

I was certain she knew it was me that had placed her in such a situation in the first place, but I had to applaud her performance.

Ever the plea of the innocent, a babe in the woods, a child abandoned in the street, she asked for forgiveness in whichever wrong I thought she had done.

I said nothing.

I had intended to ask if she had felt guilt for her fraudulent actions but in the time it had taken her to switch from mercy, to panic, to malice and then once again to begging, I myself had decided that this was a show without the need for words or commentary.

She began to struggle against the ropes as the water rose and reached the rung of the ladder where she rested her feet.

The cold must have been quite a shock and as I uncovered my delicious cold cut wrapped in a buttered sliced loaf, I stifled a smile as almost instinctively I asked if she would like some.

A chuckle was unavoidable as I poured wine into a small goblet brought especially for the show.

Sometimes the practice of being a gentleman can rub off on one's nature regardless of the situation.

As I had gathered the tide information, it was astonishing to see how accurate the account had been and also the rate at which the water heightened.

Realisation 'sank' in if you will pardon the gruesome pun around waist high for the deceptive maiden. Be it cold water or shock, she shivered violently as she screamed for help in the hope someone may be passing and hear the noise.

We had ventured too far into the dark for such an event however and at her chest she gave up such an attempt.

She had now reached the extent in which her restraints would allow her to rise no more and yet the water crept ever higher.

I had finished my wine and meat and an uncontrollable urge came upon me.

In my previous works of art so much effort had been required.

The final moments of life in others had needed some great effort on my behalf. This time however, this giver of pleasure, in the form of a woman had given me the honour of one final act of kindness.

I stood and moved closer.

With total disregard for my clothing, I lay flat on my stomach just above the ladders on the bank side upon which this tied and tormented girl struggled ever more to set herself free.

The ground was cold and wet.

It was altogether uncomfortable, but all the same, an uncomfortable compromise I was willing to endure.

As unpleasant as the dampness of the soil may have been, I tried to ignore the thought as I looked down to see the angelic face peering up and straining to keep breathing the midnight air.

She began taking deep breaths.

The cries and begging had now ceased completely.

I looked into her eyes and she into mine and, in a perfect moment of placidity, the water rushed by and took her dreams, her lies, her sins and her life along with it.

In the final instant of watching her disappear under the brown muddied water she resembled a china doll in formaldehyde and then… she was gone.

Serenity.

I stood and was embarrassed to see that my wet trousers revealed an 'excitement' I had long thought forgotten.

Even in death, the lady of the water caused an arousal. For this reason alone, I bid her a 'goodnight' and I left my written words upon the river bank, this time, directly addressing my stalker, my new biggest fan, the new mystifying Detective Howes. Although if he would know they were for 'him', specifically or not, remained to be seen, but as I had made clear, more correspondence was to follow. Finally, I hauled myself into the carriage and returned to the gaslit streets of Hull.

CHAPTER 27

Stephen had spent the night wandering the streets. How far or exactly where he had walked, he was unsure. All he knew was that his feet ached and his drunkenness, although excessive, did not seem enough.

Now back in his room, he tried to take his mind from the previous course of events but something disturbed him, yet he could not fathom what that might be.

He had seen a man murdered.

That, to him, was nothing new.

He had seen his fair share and even the manner in which the murder had occurred was far from the most brutal he had witnessed.

He kicked his shoes off, only just realising his shoelaces were untied and as they clattered to the floor, a synapse in his mind flickered. Dull at first with direct attribute to the ale, but he realised why he was so perturbed.

Like his shoelaces, they were fastened in a neat and tidy fashion previously when he had set out to work this morning.

All in order and doing what they needed to do. Holding the shoe to the foot constantly and continuing to do so.

When the fight had occurred and he had witnessed his colleagues acting together but seeing them flee afterwards, then just like an untied lace, they were now messy, untidy, unable to perform the task they were set out to do because they had let themselves be undone.

The structure and best intentions of all the workforce had been torn apart and left messy in one smooth impulsive and violent action.

He himself could manage these sorts of acts, his shoulders had borne the brunt of such actions for years but to see the foundation upon which he had based his recent moral integrity crumble, weighed heavy on his mind.

He slept for a while but restlessness got the better of him so he sat in his chair, looking out of the window, watching the sun rise until he was low on cigarettes.

Whisky was replaced by tea with whisky and then, when the clouds grew brighter instead of the expected sun illuminating the sky, he resorted to tea alone.

He did not even consider attending work that day. He had a feeling that attendance would be low and had no intention of trying to explain to anyone that had not been involved in the chaos, why the case may be.

At ten o'clock, George knocked and enquired as to Stephen's health and after a tea with a strained conversation, he left the detective alone.

When a knock at the door came at around midday, he expected to find George once more but this time it was his landlady.

She had a letter that had been delivered by, "a cheeky little bugger, he put it in me 'and and scarpered, said he wor paid to deliver, not grass."

When she handed Stephen the letter, a chill gripped him. The envelope was of the highest quality that he had ever seen. An 'off white' colour with handwriting upon it of the practised upper class.

He had no need to break the wax seal, which ensured it was read by the recipient only, to know that this letter was sent from someone who should not be sending private correspondence to him.

He closed the door unaware that Mrs Pritchard was in mid-conversation.

Stephen sat heavily in his chair and, taking the pocket knife that he carried, he opened the letter. Once again, the writing screamed elegance from its very core. Taking a large gulp from the whisky bottle that had been on the floor next to his chair, he began to read…

Dear 'Detective' Howes,

It is a shame that correspondence in this manner cannot be a two way system, but I am sure that if I want to remain free to continue my artistic work, then I see little option.

Let me begin by telling you who I am. Not exactly, of course. That would be a grand error on my behalf, but you know me, or at least you want to. You want to be close enough to hear me say, 'Congratulations, Mr Howes, you have captured the most evil creation to grace this earth.'

But this is not to be so.

At least not until I decide that I am ready.

The part that will truly irk oneself is that you have already been that close.

It was in fact my design.

I had heard, as one does around this town, that I was being specially tracked by a very competent man and this aroused my suspicion. I simply had to know more.

I murdered a young lady, not two days ago to 'draw you out' as it were.

She and I had crossed paths and I found out enough to commit the murder. Please do not arrive at the conclusion that I murdered her for a reason of passion, because this would indeed be an error on your behalf.

I severed her artery in a swift motion and as she fell back to the bed, I set about my work.

The style for this piece was not of my usual nature, I am sure you will agree… but that was my intention.

The police were told, the Chief arrived and 'the special man' looking to capture myself came along not long afterwards.

I heard your prognosis from across the street whilst I nestled upon my cab seat. I waited and as predicted, yourself and the Chief entered my ruse of a taxi in waiting.

I heard all that I needed to hear through the squawk box… your candid conversation and the grief that followed as you both wallowed in confusion and smoke from pipe and cigarette combined.

Your mention of another particular killer and how quickly you deduced the action of the streetwalker's murder told me you were special indeed, but if you were to kick yourself once you are to do it twice and thrice.

The butcher.

After I had finished my single masterpiece of many to come and my message had been left for all to read, I was startled by a dull thud from the back entrance to the shop. Mere moments earlier and I could have been crushed by the dammed body of the young gentleman you let fall from the upper floor.

Peering through the smallest of gaps, I witnessed your murder and concealment of his body.

I dare say at that moment in time you had my attention. However, at that point, all you appeared to be, was a murderer.

Had it not been for the fact that you appeared the next morning wearing the mask of a detective as you bustled through the crowd, unaware that I watched from the very same crowd itself, even having a main part to play, then I would have possibly have considered you for one of my other masterpieces.

However, I now feel you are to play a bigger role in all of this macabre story, but how big the role, I am not yet sure.

The prostitute's murder is not to be dwelled upon by yourself. Leave it to others and view it simply as a sketch, crudely scribbled on a note pad. It was personalised for you, to lure you out yet it maintained the same amount of care as my other works of art in the sense of anonymity.

My only regret is that the tune playing throughout the deed was not of a fitting overture.

It happens so much these days that I do not even commit them to my personal journal.

One day you may come to read of my adventures in the very journal I speak of, but it is not a complete work.

For instance, just the other night as the rain patted the walls and windows of my abode, I had a sudden urge grip my very bones.

I clubbed a man and robbed him of his shoes.

He lived, I am sure, and it must have appeared to be a simple robbery, but then my work changed style.

Much like the artists of years before, too poor to buy blank canvas after blank canvas and painting over their work to create something anew, I donned the shoes… they were at least two sizes too big for me.

I must have looked quite comical in my wanderings.

After a while, I found what I had been searching for, a child, who was quite simply put 'out far too late' and begged me for money.

The area was romantically empty, so a fierce backhanded swipe knocked the youth from his or her feet (I say this because the garb worn by the small, street beggar made gender unfathomable) and then I proceeded to stamp upon the cranium until what used to be the working of an inner brain contained within a skull became diluted by the downpour of British weather.

Brutal and surprising at how delicate a young child's head really is, I left, satisfied that no one had seen me commit the murder.

Especially since I had been sporting oversized murder weapons. I could have managed the degradation of arrest but certainly not whilst wearing ill-fitting attire.

I abandoned the shoes when I arrived home.

The streets were so soaked to the marrow, they had become like new with raindrops within thirty paces.

Can you begin to imagine the irony of creating murder 'in another man's footsteps'?

I cannot hear your answer, yet regardless of what it might be, that is exactly what you did with my murder of late. The young girl killed whilst candlelight remained the only witness. You made the murder someone else's.

It is with this confession that I hope you understand exactly why you have no choice but to sit, just like the others, and watch my work progress.

Unless you strike lucky, detective, or I am ready to slip softly into the night, you are nothing more than a witness to my greatness and interesting history.

Do not fear, my correspondence shall continue.

It is in the strangest meaning of the word 'refreshing' to have a glimmer of past light linked with myself walking this sheet of earth... someone sent to 'make me pay' for greatness and be paid in return.

Until next time, detective, I shall sign off simply with my location.

From Hull

Stephen could almost hear the words being spoken. It sent a chill through him. The killer knew where he lived. From this moment on he knew it was to capture the Artist or be toyed with in a manner by this psychotic madman.

The day became greyer and as the sun swept from left to right through his window, he could no longer read the words.

It was true, the letter would remain secret from all the others. Just like so many other details he could not share.

He had never felt such a weight upon him. He required something to ease the pain.

Stephen had seen enough horror in the last two murder scenes of his target to last him a lifetime.

Coupled with his 'assisting' the other officers in the precinct and the fight that had taken place at the Bay Horse pub, Stephen could feel his mind jolting. The letter was his last straw.

Pleasure and pressure struck a fine balance with him at the best of times but as of late he had been waking from his tormented sleep in fits of panic.

He must have fallen asleep though shear mental exhaustion. As before, he had dreamt of falling from the cliffs but his dreams were now altering. His two latest restless nights he had crashed through ceilings, first into the theatre, landing between the corpse of the man with his face crunched 180 degrees in the opposite direction and his accompanying lady cut so deep that when the removal of her body had taken place, her head had unnaturally tilted back at an impossible angle like a lid flipped from a cooking pot.

He tried to stand in his dream but was slipping all the while on the gore that had been left for witnesses aplenty.

The deep circles that gathered around his eyes were becoming more and more apparent when he awoke after falling in his dream, startling himself so his eyes opened rapidly day after day.

The next dream with regards to the second murder had left him crashing into another ceiling, another crime scene… the butcher's mouth gaping open, eyes never leaving Stephen.

Once again, he tried to steady himself, all the while Keen's head held back whilst the pole protruded from his jaw, and from deep inside of his belly a low murmuring, curdling gurgle could be heard which filled the room more than the stench of a decaying body.

He had woken more times that he liked to admit to the after-echo of his own calling out. Mrs Pritchard had made no complaint to the noise, however her uneasy looks made him realise he had been more vocal each night in his terrors.

His last sleep… he had woken after seeing Napier impale Armeen. As Stephen landed on his front from the fall on the cliffs, he turned his head ready for impact and fell in synchronisation with Napier's plunge of the weapon.

The howl from Armeen, which hadn't actually occurred during the fight, turned into Stephen's as he woke from his final fitful rest of the night.

Although the purple bruised sky meant that the night was just starting, he made his way as quietly as he could muster down the stairs of his lodgings.

Cold and cloudless, now the stars made an appearance and watched on as he hunched his shoulders and aimlessly travelled the cobbles. His mind absent, his sauntering led him to a place he had begun to learn more and more about.

Waterhouse Lane… the area sported a range of cultures from far and wide. Being so close to the docks with high-rise buildings of three floors high either side of the street blocking out any natural light, night or day, it reminded him of Parliament Street on which the police headquarters were located but more of a 'negative' version. Where a gentleman could leisurely saunter down Parliament Street, a hoodlum would hunch around in this particular area.

Seeing a green glow from a gas lamp-tinted frame, Stephen strolled inwards, toward a small building, already aware of its contents.

George had seen the stress and strain upon Stephen and told him of a man that helped people to 'unlock' answers within the confines of the mind. Generally, the street sleeper would remain upbeat and jovial but during a drinking session, all of a sudden, he had become serious. George told Stephen that the detective had helped him so much that he felt confident that Stephen had saved his life and that he could not stand by whilst Stephen mentally struggled with his inner troubles.

Stephen had followed George's directions without realising he was doing so and now found himself entering a low door, worn with crisping paint and perhaps more so crisping because of the almost intolerable heat that swept from the entrance, like a dragon's breath.

CHAPTER 28

Closing the door behind him, Stephen found himself face to face with Lock Key, an illegal but highly tolerated Eastern cultural pharmacist.

"What is it you seek, my friend? I have something for everything and everyone alike."

This had an unexpected effect on Stephen, his shoulders seemed to bear an excessive weight instantly. His task afforded very little time for self help, but being asked by a stranger how they could help him felt as disarming as Lock Key's accent. He had an almost Asian appearance but his wording could not have been more western if he had attended England's finest schools.

George had told Stephen that Lock Key was short and warming to his customers, known to a select few but well regarded amongst those who frequented his trade.

He stood behind a counter that was draped in dark green cloth, almost like a billiard table's felt, but instead of billiard balls upon the counter, it was littered with small boxes, labelled in symbols rather than the titles of their contents.

Stephen felt almost dirty to be associated with this 'hole' to which people would scurry willingly, just to find whatever concoction they were seeking.

The room seemed to crawl around him, its small confines radiating people's guilt, passionless escaping voids ingrained into the very brickwork.

"To sleep," Stephen admitted uneasily. His mind had toyed with the idea of turning around, right then and there to take solace in alcohol, but he had tried that route already, undoubtedly a little too often and no answers had been discovered as of yet in absinth or ale alike.

"We all sleep, my friend. It's staying in the dream world that proves to be the problem. It is said that you must straighten out your affairs of the day to rest when the dark blanket descends. Perhaps something to void the day?"

"No, I need to be functioning during the day. I'm… I'm required for a task."

Lock Key's eyes seemed to glaze over, clearly not seeing Stephen even though they were fixed in his direction, instead pondering an answer for the deprived detective.

"Very well, then I would recommend a tiny assist to make your days seem brighter."

He bent down under the counter and opened a drawer to remove a small silver snuff box.

He placed the box in Stephen's outstretched hands. The metal was warm but rough between his thumb and forefinger. Pushing the catch, the box opened as if spring loaded.

The powder that lay in the bed of the box was almost flesh coloured.

Stephen stared at the contents for moment or two… Lock Key's voice brought him from his wonderment.

"The first payment is a little expensive but that is however for the box. A gentleman's fondness of snuff is never questioned. After that, you come again and I will increase your depletion for a much more comfortable fee. Be sparing in the beginning… after that, the ingestion is totally to the gentleman's choice. The effects take no more than one hour to manifest."

Stephen dipped in his finger and lined the tip of skin on his digit that was already wet with the perspiration from the heat of the room. As he was about to sniff the substance, Lock Key raised a hand.

"Forgive me, detective, but a payment will indeed be needed first. Shall we say a guinea?"

Stephen closed the lid and dug into his pocket, and paid Lock Key what he wanted.

He stopped as something crossed his mind suddenly. "How do you know I am a detective?"

"Even were it not for Sailor George informing me that you may frequent one time or another, nothing gets past myself, detective. Where my trade is involved, I make it my business to collect investments and information. Not to mention, you have made quite a stir upon the fine trading streets of Hull of late and in such a short space of time nonetheless."

Stephen paid the words no mind, his curiosity satisfied. Lock Key continued to speak as he inhaled the flesh-coloured powder.

"Please feel free to return any time, detective, but I insist upon being exclusive to certain patrons and hope you will keep my secret of trade as safe as I will your profession?"

"Of course. If you make information your business, can you help me find who I seek?"

Lock Key looked towards Stephen, thinking for a moment before he spoke. "Whom you seek is yourself, the fiend you seek will not bring you peace, but you reign in chaos, embrace the chaos."

And with a wry smile, the shop owner pointed to the door. Deciding not to deal in riddles or digest the wisdom bestowed any longer, Stephen turned to open the door and before ducking to exit, he saw the plaque above it.

'Whom you seek is yourself, the fiend you seek will not bring you peace, but you reign in chaos, embrace the chaos.'

Stephen laughed and realised this was not the place for answers as he exited to the street.

CHAPTER 29

Walking into the town centre, he felt like he needed a strong drink. The hour was not so late and he did not think this would be a problem.

Finding a public house close to the Paragon region, he entered and ordered ale before making his way to the rear of the room to where he could only assume would be the lavatory.

The place was surprisingly bright and instead of the majority of mixed young and old patrons, this place seemed more to attract younger customers.

He entered the only cubicle of the outside toilet, locking the door and, staying as far away as he could from the latrine slop, he pinched thumb and forefinger together inside the snuff box and once more he took a large sniff for each nostril.

He leant upon the lavatory door and took a few deep breaths, his thoughts wandering to the places he had seen since arriving in Hull.

He was amazed at the drinking abodes throughout the town.

Although they were mostly dark, damp and, at the best of times, foggier with smoke than the morning mist upon the calm river waters, they seemed hardly ever closed or empty.

There was a reason for the name 'public house' given to the establishments because to most that's what they were, 'houses'.

Homes to man, woman and, often, children.

Communities enclosed with a friendly smile and places to unwind from the back-breaking shifts that were needed to keep bread on the table and beer in the belly.

The alternative was more shift working or to sit at home in the cramped cold rooms of all shapes and sizes littered with children or nagging, tidy wives.

The pub was a sanctuary for all and for him also. He had only been around for a short while yet he was needing this type of atmosphere for his sanity.

What else did he have?

Death and murder in an office whilst he waited for a mistake to be made by the biggest and most feared murderer of all. Worse than the Ripper himself, even though Stephen was confused to the lack of mention of the London ghoul, old slippery Jack.

His mind wandered further and fell upon his new work colleagues.

He knew he was not in Hull for the long haul… as soon as the Artistic Killer had met his end, Stephen would slip away into the night, a much richer man. However, he could not help but feel a warmness, an affection almost. Each person contributed something different to the environment.

Flint had shown Stephen just how the office mentality had become a tram with regards to information, heading in a single line of enquiry, hoping the person committing the crime would simply step into the light with hands raised because everyone around them were pointing in that direction.

With no family to speak of and his free time taken up by what Stephen had suspected were opium dens and whores, he could see why the mentality of coasting through the week's work had developed in Flint. He was quite clearly on the receiving end of funds from criminal fraternities but Stephen could not judge too harshly on this fact.

Crimes against women, children and the aged were mainly what the police were summoned for.

Crimes that people deserved to swing for.

If in the quite hours of the morning a few thugs captured bruises and Flint received money to not pay attention, then who was he to judge if this was wrong or right?

O'Connell was a man of honest intentions with the heart for the job yet perhaps not the skills, although spotting something was amiss at the jewellers before it happened took a certain insight. He had spoken briefly about his time away from work, educating himself through literature that meant he had a wise word for any type of situation.

He often offered advice to assist personal problems and any time he spoke, people listened. If it was a family, he would certainly have been the grandfather of knowledge.

Napier for the majority of the time appeared nonchalant, and Stephen could not figure out if he was 'capable but not interested' or 'incapable and ignorant of the fact'.

With what had happened with his lover, Napier more then likely had lost the will to uphold the law when he was wanting to break it by killing Armeen.

Now that he had completed the task, Stephen knew he wouldn't have time to work with Napier.

His absence from work would be immediate and probably permanent.

No doubt if anything had been reported, Rudyard would insist he take leave whilst inquiries were carried out, but assure him that it would be regarded as an accident or self defence.

Napier had killed Armeen. He would not be willing admit to it, but alas the deed was done.

Ford was a gentleman of rare talents. He had the aura of a man that could make anyone feel welcome within the office. He was a very articulate and more than willing to help out as and when he could.

A dedicated family man, Stephen knew from meeting him that his love of the job was to try to make the world a safer place for his wife and daughters.

Out of all the detectives, Ford seemed to spend the least amount of time in and out of work with his other colleagues, but Stephen knew he would instead be rushing home to sit with his family and appreciate every moment he could.

The stress and brutality of the job did not seem to affect Ford and for this, for his entire situation, Stephen was envious. Not in a bitter sense in the slightest, but an admiration of sorts.

Of all the detectives the only one left to ponder on was Raffle.

Rudyard being Chief Inspector ran a tight well-inspected ship.

His involvement with any case was minimal. This seemed to suit everyone involved just fine as long as everything remained above board or at least appeared to do so.

He was the kind ear upon which problems could be shared and dealt with accordingly… but Raffle? He seemed the ever-threatening back hand to those that did not show courtesy.

The detectives of the office tended not to approach Raffle unless with carefully chosen wordage and a confidence that what they told him did not require questioning.

Stephen had learned from others that Raffle lived in a house of good standing and had previously been in the army but rarely spoke about it. He and his wife had two grown children and to all intents and purposes lived an extremely straightforward existence, but Stephen firmly believed that certain people have an awareness of others similar to themselves.

'Evil knows evil' was once how he had heard it described. The feeling that creeps into you when you first meet a person and instantly it's clear, some form of primal instinct, that you could become the worst of enemies or the best of friends…

CHAPTER 30

"You going to be much longer, mate? I'm busting!"

The knock and voice brought Stephen back to the present.

Stephen looked at his pocket watch and saw that twenty minutes had gone by in an instant. He laughed but was not entirely sure what he was laughing at.

"Won't be a tick, my good man." he said, the words spoken in an extremely jovial manner that he had not expected, or intended, from himself.

After rubbing his face, he left the cubicle and made his way back into the bar.

A few more patrons had joined the crowd in the drinking and a tattered young woman with Rubenesque cheeks began to sing, men joined in on the chorus and the entire audience were involved.

An hour later, Stephen walked out once again into the street. His throat hurt through uncharacteristic singing. As and when he could join in, he had even though he didn't know the words to any of the songs of this unfamiliar time and place.

Eventually, he decided it was time to move on.

He was amazeed as to what was going on. It wasn't till he tried to find his cigarettes that he felt the snuff box and realised that the singing, mixing with strangers and time skipping by like a child playing hop scotch had to all be accounted to the powder Lock Key had supplied.

He was unsure as to how he felt about it all. Presently he felt happy, but it was not a mindset he wanted to constantly be involved with.

He made a mental note to reduce his intake.

Merriment was needed, that was for sure, but he knew more than anything that he could not lose track of his original intent.

He walked the cobbles, turning right and heading towards the train station, the night air still as clear as before but the temperature taking a considerable drop.

He was dressed adequately but feeling the cold on his hands and untrimmed whisker'd face, he hastened in his step for the next place to sooth his vocal chords with a pint of mild ale.

One or two hansom cabs were sitting outside the front door of the Royal Station Hotel. They had clearly been stationary for quite some time as the horses' manure piles were stacking up and being trodden in by the hooves.

The hotel was of a fine build and supposedly hosted parties to the finest of clientele. He suspected this was why the cabs looked like private hire spider cabs. They waited for the higher class patrons to exit, as they knew they would be tipped extremely well.

Stephen passed the iron gate entrance and was making for the arched double door when a man dressed in a fine garb pushed his hand roughly into Stephen's chest.

"Not tonight, squire."

Before Stephen's brain could protest or reply at all, his imbedded muscle memory took over.

He gripped the man's right hand with his own, his palm flat across the back of the assaulting hand. Stephen's fingers wrapped round and then twisted the offender's wrist, pulling his arm towards his own chest, the smartly dressed human blockade soon letting out a half grunt, half yelp as his arm was forced around into an unnatural position.

"You should really be more courteous to people," Stephen said. "You're the doorman, I take it?"

Before the bouncer could answer, Stephen twisted his arm further round which caused a further gasp and an agreement from the doorman.

"I'm Detective Stephen Howes and I will be drinking here tonight. Have you any protest to that?"

Before another word was uttered, from behind the bouncer a shrill voice echoed from within the safety and warmth of the hotel.

"What on earth is going on here?"

Stephen looked beyond his present company and saw a tall thin man in a tuxedo now storming toward them.

He considered if he should directly assault the approaching concierge, made obvious by his slicked back hair which would only be styled so as if to demand an air of importance. He reminded Stephen of a well-groomed Officer Allen, attempting to command respect with nothing more than an annoying barking voice and little else.

Stephen almost felt pity towards the man and decided to spare all around from his wrath, when suddenly he heard a soft yet direct voice from behind him.

"It's okay, Malcolm, he is with me. I will make sure he behaves himself."

Stephen released the doorman's hand, allowing him to nurse his wrist and pride, and turned to where the voice had come from.

Before him stood a young lady dressed as exquisitely as her voice suggested she might look, the lights from within the hotel illuminating her features. Her hair dark and clearly visible under her hat, she was fashionably styled from head to toe, her posture suggesting nothing short of elegance.

How long the moment took to pass between them, Stephen had no idea, but he was all too aware of appearing dumbstruck by the lady. He was saved from his empty headedness when she spoke first.

"You won't be any trouble, will you, Detective Howes?"

Remembering himself, Stephen shook his head slowly. "Of course not, madam. I'm sure I can be the complete gentleman to accompany a lady."

She smiled and lowered her head slightly as she took his arm to allow him to assist her up the mere three steps that led into the Royal Station Hotel lobby.

CHAPTER 31

Stephen and the young lady appeared quite the striking couple as they passed into the vast reception area. It was noticeable to him that this was possibly the brightest lit room he had ever entered after the hours of darkness.

Whether it was the gold decorations with the lightly varnished mahogany or the vast amount of gaslighting he didn't know, but it was an immense contrast to his usual clouded entrance in a place of drinking where the hollows of people's eyes followed him, sullen with the grief of escapism. Instead, the watchful gazes of the staff and upper class guests that had seen or heard the commotion in the doorway eyed him in near amazement.

It was obvious that these sorts of people were not used to the vulgar nature of Stephen's more base instincts. Hull had an amazing ability, it seemed, to offer exclusive living to the upper class while the remaining labour-based population huddled in the squalor. From the dregs to the downtrodden.

The young lady gave and received courteous nods from the staff and even the odd bow from the well-dressed gentlemen. For the first time in a long time, Stephen felt out of place and almost ashamed.

His entrance had been dramatic but now beside this voluptuous, grace-filled young woman, he felt like a man with rugged looks and tattered clothes.

They passed near the reception and she guided them along to the right. Stephen opened a door on the mere assumption it was their destination, as there were few other places to go, but it seemed he had assumed correctly as the lady nodded. When she passed by momentarily and almost teasingly, he managed to catch a scent of her.

Without time to savour the essence, Stephen followed her into a huge, vastly-populated room, that appeared to be hosting a function that quickly diminished her aura, as a plume of expensive cigar smoke consumed them both and clouded any pleasant senses.

A string band was setting a merry tone amongst the inhabitants and the whole event seemed of an upbeat manner.

The lady leant towards him and whispered, obviously aware to his shock at the amount of people that were seated in the room, "Don't worry. You're just my escort and I am invited."

This did little to settle Stephen's paranoia as all eyes now turned to the couple.

His company walked directly, with Stephen closely in tow, to a small table that differed from all the others as it was free of occupants.

Once again, his manners swept in subconsciously as he pulled her chair out for her to be seated, and with grace and glamour, his accompanying stranger sat with all the elegance of a duchess.

Stephen seated himself next to her, but with his back to the rest of the room. He could feel the glares burning into him, but he cared a little less when he could not see the accusation in the looks.

Clearing his throat, his curiosity got the better of him. "It appears I am in your debt, Miss…?"

"Sanberg, Miss Sanberg. And yes, Mr Howes, it certainly would appear so."

His determination to find the origin of her name, as it was that of a curious one, instantly became lost with the shock of another matter entirely.

"How did you know my name?"

The corners of her lips raised slightly in a devilish smile, her eyes brimming with mischief.

"In a room containing the 'gentry of Hull', Mr Howes, it would appear that your name will have more than likely been mentioned by at least a dozen men in here over this last week or so. You are quite the subject among the shameful elite."

"And how, may I ask, did you know I was the 'said' talked about gentleman?"

Not diminishing her playful smile, she answered whilst leaning a little closer to avoid others who might be interested at her response from hearing.

"You were described to me by a close friend. I have to say, Detective Howes, she was not wrong in her description, not to mention you are dressed as close to a detective's attire as one could muster."

She had a point. He had not differed in his garb too much but this was a conscious effort to try and blend in more with his fellow workmates. Not wanting or needing to pry upon her meaning, however flirtatious, Stephen altered his track of inquisition.

"What is this 'event' I am unwittingly attending and how do you fit in, Miss Sanberg?"

As she altered her expression to one of over-exaggerated exhaustion, Stephen realised Miss Sanberg had not a care in her world and was enjoying toying with him. If this had been a matter of work, his patience may have worn quite thin, however she had an alluring nature and whilst talking he had completely forgotten the watchful gentry.

"I'm sure as the latest and greatest detective of Hull, you will soon be able to figure that conundrum out for yourself."

The band ceased as if in tandem to Miss Sanberg's tease.

The violin player demanded 'pray silence' of the room and announced that he would like to ask upon stage the organiser of the fundraising event.

Curiously, Stephen turned as it was only at that point he had realised this was the reason for the collection of upper class, but as to what the funds were being raised for, he was still none the wiser.

"And now, gentleman and the most esteemed of ladies…"

Stephen scanned the room. It appeared Miss Sanberg was the only lady present.

"I give you… Victor Sören."

The room erupted at once, clapping hands hindered by cigar clasping fingers or whisky filled glasses.

For a second nobody seemed to appear to rise and take the mantle, but Stephen was eager to see this 'Mr Sören'.

This was a coincidence of the highest order and certainly not one to be missed as it transpired that the honourable Mr Sören had been the one the Peacock was delivering the collection money to… Mr Sören had been the one The Barge answered to… his name had been whispered in hushed tones around the office when others feared an apple cart might be upset by Stephen.

Mr Sören, it appeared, was the so-called 'organiser' of any crime worth committing around the streets of Hull.

Stephen expected to see a giant of a man due to his reputation but when Mr Sören stood and took his glass to raise a toast, he was a tall man but the thinning blond hair and sylphlike limbs didn't seem to do the expectation justice. He did not make his way to the stage but spoke where he stood, the accent Dutch and booming with an authoritative tone.

"It is great that you can all make it to the party. I hope that all your needs are catered for, one and all. If any of you need anything…"

The word 'anything' was clearly emphasised to have an abyss of meaning.

"…then please do not hesitate to ask, yes?" Victor Sören raised his glass further into the air and continued, "We all know here that the transportation of certain 'goods' keeps this town afloat…"

To this quip, a whole manner of 'gafforff's' were given by men wearing suits more expensive than a dock worker's annual wages. This in itself was a tragedy because for a night or two the suits would be a signal to peers about just how much each individual was worth, but certainly not in relative value of the person's personality.

When the crowd had quietened down, Sören continued, "And this fundraiser, yes? Is dedicated to the safe transport of these goods to and from their destinations. However, it appears we have a special guest who can also have you arrive home safely, as I am told Detective Howes is more than capable of the task."

The breath left Stephen's body like he had received a blow from a hammer to the gut. He had not even expected to be noticed, never mind be spoken about so directly. The words shocked him but the look that Sören had on his face turned Stephen instantly as cold and dead as the river bed.

He knew in that second that there was something more to Sören than the ice chilled exterior.

Stephen was now the guest of honour himself at a party he had not been invited to. Even the band members craned their necks to see who was being spoken about.

Stephen felt he should stand to the non-existent spotlight that had been placed upon him, uncomfortable for the first time in a long time. He sat and said nothing, every eye scrupulously surveying him.

Breaking the silence, Victor Sören continued, "It seems you were certainly more than capable of accompanying my daughter to this 'gathering', so a few merry men of the high classes should be of no trouble to you, yes?"

Stephen regained himself as he heard a challenging 'menace' creep into Sören's voice. Avoiding the fact that Miss Sanberg was Sören's daughter, an issue that could be raised at a later time, Stephen would not tolerate a threatening manner from anyone. When provoked, Stephen was nothing short of a malevolent force and Sören's attempt to belittle him would not be accepted.

He stood with all six feet two inches of him, aware that not a man in the room was a match for him if physical confrontation ensued, but he had decided that words would do for now, unless other actions were required.

"From what I hear myself, Victor…" Using his first name was a clear sign of disrespect to the Dutchman and Stephen wanted to see how he would react as he continued, "I doubt I will be needed for anyone else's safety. If anyone here tonight were to be set upon as they made their merry way home, it would be under your ruling."

Stephen had to hand it to the 'organiser of events and crime', if his English be slightly impaired, Victor's retort certainly was not.

His eyes never left Stephen for a second and were near impossible to read for any kind of emotion. All the while he had not changed stance from holding his glass aloft, like a looming statue ready to collapse on anyone who may try to shake its foundation.

"I can assure you, detective, that if a man has specifically been invited to attend my gathering, his safety will never be in question."

His meaning was clear. Venomous to the point of a threat. The room was a vacuum of silence. The breathing of all had seemed to stop as to not disturb the verbal conflict or distort a word passed between the two.

Stephen played his highest card. This was an all or nothing shot. After this it was a collision or a back down from one of the 'stars' of the show.

"I'm sure that is certainly the case for all of these fine gentlemen, however I am unclear if that extremely bold statement covers your daughter? As I have done such a good job so far as to take care of her, I suppose I should continue my gentlemanly duties?"

Victor Sören remained unperturbed. Like a chess player contemplating his next move from afar, he had Stephen locked in his gaze.

And then Stephen saw it.

Be it submission or mischief, he recognised where Miss Sanberg had gotten her devil may care look from. An almost friendly grin passed Victor's lips and, almost impossibly so, he raised his glass further still.

"How could a father turn down such a gentlemanly offer, Mr Howes, yes? I will leave my dear Sophia in your care and trust she will come to no harm."

The room seemed to expand and reverberate in relief as the majority of men present began to laugh in what could only be the result of nervous tension.

Stephen gave Sören a courteous bow, outstretching an arm before once again taking his seat.

CHAPTER 32

"Well done, Mr Howes, I am thoroughly impressed. You are not only a handsome face, are you?"

"Am I to take that as a compliment, 'Sophia'?"

"You are indeed. Would you care for a drink?"

"I would say that's a sterling idea, my good lady. Allow me?"

Stephen rose to make his way to the small serving area that seemed as busy as the band that had once again taken up playing.

After a short while, he ordered his drinks and made his way back to the table where Sophia waited for him. As he sat, this time closer, he contemplated where to start with his line of curiosity.

"Where to begin?"

"Take your pick, Mr Howes. No doubt we have limited time as the hour is late, so you will have to be selective."

He sipped his whisky, all the time looking at her. She was beautiful, there was no denying it. But beauty only raises so much in curiosity. There was something else. Something more alluring. Her nature and mischief made her a flame to which he was becoming a moth.

"Your surname does not suggest that you would be Mr Sören's daughter?"

"I can see why you would think that, detective, Sanberg was my mother's maiden name. I didn't know my father for most of my life, but he provided for the daughter he knew he had conceived but chose to conduct his business in Holland just before I was born. As they were unmarried and my mother did not approve of his business, I took my mother's name. My mother passed away due to illness a few years ago now, but before she passed, she had taken up regular correspondence with my father."

As was only right, Stephen interrupted by passing his condolences, yet the conversation flowed from her as if a woman unaffected by the death but eager to relay her story.

"When she did pass away, my father took up business in Hull and began making his mark here, I've been under his watchful eye ever since."

As she spoke, she looked in the direction of Mr Sören, who indeed at that moment was watching the conversation but unable to hear the detective and his daughter.

Stephen raised his glass to him and a practised smile of self control whilst brimming with rage was the reply received to the gesture.

Stephen turned back to Sophia as she radiated a lot less maliciousness than her father. In fact, she was inviting.

"What is it your father does, Miss Sanberg?"

"Detective? And here I thought you were interested in me?"

Once again with a teasing smile. It was a smile that could deliver a death sentence and you would not hear the words.

Stephen chuckled, almost forgetting himself. "Forgive me, detective's curiosity. In that case, what is it that you do, Miss Sanberg?"

"My father owns a flower business. Mainly transportation of those and other various goods. He now owns property and shops in this blooming industry, if you will forgive the terrible pun. I can turn my hand to many things but currently I work in one of his shops. As a manager. I manage accounts… it's not exactly strenuous labour, Mr Howes, but it gives a girl something to occupy her time."

Stephen's detective nature spoke with his usual manner of inquisition.

"You said a moment ago that your mother did not approve of your father's line of business… why was that?"

She grinned and appeared to be deciding or not to take a leap of faith in this newly aquatinted stranger.

"As you are a member of the police force, I shall choose my

words carefully, detective… flowers are not the only goods that are required in Britain."

"Feel free with your words, Miss Sanberg. You have my strictest confidence."

"Well, let's just say although things can be readily sought through various shops in Hull, the rich enjoy accumulated and unrestricted amounts of 'whatever takes their fancy' as it were. That is where my father comes in. Of course, this could all be speculation so please don't pursue the matter."

They both drank and laughed. The statement contained more elements of truth then either cared to admit, but they were far too concerned with each other to think about anything else. They chatted for a long time, but it was not like either noticed for how long, Sophia recommending some of her favourite establishments in the town, and mentioning places he might like to visit… with a distinct hint that she could perhaps show him around sometime.

Stephen didn't want to talk about himself, so he began to ask Sophia about her life. They found an instant ease with each other. The rarity was not lost on Stephen and as they delved further into knowing, a sudden interruption was extremely unwelcome.

Whilst the two laughed about a quip, made to their chance meeting, both lost in conversation, Mr Sören appeared.

"Detective, it appears I must take my daughter from your care. She and I must be courteous to our guests, no?"

"Mr Sören?" said Stephen, trying not to appear as startled as he was by the unexpected presence. "Of course. I understand. Forgive me for intruding in such a manner. I must admit, however, it is a pleasure to meet you finally."

The manners were not lost upon Victor and shaking Stephen's outstretched hand, he attempted a vice-like grip that would have been effective had it not been for Stephen's strength.

"That's quite the handshake you have, Mr Howes. Safe hands, I bet. Now you must excuse us."

Sören let go of Stephen's hand and held his arm out for Miss Sanberg to take, to be led away.

"Until next time, Mr Howes. My thanks to you for your company."

"Think nothing of it, Miss Sanberg. Until we meet again…"

And like that she was swept away in a low cut field of high-class, pawing business men.

Never outstaying his welcome, Stephen finished his drink and left. He didn't so much as look back but he knew his exit would have been noticed.

He took a final sniff from his snuff box and made his way home.

When he arrived back in his room, the letter still lay on the floor beneath the window where he had left it. He picked it up and put it in the closet next to his other items that were to forever remain a secret.

As he undressed for bed, he realised that since leaving The Royal Hotel, he had not stopped grinning like an imbecile.

His sleep was an almost peaceful one and this time upon the clifftop edge, before he fell, he heard the calls from his work colleagues.

More appealing to step back then ever before, as he leant forward to fall, a hand almost grasped his own. Soft to the touch and, before he could turn to see her face, he awoke to a new morning, aware of how much more positive the day seemed.

CHAPTER 33

Each morning when Stephen awoke, it was usually with a groan. Today, however, due to the lack of alcohol and an increase in his use of Lock Key's powder, his cranium did not cause him any suffering. Capitalising on this, he washed himself in a bowl of soapy water, dressed for the inclement weather and knocked on George's door.

Their landlady, Mrs Pritchard, shouted venomously that George had left early, and probably for early morning sermons. "The silly old sod," she added for effect. For all George's niceties, Mrs Prichard was a polar opposite. A yin and yang in the truest sense of the words.

Stephen took out to the cobbles and walked towards the River Humber.

Everything was brighter. Even the overcast sky was a gleaming grey. He was fully aware that this had to be the effect of the powder that Lock Key had given him, but deep in the recesses of his mind somewhere, he wondered if meeting Miss Sanberg and enjoying her company the night before, had also played apart.

He took to thinking of her… they had chatted for no more than an hour but already he felt comfortable with her. Her ease of nature gave him a confidence. Maybe she reminded him of someone but he couldn't think whom.

With his head high and his shoulders back as he walked, he was noticeable in a crowd and hearing his name shouted and followed by a "God bless you," he didn't have to turn to know it was George hurrying towards him.

They greeted and decided on a morning stroll, before a potentially inevitable visit to a pub. Arriving at the river, it was sight to behold. Brown water and a view of Immingham's fishing docks… it all made Stephen grin.

His perception of such sights previously put him in mind of mud, dirt, grime, fish odours, slippery stone, blood, discarded fish scales and swills of spilt beer. But today, he had seen something almost devilishly pure the night before and he had a substance in his blood stream… they changed his perception.

Now when he looked, he saw a way out from poverty, togetherness, rewarding turmoil, families provided for, the smell of the sea, fresh air from the water, merriment in the collectives, the joy of returning vessels, the exhilaration of a boat's holding line thrown to the dockside allowing the crew a warm welcome ashore.

'It's all a matter of perception,' he thought.

He turned to George and asked if he missed being at sea.

"Every day, God bless you, sir, but I believe I now have purpose, sir, God bless you. You have given me a hope, sir, God bless you. You have helped a man like me for no other reason than a goodness in your heart, God bless you, sir, and I've seen a change in you, sir… why, you haven't stopped smiling since we met this morning and I truly believe it has not to do with me, sir, God bless you, but I have perhaps played some small part."

"You are a perceptive man to be sure. I visited your recommendation last night. Mr Lock Key. But alas, my friend, that is not the only reason. I met a girl last night also, George. We met under a strange collection of events and I feel there is a connection. I even met her father. Not under the best circumstances, I must admit. There is 'something' about her, that's for sure."

"A lady, sir?" George asked. "Well, she must be quite the catch, God bless you and her, sir. Who is she?"

When Stephen explained more, George seemed disgruntled, a demeanour that was alien for him.

"Sir, God bless you, sir, but I hope you know what you are doing."

"I feel I am doing something wrong, when I have done nothing at all. But I do catch your meaning, George. I may never see her again but I shall try my best to make it happen. It's been a long time since I have felt anything in this way for a lady, I've been so very busy. Perhaps your friend's powder has helped clear a little fog in my mind."

"God bless you, sir," replied George. "Mr Lock Key knows his treatments, sir. A true visionary. I don't agree with clouding the mind unless in ale of course, sir, God bless you, but clearing the mind, sir, I struggle to argue with that, God bless you."

"Speaking of ale, George, would you join me if I offered?"

Stephen asked but knew the reply would consist of a "God bless you, sir," and maybe another "God bless you" for good measure. With so many blessings, Stephen had to wonder why he had not found his killer, but he had found Miss Sanberg and wanted to know where that path may lead him, if anywhere.

Right now their paths led to the Minerva pub near the dock. A small area with a bustling atmosphere. They set out drinking on what transpired to be a day of switching from historical lessons about the town to Stephen talking about the unknown depths and qualities of Miss Sanberg.

Soon enough the pub collectively recollected with George various tales of fishing trips and Stephen admired the family-like attitude. Laughing loud at the jokes and banter seemed a law unto itself with the seafaring folk.

Finally, Stephen decided to call it a day and unsteadily rising to his feet, he realised it was no longer daytime.

George remained in the public house and wished the detective a 'good night' as he exited and took in the sharp breeze of the night. Tomorrow was a fresh start. A new day in the office. He paused, only just remembering and secretly hoping the murder of Armeen had been swept away. His optimism was foolish, but as he sniffed some more of Lock Key's powder, he forgot to care.

CHAPTER 34

The following morning, he took another sniff of the flesh-coloured powder before setting out for the office.

The day was bleak but all seemed brighter. He bought bread on the way to eat throughout the day and an early beer at the George hotel, which placed Stephen in the mind that he could deal with any problem presented.

He had almost forgotten about the pub fight altogether until he entered the office and the clouds seemed to follow him indoors.

Raffle appeared the only one present who was not out of sorts.

Ford was a grim white and Flint was, for once, genuinely working hard at some form of paperwork.

Napier was absent and as Stephen sat, O'Connell appeared from the CI's office, still talking as Rudyard followed.

"It's a mate of mine, you see, sir. He's asked me to have a look into his daughter going missing. It's only been a day, mind, so I'm only keeping my ear to the ground but I am sure something will turn up."

"Of course, John, keep me up-to-date."

Rudyard looked at his seated squad and simply shook his head as he walked back into his office and closed the door.

If he knew anything, Stephen was unsure but he did not want to ask aloud in case any questions were raised by O'Connell, who was the only detective not present during the pub brawl and subsequent murder of Armeen. He decided to wait until the time was right.

The morning was spent looking over facts from the Artistic Killer's crime scenes. He asked for the report on the murdered girl of 'Prossy Lane' but did not reveal that it was indeed his target that had committed the crime.

No further evidence had been taken from the murder scene and the coroner had confirmed the cause of death was as Stephen had described it. The taunting tone of the letter made his skin itch.

He had hoped the girl had died quickly even as he wished she hadn't had to die at all.

He tried to cast his mind back to the taxi driver but he knew he had not seen his face.

Stephen knew he had not seen his face because if the driver had rightly been the Artistic Killer, he would have recognised him, for this was one of his secrets that he could not share. He knew the killer's face. Or at least what it once was.

It had been shown to him by Craven Wilkinson when the initial stages of the assignment had been undertaken. The picture had not travelled with Stephen however… it was agreed that the risk was too great and that Stephen needed the upper hand in the capture. If a policeman recognised the killer through a wanted poster or the newspapers then an arrest would be made. This would mean prison and the hangman's handshake.

This was not what Stephen was to be paid for. He was to make the target pay in pain and anguish before his eventual demise. Craven was paying enough for the act and Stephen was more than willing enough to commit it.

His thoughts trailed along the same track until a deep voice interrupted him.

"Detective Howes, let's go for a walk."

The break was extremely welcome, however the mannerisms of Detective Raffle was nothing short of disdainful towards Stephen. As much as recently he had seemed a little warmer to Stephen, Raffle still sported the furrowed brow when communicating with him, mere moments before when he wished him a 'good morning'.

Half-heartedly arranging his paperwork into piles so as not to hurry after Raffle's command, Stephen stood and made for his hat and coat.

As he put them on whilst exiting the door, the daylight shining through the clouds, although scarce, was a vast contrast compared to the office, not to mention the blast of smoke-free and chilled air that instantly refreshed his mind. It was amazing how an office of smokers can soon clog up the work area and make an appreciation of the day's breeze so welcoming.

CHAPTER 35

Detective Raffle stood waiting in the street for Stephen with his back to the police station entrance, his stocky frame bulked in his smart detective's suit, obviously a man careful about his appearance. This was surprising to Stephen considering he had seen the detective with nothing short of the devil's fury once the tension had risen in the Bay Horse brawl and murder.

Taking a slug from his concealed hip flask, Raffle began to walk, knowing that Stephen would surely follow.

"Where are we heading, if you don't mind me asking, Detective Raffle?"

"I need a word with you and I fancied a drink, so where do you reckon?"

"Public house by any chance?"

"Nothing gets past you, eh, Detective Howes?"

Stephen could not be certain and he was clearly no fool, but the way Raffle said 'detective' hinted at a form of insincerity.

The walk was not a lengthy one, yet the rest of it was taken in an anticipated silence.

Stephen had no idea what it might be that Raffle was wanting to talk about. From day one, the detective had shown only a suspicious eye toward Stephen but it mattered little. Stephen was sincere in the attempt to catch a killer and had already shown enough gumption to prove his worth.

Every other member of the team had warmed to the mock detective, all but one. The one now entering The Empress public house. The low ceilings and the much needed candlelight, because of the shabby windows, radiated the impression of an illegal gathering hole, the type of abode Stephen preferred to spend his spare time in whilst away from shift.

He half expected the likes of George to be seated along the bar, spending his earnings of being 'Hull's unofficial tour guide', were it not for the fact that George still remained faithful to the church during the day, as if using the stone work and sturdy reassurance as a replacement for his dearly departed wife.

"Take a seat over there."

Raffle pointed to a corner that was empty of occupants and certainly an area clear of any intrusive eyes or ears.

As much as the command seemed expressed as an order, Stephen was already formulating that Detective Raffle, up to now, may have been misunderstood. His manner, although aggressively forward, may not have been the malicious intent originally thought by Stephen.

Stephen took off his jacket, then his high bowler hat and hung them upon the old wooden stand by the door. In this light it would be impossible to see if anyone were to walk away with his possessions from where the detectives would be seated, but he observed the welcoming reception Detective Raffle received from the patrons and severely doubted anything would be taken, including liberties where Raffle was concerned.

Detective Raffle held a magnetism that people were compelled to orbit, including Stephen himself, all the while with a cautionary step, pointing in the opposite direction in case flight would be required from an angered detective. Almost as if in the company of a sedate bear or tiger.

The air in the public house hung thick with a plume of choking smoke, clogged enough to make a regular pipe user want to cough. The natural light was slim and scarce as the only windows were small and covered as to avoid prying eyes into the dim interior.

Stephen seated himself and sat back, lighting his own cigarette whilst waiting for the delivery of his drink and curious about the conversation that was no doubt about to take place. He felt the snuff box in his pocket but he decided to remain in the moment for whatever it was Raffle wanted to talk to him about.

Detective Raffle appeared without the coat of his three piece suit, his shirt sleeves rolled up revealing tattoos on his forearms. The new appearance had taken place at the bar which was out of sight from the seating area and, if he were not carrying drinks for Stephen, it could have looked as though a Queensbury rules style challenge may have been coming.

"It's a new brand stout. The bar man brews it himself."

It was as if Raffle had transformed. Stephen could not fathom the detective from one moment to another. The attitude now seemed as if the two were long term friends and according to what he was expecting, Stephen had prepared himself for animosity.

"Thank you, Detective Raffle."

"I think we can drop that for now, don't you?"

"Sounds a stellar idea to me."

"Right, I think we need a good word, don't you?"

"Do we?" said Stephen, sounding more questionable then he intended.

"I'm usually pretty good at reading people. If there is something not right with someone, I can tell. I had my doubts about you when you first came and after the butcher murder, when we found that kid in the alley, I knew something was definitely off with you."

"Do you mind what if I ask where this has come from?"

"Well, Mr Howes, when you came in to ask where the Chief Inspector was the night before the butcher's 'butchering', I was in the office at the back. You went into Rudyard's office and come out after been in a few minutes, even though the chief was not there. I went in after you and had a look around. I saw that the chief's gun had gone. I know he didn't take it because we only use it for the extreme cases. But where else could it have been? I also know that Ford gave you the Slick case that very same morning."

Stephen took a drink of his pint that had now settled, no longer looking like a bruised and tainted mist upon the streets of Hull.

He remained silent, not sure what Raffle thought he knew or what he may have in fact known.

"The gun gets later replaced and a body found in the alley

behind one of the Artistic Killer's killings has a crack in his head that come from something large and heavy, something the size of Rudyard's gun could have made, could have been anything… I can practically hear you thinking of an excuse. I know who that little bastard was that we found behind all that carnage in the butchers. It may be a massive coincidence but the way you handled yourself in the Bay Horse the other night…"

Stephen took a large drink of his stout, which was refreshing as his mouth had gone dry.

How had could Raffle have made those leaps in his assumptions and be so correct?

He still knew nothing for definite, and all of this was guesswork, but it made Stephen feel no better.

"All of the 'gun thing' is irrelevant though, that's not why I got you here. You've got balls, Howes, and you're not totally on the side of the law, which is what I need right now. Not to mention the fact that you can keep your head in a situation if needed."

Another drink of the stout for them both and Stephen was as confused as he had ever been with regards to where this conversation was leading.

"Okay, Raffle…"

Stephen's upper class gentlemanly nature now thrown aside, it almost felt a relief for him to not have to falsify the appearance of a mild mannered upholder of the law.

Detective Raffle had a distinctive personality, which made Stephen feel that certain truths or ruses could be affordably done away with.

"Let's say you're right about the gun situation or even at a push, the Martin Slick murder, what is it you want from me?"

"Funny you should ask. I want your help." If it was for dramatic effect or simply for thirst purposes, Raffle took another drink from the instant heartburn-causing stout. Waiting a little longer to savour the taste, he looked around for people who may be listening and, satisfied nobody could catch what he was about to say, he dropped his voice regardless. "You show up in town and murders start happening. Bad ones. Although on the plus side, cases start getting solved. One pearler in particular was the arrest of a man who was extorting a small Jewish jewellery shop and for his efforts he got hammered pretty well. Bully for John, but we both know it wasn't O'Connell that solved that case. We also both know who he took to help him out with the case that day. He comes back pleased as punch and not a mention of your name is put in the picture. Later that day and with the crime of extortion not even dried in ink on his charge sheet, the bloke committing the crime is let out and sent on his merry way."

He paused and raised his eyes at Stephen before continuing. "You don't know this and neither does John. You know why? Because you're new around here and John is far too straightlaced to be involved in what I know for a fact is happening. The fight you had with The Barge the other night? He's another enforcer for someone who holds the majority of the cards in this town. The cards and also the top end of the police force. At our level we are hardly worth buying, but all the hobnobbing pricks at the top are all firmly paid off and in the grasp of one particular person…"

Another pause and Stephen knew the name that was about to crop up, again.

"Sören, Victor Sören," Raffle said. "A Dutch businessman that made his money in mass trading under the counter and then advanced to property and business in Hull."

Of course, Raffle had no idea that Stephen had already met Sören and his delightful daughter the night before, but as Raffle was on a roll, the fact hardly seemed worthy of mentioning.

"From then he has evolved a criminal web in and around the town and lining the pockets of the authorities ever since," Raffle continued. "His men, if ever arrested at all, barely spend more than a day in the nick and, trust me, I have tried to keep them there, but the order always comes down from up high and the doors get magically unlocked."

Another sip taken by both men, Stephen finished his cigarette and dotted it out in the ashtray that sat between them. He did not light another as now it appeared Raffle was reaching the conclusion to this tale.

"After a few times," the detective said, "this all really starts to get on my wick and after a bit of digging, not to mention 'extracting' information from felons, it turns out that the fucker is running the whole show. I, in the meantime, am told under no uncertain terms to drop the issue and if I continue my course then it will either be 'the force' or Sören's force that answer my inquiries with severe consequences. It's around that time, I lose faith in our glorious chain of command, or at least the organisation of it. So I continue quietly in my work. Do the best I can to solve that which needs to be solved and all the while appearing docile. But here is where it gets interesting. I'm not the sitting back kind of person. Sören needs hurting but I can't commit a direct attack on him, I haven't got the manpower or resources, so I hit him another way."

He stopped to take a drink. Stephen resisted the urge to hurry him along with his story.

"One day," Raffle resumed, "I am sat having a well done bacon sandwich and I see a fella leave a shop carrying a briefcase not unlike the bloke you arrested at the jewellers. Call it what you like, divine intervention, moment of clarity, foolishness, but my exact thoughts were 'fuck this'. I followed the bloke, crossed the street and when he was near a side alley, I crossed back towards him and before he knew it I shoulder barged him down the alley. He didn't even see me coming before he was out cold, sprawled on the floor. I took the briefcase and walked away. No running to arouse suspicion and not a care in the world. The crime never even got reported. Not the slightest mention. It was all too easy. I got the briefcase home and inside was money. More than I would need for my simple living. I bought new clothes and spent money on my wife and boys, then the rest… well, I simply gave it to a children's home. I left it on the doorstep with a note to make sure the children eat well and to expect more deposits. A couple of weeks pass, a different collector, a disguise on my behalf and a crack on the head to the previous owner of the briefcase and away we go."

Raffle looked right at Stephen as if expecting him to react but

Stephen just gave a slight nod and Raffle continued, "I've been shaking down snitches for delivery times and robbing them every few weeks ever since. I take a small amount for myself and the rest goes to various children's homes. I've been leaving money at different ones to avoid being spotted by anyone willing to give me up for a shekel or two."

Stephen could not believe what he was hearing. He knew the man may not be straight with the law, but carrying out robberies on Sören's money collectors was some serious business for anyone, never mind a member of the police force.

If he were caught it would be a matter of days before either the money was retrieved or the perpetrator's head given in exchange. Stephen could only admire Raffle's guts for carrying out the robberies and had to admit the thrill of it all enticed him.

"But here lies the problem," Raffle said. "They expect it now. One had a gun on my last job. The job before that, another fella was following the collector a few paces behind him as protection. I cracked him first and then made for the collector but it's all to regulated now, so I have a new plan. One to really stick it to Sören. That's where you come in."

Inside Stephen was bubbling with eagerness to be involved but his cautious nature prevented him from appearing too interested.

"What is it you want and why would or even 'should' I help you?" he said.

"Because you're like me, Howes. As much as you've tried to give this 'butter won't melt' appearance, you're just as crooked in nature as I am. Maybe not crooked to the laws of nature but certainly to the laws of this police service. I have a feeling that with you, I don't know the half of it, but what I do know is that out there is a businessman controlling what he likes and for all the crimes you've been solving, he has simply been clicking his fingers and all that good work becomes undone. It does not sit easy with me and I am more than confident it won't with you. I can rely on very few things to cover me throughout my time here… my two lads, the love of me missus and the ground that covers me casket. If you are as loyal as I think you are, you are as close as anything else is going to get to covering me during my next take."

Stephen couldn't have worded it better himself. Raffle was right, after hearing the Peacock had been released immediately and that only Stephen's inflicting injuries slowed him down, had caused instant bitterness. He couldn't personally care for the corruption but what was the point in this town's police force if it were orchestrated at the hands of a Dutch crime lord.

He lit another cigarette and decided he would listen to Raffle's plan.

"What do you need?"

CHAPTER 36

The rain beating heavy upon the ground could not be perceived as anything short of rhythmic. Stephen was convinced that its drumming resonated a similar sound to his now palpitating heart.

War beats designed to grumble in the core of the bones.

This was new to him.

Armed robbery… he simply had no need for it previously but the feeling now surging inside of him mirrored that of the anticipation of a kill.

A planned murder he had been paid well in advance to commit. This time no payment had taken place. The pay off would be the result of the act.

Raffle was not late, Stephen was just early. He did not want to arouse any suspicion, but the chance of that lay extremely slim.

These streets, close to the docks at this late hour, did not bode well for the average member of the public. This time of night and this sort of place was reserved for the degenerates and ruthless.

It seemed only fitting that he should be standing in the confines of a graveyard, a six shooting gun in the pocket of his long draped jacket, both jacket and gun dark, as specified by Raffle. Another smaller snub-nosed pistol tucked into the front of his belt.

With his coat closed and his western style hat brim pulled low, he looked more of an American lawman than a British police officer, but that was the intention. Not looking like a bobby was an essential element to this kind of work.

Confident he couldn't be seen, even if someone did happen to pass by, he removed the gun from his pocket, dropped the holding latch, pushed the barrel to the left and checked for the bullets. Nothing could have removed them whilst the gun lay in his pocket but it was reassuring to see the gold-tinted instruments of death waiting and willing to be fired if need be.

The gun felt cold in his hand. The weather was playing a major part in that feeling but also the thought of someone 'playing the hero' inside of the establishment and he having to pull the trigger… it sent shiver upon shiver down his spine.

Stephen only carried out kills on 'the deserving' but someone being greedy with possessions was not entirely fitting of his natural law of murder.

He clicked the barrel back into place and slipped the gun into his pocket.

Releasing the grip, he hadn't been aware of how hard he had been holding the pistol. His hands now regaining feeling in the fingertips, he made to check his pocket watch.

"Been here long?"

Stephen kept his voice low. "No, just got here a little while ago."

"Well, as far as I can tell, only one on the stairs. Maybe six or so inside and no other exits or entrances, barring the windows, and being an upper floor that's not exactly an option. You ready?"

Stephen took a breath, his eyes dropped from bright-eyed anticipation to coldblooded readiness. The crime was new to him but his 'war face' certainly was not.

His stomach churned with the building 'fight or flight' reflex.

He had spent years learning that if your body can give you the option of flight, sending blood to your legs and away from your organs, causing the nausea feeling, then to choosing to fight would cause another bodily shift, producing all you would naturally need in any situation.

He nodded, then turned to the intended location, pulled his handkerchief up to cover the lower half of his face and stepped into the cold night air. The cobbles underfoot, wet and slippery, would have called for caution any other time but now he was surefooted. His upper vision covered by the brim of his hat, he had his hand in his pocket, clutching his gun.

Raffle walked on his right, both unsynchronised in step, they made the sound of a horse thrashing through the rain as they were now no more then ten paces from the base of the stairwell guarded by one man alone.

At that moment in time, the bouncer had chosen to light a cigarette. Turning slightly to help the match avoid the rain, he had unwittingly blocked his view from the two would-be robbers.

As the doorman, who was a large man dressed for the expectation of heavy rain, straightened up, the drops trickled down his face to his mouth as his lips pursed for the first drag on his cigarette clear of the match's sulphuric taste, and the gun that was gripped in Stephen's hand now rested safely under the bouncer's chin.

It was Raffle who spoke. "Not a fucking sound." His voice was a sheet of ice cutting into the night sky. Slow and deliberately, he tapped down the doorman to ensure he was not armed. Finding a knuckle duster and a black jack club, he attempted to place the duster upon his own hand. The shovels that hung from the base of his arms were far too thick and wide for the brass fist. He gave up the attempt and tossed the duster to the gutter.

All the while Stephen kept the gun resting under the now shivering bouncer's chin. Motionless and malevolent.

"How many up there?" Raffle was not a man to mince words in these scenarios and he certainly wasted none now.

There was no immediate response, so Stephen pushed the gun up, forcing the doorman's head back a little, the gaslight giving clear vision to his windpipe.

He took a large gulp and stammered the words, "A… a… around seven or eight."

"Good lad, we are going up there. You first, and if you try to run, my associate here will shoot you in the spine, you will be paralysed, and on the way out, I will shoot you again. The face this time. Am I understood?"

His nod pushed against the rain-soaked gun, his whimper

feeble in the night air was almost inaudible. He raised his arms in surrender but it was neither requested nor needed, and turning to the steps, he almost fell and but caught the handrail with shaking hands.

All three reached the top where they resided in near perfect darkness.

With the rain beating in the streets below, the only other noise that could be heard was from the bouncer. A quiet sobbing. Stephen had no idea that the gun now pushed into his back would cause so much anguish for the man, yet here he was, crying.

A final thought crossed Stephen mind which he had forgotten to ask. "Is there a knock required so as to not alarm the inhabitants…?"

There was no answer, only a sniff and another sob.

"Look, don't make any silly mistakes and you'll get out of this unscathed."

"It's not you," replied the doorman. "When my boss 'ears 'bout this, 'e's going to do far worse than what any of you can."

Before now, to Stephen, Sören had just been a thug in a ballroom suite, a target, someone to pass his time on, terrorising from a distance through the medium of hurting his men, albeit unknowingly, but here he stood with a loaded gun pushed into a man's back and the bouncer's main worry was that of Victor Sören.

That took power on Sören's behalf. That was 'real' demanded fear. That was a rare achievement and, for the smallest of moments, Stephen held an ounce of respect for Victor.

That respect turned to anger as Stephen was not having his moment taken from him. He took the gun and pointed it to the doorman's cheek. With his voice low and his anger high, he snarled, "Listen to me, you fucker, your teeth have nerves inside them that when hit correctly cause agonising pain. If you think for one second to disrupt what's about to happen, I will personally save a bullet to put through your cheek. You won't die, not at all, but the pain you go through will make you wish you had and whilst you writhe on the floor, I'll then take the knife from my pocket and do things to your eyes that will a cause morgue attendant to vomit. Do you understand?"

The blubbering started to worsen and, as the noise grew louder, Raffle's patience finally gave way. He struck the doorman hard on the head with the previously acquired black jack. It was hard to make out in the darkness of the upper stairwell but the weight of the bouncer slumped to the floor.

"One less person to worry about. Let's get this done." And with a firm shoulder barge, Raffle all but shattered the door from its hinges, bathing Stephen in a gloriously warm welcoming light.

Raffle rushed in, kicking a table over to further dramatise his entrance. The table slid across the floor, knocking the poker chips and cards strewn across the cloth. Stephen was soon behind him and he pressed the gun for the second time to someone's head as he threated a gambler rising from a wooden chair.

"Gentleman! This is robbery and unless you are eager for it to become a massacre, I suggest you all keep your hands where I can see them."

The interior was well decorated and extremely deceiving. Externally, the whole building looked ready to collapse but stood now in the dry confines of the room, he saw that he could quite easily be attempting to steal from these well to do's from the higher end area of the town.

Stephen had practised his line in his head and, delivered with confidence, it completed his need for attention.

All hands at the tables were now raised, and as he scanned the room to ensure all the inhabitants were obedient, he looked to the back of the room and caught sight of her…

CHAPTER 37

Sophia Sanberg stood in the far corner of the room next to a man with his hands in the air. She, however, had not obeyed the command.

Of all the scenarios, of all the probabilities of chaos that Stephen had imagined, he did not for one second even consider that Sophia may be present in such an establishment as a late night, high stakes gaming den.

The moment seemed to last a lifetime and all he could do was stand motionless, his gun now pointing at nothing in particular, trying to figure out why she should be in such a place.

Feeling the momentum had shifted or indeed halted, Raffle took up the mantle of relations manager. "My friend here will cover you all. Any attempt to move and he will gladly put bullets in you and anyone near you. Tonight, you will lose money but I assure you, you will not lose your life if you do as we say."

Raffle walked between two tables, both with a separate game playing in tandem, three players, one man dealing cards at each table, an overseer to both games and three men situated on high stools at the back of the room. Presumably these men were escorts to some of the players and fell in to the 'to render immobile' category, the exact terminology used by Raffle who had already planned the job with possible scenarios.

With Miss Sanberg, the tally of the room made ten. The doorman had clearly lied but it made no difference at this stage of the robbery.

"Oi!"

The sudden noise from Raffle brought Stephen back into the room, shaking his head as he remembered the task in hand

and barked for the three large gentlemen dressed like monkeys in expensive suits at the back to "lie down on the floor, arms stretched forward." They did as they were told and Stephen walked across the room in a direct line to Sophia.

His own heart was reaching impossible levels of pounding, a rush in his body that felt like a sudden surging wave, as he neared her in five large strides.

"If you would be so kind as to collect the men's winnings, Miss."

He handed her a large sack. He was so close to her that he had not needed to outstretch his arm to pass it across and in delicate hands she took the bag, her eyes all the while not leaving Stephen, her face remaining neutral.

She showed no malice to the man who was asking her to relieve the associated gentlemen in the room of their night's takings. The way she looked at him was with an air of familiarity. It was as if his face were naked of any items intended to keep his identity hidden.

She gave a slight bow whether it be mock or honest courtesy, he almost felt badly for asking such a thing.

She bent with elegance, picking up money that lay upon the floor after the table had been brutally assaulted and he could not keep his eyes from her, and as she collected money from the men that held their hands high, Stephen did not notice the large man not far from his feet who lay upon his belly, attempting to rise.

Fortunately, Raffle did and with a savage brutality he brought down the sole of his boot onto the hero's head. The suited monkey's cranium cracked as it hit the floor and he attempted nothing else after that.

"Keep your fucking head on the job, Romeo."

The notion was intended for Stephen and was duly noted. Stephen took to keeping his eye and gun on the rest of the room.

Sophia passed through the occupants like a thief in the night and after she had taken the final pile from the table she handed the sack back to Stephen. Looking into his eyes all the while, she spoke quietly and softly, barely audible to him let alone anyone else. "Try not to spend it all in The Royal."

His breath left his body. His face could not be seen with the handkerchief in place, his hair was covered by his hat and body shape concealed due to the large coat but she knew… she knew it was him.

She smiled a little, and with her face hidden from the rest of the audience, she gave him a slow and mischievous wink, her eyelashes fluttering just the once. It could almost have been missed were it not for the fact he could not resist taking in every single detail of her.

Stephen was once again locked in a trace of her charm but the next thing he knew his arm was being pulled. Raffle had had enough of words to try and distract Stephen and had taken to dragging him from the room.

"Anyone follows and we shoot you as you leave."

They both strode out with haste. Carrying the bounty in one hand, Stephen held his gun in the other, wistfully scanning the room, not attempting to find a specific target.

Raffle had a service revolver in one hand and a black jack in the other. He clenched it into a fist and proceeded to slug the dormant doorman for his inability to count. He then stood, readjusting himself, and both robbers made their way down the stairs and across the street into the night without a pursuer in sight.

After a while, Stephen and Raffle stopped running, surrounded by darkness with water lapping close by. Raffle took the sack from Stephen and dug his hand inside. Taking a hand full of notes, he passed them to Stephen, and mirroring the motion again he placed a second amount into his own pocket.

"I'll go drop the rest of this at the kids' home. We should split. I'll see you at work tomorrow."

Stephen hung his head, his breathing still laboured from the exertion. "Raffle, about what went on in there, I'm sorry. I don't know what happened."

"Don't worry about it, pal. It couldn't have worked out better."

"What do you mean?"

"It's clear you two have history or if you don't, you soon will have. It doesn't take a science degree to fathom that out and no matter how badly we hurt Sören tonight, it will be nothing compared to what it will feel like when he finds out his daughter is with a copper." Raffle turned, laughed and strolled off into the night.

The situation could not register with Stephen. His head hurt and more than ever he needed a drink, or at least something, to take his mind from the unexpected turn of events.

CHAPTER 38

An hour later, he and George rested their feet but Stephen could not relax his mind. Once again, he pondered the snuff but this was a mystery he needed to solve, not glaze over.

George could tell something deep troubled him to the core. Stephen drank, but the whisky tasted sour as his blood still rushed from the robbery. The taste it left in his mouth was far from welcome.

His mind wrestled with an uncertainty… had Sophia known it was him when they had locked eyes during the raid? It was very doubtful but there was a familiarity there. A knowing of sorts but no certainty.

A true sign of his nature resonated as he pondered with worry more to the problem of being recognised by her, than the guilt of carrying out a robbery. There had been a thrill of excitement unparalleled, but when he saw her, it all seemed to disappear into a hole, clouded and frozen by the thought as to her opinion of him.

He was unaware of his deeply furrowed brow when he heard a voice.

"I've seen that look on many a man before, Mr Howes."

Stephen was half in a daze and was subtly unaware if he had heard George speak at all or if it was a voice from deep within the recesses of his mind.

"Sorry, George? Forgive me. I'm a little out of sorts this evening."

"Not to worry, sir, God bless you, but I know a woman's touch on a man's mind when I see it. Still, sir, as much as I enjoy our company, sir, and I hope you don't mind me saying this, God bless you, but it's a woman's company you'll be needing of an evening, not some know it all like myself."

Not a truer word had been spoken throughout the evening, but alas it was not a woman's touch he required, but a certain woman's answers.

He made his apologies to George and set out with a determined nature to seek out Sophia.

CHAPTER 39

During their idle chit chat in the Royal Station hotel before Victor Sören had interrupted them, Sophia had told him of a place that she frequented.

He knew the place in passing and did not think a lady of her calibre would be present in such a dwelling, but he had also thought she would not be in a gambling pit amongst such company. It clearly established just how little his knowledge extended.

As he walked unsteadily amongst the cobbles, only an hour or two had passed since the hold up but even if she were not present, he felt the need to be lost and faceless in a crowd. A drunken slurring crowd at that.

The Old White Hart was a strange establishment to reach, through a darkened alley barely lit with the space to allow single file walking. His imagination seemed to grab the walls each side and drag them in before him, determined to shut off the entrance to the public house.

The fireplace that burned inside seemed excessively large and the open mouth of its archway threatened to swallow anyone who stepped too close. The fire was minute in comparison to its potential but altogether reassuring in its infancy.

The public house itself was dark yet glowing. It seemed to vibrate so smoothly that it was barely noticeable apart from within one's core.

Opposite the door through which Stephen had made his entrance was a set of stairs. To his right was the bar, directly facing the large fireplace, and, to his left, a smaller room with a few seats and scattered book shelves.

When the barman noticed Stephen surveying the interior, he made no attempt to serve him.

"They are upstairs, mate."

Stephen hadn't the slightest idea what he was talking about and told the barman so.

"Arn't you wiv them lot upstairs?"

"No, no, just having a drink if there is no objection?"

"Well... I'm not normally open at this hour but while they're all talking, there's no 'arm in you suppin', is there? What'll it be?"

Stephen ordered and whilst the barman pulled the pint of stout, he approached the far corner wall in the room to his left to inspect the few books that scattered the shelves.

He picked out Bleak House by Charles Dickens and as he flicked through the pages, he heard the heavy footsteps of around five people descend the stairs.

As he was about to look around, he heard a familiar accent. The Dutchman was assuring his companions that all measures would be taken to find who had stolen their money.

By chance, the book Stephen had picked up had placed him close to the wall that was out of sight of the occupants. He edged closer to the bookshelf when he heard the door open and the loudly-voiced threat that the culprits would be dealt with and the money restored. The voices died out as one by one his unwelcome company left the abode to clatter down the narrow alley.

A farewell was paid to the bar owner and when the door was closed by the last of the not so merry band, Stephen waited.

His breathing was heavy. The heat of the room seemed to increase ten-fold as the realisation that potentially the people he had pointed a gun at only hours before had walked within feet of him just now.

Even though he was certain that they would not recognise him, it still felt like it was the closest he had ever been to being caught for wrongful doing since he had started wrongfully doing things many, many years ago.

His capture may however have been almost inevitable due to the glaring fact he had not changed his clothes, and simply removed his facial cover and hat. With his determination to live free of fear, to feel these effects of perspiration and panic was an unwelcome experience.

With shaking hands, he replaced the book and glanced into other side of the establishment to ensure all the men had indeed left.

They had.

He took his drink, which had been placed to wait for him whilst it settled, and drank half of its contents in one swoop. His mouth was so dry he felt like he had been living on salted water all his life.

As he placed the glass down, he heard a voice behind him from the stairwell.

"It seems you just can't keep away can you, Mr Howes?"

His heart skipped and had it not been such a feminine yet bold and recognisable voice, he was sure his heart would have stopped beating altogether.

He turned to see Sophia who was standing a couple of steps above and leaning against the handrail. She was alone and appeared almost fragile in her elegance. She no longer seemed the confident lady strolling around the room, looting the takings of rich gamblers. Albeit at gun point, but the way she scooped each load of large bills and coins into the bag, she'd seemed almost pleased to be doing so.

Previously he had only been locked into an entrancement with regards her face. Her eyes had a hypnotising effect, like a cheap parlour trick showing a pre-warned member of the audience who remained unable to resist the words of the entertainer or a snake hovering from a basket to the sound of an Indian tune. Only for Stephen, there was nothing cheap or pre-warned to any of it. It was all genuine and had a planet-sized gravitational pull.

As she now stood a few steps higher then he, he could now take in her entirety. Short and quaint in her lady-like green dress. The situation they were wrapped in seemed so surreal that he had a mind to gamble everything and ask her to run away with him.

Never before had these desires seemed so prevalent in his

mind. Looking at her lips, he wondered how they tasted as she broke the room's silence with her honey-covered voice.

"I think we should talk."

She turned and made her way once again up the stairs. He followed sheepishly, but not after finishing his drink in one last guzzle.

She was out of sight when he ascended the stairs but as the rooms were so few and far between, it took no time at all to locate her on the top floor.

She had seated herself next to an old piano. As was the custom of most ladies, she perched upon the edge of the chair to allow the framework of her long dress to settle.

Stephen sat on one of the many scattered chairs a foot away from her.

His mind raced with questions, and even to the extent of a lengthy apology, but at present he was unaware of how much she knew and what her next course of action might be.

He waited and let her pour two healthy measures of whisky for each of them.

As they drank, they maintained eye contact. It was becoming a habit within the short space of time that they had held company. It was a deepened sense of curiosity for one another. A subconscious reach to attain if the other were thinking mirrored urges, but altogether cautious in case they were not in the shared frame of mind.

Her dislike for the drink was obvious as she placed the glass upon the piano key cover.

"I don't usually drink such a large amount, detective. But I am sure you can imagine I may require such a measure to calm my nerves?"

Her practice of concealment was very well performed but a single slip and Stephen knew she was teasing him.

"I'm sure you do, Miss Sanberg. Crime is such an unsettling occurrence."

She continued to play the game, but he was relieved to see it was in good humour.

"And what made you think I had been involved in a crime, Mr Howes?"

Stephen filled his own glass from the whisky bottle once more and eased a more lady-like portion into Sophia's.

"You have forgotten the most important aspect of our acquaintance, Miss Sandburg. I'm a detective. Why don't you tell me all about it?"

She smiled in a silent admiration for Stephen's ability to play along and keep a straight face. Taking a sip from her refilled whisky glass, she let the burn reach her throat and the tingle linger upon her lips before she spoke once more.

"You were very lucky my father was not present, Stephen, if I may call you that, seeing as though we are now so well acquainted. He's not the type of person to let the small matter of a gun get in the way of his anger."

This was confirmation that she knew and for a fraction of a second he worried that others may have recognised him, but to hear his name from her lips clouded any worries he may have had of… anything.

"I think the gentleman I accompanied may have been inspired by your father's presence or attempts to stop us, but as you say, Sophia, it was lucky he was not there."

He took a drink and did something he was not accustomed to doing. "I'm sorry for pointing a gun at you."

"That's quite alright, Stephen, but I would prefer we didn't make a habit of it."

He laughed and so did she.

He rarely enjoyed the company of a woman, mostly due to circumstance and not choice, but now here he was, sharing laughs and drinks with one so comfortable in her own skin. It made him feel uneasy at the prospect, but at ease in the situation.

"If it makes you feel any better," he said, "the idea was not mine."

She simply nodded her head respectfully.

"I know why I had made my way to that late night gambling

den, Miss Sanberg, but I am still curious as to why you may have been present."

"You make a very good policeman, Stephen, as I feel I can be open with you, but I trust our conversations remain in the strictest of confidence."

"Of course, Sophia, I want you to feel at ease with me as I do you."

As he spoke, he suddenly became aware of how honest his words sounded. Not just to her but to himself.

For all her jovial nature and teasing in conversation, he saw that, in her own way, she was as delicate as a violin string.

He was old fashioned in his attitude that women needed protecting from bad people and he himself was bad, there were no two ways about that fact, but in a world where badness seeps into the skin from the very foundations of the roads and ruins, a dark nature was required to some extent.

It came to him whilst she sipped from her whisky glass that he wanted to be her 'necessary evil', her 'needed badness'.

Her voice broke his train of thought. "My father owns many businesses in Hull. This public house being one of them, in fact. He also owns unused properties and the room you intruded upon this evening is such a room. There are many men in this town that enjoy a safe place to gamble. You, Mr Howes, made that place a little less safe tonight but if he catches you and your companion or some street sleeper to take the blame, the rich will be safe once more. I usually attend the evenings for a number of reasons. Mainly because a woman's presence makes men feel more at ease, as I have a way to address a courteous fellow, and they know I am not to be harassed in any way or woe betide the man that does, I am sure you can imagine… Also, because my father cannot be present constantly and I am the only person he wholeheartedly trusts, or so he says."

The reasoning was sound the more Stephen thought about it. It was a very clever move made by Mr Sören. He would make money as the men gambled, keep them in favour and he did not have to be present to experience the expectant nature he had seen at the rugby field. Although he wondered as to the meaning of the last words in her statement.

Stephen imagined that businessmen attempting to create business opportunities in a formal environment soon became tiresome if every formal occasion were impeded.

After a while, it was clear Sophia had to stifle a yawn in the most ritzy of manners. The hours had passed without notice whilst they had chatted and as she told Stephen she would have to retire, she also told him that although her father had a house on the outskirts of Hull, she would often spend time in the place they had for late nights such as these, a property next to the River Hull, mostly purchased to avoid late night travelling for Mr Sören but since having been adopted as a preferred home for Sophia.

The detective told her he would see the lady home and as they left, Sophia wished the barman a farewell. Stephen knew this would be reported back to Sören but it was too late for any avoidance.

The night air had taken a dramatic chill and Stephen, ever the gentleman, removed his jacket and placed it upon the shoulders of Miss Sanberg. They walked and the conversation flowed like they hadn't a care in the world. Extracted from the surrounding and situation entirely.

Stephen knew that in her company he could be sincere and as far as he could tell, she was being the same with him.

There was, unfortunately, the biggest of secrets that he held from every single person which he could not share... his past, when asked about, could only be relayed with gaps and recounted with significant happenings but no details due to the nature of his arrival in the town.

He longed to tell her the truth, not just his intended murdering of the Artistic Killer but all of it, the unfathomable truth, even if it was just to one person alone.

At one stage he had to remind himself of the dangers as to what might happen if he did confess. Not to mention that she wouldn't believe such a story. He'd likely be in the madhouse before noon.

In no time at all they had reached Miss Sanberg's destination and the moment suddenly became awkward.

Stephen was unaware of how to stand. She took the jacket from her shoulders and handed it back to the nervous detective.

"Thank you, Stephen."

"That's quite okay, Miss. Forgive me for being forward but perhaps you'd like to do this again some time?"

"If you mean the start of the night then I am afraid I will have to pass, but if your intention was accompanying each other then I would like that very much."

Stephen took a moment to register what she meant by 'the start of the night'.

It was amazing how she had the ability to render him so child-like. 'Smitten' was the only word that seemed to spring to mind when thinking of the effect she was having upon him, as any other word that may have seemed appropriate also seemed absurd in the short time they had known each other. Stephen could only hope that she felt exactly the same. He hoped her heart danced when she caught sight of him and although she knew the dangers of such a coupling, not to mention the outing from those who were closest to her, she could not help her emotions.

She bowed her head to wish him a good night and for the second time in one night, her lips tingled.

First with whisky back at the pub as she drank and secondly as Stephen stepped forward boldly and kissed her. The warmth seemed to radiate from them both in a blanket, blocking out the ever-present mist. Tense at first, they both soon began to relax.

Stepping back, Stephen said, "Forgive my boldness, Miss Sanberg, I don't know what came over me."

"Think nothing of it, detective." Her words were civil, yet playful once again as she bowed her head to hide her blush. "Stealing money from my father is quite a nasty habit but stealing kisses from myself is not so disagreeable. However, I do intend to keep my reputation, so perhaps not so public or so forward next time, Mr Howes. What would people think if they caught me kissing a detective?"

If he was honest, he could not care less what others might think. Her 'devil may care' attitude was like a virus and one that he had no intention of fighting. He played along with her romantic mocking.

"Then I guess I shall have to wait until we are far more familiar and alone next time?"

Once again, she bowed, with a simple yet teasing word of, "Indeed."

She disappeared into her town retreat and left Stephen to wander home with Mozart's Piano Concerto No. 21 in C, 2nd movement playing in his heart. He hadn't felt so free from worry since having a snifter from his snuff box but as soon as he had started to use the powder, he had no need for it. Sophia Sanberg had created a sense of elation in him and, although he was unsure of how long it would last, he wanted to hold onto that feeling.

The rainbow that danced lovingly in his mind soon became cloud and then thunderstorm as he entered his lodgings.

He passed George's door unaware if his tour guide had retired early or not and as Stephen settled into his own room further down the hall, he noticed in the candlelit radiance upon the table that a fresh letter awaited him. Unopened and crisp in its malevolence.

Stephen reluctantly read the menacing letter that contained soul-constricting words. It seemed fate entwined him to never forget his job in hand.

Dearest Docile Detective,

It seems we have a trade to make.

The terms you may not agree to, of that I am sure but the truth of the tale is, I am giving you no choice in the matter.

There is a victim awaiting your attention with a message attached, but in my caution to remain undisturbed in the act itself, I may have left the deceased too far from prying eyes altogether. What good is an act of murder if no one is to witness the outcome?

Her death is not one that is gruesome in the details. This time all of your officers can witness it without wanting to empty their stomachs of the dank and dreadful foods from breakfast.

The beauty remained angelic in the final moments of the harlot.

She was a being of manipulation but on this very occasion she found herself unable to manipulate the tragedy that became her demise.

No doubt the story on her behalf will play its own little performance, as a lover scorned is a force to be reckoned with, but with multiple scorns…? The rage would be worthy of a level of hell from Dante's Divine Comedy itself.

If you follow the River Hull for long enough until the lights of the town cannot be seen to interrupt the blackness of night, then you are sure to stumble upon the dreamy drowned damsel.

And now, my price for passing along this information:

It seems perhaps the information of one lady's whereabouts deserves the disappearance of another?

Someone you know, perhaps?

Someone you have recently encountered and are growing fond of?

Do not worry, Mr Howes. I have no intention of calling in my debt for a while yet. I have time and people to kill for now, but rest assured, the love that I am sure grips the pair of you star-crossed lovers will require a divine force to pull apart?

Sincerely

A divine force

He crumpled the page in his grasp and was ashamed for his in own recklessness and incompetence. He had inadvertently become distracted by so many different items throughout his new life that he had found something good, then something astounding and then he had put that one redeeming factor in harm's way. Miss Sanberg.

The worst possible force of evil had set its gaze upon someone Stephen had just met. He cursed aloud and kicked the chair that was next to the door. He had no idea how, as their meeting had been brief and practically non-eventful. How could this killer know his movements so intimately when Stephen had only just become aware of his feelings?

Stephen felt an unequivocal rage.

As he was about to pick up the table and attempt to dispel some of the tension, a knock came to his door and without being totally conscious of the exact course of his actions, Stephen had his gun in his hand and was flinging the door open with such speed that the timid figure of George cowered at the fury which burned in Stephen's face.

Stephen lowered the gun and clasped George by the collar.

Had he been within any sorts of sense, he would never dream of such an act but he was incensed. Pulling his face close to George's ear, as the former street sleeper raised his hands to act as a barrier to any attack he thought may come, Stephen voiced through gritted teeth, "Who left this note here?"

George pleaded at first, the figure he resembled that of a terrified fragile man, and the disdain from his friend shook him to the core.

"Sir, please, God bless you, sir, bless you, I did, sir, bless you, sir, please. It was left at the door no more then an hour ago, sir, and I saw it was addressed to your good self, God bless you, sir, please, I'm sorry."

A flush ran through Stephen's cheeks and, like a hypnotist clicking his fingers, he was once again in charge of his faculties. He let go of George and attempted to right his wrong by smoothing down the man's collar.

Stephen stepped back ashamed of himself. "George, George, forgive me. I'm sorry, old friend. The letter, you see? I'm sorry, please forgive me. Come in and I will explain."

Reluctantly, George obeyed sorrowfully and gave Stephen yet another reason to feel like he was swimming in tar-filled grief for his mistreatment of such a loyal friend.

"George, please, I am sorry. Please sit. I… I just need a moment to correct myself."

Stephen poured two drinks of a brain-numbing measure from the whisky decanter and slugged half down in one foul gulp.

For a moment, his hands rested upon the table by the window and he took a deep breath before handing the other drink to his still wary friend.

CHAPTER 40

"There is no easy way to say this, George, but I fear I have put everyone in danger. The letter was from the very killer that I am hunting and within its words he mentions Miss Sanberg. He knows of my association with her but to what extent he knows about her, I am not sure. You see, I met her again tonight." Stephen was thinking on his feet. The killer had announced something drastic which in turn required a drastic retaliation. "George, please, I know I must have frightened you and for that I am truly sorry but I need your friendship more now than ever."

As George finished his glass of whisky through shaking hands, he looked to the detective and in a proud manner to be able to be of assistance he told Stephen, "God bless you, sir, anything you ask shall be done, sir, God bless you."

An hour later, George was carrying a letter addressed to Miss Sophia Sanberg. Stephen did not know if the killer knew of her town house, so to as not to risk the possibility of being followed, George was to be the carrier. He penned a letter to ask 'that she remain with her father in the country and to take all precautions as to her safety'. His worries were also stated and the urgency in which she must obey but could offer very little in the way of an explanation.

George, ever the gentleman, obliged and was swift to make his way to place the letter in her hands.

With his gun by his bedside, Stephen contemplated his next move, but with fate being ever the obstacle, his best laid plans soon came to a halt.

The light had been creeping over the horizon for some time,

but now the sun was making its dramatic entrance, a signal that a new day had started.

Stephen heard the boots ascending the stairs, and not waiting for the knock at the door, he crept as silently as he could muster and held the gun chest high at the door. If danger lurked upon the other side, a blind headshot would be nothing short of a miracle, however aiming at a guessed torso level upped his odds.

The knock came finally.

"Who is it?"

If his own tone was intended to be stern or not, he was unsure, but that is exactly how the question came out nonetheless.

"Detective Howes? My name is Constable Matchett, sir. I've been sent to fetch you most urgently."

"On what business?"

This could still quite easily be a trap set by his target, so before Stephen offered up opportunity, he required more convincing.

"It's Detective Ford, sir, he has been injured and Chief Inspector Rudyard requests your assistance"

If this was indeed a trap for Stephen, then the mention of those names made it even more clear that the Artistic Killer was more aware of Stephen's weaknesses. Stephen swung the door wide to find a young fresh-faced constable and any suspicion of lies were soon forgotten. He collected his hat and coat and followed the constable down the stairs.

CHAPTER 41

Stephen stepped to the driver's mount and removed the man's cap. The driver looked shocked for a second before Stephen apologised and took a seat inside of the hansom. He had entered a cab previously and unbeknownst to him the driver had been the Artistic Killer. He was no longer taking those types of risks and as much as the thought of Ford being injured disturbed him, he knew now would be an ideal time for the killer to act.

Stephen questioned the young constable who was only too willing to provide answers. He told Stephen how Detective Ford had been brought to the hospital to which they were now heading. His injuries were drastic and seemingly he was certainly in a bad way. But when Stephen asked how he had come by his injuries, Constable Matchett answered, "Shot in the line of duty, sir. He was around the docks when they found him. We've cordoned off the area but he has requested to see you immediately," and said no more on the matter.

Stephen asked no more questions, sitting sedately and appearing lost in thoughts. He would find the details soon enough and knew that if he worried or not, the matter still remained that Ford had been shot.

He could only remain thankful that the shot had not been instantly fatal. This did not seem like his target's style but as of late he had learnt to dismiss everything he knew about catching or tracking a target. He was on totally new ground and the very notion terrified him.

The horse came to a stop outside of the hospital and the driver remained seated, almost wary of Stephen after his surprise and forced unveiling.

Constable Matchett opened the carriage door and Stephen felt like he had lead in the soles of his boots. He thought about everything that had happened to him whilst being in and around Hull. His time here had been frantic to say the least.

He had made friends, enemies and found a person he wanted to see himself sharing something more with. He did not know what might happen between him and Sophia or even if their time together would only be short-lived, but he felt, and was sure she felt, like there was a possibility for something 'real'. Something that had escaped him for a long time previously in the past, but now unveiled itself to Stephen in the most unexpected time of his life.

But before he could consider the danger that lurked around any corner for Sophia, his friend was now in need.

Detective Ford was a good and honest man. A rare breed in the surroundings of the town. To think that anything may have happened to someone he now regarded as a friend, churned his stomach into a belly full of knots.

He tried to clear his mind. In situations that were high in stress, he reminded himself yet again, worries and dread helped nobody.

He opened the door to the smell of disinfectant that was almost enough to cause dizziness. Since the talk of bacteria had become the forefront of everyone's mind only recently, boiling water and cleaning surfaces with coal-laced products had become common place in official buildings or assemblages.

Asking a passing nurse the location of Detective Ford, she changed her direction and helpfully showed Stephen to a corridor and informed him that it was the last room on the left.

As his shoes echoed, he passed rooms of people either in pain or asleep. At the end of the hall sat two young girls clad in dark colours but dressed immaculately. He could only assume these morose minors were Russell Ford's daughters. Seeing the pair of them, he could no longer clear his mind of dread. An invisible force pushed him faster to the door to find out the current well being of his co-worker.

He nodded to the girls and tried to force a smile. They looked pale with worry as he walked into the room without a word.

CHAPTER 42

Russell lay upon a bed of off-white sheets with a bandage that was heavily saturated in blood wrapped around his torso. Next to him stood his wife who held his hand and not noticing Stephen enter, she talked to Ford in a low and soft tone, willing him better with her reassuring words.

When Detective Ford turned to see Stephen, he attempted a half smile but being pale and obviously in agony, the effort seemed understandably strained.

Stephen could not find the words now either. Ford's wife looked stricken as she turned to see Stephen, as if he had come to put her mind at ease, almost silently pleading for some form of miracle but, unable to offer anything of the sort, he hung his head and said nothing.

Unexpectedly it was Ford who broke the silence. "What an awful time to introduce you both."

The tension immediately left the room. Both Stephen and Ford's wife half attempted a laugh but neither managed anything of the sort.

"I've seen you in better condition, my friend." Stephen turned to Ford's wife and held out his hand. "Mrs Ford, I'm Stephen Howes."

With the lightest of touch, she took Stephen's hand in her fingers. "It's a pleasure to meet you, Mr Howes, such a shame in these in circumstances. I've heard so much about you."

Without another word she turned to Ford as if his condition may have changed in those moments of distraction. It hadn't.

"Mary, could you please give me and the detective a moment?" Ford almost rasped.

His wife seemed hesitant but, after kissing him on the cheek, she left.

Stephen stepped forward. "I leave you for a moment, Ford, and this is what happens."

Ford smiled at either Stephen's joke or knowing that Stephen possessed an inability to deal with tense situations such as these and resorted to quips.

"Well, rest assured, Stephen, I did try to find you."

It had not been intended, but Stephen felt a pang of guilt. He did not know what had happened but sensed he was about to feel a whole lot worse with Ford's account of events.

"Tell me what happened if it does not pain you too much?"

"No, no, I called you for a reason. I came to find you but was unable to. Let me explain. For a while I have been following a lead that gold robberies around the town have been organised by one person. The robberies were before you came to Hull but they were frequent and usually, it's not hard to spot people who suddenly accumulate wealth." Ford paused as if to catch his breath and gulped deeply before he continued, "Murmurs were circulating that the stolen goods, mainly jewellery, were being shipped out of the country via a boat in Hull, and opium shipped back in return on the same vessel. I had no idea of the details but after asking around, with a few stern words here and there, I began to make progress. After threatening a street hoodlum with a serious charge, I finally got a name, the first real break in the case… Colin Appleton is nothing more than a bottom feeder known for snitching mostly, the connection never became clear until I thought about it, but he stopped telling his tales the same time the robberies started."

Another pause from Ford but this time with a rasping cough. Stephen was beginning to wonder if the diagnosis as to his health had been accurate.

"I knew where he lived," Ford said, "and where he frequented so I decided to try to find him. A few days ago, I was asking around and came up against a brick wall. I was told by someone that "bad things happen to people who ask about that gang" and it was then that I knew he had perhaps moved up the criminal ladder or he was frequenting with someone who was worth fearing."

Ford began to cough loudly and Stephen poured water from a decanter at the side of the bed, holding the glass to his lips for him to drink.

Already Stephen could see where he was going with the story but he could not understand why he could not just simply go out and arrest Appleton, or better still for the anguish he had caused Ford's family, simply dispose of him in a way Stephen saw fit.

"As you can imagine, this made me all the more determined so I pressed further. Yesterday afternoon I received a letter on my desk. It left no doubt that I had stumbled upon something bigger than I had ever imagined. The note was short and to the point that I should no longer progress in my investigation and needless to say, it was anonymous. Yourself and Detective Raffle were nowhere to be found and obviously Napier was not an option. O'Connell is still on his leave of absence, trying to find his friend's daughter in his own time, so I had no choice but to request Flint to accompany me to a public house near the docks. I entered, asking Flint to wait outside in case Appleton was inside of the pub and tried to flee. I walked in and saw Appleton. Not wanting to make a scene, I asked him to make his way outside so we could speak. When I began to follow behind him to the door, he turned and pushed me. I lost my footing and fell but was soon behind him and expecting him to be apprehended when he reached the exit. I was unable to fathom the reason why he had not been stopped when I got to the open air outside, but I was to find Appleton still running and Flint nowhere in sight?"

He stopped, composing himself.

"What happened then?" Stephen asked.

"I gave chase and Appleton made his way onto the private docking area. I lost sight behind some stored items and to cut a long story short, as I reached near the single entrance pier, the fool shot me. I felt the pain in my stomach and hit the floor, reaching for my own gun. He disappeared out of sight when I returned fire. You are the only one I can truly trust. Perhaps Raffle too but I need to remain careful. Moments later Flint came, looked stricken at the sight of my wound and was apologising. I told the useless double dealer to go and get help. I sat up and had my gun pointed down the pier. Soon enough officers turned up with a doctor and once again Flint had disappeared. I had my suspicions he was on the take, but I expected more than to be abandoned by him in such a situation. Anyway, that's by the by. A man can have his reasons. The point I was trying to make was that there was only one entrance to that pier, the rest of it is surrounded by water. Whilst I lay there, Appleton did not pass me. When I was carried away, I gave strict orders that nobody was to pass. A guard has been stationed ever since and unless the blackguard has made a swim for it in impossibly cold waters, then he is still somewhere hidden on that pier. My guess would be hiding in the very vessel I have been trying to locate, the one that regularly ships the missing goods out and that dire drug of the degenerates in."

Ford reached out a weak limb to grasp Stephen's jacket and pulled him closer in case anyone was in hearing range.

"I need you to do something for me. Find him, Stephen. Find him and bring him to justice. If not for the crimes previously committed, then for the sheer hardihood of the hound."

Stephen could not believe his ears. These words from Ford seemed so out of character but then again seeing the pain caused to Ford's wife, he realised that this was more than likely where the malice had originated. Wanting revenge for causing his family agony. It was the exact sentiment he expected from such an upstanding family man.

Stephen placed his hand on Ford's shoulder.

"Don't worry, Russell. He will pay, that's for sure. For the sake of your family. You just get better."

Stephen could not handle the sight of his friend in this condition and could no longer listen to the spluttering coughs, so without another word he left and set out after another target.

For a single moment, Stephen forgot everything else that may have occupied his mind, even Sophia, because as he left the room, Mrs Ford stood up from her seat in the hallway next to the two girls and moved closely to Stephen. She had a sadness in her eyes but a stern look as she spoke.

"Detective Howes?"

"Don't worry, Mrs Ford, I will do all I can to find the man that did this."

"Of that I have no doubt, detective, and I trust you will do all you need to do to make the man realise he has made a mistake against my husband and our family."

The words hung in the open area like a threat or an angered promise, rather than a question. With a curt nod and a determined stride, Stephen left but not before replying with an utmost certainty, "You can rely upon that, Mrs Ford."

When Stephen reached the exit, the air was refreshing. The clothes worn by the Fords were of mourning and the conversation of revenge. He needed something totally different and the daylight certainly provided that.

Constable Matchett stood sentinel by the hospital door. Stephen spoke to him with the air of respect that he felt Matchett was unaccustomed to.

"Tell me, how do you feel about a fellow man of the law being shot?"

"Like I want to do something about it, sir, and I am told you may be the best man for it by the lads on the beat, if you will excuse my forwardness, sir?"

"Good man, of course. Can you handle a weapon?"

"Five years army, sir, with efficient combat training including weaponry."

"Good to know, Constable. Now take me to where Detective Ford was found and stop somewhere if you need to arm yourself with a pistol."

Constable Matchett did just that and after stopping at a small house on the way, he returned with a holstered revolver. It had been his old service weapon and after informing Stephen that it also had spare rounds if they so required, they both sat in silence as the hansom carried them to their destination.

Before long, they arrived at the pier. A single officer stood by the entrance and Stephen recognised him from the Waterloo Tavern murder scene.

"Officer Brent, isn't it?"

"It is, sir. Good to see you again, sir."

"Has anyone been in or out of this area? Has anything been out of the ordinary?"

"Nothing and nobody, sir. I've kept an especially keen eye out, sir. How is Detective Ford?"

"He will rest more easy if we find who did this. Officer Brent, I have another task for you. I want you to find Detective Flint. Search high and low, although you are better to start at the low and if he will not return of his own free will to either here or the station, then you have my permission and the future backing of Chief Inspector Rudyard once I speak to him, to use whatever means necessary to change his mind. Do you understand when I say 'whatever means necessary'?"

Brent seemed unsure at first as to what he was being asked. He didn't know why the request was being made, but being previously impressed with Stephen's methods, Brent assured that he would do as was asked.

When Brent was out of sight, Stephen turned to Constable Matchett and spoke honestly. "Matchett, I need you to play a part in what may or may not be about to happen… are you okay with that?"

It was evident the constable had metal in his stomach. He nodded and asked no questions.

"I'm going to search the pier. I know time has passed, but I have reason to believe our culprit may still be here somewhere. As I make my way down, I need you to have your pistol drawn and if you see our man then you shoot. It's clear he is dangerous and not afraid to kill a man of the law. I have no intention of being a victim today, do you follow my meaning?"

Again Matchett nodded, drew his revolver and checked his chambers were full.

They were.

Stephen turned and walked down the pier. He had his own pistol drawn now and crept foot over silent foot across the boards and towards the first of the private boats that lay few and far between on the rolling of the dock waves.

The first was rotten wood which matched the same mud brown colour of the water. Ropes held the doors shut and it would be impossible for someone to stow themselves inside the small boat's cabin and bind the ties to secure themselves in.

He walked on and stepped onto the rear of the next boat along, as noiseless as he could manage. He opened the hatch that gave access to the cabin of the vessel.

It was as clean and proper internally as it was externally.

The only noise that he could hear was the lapping of the water upon the sides of the watercraft. Besides a small charting table and an area for storing items, the room he was in contained very little else.

He stepped into the front to find a small bedroom. Stephen checked in the tiny spaces a person might conceal themselves, but after a short while he realised the effort was fruitless.

Upon resurfacing, Stephen gave a shake of his head to the ever alert Constable Matchett to inform him nobody had concealed themselves inside the small confines.

Only two more of the four crafts remained to be checked.

Bearing a strong similarity to the last boat checked only larger, Stephen stepped aboard but not before noticing the Dutch registration of the vessel.

The strong smell of salt filled his nostrils and something unfamiliar yet sweet. Unable to place the smell, he thought no more of it and slowly pulled back the hatch to the inside of the boat.

He stepped in with his gun pointing at all areas of the room. The interior was much more spacious than the last. Cupboards lined the bottom of the walls, windows lit the light wooden decor.

A table with seating and a separate table for charting hung on one side and upon the other, a wall held pieces of recreational fishing equipment, creating a clear centre walkway to what Stephen assumed was the bedroom.

He stepped further in, attempting to listen to any kind of movement that may be within the back room.

He heard nothing.

Keeping the pistol pointing at the door, he stepped forward.

Before he reached the entrance, his head brushed the roof. Stephen startled as the touch upon him had been so unexpected and every fibre of his existence tingled with anticipation.

He quickly entered the room and swept his gun around, covering all angles in case the criminal was hiding there.

Empty.

Checking around, Stephen found nothing more than hidden bottles of liquor and maritime books and maps.

Once again, he surfaced and Matchett had not moved. Another head shake and Matchett nodded that he had seen the signal.

The final boat was in much the same condition as the first. Extremely secure and impossible to be locked from the inside.

Disappointed, Stephen retraced his steps to the entrance. Matchett enquired if anything at all had been found.

With nothing to report to his new found back up, Stephen pondered if the culprit had jumped into the water even though this seemed unlikely as the temperature at this time of the year would make very short work of the cad, not to mention the noise of the splash would be a giveaway or, even if Ford had passed out at any point and missed his attacker scarpering.

The day had begun to bring onlookers as the pier, although private, was situated near the working side of the docks.

As Matchett lit a cigarette and kept a watchful eye on the area, something lurked at the back of Stephen's mind. He did not know what, but something in his search had struck him as odd… it was only instinct and memory that perturbed him now.

What was it? The boats seemed unproblematic in design. The lack of space made it almost impossible to conceal someone, so why this feeling he had already laid his hands on the information he needed?

He requested a cigarette from Constable Matchett who offered a fair warning, "Careful, sir, it's a strong brand. They will go straight your head."

The words opened the door within Stephen's mind that had held the answer. The larger boat! He declined the cigarette and told Matchett to wait once more.

"Don't let anyone down the pier," he said. "No one at all, do you understand?"

"Of course, sir," and without being prompted, Matchett once again drew his pistol.

Stephen walked confidently to his destination and, reaching the larger vessel, he slowed his pace and attempted his utmost to remain soundless. As he descended into the cabin for a second time, he removed his coat. Gently laying it upon the charting table to his right, he looked and found what it had been that had unsettled him within his psyche the last time he was here.

When his head had hit the ceiling, he had not paid much attention as to the reason why. Now it was evident. The floor from the rear of the cabin to the front had a slight and almost unnoticeable raise. Crouching down, a thin beading that ran along the length of the vessel at closer inspection revealed the concealment of a tiny gap. It was a hidden hatch two feet wide and running the span of the internals. A hidden compartment lay in plain sight.

Standing back up, Stephen removed a piece of fishing equipment from the wall. The rod would stand around six feet but when Stephen snapped it forcibly over his knee, the piece he held in his hand making a solid club.

Taking a knife from the wall, he jammed it where the seam concealed the hatches and wedged it open. When he had gained a sufficient grasp, he swung the hatch open in one dramatic and purposeful motion.

What lay within was a tall man facing upwards and blinking at the intrusion of light. His hands were raised, either against the harsh sudden influx of light or to protected him from an unknown assault. His hands did little to protect him from either.

Stephen used his newly acquired club to its full potential four or five times. The cries from Mr Appleton echoed in the small confines but did little to bar the attack.

The genius of the hidden hatch design was not lost on Stephen and that is where he left Appleton sobbing whilst he removed his own shirt.

"Please... Please... I'll come quietly. It was meant as a warning shot. Please, I'm sorry."

Thinking back, Stephen could remember very little of the act itself. Beating Appleton to death crashed through Stephen's internal yearning like a devastating wave, leaving a coastline without traces of life.

As he de-robed any light-coloured clothing so as not to drench himself in incriminating evidence, Appleton ranged through typical reactions, begging, threatening, pleading, trying to escape and when that had been quelled with a forceful impact, he resumed to trying to reason with Stephen.

Becoming a waterfall of information that was essentially useless due to the inevitability that he was about to die, he told Stephen that the boat was used for exporting stolen gold and importing opium.

All of this information came for a while, until Appleton told the name of the boat owner. Indirectly owned for legal reasons but still the property of one Victor Sören.

The revelation that Sören would also be related to this type of business was no surprise to Stephen. It was more or less an accepted fact by all, but to have unearthed and disrupted Sören's business in this manner, in such a short space of time, brought the realisation to Stephen that Sören would do one of two things. Either lash out or flee.

Both situations would not bode well for the blossoming relationship of Stephen and Sophia.

If Victor Sören fled, he may take her with him.

If Sören attacked Stephen, then one man would ultimately suffer, meaning so would Sophia.

The thought that she would be upset or absent from his life shifted the dark clouds into the recesses of his mind.

The release of pressure came instantly as he brought the club down upon Appleton's forearm as he held it up to defend himself. An audible crack and a yelp were the last thing Stephen remembered.

When he had calmed himself, Appleton's head was nothing but a crumpled mess. For a moment Appleton lay in the stow away hatch, motionless but with the death twitches that rattled his body and the light catching the blood evacuating his carcass, there was a similitude of life.

The familiar taste of copper lingered in the air as a reminder of vast sin. But also like a responsibility acted upon.

Stephen closed the hatch and tried to clean any blood or chunks of flesh that may have splashed onto him during the flurry of rage.

Dressing once more to the exact extent of when he had entered the boat, he left and tasted the fresh and salty, untainted outdoor sea air. With the inrush of air to his lungs along with the adrenaline still pumping around his body, Stephen felt his legs buckle a little.

Stepping onto the pier, he felt a relief and trying to appear like nothing had happened, he walked back to where Constable Matchett had remained throughout.

Matchett held out his hand, downturned. Stephen assumed he was passing a cigarette so he took the intended item. A handkerchief dropped into Stephen's hand and with a wry grin Constable Matchett asked the detective if he thought it wise to clean his face a little before anyone 'caught glimpse'.

"Much appreciated, constable."

Stephen had no idea how to approach this situation. He had only met Matchett hours before but had a slight inclination as to his mentality.

"Anytime, detective. I take it everything is taken care of?"

"What exactly do you know about what has just happened, constable?"

Matchett lit a cigarette for himself and passed Stephen one. Taking a drag and letting the adornment of smoke danced in the air, he said, "I heard a muffled noise and was unsure if you required assistance. As I approached, I observed through one of the portholes that you had the situation well in hand, so I resumed my guard and waited, sir."

The delivery of testimony was given nonchalantly and both men let the smoke and explanation hang between them.

"You have no need to worry, sir. Detective Ford or anyone for that matter, never needs to know details and if I am honest, I believe I would have done the same thing if I had found him, justice in a sense, as I have met Mr Ford's wife and she doesn't deserve to be a widow, or his children orphaned."

Stephen held silent. He simply and solemnly nodded.

"I take it the body is not to be discovered, sir?"

Stephen had a feeling he knew why Constable Matchett had seemed so trustworthy from the outset… they were cut from the same cloth.

"Indeed, it will be a while before he sees daylight again."

Further from his worries of the current situation, yet all seemingly connected, he knew he had to find Sophia.

Prioritising his next actions, he decided he needed to see Ford first to inform him as to not to continue his search any longer for Appleton, but Stephen decided he would disregard any graphic details.

Officer Brent had not returned with Flint but that was far too low on Stephen's agenda to pay it any mind.

CHAPTER 43

He walked a little before hailing a passing cab and directed the driver to the hospital. His thoughts ran as quickly as a March hare whilst the horse clattered down the streets. In Hull, he had committed and solved murders. Made friendships and antagonised enemies. Loved and lived more than he ever thought possible.

In comparison to his origins before becoming a mock yet competent detective, he wondered if he would ever want to go back at all. His instructions from Craven Wilkinson were very clear on what needed to take place after his hunt had ended, but the life he knew elsewhere was bleak and dismal.

Still unable to share anything with anyone at all, he could not even seek advice. Even George, who believed in the impossible notion of a higher power, would think him mad if he were ever to explain his previous situation.

All he knew was that he wanted see Miss Sophia and whatever or wherever it went, made no difference as long as he tried. He knew if he never knew, it would haunt him more than the faces on the cliffs in his dreams.

She radiated the 'courage and roll the dice' attitude he had so often lived by. So he could speculate that she may take a formidable risk with him, he would see that they would want for nothing but that was, once again, not a concern nor hindrance at present.

With the murder of Ford's attacker out of the way, he felt he needed to confront Sören and rid the weight of distress from his life and whatever happened afterwards he would simply have to deal with.

The carriage stopped and he exited as before. This time alone and glad within the pit of his stomach that he had done the right thing.

He followed the same steps as before, yet only checking momentarily that he had not walked any blood upon the soles of his shoes into the gleaming hospital. The chances were very slim but it did not stop him mentally picturing the scenario.

Nothing had changed. In positioning and condition from mere hours earlier. He was glad in a way.

Mrs Ford stood lovingly by the side of her husband and as Stephen entered, she nodded and took leave without a word.

Stephen pulled a chair close to Ford's bed and asked how his friend was doing.

"Still the same. I slept a little but woke with my own coughing fit. How did the search go?"

For a moment Stephen diced with many possible answers. The truth, the necessary details or a lie.

The truth to a friend of such calibre seemed only right but he knew he needn't tell all.

"Russell, you were right. The boat had been used to smuggle. However, it is now safe to say the man who shot you, and the boat used to smuggle, will no longer be any concern or any future problems. I do not wish to dwell on details, but as a friend, you can take my word for it."

Stephen was unaware that blood had flecked upon his collar and as Ford looked and obviously noticed it, he did not press any further for details regarding the matter at hand.

"I truly cannot thank you enough, detective. You have given me good reason to call you friend. Even more so."

Such a situation was nothing short of alien to Stephen. Thanks for dreadful acts that usually came in the form of payment in his past. He had been paid to kill quite often, yet payment of honest words shook his very core.

"It's the least I could do, Russell, but I hope you know this is strictly confidential."

Russell Ford nodded slowly as if insulted the matter had been raised at all.

"As is the next thing I am about to tell you…"

Stephen knew he was taking a huge risk in his next words but also knew that another matter needed to be put to rest. It had become evident that Detective O'Connell had taken leave to locate his friend's missing daughter.

When Stephen had received the letter about the drowned girl, he had a suspicion that the two might be the very same person. For this, he needed to divulge his knowledge to help Detective O'Connell and the grieving parents, but other than a reason of admitting he had the letter in his possession, he could not find any other excuse.

"I… I have had correspondence from the Artistic Killer. He has written to me recently and revealed that he has killed again and left the victim too far out of town for her to be found. He told me more or less where to find her and I am passing this information onto you because I need to keep his letter a secret. I have many secrets, my friend, secrets that could have led to the capture of the Killer long ago, but just like your attacker, the killer cannot see the inside of a prison cell."

Ford appeared downhearted.

In Stephen's mind he saw the reaction and thought the reason that Ford was disappointed was because Stephen had lied to them all.

But Ford spoke timidly, "Why have you had to carry this all to yourself, when others could have helped you? Even if the result were to be the Artistic Killer's death, someone could have helped you catch this madman."

Stephen shook his head. "There are too many reasons to explain, but right now I need to tell you that after this has all come to a conclusion, I intend to leave Hull. Before it happens however, I want to thank you for all that you have given me. The whole team. These past few months have given me purpose beyond belief and I wanted to thank you. I hope one day we can meet and I can tell you all everything… however much I doubt I ever can, I would want nothing more."

The nurse entered at that very moment before a response could be mustered and Stephen took this as a better time than ever to leave. He squeezed his friend's hand and, as the nurse checked the blood-soaked bandaged, he departed with words he truly meant, "Get well."

He bid Mrs Ford and her children a good day and was out of the hospital before he confessed his whole truth. The urge had been so overwhelming that only to exit hastily stopped him disclosing his story from the outset.

CHAPTER 44

Without a cab in sight, he decided to briskly walk to Sophia's town house. By now George would have delivered the letter and she should have set off for her father's, but he had to make sure. Stephen had a mammoth-sized bone to pick with Victor Sören, from extortion, corruption, gambling, intimidation and the ability to spring criminals from within prison walls straight out of the front gates, dissembling his colleagues' hard work on catching criminals. Victor Sören was a cancer that needed to be cut out, but, if he even tried, the act itself could dislodge his entire situation.

While he walked, he finally had time to think.

For a change, he was not drunk or using Lock Key's powder.

Somehow, the focus of everything he held dear being in jeopardy made him not even for a moment 'need' a drink.

His target was clever.

Obviously too clever for Stephen so far, but he'd had that sort of mission before. Granted he had always caught his intended, but it was now different.

He had found friends and a situation that was distracting him.

Ford had suffered, Flint had fled, Napier had exacted revenge and O'Connell had absconded to tackle his own case due to the lack of interest shown by the force.

Regardless of the outcome of the things that lay ahead, Stephen was confident that the area had improved for the better in some distorted kind of way, but couldn't help think that perhaps with him around, it had all tumbled into a pit of wallowed grief.

The circumstances all depended on how it was all perceived.

Ford had been shot, but with assistance from Stephen, the

attacker had been caught and dealt with and he was now confident that the shipments that Sören had orchestrated would cease.

O'Connell would inevitably be looking for the missing girl of his friend, Stephen's target's victim but he had told Ford where this girl would be found. That was some solace.

Napier had wanted revenge for a very long time upon Armeen, and Stephen knew if Detective Napier had entered that pub alone, without help, he would never have been seen again.

And now Raffle had hurt Sören financially more than ever. Robbing money from his protection racket had been small claims, but with Stephen assisting in the robbery of people who trusted Victor, it had picked away at part of his foundations. If the rich don't trust where their money is being held, they will always find somewhere else to put it that they do trust.

CHAPTER 45

Stephen knocked at Sophia's town house door and after several long moments he was satisfied nobody was home. He checked the letter box and looked through the window. There were items that indicated someone had been there, but now all candles were extinguished and nothing stirred within.

He then made his way back to his own lodgings. He wanted to pick up his black jack club in case something were to happen. He had his pistol with him, that went without saying, but if Victor Sören were to react badly to Stephen's arrival then he would only want to use the gun as a last resort.

As he walked towards his digs, he could not help feeling that something was drawing to an end. Like this moment was the beginning of the end of it all. He had no notion as to why… all he knew was that if this was indeed the final act of the play he had so recently been drawn into, he wanted Sophia by his side.

Walking down his street at a rapid pace, a slab of dread pitted itself in his stomach. He could see George frantically pacing up and down in front of Mrs Pritchard's house, and speeded up until he was almost running, reaching George just as he turned to notice the detective.

"God bless you, sir, I've enquired everywhere, sir, God bless you. I could not find young Miss Sandburg, sir, God bless you and God help us. I didn't know what to do, sir, God bless you. I left a message at the police station, God bless you, but they said you had important business, sir, God bless you, and that wretched desk clerk would tell me no more, God forgive me for cursing, sir, but he's quite trying on the patience, sir."

Stephen's mind was racing as to what to do next. He told

George to calm himself and not to worry. He would find Sophia himself and George was to wait in the lodgings until he sent word.

He hailed the first cab he saw and gave the address to Victor Sören's house. Although it lay in the countryside upon the outskirts of Hull, Stephen could not appreciate the beauty whilst he was unsure of the outcome of the next situation or the safety of Sophia.

The journey was a morose one that left him tangled in knots.

CHAPTER 46

When he finally reached the house, it was everything he had expected. Sophia had described it to him, and it had sounded like a farm or plantation, and, reaching the property, he could see that his imagination had not been too far off the mark.

Stephen had the cab wait at the main gates that led up the entrance to the house. A long lane with trees either side greeted him and he decided to walk the way as to grasp a layout of the area. Plus he felt he had further work to do on the construction of his very delicate sentences.

When he got within sight of the house, he saw a woman weeping on the steps of the front entrance with a man consoling her. He began running at a rapid pace. Dread once again enveloped him just like when he had seen George outside of the lodging, no more than an hour ago.

The adrenaline filling his system for the second time in one day would surely have a fatiguing effect on him but the way he presently felt he could rip the house to pieces to find Sophia. If something had happened to her, it could only be placed at Stephen's door.

The man holding the woman by the shoulders saw Stephen and it appeared he too was as sullen as the woman, but he was clearly the more responsive of the two, so Stephen addressed him first. "What's going on here?"

"Gone sir, just like that! Gone..."

"Who has gone? What are you talking about, man?"

"The owner, sir, Mr Sören. Last night he comes 'ome in a whirlwind and flurry. Next thing 'e 'as me loading up the 'ouse,

’orse and cart, then this morning before the sun comes up ’e’s gone. Taken off. Like a thief in the night.”

Stephen for all his metal and guile for the first time felt real and unadulterated fear. He asked the next question but he was not sure he wanted to know the answer.

“What about his daughter? What about Sophia?”

“She came by a few hours later, sir. After we sat ’er down and explained it all, we gave her the letter Mr Sören had written her, she went to her room, fetched a few items of clothing and was away, sir. She gave us this letter in turn to pass to a Mr Howes who may come by and was gone too. She told us she was to have nothing more to do with ’er father’s doings and left. That she knew he was the type of man to abandon his daughter. Me an’ me wife here. sir, we have nothing now. We’ve been in this ’ouse and tending to it for years and now it’s all but abandoned. Damn the rich! Damn their callousness!”

As he spat his last words through crooked teeth, his wife gave out a howl of desperation. Stephen sympathised with the workers, but right now he cared for only one thing. “The letter? Where is it? I am Mr Howes.”

“Inside, sir, on the table by the hat stand.”

For an old country residence, the interior was very blank. This truly matched the Dutch minimalist love of all things pure. Besides a few items of furniture, it seemed as though Victor had cleared the essence of the house out. Perhaps it was a subconscious style as to not have to carry much when the time came to flee, as he had clearly done so now.

For all of his high class antics and his organisation of criminal activities, it had finally been revealed that Victor Sören was a coward. So much so that he had abandoned his own daughter to run to a life free from bars.

Knowing how alone this would make Sophia feel, he was glad Victor had taken to his heels and run… it would save Stephen having to kill him.

He opened the letter with a ravishing thirst. Ink and paper within his hands deciding his next port of call.

Dear Stephen,

If you are reading this then you will already be aware of my so-called father's actions. We shall talk more when we meet next. I am currently staying at the place we first met.

I do not wish to return to the town house in case my father is there, but I doubt he would remain around the area. It appears you have had quite the effect on both our lives in this empty household, his for the worse, mine for the better.

Please hurry, I await your arrival.

Sophia. x

In such circumstances he knew he should not be, but Stephen was grateful.

He knew she was safe up to the point of writing the letter and the man that stood between them had shown his true colours in his flight.

Although the scene upon the house's main entrance steps was melancholic to say the least, Stephen could not help but have a spring in his step as he wished the couple luck and took off at pace to his awaiting cab.

"The Royal Station Hotel if you would and don't spare the horses."

CHAPTER 47

The return journey could not have been over quickly enough. Victor had gone, Sophia had asked for Stephen and that was more than enough for him at this moment. His fear of conflict with Sören could be done away with. Stephen liked to put each of his issues in a box with a solution close by and once the problem was no longer as such, he paid it no mind.

Victor's disappearance now fell into his 'pay it no mind' category. Even though for all the fear and anguish he had caused, Sören had taken to his heels like nothing more that a common criminal.

The day had been a very eventful one and up until now he had not stopped for a moment. Nothing was ever simple in his life but he believed there was no fate but what he made.

His path had been pushed in a certain direction. He had the ability to make things happen or avoid them. Indelibly but figuratively Appleton's blood still burned fresh on his hands. Even though it seemed a lifetime ago already. This should worry Stephen that the act of murder had come and gone all too easy, but strangely it didn't.

He pondered whether the reason was because he had killed for a friend. A rare title for someone he had worked with, as he mainly regarded people as associates, but Ford was truly a friend and the deed had been committed with a heart of the purest intentions.

The cab came to a stop and Stephen crossed the driver's palm with plenty of silver.

This time upon entering the Royal Station Hotel, it was with more ease than previously. His last visit had resulted in the injury of the doorman and the scolding looks from the concierge.

He enquired at the desk as to Miss Sanberg's room and the hotel reception placed an internal call, to ask permission of the young lady. Relief filled his heart when he had heard her voice faint through the speaker, giving her approval to the receptionist.

He was told the floor and room number, but rather than wait for the elevator, he bounded up the stairs evermore eager to see Sophia.

CHAPTER 48

She answered with a look of relief, elated to see the face of the man she knew would not let her down.

Stephen entered and without a word, they kissed. Holding her in his arms, he felt so joyous that he could have held much tighter had she not seemed so fragile, probably after being abandoned so readily by her father. When they parted, neither could think of anything to say.

Finally, and regaining her boldness of character, Sophia broke the silence.

"This is becoming a habit too quickly, is it not, detective?"

He laughed as best he could and she pulled away with the embarrassment of where to place herself. Stephen stepped back and poured them both a drink from a decanter on the dresser to make her feel more at ease, aware of her situation.

"I was worried about you. I sent you a letter this morning but you'd left before it could be delivered. I headed straight to your home in the country but found it in quite some turmoil."

As he handed her a drink, she lowered her gaze almost ashamed. "That is not my house, Mr Howes. It belonged to a man claiming to be my father, but no father would abandon his daughter in such a manner. He left a note in a vain attempt to explain what he was doing. Naturally it turned itself around and became my fault. That you and I had met and become acquaintances in such a short time did not bode well for him and after many of his 'business ventures' had been brought down so swiftly by the untainted and revered detective Stephen Howes, he was living on borrowed time. He had always had an escape plan in case something like that should take place and when you robbed his business partners, he took their investments and fled to who knows were? Quite frankly I don't care but I am sure the people do whose money he absconded with. That is why I cannot stay here, Stephen. People will be more than mad with him and assume I know more."

"Do you?"

"Of course not. I make a promise to you now on my life, I will not lie to you. I never have and I never will as long as I shall draw breath. You came here for me knowing what a cad Victor Sören was, knowing I was his daughter but still, you came."

Stephen lifted her lowered head and kissed her again. He knew there were things she hadn't said, but she didn't need to.

They talked a while longer, more affectionately and then seriously about what prospects and roads she had and already a natural assumption was that Stephen would be part of those plans. It had been obvious they could not stay in the hotel and the only other place Stephen knew to be safe was his lodgings.

With only one entrance, a locked heavy front door and George's room in the path of Stephen's, he felt sure he had the safe haven he would need for the time being.

They both decided they should leave her things in the room. If people thought she was remaining at the Royal Station Hotel, then they would waste time and effort in waiting, rather than searching for her at Stephen's abode.

She changed in a separate room whilst Stephen waited. He kept close to the front door, ever ready for any intruder.

Businessmen and their heavies were relatively easily to deal with, however a threat from a sadistic, calculated psychopathic killer remained a completely different risk in itself.

Since the indication had been made that the Artistic Killer had intended to hurt Sophia, Stephen had kept the information burning deep within him. Money was now irrelevant in the death of the killer. Protection of someone he held dear and the demise of an evil abomination were now Stephen's main concern.

"Are we ready, Mr Howes?"

Her voice interrupted his seething anger and softened his rage when he turned to see every angelic yet devilish inch of her.

"We are, Miss Sanberg. Let's leave."

They walked the stairs and he told Sophia to wait thirty seconds and pull her hat low to exit through the lobby. People or a person may be on the look out for her and he could cast an eye over the other hotel guests for anything out of the ordinary before they were to leave the place behind.

The lobby was as well illuminated as ever and stopping to light a cigarette, Stephen cast a trained eye over the people mulling around the area. He saw nothing of concern and made his way to the exit.

Standing in the doorway, he surveyed the streets. The cold air brought the nights in swiftly and after such a long day he was not surprised that the sun had already begun to darken the smoke-filled sky.

Taking another drag of his cigarette, he looked but saw nothing out of the ordinary as he turned to see Miss Sanberg gracefully exit the hotel. He walked a little in front and she followed.

It would be a bad idea to use a cab from the hotel as that would mean they could be tracked if someone were to try hard enough.

They crossed the street, ever careful of the soundless trams that claimed so many lives, and reaching Paragon Square, Stephen hailed a cab once they were out of sight of the hotel.

As one stopped, he opened the door to let Miss Sanberg enter. He held her hand as she ascended but before he could follow, Stephen cast a glimpse to his right. He was half risen, but what he saw, stopped him dead.

Within the bustling crowd he saw him. His target. The Artistic Killer. Creed Winters.

In an instant, he jumped from the cab step whilst shouting for Sophia to stay where she was.

He knew the face. He knew it was him but when the crowd cleared to where Winters had been standing, he was no longer there. Stephen had seen that he was dressed in black and scanned the area frantically for Winters.

He could see nothing. No sight nor sign. Like an apparition, Winters had vanished. It had been only a glimpse but Stephen was sure it was him. He had his gun in his hand and the people around him looked scared at this panicked man wielding a weapon.

The crowd soon became scarce but without provoking any further reaction from Stephen.

He could not believe he had seen him from chance as the coincidence at such a time was nothing short of unbelievable, but he also now doubted that he had seen him at all. It would have been near impossible to disappear at such a speed.

Stephen made his way back to the waiting cab to find Miss Sanberg looking worried. He told, rather than shouted, the location they wanted to go to the driver, cautious now to have them dropped off a street or two away from his lodgings. He used the short time they were in the cab to explain to an almost uncharacteristically scared Sophia what had happened and also about the letter he had received.

She was understandably apprehensive to learn that a direct threat had been made against her by this barbaric murderer that haunted the streets of Hull. The papers had made cartoons of a ghoul creeping along the brickwork ready to commit the most horrific crimes, but up until now she had thought him only a threat to the gullible and sapless.

The stories had been played down within the media but this was to avoid widespread panic. The Hull Daily Mail had been guilty of dramatising a story now and again. The stories they told about Harry Keen seemed too far-fetched to have much truth in them, but as Stephen told how the papers had not gotten half the facts, she now seemed wholeheartedly worried.

Stephen reassured her that whilst they were together, no harm would come to her. She believed him and knew that he felt for her as she did for him. She had heard that love could be only a heartbeat away, a notion she found comical until it had happened to her…

CHAPTER 49

They arrived a street away and Stephen kept a watchful eye on any persons around the streets. The population had died away with the night sky and with the gas lamp lights shadowing the pavement, pursuers would have an ample opportunity to remain out of sight, but taking a walk down one street and back up another, he was certain that if anyone had been following, he would have surely spotted them.

They arrived thankfully at Mrs Pritchard's house and, securely locking the door behind them, they climbed the stairs. The avoidance of noise was impossible as each foot fall creaked. And as they neared the top level, George appeared.

"Sir, there you are, God bless you, sir. I was so very worried god bless you…"

It was at that moment George noticed Sophia and stopped talking.

"George, I would like to introduce you to Miss Sanberg. She is the lady you were to deliver the letter to this morning."

"God bless you, Miss! God be praised that you are safe. I do say I was mightily worried that the letter never reached your hands, God bless you, but here you are, and thank the Lord if I do say so. God bless you, as I know Mr Howes here would have been very worried, although I don't wish to embarrass him. God bless him."

She nodded and told George she was very pleased to meet him.

Stephen unlocked his door and let Miss Sanberg enter as he told her he would be but a moment, as he wanted to speak to George alone.

She made herself busy lighting candles as Stephen spoke quietly to his friend.

"George, Miss Sanberg may be staying a few days until we can get things in order. I may have something for you to do for me. Take my gun… do you know how to use it?"

George nodded with unease as he took the pistol.

"Good. If anyone comes up those stairs, you halt them where they stand and wait until I say that they can carry on. If they do not halt, then you fire. Do you understand? I have my spare pistol so I will also be armed, but, George, you must understand that we all may be in danger. I will clear any mess or mistakes but we must remain diligent until I can do so."

George nodded again and ever the ready friend, he told Stephen not to worry as he would do whatever was asked.

God would judge the actions, but he trusted Stephen more than the law itself.

George returned to his room after they had spoken a while longer and left his door open an inch or more.

Stephen wanted to tell his friend that due to the noise the stairs made, he would not have to rely so heavily on his eyes, but more his ears, however if his friend wanted to stand guard in such a way, then he was happy for him to do so.

His own room glowed in candlelight by the time he returned. Sophia had removed her hat and coat already and was in the process of pouring them both a drink.

As ever, the candlelight cast a soft and delicate illumination upon them both and as Stephen walked towards her, the enticement of her features beckoned for him to kiss her once more.

This time there was no holding back. As he lowered her onto the bed, they both knew what was about to happen. Stephen had been raised in very different times to say the least, a time where sexual encounters were not so ethereal. Her inexperience was obvious but throughout the night, her confidence grew until, exhausted, they fell asleep in unison.

CHAPTER 50

I feel ready now more than ever that my time in my current form may be close to an end.

My designs of grandiose gruesome greatness have reached their peak. Tonight I truly created a masterpiece.

I spied through the letter box, as my intention had been for others to do so, and an exact replica of a picture seen long ago burned itself in through my retinas, deep into my very soul. I saw beauty and realised that I could not better my design.

To the intended recipient of my message, the 'Detective', I'm sure if his skills and mindset are quite up to it, he can surely fathom that he who has something to lose, becomes he who can be severed from what he holds so dear.

I saw him today, before the darkness truly fell and I wore my garb of pretence. I watched as he left the hotel with his adored young lady and, in the last second, he caught sight of me too.

He chased a little but I had already gone.

So far, it is his predictability that makes it so easy to allude not only the police in this shadow of the past, but also the detective sent to catch me. Although, if I am truly honest with myself it is with a hint of jealousy that I make my next move.

My ending as it were.

I have tallied more kills now than anyone of this time. I shall be hailed in books to come but the one man who surely should be hot on my trail seems to have become almost distracted. Disinterested in my immensity.

Dealing in the affairs of a petty gangster, he has no longer been pursuing myself with the admiration I deserve, so it is with my next victim, I wished to pick something 'un-ignorable', for it is true, unless there is a moment of chaos, followed by an emotional release of realisation, nothing shall be remembered.

The Chief Inspector now whole-heartedly knows the true meaning of the word release, of that I am quite sure.

As I have most of the detectives of Hull, I kept a keen eye upon the CI. Infidelity is not a pastime I would have suspected such a man to partake in, however he was witnessed by none other than myself entering the abode of an inappropriately dressed young lady.

He stayed for a while and, upon leaving, he gave the impression of a man truly energetically dishevelled.

Checking my pocket watch and placing it back into my draped jacket, I made quite the breeze of my walk, keeping in line with his footsteps.

The nights of Hull never cease to amaze me. It's as though they were created for my work. Rain or a light drizzle often create the need for the coat and hat that can be used to conceal my features and creative tools. The cool air, fresh, yet the stench of the streets hang like a terrible habit one cannot shake loose.

The buildings that assault all of the streets seem to glow a horror show when in reflection of the gas lamps. The sky and brick both a bleak collaboration that adds texture to my palette of preparation.

The Chief Inspector made to cross the street and caught sight of my presence.

At first, he paid no heed as no doubt the rain would surely obscure his vision. To him, at the time, I was nothing but another occupant of the street.

With the peak of my brimmed hat low, I continued upon my course yet all the while keeping a peripheral and watchful eye upon him.

An old policeman's trick when noticing a potential pursuer is to stop and light a cigarette or in his case, a cigar. Chief Inspector Rudyard did not deviate from this ruse.

He stopped as I purposely rounded the corner to the point of extravagance and vanished from his list of things to ponder for the night, as his first plume of smoke rose and quickly dispersed into the wet winter air.

My path did not alter. It had no reason to. My personal carriage was situated a street or two away from my original planned act.

But that was the beauty of creation. Never are two rehearsals the same, but both can be equally perfect.

Unable to leave a horse unattended for obvious reasons, my carriage remains constantly manned by a recently-bought crippled vagabond who has no sinful doubt as to what may happen in the event he repeats to another soul, what he may chance upon to observe.

I do often remain cautious as and when circumstance will allow. The lost art of keeping secrets, is, of course, to tell no one in the first place but when this cannot be avoided, then the witnesses must join the list of listless deceased.

He would only be privy to the transportation of my artistic models, never the actual act and being too dim in mind, he was very rarely concerned as to my tasks.

One could almost fool the simpleton that I was merely assisting a drunkard home.

The issue to date not having being raised, it is my assumption that no need for concern is present with my means of transport or the born idiot that wields the whip and carriage.

On occasion I have previously followed Chief Inspector Rudyard. His address has become known to me, this moment had half been planned, but now it seemed to be gaining its divinity.

His visit to his wench had greatly reduced the chances of onlookers due to the further lateness of his normal arrival time home.

The scene from above would quite simply have been nothing short of magnificent. God's own view. Picture if you will my cloaked and well-hidden motionless figure on the darkened side of a high, rotten wooden fence, damp from years of sturdy solace. Out of sight and out of mind from the streets and stage.

And now to the right of the stage, the most significant member of Kingston Upon Hull's detective squad, Chief Inspector Rudyard.

His late night cavorting could almost be the undoing of his living soul, but in actual fact his demise is to be simply, my own will.

I could not see this but his head was hung sullen, deprived of all goodness and stooped with the misdoings of marriage. My assumption that he had been visiting a mistress must have been correct as no man carries that weighted walk with a clear and angelic heart. First comes joy, second comes guilt, as I have heard many confess.

During the day, Rudyard would certainly cast a formidable shadow, one to not cross paths with, but during the hours of darkened skies there are no shadows of men.

Only what lurks in night winds. I myself am a creation of the blackest of nightly winds and tonight I gust upon the self righteous.

My eyes adjusted to the dim street gas lamps as I waited tentatively.

A slight grip upon my blade so as to not moisten the handle, its sharp, almost carnassial blade ideal for what was required with the attention to detail needed.

As sole occupant of the streets, Rudyard's footsteps echoed, allowing a pin point assumption as to his whereabouts in regards to my own.

Slowing my breath and mind clear of any form of delightful music, I felt almost solitary in the world myself.

As if in a large theatre hall, lifeless and still, but with a slow and simple rhythmic drum, tap… tap… tap… tapping… Gaining momentum and decibels as to give the impression of growing closer rather than louder.

I hadn't realised but I had closed my eyes to focus on the sound and light-headedness swooped upon me like an owl gliding low above the equal heights of a cornfield's growth.

It was only the ceasing of the footsteps that caused my mind to sharpen.

I held my breath desperate for any form of indication as to the location of the perceived hero of tonight's show.

A scrape and a flare.

He had stopped to light his cigar once more upon the other side of the fence.

A puckering of inhales in an attempt to reignite his cigar and the sound was so close, the rain-drenched fence and a couple of inches of night air was all that separated us now.

The curtain had risen and it was time for the first act.

My left foot forward, followed by my body weight, brought me into the gas lamp's glow. A turn on the same foot and a planted right step had me facing the opposite direction to which I had begun and directly facing Chief Inspector Rudyard.

The movement was so swift, by the time my blade reached flesh in an arcing motion from left hip to my right shoulder, poor dear Chief Inspector Rudyard barely had time to blink.

First the gurgling, then a comical plume of previously inhaled cigar smoke from the sliced throat and gaping mouth and then the feeble clasping of hands to the neck. Of course, a human reaction of the highest natural order, but feeble nonetheless.

Stepping back and enjoying the dark liquid flow from the internals of his body to the external, seeing its surroundings for the first time, I surmised that with a kill this simple, I had a mind to be rid of all of my pursuers, but then where would the fun be in that?

His white beard stained yellow through years of smoking was now thick with his life's blood.

His jacket reminded me of a country manor owner of a fine breed taking a midnight stroll on his grassed acres of land, dressing, not to his highest of standards but in expensive attire all the same.

Indeed, Chief Inspector Rudyard was strolling on his acres, but tonight was to be his last walk.

He tilted his head back and I beheld the immensity of his desperation, as he appeared to be facing the heavens for some form of salvation.

This caused a blessed almighty fountain of fluid from his neck and as it wonderfully became lovers with gravity, so did Chief Inspector Rudyard's aspirations and hopes.

He slumped forward, his head giving a shuddering thud to the path cobbles.

Before he bled out, I had the unfortunate business of moving his body.

My creation was not quite finished, for in the moment he tilted his head back, asking for something from the Lord above, it reminded me of something I had once had the pleasure of beholding.

A picture painted, a divine historic event, no doubt, and I knew in that instant it was my task to recreate it.

Behind the cover once more of the old wooden fence, my blade removed the head with only a small amount of effort, gliding back and forth, almost thankful as to have brought this blade. A chopping instrument would have caused that altogether annoying sound of wet flesh thudding until a final thud of skull leaving neck.

After slicing angelically, the real task could now begin. Still clad in darkness, I left the colours on the pallet whilst I fetched the carriage. We – he and I – were to return to his recently departed destination and make art in its most beautiful form.

CHAPTER 51

The midday sun intruded first on the mid-section of the door. As if softly appealing for permission, it crept along the wall with the passage of time until the reflection caught in Stephen's shaving mirror then to his face at a near perfect angle to disturb his deep contented sleep.

At first, he stirred and then, before the memories of his current whereabouts returned, he tensed to the feeling of Miss Sanberg's body as a foreign object in his bed.

He opened his eyes and to his relief it was not another absinthe-induced hallucination.

Instead, he could not think of a more welcome sight than to see her still sound asleep in a lost and content world he could now relate to because he felt some form of completion himself.

The room was warm with the day's cloudless sky, giving everything softened features with the tiny floating pieces of lint that hung in the room.

Seeing the tiny specks float aimlessly always put Stephen in mind of being in space… it was as if the world continued to rotate but had somehow forgotten to take them both with it. Now drifting in an orbit of their own making, delicately above the heavens.

Carelessly, they had slept through most of the day as it had been a long night, not just within passion but drama built up throughout the weeks that had predated the latest encounter. He had killed someone the day before, Victor Sören had absconded, he had seen his killer, and had laid with the woman he now never wanted to be apart from. Even for him, this was a day of a grand scale.

With his bed sheets in an entanglement of previous vivacious pleasure, he took in her looks as if once again for a first time before he was to raise from his bed. It was, in fact the first time the light of day had shone upon her face after they had held each other in sweet embrace.

The night before was now etched into the highest point of his memory, he thought of the breath she had taken as he entered her and once again it made his loins ache.

She had closed her eyes as he kissed her and when she opened them, he saw something different in them altogether. A lust they had both waited for and were now able to indulge.

They both had reason to be satisfied. The energy expenditure had been vast and both of them left with their thirsts wholeheartedly quenched.

Now, in her sleep, as if sensing someone was watching her, she turned her head to unintentionally profile for Stephen, but still sleeping.

Stephen knew she could have her choice of any man, yet she had wanted him. He also knew better then to question his luck, and this was a blessing of nature itself.

It was at that moment the stark realisation hit him. He knew.

Right then and there, he just knew.

He knew that he had to tell her everything. She may not believe him at first and not want to believe afterwards, but he needed to know that she felt the same way for him as he did her, then his truth was a true test of feelings. It would all seem like a cruel joke upon her pride, but if she believed him or not would be a totally different matter.

He kissed her cheek to wake her and to also savour the moment that may be their last, wholeheartedly depending on how 'open' her mind was.

Sophia's mentality was abnormally strong. It's what made her so appealing to everyone and anyone that had the pleasure of knowing her, but for the news she was about to have to digest, it would take a near miracle.

It was all or nothing as she sleepily opened her eyes and, raising her soft hand to his face, she raised herself a little to kiss him on the lips. Leaning back with an attitude to project her devil may care ways more now than ever she half-mockingly asked, "Hello, detective. Why so serious?"

CHAPTER 52

"We need to talk." His voice sounded worried, but was as stern as he could muster.

She looked at him, almost immediately awake now, and the slumber she had only moments before been so divinely wrapped in was well and truly passed.

"Have I…? Have I done something wrong? Is it because we shared a bed last night?"

"No, Sophia, it's nothing like that. I have to tell you something you may not want to hear but I have to be honest with you from here on out. You deserve to know all about me and what I am about to tell you will sound completely deranged and insane, a lie almost but it's the truth all the same. I'll make us some tea."

As he attempted to stand, she gripped his arm with her delicate hands holding him stationary for a moment.

"Is everything going to be okay?"

Her voice had a child-like softness and it was the first time he had seen a disquieted side to her.

"That depends on how you react to what I am about to tell you."

She sat up in the bed, waiting patiently, not entirely sure if she wanted to hear what he had to say.

She knew he was not an average detective.

She had heard the stories, but there was no true malice in him. He was more of a gentleman then the majority of gentlemen she knew.

Was he married?

That had to be it…

She had laid with him not only out of wedlock but also whilst he was in wedlock with another. Her stomach churned. She didn't know how she felt about that kind of situation, she only knew how she felt about him and she suspected his feelings mirrored her own.

Stephen poured tea into two cups and brought them over to Sophia.

He placed the cups on the bedside table.

Whilst making the tea he'd tried to think of how to word the madness he was about to share.

"Sophia… I don't expect you to believe any of this. I wouldn't blame you if you didn't but I assure you I have no intention of keeping anything from you. If what you said last night was true then I also want to spend the rest of my life with you, however if we are to do this, then the most extreme circumstances may have to take place beforehand."

"Oh my lord, you are married to another?"

"No, no, that's not it, I wish it was as easy to explain as that."

Sophia's features hardened. "You wish it was as easy as that? What on earth do you mean? How could it be worse?"

"Well, if you let me try to explain, you will see."

Stephen sat with his face a foot or two from hers and began to explain. He would have to explain the best he could as to why he was hunting a man in Hull and how exactly it had all come about. He took a deep breath…

"My dearest Sophia, please try to keep an open mind. At no point did I expect to have to explain this to another soul. Please forgive me if I seem out of sorts, but I am sure you will understand why afterwards… you see, I'm not from around here. I don't mean Hull. In a sense I am from Hull, just not the Hull that you know."

She wanted to say something and almost did but decided against it.

"Near enough everything you know or you think you know about me is a lie. I'm not really a detective. I am, however, an investigator hired to find a man and kill him."

He paused and let this small piece of the truth sink in. Sophia did not react to this information. Before he had chosen to abandon her, her father had been on the wrong side of the law for all the years she had known him, so a hired killer was not the worst information she imagined. Again, she attempted to speak but this time was cut short. Stephen's story was far from over.

"I was approached by a man named Craven Wilkinson. He'd had his wife taken from him in the most bizarre circumstances at the hands of a work colleague. Craven wanted revenge and peace of the mind. I am in the business of finding people and for the right price I also dispose of these people. You have to believe me when I tell you that not one of the men I have killed deserved to be living and breathing. I hope you do not judge me too harshly in this but that part of my tale is the most understandable in comparison."

He stood and Sophia's eyes never left him as he walked to the window and leant against the sill with his back to her. The sun now firmly set behind the clouds, the grey daily life outside seemed so easy to him now.

He did not want to have to explain the next part, for however ridiculous it sounded in his mind, it would be even more inconceivable to her. He looked out, staring at nothing in particular and, keeping his back to her, he chose his next words the best he could. "Imagine if you can, a time years from now. Countries battle the same as they do now and there is an equal amount of squalor and destitution, if not worse than what sits right outside this very window."

Turning to her, he seemed to have aged since standing there.

"One country in particular, gaining momentum and power, decides it has taken enough abuse and mockery from other countries and then, falling out with its allies over some rash actions, that said country does something very stupid. You see, in this time years from now, I want you to imagine that countries have bombs that can end an entire existence with the push of a button. The blast is so powerful that unless you are very far away or underground, there is no escaping the devastation. The trouble with one country pushing this button to send a bomb somewhere else, is that a country near or next to the target gets mad and does the same, before you know it and within hours, all the things that used to exist, no longer do."

It was difficult to speak but he continued, "The same happens in all of the remaining countries. Whilst all this is taking place, the men in charge head for places underground that have been built well in advance and prepared for this very type of event, because these bombs are no secret and the countries responsible have been simmering with rage for a very long time. However, the men in charge need other people to actually be in charge, so they take with them selected people. Understandably the selection of people is narrowed down to the finest minds and brains of the surrounding lands. Scientists, doctors, chemists and so on. To keep everyone in line and safe in case of the bombs ever being followed by invading armies, they also take their own armies, elite and capable. The brains and soldiers won't come alone so the families of these members also come along. Before you know it, you have a small city population gathered in a safe, manageable underground haven. So imagine, if you can, a place where the men and women with immense knowledge have to sit and wait for the dust to clear and the bombs to no longer fall. All they can do is simply wait. To have overactive imaginations and the need for all kinds of enhancements to the surroundings, with technology to play with and nothing but time, imagine what kind of things can be dreamed up by these minds and made reality?"

Sophia all the while was silent, watching Stephen at the window, waiting for him to laugh or make sense of these crazy notions, not knowing what on earth he was talking about or what this had to do with him or in fact her.

He walked across the bare floorboards, his feet heavy as they brought him to her. He sat on the bed, close enough to her to smell her sweet perfume and continued.

"Imagine a year or two passing in these conditions and all the people become either restless or entranced in important works at breakneck speeds. Things that would have taken years to develop under the old strict rules, are now rushed through processes to improve standards of living. Materials are fashioned that can be used against the dangers of what is happening on the surface of the once clean and clear Earth, vaccines to illnesses that no longer have 'waiting periods' can be speedily approved… by ridding three quarters of the population of countries and condensing the remaining 'elite', the things that can be achieved become limitless."

Sophia had been so worried about what Stephen had to say and now he was telling her about magical bombs and clothing that meant you didn't get ill. She wanted to scorn him for making her so worried over nothing but such a far-fetched story.

"Stephen, why are you telling me all of this? What is going on? You're not making sense. Why are you telling me a 'fairy tale', for want of a better word? Is this a dream you happened to have? You were speaking in your sleep… is that what this is all about?"

"Sophia, none of this will make much sense but let me finish what I have to tell you."

She almost seemed nonchalant now. He was clearly playing some kind of prank and she was not one to be toyed with in such a manner. If it was a dream then she certainly hoped he would conclude it shortly as the room had turned cold and she felt the need for his company beneath the sheets. The only thing stopping her playfully mocking him was the cold, grim look upon his face, his normally sturdy manner seeming almost defeated.

Stephen took a drink from his tea cup. The truth was that he was not defeated. He felt almost relieved to be telling this truth of grand proportion.

"Please, I understand how this all must sound but hopefully it will all make some kind of sense soon. The issue with returning from the undergrounds is that it has to be supervised and regulated correctly. Special teams from the army divisions only are allowed access to the surface. Small groups at first, all fully protected with clothing designed for such excursions, these groups are needed to reap information about the kind of situation in which the world now resided. Years and years after the last of the bombs are dropped, the 'Britain Delta Bunker', located in the north of England, surfaces. The team at first only progresses no more than a few hundred metres, collecting samples and then returning to the Britain Delta. They report back and tests are run upon the collected information. Soon after, the second group go a little bit further then return. This continues until all the information is collected and the results show what everyone has hoped for. The surface is safe to inhabit once again."

Sophia looked confused but Stephen continued.

"Unfortunately, near the end of a latter excursion something unexpected happens. The team returns and as the doors are about to close, someone else makes an attempt to enter the bunker. Not a member of the army or the Britain Delta bunker. It is a very feeble and unsuccessfully attempt. The person is taken and tested. The 'would be' intruder has been living on the surface, with nowhere to hide but a makeshift home, parts of the country were not hit with the blast and people have been living, scavenging whatever they can find and almost creating their own existences wherever they can maintain life. But these existences are not without consequence, it seems…"

"Illness from the bombs' aftermath," he continued, "take a terrible effect upon the surface people. They are frail and a shadow of what they have been. Hairless, savage, wild of mind and dying, as it seems the water of worlds has become dangerous to drink and live on.

They strive to survive and by whatever means, one can only begin to imagine, it is taken as a collective decision that if the world outside is once more to be 'inhabited' these survivors will have to be dealt with.

The army teams are no longer collecting information on excursions, they are sent out to cleanse the surrounding areas of the sick and desperate communities that have gathered.

Some have turned almost primal but, with deteriorated bodies and half-starved minds, they are a very poor match to the organisation of the Britain Delta army squads.

Meanwhile, the families, scientists and great thinkers below ground have developed an idealistic community. No need for crime in any real fashion, no need to steal, as everything that is essential is already provided, everyone does their own part in making the machine of tranquillity work.

Chemists work, scientists experiment, mothers care for babies, educated parents educate their kids. When the children grow, they either join the army divisions or become useful to whichever tasks they are suited best for. Imagine the place as an ant colony with better resources."

Sophia could stand no more. In as stern a voice as she could muster given the early hour of the day, she spoke. "Stephen, I've heard enough now. Will you at least tell me the ending to this… this fantasy or come back to bed?"

Stephen was nothing short of understanding with her reaction. He could empathise with how all this had sounded so far. But his tale was almost told.

"Very well… I am almost finished. You see, I don't have to imagine all of this 'fantasy' because it was exactly the world I was raised in. When the bombs fell, my mother was pregnant with me. My father had reached a top level in the army and our small family was given escort to the Britain Delta bunker…I was born a few months later below ground and, growing up, I would watch my father leave with the task force to hunt the survivors. His army mentality and the reasons he would explain to me was that the surface world was littered with these people. They were stopping us from being able to live safely on the outside. His job was to make us and our family safe so he could take me to the seasides of Britain and he'd one day teach me how to swim."

Stephen paused as if to reminisce, which in itself for him was rare.

Sophia took this opportunity. "Stephen, why do you mock me with such a tale? This isn't the least bit amusing, I can assure you of that."

"Sophia, I know how this sounds. And I understand it is a lot to take in but I assure you, not a word of this is false, please let me finish."

She placed her cup down with a thump and sat back, her arms folded and pouting in an out of character huff.

"Well, the years passed and the children around me became close friends. We progressed through the school years, and the Earth above us became more and more rid of the strays who were most certainly dying out if they had been left to their own devices, but everything continued with the normality of civilisation.

Or so people thought..."

He continued, spilling the rest of the story without a break. "It was not noticed until it was far too late that a soldier, still not known to this day, had brought back into the bunker the only given risk presented on the surface of the Earth from the bombs.

Infertility.

It spread the moment it came into contact with the civilised world that remained. To each and every person, young, old male or female. The ability to breed had ceased.

Babies were no longer being born and this news hit the colony hard.

The future seemed to cease for the human race.

People no longer radiated hope and good nature, gloom set deep in everyone's foundation. We were to be the last survivors of the planet. Scores of people took matters into their own hands. It was a terrible thing to hear of families no longer being part of your community because of the inability to multiply.

Scientists grouped and gathered, worked furiously with all the tools and abilities they could muster, although they managed to eradicate the defective 'virus' the damage was already done. The population was still set for dying out.

With no further threats from the aftermath of the bombing, people were allowed to return to the surface.

The mindset of everyone had changed. Because of the 'type' of collective culture, something happened to the present society.

Clothes were made of an older fashion.

Music reverted back to a time, not far from the style of this year now. Due to the class of civilians drawn together in the bunkers, language refined from what was once apparently a bastardisation of word usage, to its once correct manner and clarity.

The style of everything reverted, yet the technology and ideas remained the same. The buildings that still stood shabby in small villages were those of a solid ancient build and these were used as the new settlements. I myself resided in one as there was no longer a need to dwell below in Britain Delta.

Around this time, I was coming of age and joined the army at the insistence of my father. I had been out on the surface long enough now to know the surroundings and specialised in locating and tracking.

By now the only surface survivors from the blast were well hidden and the strongest bunch of the weak. I excelled in locating these people. It was second nature and was part of a premium selection.

Slowly people began to further give up hope. More years passed, civilisation decreased a little as people saw more and more people die and knew nobody would ever be born to replace the loss.

Slums became more apparent as the civilised, intelligent chose to remain below ground and try to do all they could to find a solution to the Earth's problem. Clean running water and other essential needs were indeed being restored but at an almost snail's pace. Everyone knew they were not building for future generations.

Something drastic was required for the cause of humanity itself.

Thankfully, two scientists in particular were very much thinking outside of the box.

In the early days when surface people were captured, most assumed they were being eradicated. This was not the case. They were been kept. Stored for further testing.

When a need for an experiment subject came along, it was inevitable that someone would suggest what eventually began to happen.

The scientists began to attempt something that seemed something from a novel… time travel. By sending people back they could change what had happened or at least warn others. If not that, then bring people forward who were not infertile and begin repopulation. The possibilities were very real with nothing but time to work, unlimited budget and readily available test subjects, the high IQ minds were free to exercise the brains that would do the unthinkable. It was all like something from a H. G. Wells novel…"

"Who...?"

"Never mind."

Stephen continued. "Craven Wilkinson and Creed Winters worked endlessly, mostly in secret due to the nature of their work, although this began putting a great deal of strain upon Craven's marriage but he knew how much his young wife wanted children. He wanted to succeed for her more than humanity, as romantic as that may or may not seem.

He devised a theory that the time we live in exists as if you are looking down at a sheet of paper. Our entire history is written upon this. Just below that is another history or piece of paper set only a tiny piece of a second behind. Exactly the same just slightly behind. Below that, another 'time sheet', again slightly behind and so on right through till the beginning of everything.

After years and years of turmoil, Craven and Creed were convinced they had achieved their goal.

The machine was ready and all it needed was a test subject.

This would take approval from the current government, which in turn would take time.

Creed however, with a collection of, more than likely, envy through Wilkinson's devotion to his wife and perhaps a festering insanity exacerbated by years of work and living underground in near isolation, decided he could not wait.

He kidnapped Craven's wife. She was to be his test subject. He had convinced himself that he was giving her all she wanted. She would be sent to a time where she could have children.

His mind had well and truly shattered. Nobody knows what happened to Craven's wife in the final moments.

What is known is what condition she was found in. Something had gone horribly wrong. Creed Winters stood motionless in the room as Craven entered and saw the devastation that was left of his once beloved.

According to Craven, rage took over him… they fought and although he was injured, leaving him with a permanent limp, he managed to render Creed unconscious.

He dragged him into the machine and attempted to inflict the same fate that his wife had suffered.

But something had changed during the struggle, a fateful fall onto the machine had rectified the problems that had caused the death of Mrs Wilkinson.

Craven started the machine and instead of mutilating Winters in revenge, the experiment worked.

He was sent back to a different 'sheet'.

This 'sheet of time' to be exact…

Upon realising what had happened, Craven was distraught. He had unleashed a monstrous abomination upon this past and there was nothing he could do. Until… he realised there was something.

That's where I came into it. He somehow knew of my reputation and found me, visiting my flat, not unlike this one, only more torn apart through neglect, as hard as that may seem to believe, and he explained to me what had happened.

At first I thought he was mad. His story seemed to me then as this must to you now, but he took me to the laboratory, showed me everything. The smell of something similar to sulphur hung in the air. I will never forget that smell. Rancid and eye watering…"

Stephen was now in full flow of his tale, hardly stopping for breath. Sophia's eyes were wide open as though she were a child listening to a Grimm tale or dragon being slain by a handsome knight.

"And then he made the proposal. He told me about his plan… he would send me back to catch and kill Creed Winters.

He could not take the risk, knowing that blood spilt by Winters would be on his hands, that the police of this present time, now, here, would not catch him.

It was Wilkinson's actions, unintentional as they were, that set this malevolent force free within simpler times and surroundings.

With forged documents of this time, I was to infiltrate the police force under the guise of a detective, as this position would allow me to means I would need to catch Creed.

To track down Creed, with the full intention of murder to be more exact.

I was to carry gold in my travels as it is as valuable in my time as it is in this. This would pay for all that I would need to assist me.

With no hope of any kind of future and only drinking myself to death with the rest of the dying breeds, I impulsively agreed. Obviously, I witnessed tests of animals transported back to this time, just to make sure there was no chance of ending up incinerated like his wife.

I sat in his machine. The smell of sulphur rising, I closed my eyes and when I opened them, I lay in a field close to the coast.

The air was clear such a freshness I had never known. My skin tingled to all new manner of feelings. A dustless sky, clear fields instead of scorched earth. It was overwhelming. Once my senses were gathered, I buried the gold that I could not carry and set out for a nearby village.

I had clothes handmade and posted the documents needed for my police deception. I took lodgings in a tavern and retrieved my gold. It now resides in a bank and I can access it via order in Hull at any time.

My only goal is to kill Creed Winters, though I must admit, accustoming myself to the times and land has proved difficult. With his advanced mind, he rarely makes an error, but I have in the meantime helped many of the officers and am proud of that fact. I am close, I can sense it, but when I am done, my mission will be over…"

The word 'over' hung in the room for what seemed like a timeless existence. Sophia did not so much as blink until finally she crumbled and began to laugh out loud. At first it was a full hearty, belly laugh which Stephen truly loved… which he would have loved, had it been any other situation than this.

After a while she finally began to simmer down and noticed Stephen's grim expression had not faltered. Her laugh turned to a chuckle then died down. "Stephen… Stephen, you can't expect me to… you don't expect me to believe that surely?"

"Sophia, I know you may not, but that is my story. I swear to you, that is my honest truth. I cannot and will not lie to you ever again. I meant what I said to you last night. I think I love you and never want to be without you."

"Stephen, even if this far-fetched time travel story is true, and you still intend to kill a man, what will you do after that? Return to the future? Do you understand how far from reality that sounds?"

Stephen hung his head. He knew exactly how it sounded. He did what he thought he could to show her the only small piece of truth he could provide.

He walked over to the cupboard of the room in deathly silence and retrieved a small metallic case with a rough surface that felt cold and heavy in his hands. He had no idea if it was the information he had revealed or if he had simply forgotten how heavy it had originally felt.

It was cube-shaped with a bright neon blue light shining from the centre of each side in a time that 'neon' did not exist.

A circle of entrancing colour burning brightly.

He placed it upon the bed.

Sophia had never seen anything so beautiful in her life. It seemed to call to her. She reached out to touch the cube and when Stephen spoke, she jumped with fright.

"This is how I get back. I press the lights in a certain way and whatever is in a six foot square around it, travels forward with me too. If you believe me or not, Sophia, I want you to be in that square with me."

CHAPTER 53

Whilst Sophia sat and stared at Stephen, unsure whether to he was about to break into laughter at any given moment, she began to feel solicitous at the notion that he was indeed mad and believed his own story.

The story of fantastic worlds in harsh, outlandish conditions. It was verbalised flawlessly and she had to give him credit in that sense.

The silence was finally broken by Stephen himself and, for that, she felt relieved as she had become lost for words.

"I can only imagine how this sounds to you. I wish I could prove the slightest aspect of it, but the truth is I can't. These are all simply words until they are actions but I had to tell you, for my own sanity more than anything. When this is all taken care of, a decision may need to be made as to our future and I want you to be at least aware of the truth."

He sensed her loss and also the slow deliberate movements she made whilst taking her tea from the night stand and drinking.

The weight felt lifted from him but it had now been replaced, knowing she might think him insane.

No more discussion would do any good for either of them so he reassured her that until the time came, it would be useless even to ponder such a far-fetched notion and he made a feeble attempt to focus on her own sudden misfortune at becoming, in a sense, nothing short of an orphan.

She talked and told him she had no idea what to do and soon enough they were engaged in conversation, however, with the past conversation still within the forefront of their minds. In a way, she could almost imagine she had dreamt the whole thing or that he had at least. And, in a fashion, she would treat it as such.

She listened as Stephen told her that he was sure soon enough the killer would make himself known.

When the opportunity came, he would slay the man in question and from there they would ride the wave of uncertainty and love combined. She liked the sound of that more than any fairy tale of time travel and mass destructive bombs.

Once he had explained the situation of the police force that he had so easily deceived, but in no way hindered, the absence of some of the detectives, the surprises from others and the general disarray within the unit, she placed her cup down and kissed him.

He returned the affectionate gesture and soon enough they were lying once more upon the bed, the intensity of what Stephen had said soon forgotten as he began to kiss down her neck, along her bare shoulders and down her body. When he reached her stomach, she asked, "And what on Earth do you think you are doing, detective?"

Before Stephen could offer a tantalising answer, he heard it…

A footstep creak outside, climbing the stairs. His face paled and he was on his feet with his gun in his hand before he heard George boom aloud, "Stop! Who goes there, friend or foe?"

Before an answer could be given, Stephen was out of the door and pointing his gun in the same direction as George.

CHAPTER 54

The stairway was dimly lit but even so, the uniform was easy to recognise.

It was Officer Brent.

He had his hands raised high and was able to see he had caused an amount of panic, but was unsure as to why. "Tis I, sir, Officer Brent, here to collect you, Detective Howes. You are to come at once, sir. Grave news."

"Well, what is it?" demanded Stephen, adrenaline coursing through his entire body.

"It's Chief Inspector Rudyard, sir, murdered in the small hours. It's… it's the work of your killer, sir."

The sentence had obviously not sunk in, Stephen demanded his next question because it was instinctively his train of thought.

"How did you get in here?"

Brent hesitated. He was not sure if he had made himself quite clear enough and thought best to make sure. "Your landlady, sir, she let me in. Did you not hear what I told you, sir?"

As he spoke, Stephen had suddenly realised exactly what the young man had said. The Chief Inspector had been murdered. The backbone of the unit and the stout man who gave the orders and praise when needed. The Artistic Killer had chosen another victim and in that very same moment Stephen swore it would be the very last.

He told Brent to remain where he stood and returned to Sophia. He sat on the bed in which she had pulled the covers up to protect her modesty, a wide-eyed expression of uncertainty on her face.

"Sophia, I need you to listen. The killer has struck again."

She nodded as she had heard it all but let him continue.

"I need to see what has happened. I have to catch this man or we may never be able to be happy and free but I don't want you to worry. I will leave a policeman to guard the front door and George will also stand sentry in case you should need anything. I promise you this, I shall be back as soon as I am able and hopefully with the good news that my mission is complete."

He kissed her quivering lips and began to ready himself. His gun was standard and the rest of his outgoing items were a matter of habit by now. He sat with her once more and could see the tears forming in her eyes.

"Stephen, you are all I have in this world now. Please, for me, be careful. I cannot lose you, not now, not ever."

She held back a sob as he told her not to worry and left the room as quickly as he could before he changed his mind and decided to flee with her there and then.

His told Brent, who had not moved an inch on the stairs were simple, to wait outside the front entrance and not to permit a soul to enter.

To George, he asked that he watch over Sophia, asking that he be a guardian over the one thing Stephen presently held dear. The pride of such a duty was evident in George.

"You need not ask, sir, God bless you, for I shall protect her with my very life, sir, God bless you. Like a guardian angel, sir, I shall make sure no harm or ill will befalls the young lady, sir, God bless you, as God is my witness, God bless you. As you have surely looked out for my life, sir, a million blessings would not be enough for what you have done for me. I shall give you peace of mind, God bless us all, sir, that she will remain in my care. I only ask in return that you catch this demon, sir, God bless you, so that we all may sleep easy in our beds, God bless you."

Before another blessing could be uttered, Stephen put his hand on George's shoulder and said before he left, "God has blessed me, George. With a true friend such as yourself."

Stephen descended the stairs and tried to put what he was leaving in the house, out of his mind, but not before informing Mrs Pritchard that she was not to answer her door to a living soul.

Once he was sure she followed his meaning, Stephen entered the street and took the carriage that had brought Brent. The compulsory check of the driver confirmed that he was not the Artistic Killer, merely a simpleton who probably knew the streets well and could manage a horse. And with that, he set off with firm intent on hunting his murderer.

CHAPTER 55

Once again, the carriage ride offered a rare kind of peace in which Stephen could gather his thoughts and assess his current situation.

He had told Sophia everything. He had felt an overwhelming urge to tell her the whole truth, not only because she had given herself to him physically but because he now felt certain that they shared the same amount of love for one another.

From all he had gathered, Stephen had only heard amongst rare occasions where true love may be possible, not everyone had the joy of feeling what he felt within the pit of his very core.

The truth was dramatic. It was simply unbelievable. He wished it was in itself a lie and that he had not had the entire weight of this unfathomable tale hanging over him from the very beginning.

When Craven Wilkinson had first told Stephen that he would be travelling back in time, he had laughed.

He soon realised it was not a joke.

Craven had shown Stephen the machine itself and for a minor demonstration he had sent a small rabbit back.

It was a fantastic show to behold and when he brought it back, he felt a little more like he was being shown a parlour trick. Like an illusion.

Over the following days, Craven explained the principles, the theory and the sheer relentless manner in which Craven and Creed had made science fiction become science fact. The idea was sound and the demonstration a success.

As he had told Sophia, Stephen's life before this final mission had been squalor, depression, drinking, wild women, wanting to forget and bleak outlooks.

The night before he was sent back to the year 1890 to capture a killer unlike any the world had seen so far, he drank and thought long and hard about his prospects.

The spiral his life had entered was much like his dreams. The dreams that had become less and less frequent but still as powerful.

Falling into certain death with no chance of survival… falling towards the water… but it struck him that he had never actually hit the water.

It was the night before the 'transportation' that he realised he had never hit the water previously because he was heading closer towards the cliffs.

The final face to join the ghost-like shapes he had placed there.

If it did not happen at the hands of another, Stephen knew that he would in all likeliness take his own life. The life that had taken so many, that had no future prospects. He imagined that perhaps if he had killed himself, his final thoughts before he slipped into the abyss would be to look out from the cliff faces. Like all the others, watch himself fall and finally slash the surface.

But that was then. Now he had something to live for. An opportunity that seemed a very real and very fortunate prospect. An itch in his mind whispered a question he knew that he already had the answer to… what would you return to your future time for? What awaits you?

The chance to start fresh in this life, this time, was something he was enjoying the thought of. Beginning anew with the one person who could make it all seem… worth something.

He allowed himself a smile at the warmth in his belly, like a well-poured measure of brandy, and relished in the possible future.

His daydreaming came to an abrupt stop however as he jolted forward with the halting of the cab. Remembering the news he had just received, Stephen readied himself for all kinds of madness. The final act in the grim tale was about to begin and he knew today it would all end.

CHAPTER 56

The scene at which Stephen arrived was a mass of chaos and carnage. The street bustled with journalists, concerned townsfolk, policemen attempting, but sadly failing to uphold the peace. Finally, leaning against the wall next to a clearly barged open door, stood Detective Raffle.

He was smoking and staring into nothingness. Stephen was admitted through the blockade.

"Is it true, Detective Raffle?"

Raffle, without turning towards Stephen, told him he had better have a look for himself.

This confirmed two things to Stephen, that it indeed was true that the Artistic Killer had claimed Rudyard as a victim and that the scene that awaited him was not for the faint-hearted.

Like wading through tar, he walked foot over reluctant foot into the two story house. The flash of crime scene photographer illuminated the innards.

In years to come, Stephen knew that nobody would be allowed to enter a crime scene until the forensic team had covered every single inch, gleaning all evidence that may have dripped, dropped or imprinted itself onto the surroundings, but by the time he had come to work his trade, after the bombs dropped, the police work was much the same as it was now. Photos, witnesses, possibly fingerprints and clues that didn't require a microscopic view.

The front door gave way to the living area. To the rear lay a door that allowed access to the stairs and, potentially, kitchen. The house was certainly not in a respectable state, but the contents indicated the lady of the house had high taste.

Along the wall of the fireplace, certain paintings hung which he did not recognise but at the same time he did not wholeheartedly dislike.

Even with the cold winter air allowed into the dwelling, the atmosphere could not produce a chill of the same magnitude to what stood in the centre of the room.

A lady of around forty-five years of age had been hung from the ceiling, a short rope from a tatty chandelier keeping her on her tiptoes. This was however quite obviously not the cause of death as the cloth that had been forced into her throat bulged from her windpipe. He eyes were in wide open shock, a moment of demonic terror frozen onto her face as quick and eternal as the photographer's next flashbulb.

The rope had been used to secure her in a standing position, her arms tied in a way to give the appearance of holding a serving tray aloft as if delivering a drink or a meal for a master, but there was no meal or refreshment.

A wide silk scarf of a variety of colours covered what lay on the tray… it did not take a peek underneath to see what she was serving.

The breeze that taunted Stephen lifted the silk enough to glimpse the severed head of Chief Inspector Rudyard. His white beard matted with blood. The lifeless eyes were enough to turn Stephen's stomach.

He did not retch, as he had nothing to offer the floor due to not having eaten for some time. He simply wished the two had not suffered before they had been placed in this macabre presentation.

The reason, he was not yet sure, but Stephen knew what this represented.

It was a recreation of paintings he had seen a long time ago in the future.

The painting had been the beheading of St John the Baptist. At the request of St John's stepdaughter, King Herod had beheaded the saint in reward for a dance and placed his head on a platter. Did this mean the killer was offering the head in exchange for his own 'dance' with Stephen, a grand finale for one of them?

The similarity to the painting was breathtaking and an admiration could be held were it not for the death of his friend and temporary boss. Stephen could only guess that the lady was Rudyard's mistress.

Stephen felt hollow at the sight. It was not the head of his friend under the scarf. It was something to observe, almost sure it had been created to capture his attention. He felt detached from the situation because wallowing in the grief would provide nothing but hindrance.

Upon a dimly-lit table near the window, lay a letter. He saw the writing and for a second didn't think it was his Artistic Killer's handwriting.

The wording was similar to all the other murders. Rantings of a madman usually written in blood but this time there was more and it itched within Stephen's mind that it had been done with purpose rather than scribbles to convince others of his insanity.

be careful what you wIsh for.
A high price Must be paid for such a high reward.
The clue sHould makE you aware for our finaL wORk of art.
let this all be finisheD, for my work iS complete.
we are Very clOse to endIng out partnership.
Calm music will Enrich my CONFESSion.
Anger shaLL play no parT in what we must
accOMplish you and mE

Stephen read the letter once, but this time the capital letters were more obvious. When they had been scrawled in blood on walls, it was assumed they were something created for the ease of the writer.

Taking out his notebook, he read through the previous bloodstained wall scribbles.

It was such an obvious statement when on paper… how had he missed it until now? Stephen began to jot down each individual capital, placing a slash where he though there should be a space:

my work mIrrors tHe gEnius of the music
soon you will AdmiRe My art, UnderStand Its creatioN
dead And unwoRthy to behold the delighTs of beethoven. now it begins"
wIth my CREATion evEn the most disGraceful beings becOme beautiful in my DesIgN of DEATH

The first:
I / HEAR / MUSIC / IN / ART

The second:
I / CREATE / GOD / IN / DEATH

And finally:
I / AM / THE / LORDS / VOICE / CONFESS / ALL / TO / ME

Clearly the words of a crazed lunatic to have such single-minded belief, or, if not that, then the words of a… priest.

CHAPTER 57

Like a demolished building, like the great bombs of the 21st century, everything clattered into a collision.

The priest had been present at Harry Keen's murder. Stephen had not seen his face as he had his back turned to him the whole time, and back then it hadn't seemed so irregular, but he remembered seeing the garb the vicar had worn, when he thought he had seen Creed Winters only yesterday the black clothing seeming familiar, but he could not place as to why… it had been one and the same.

George had talked about the arrival of the priest not months before Stephen had arrived in Hull himself. The role of priest would have been perfect cover to gain trust, to hear the sinners tell how they lived their lives and to revisit crime scenes as/was/ is often the case in this day in the age of psychopaths.

When George had told Stephen about his closeness to the new priest, he had paid it no mind but now… now he searched mentally for any information that may have been divulged. It now made sense that that was how the letter arrived so fast about Sophia. George must have told the priest in conversation, probably orchestrated purposely by the killer. It mattered little… he now knew where his target had been hiding all along, in plain sight.

There was nothing more to detect at the scene. Once again, he was striding speedily to avenge the harm upon one of his new-found friends. This time, he was avenging a death but with the knowing that this retaliation would be the prevention of a future horrific demise.

CHAPTER 58

Stephen was away from the street so swiftly and making his way to the church that he didn't hear Raffle call after him.

He was all too aware of something else calling him. Something gnawing at his core.

The crime scene had given him exactly what he needed and had more or less pointed exactly to the whereabouts of Creed. So why did something etch into his brain? Something that didn't sit equal.

Why would Creed give it all so easily? Why would he want Stephen to follow him to his lair?

It was as if he wanted Stephen in a particular place to ensure he was not somewhere else. Somewhere like his lodgings!

The clue. The actual sentence had tallied in within Creed's final letter to Stephen.

It had talked about taking Sophia away from him and the reference made to 'a high price to be paid' and his 'final work of art' was not in reference to Rudyard at all, but to her.

CHAPTER 59

From Holderness Road, Stephen knew he had to quickly make it back to his lodgings. He literally stood at a crossroads around a half a mile from where he stayed.

He began to hotfoot back towards the town centre and made a check that he had his pistol secured and his black jack to hand.

The cold was setting in with slush grey clouds whipping the sky, but the heat from his rage could have melted an iceberg.

The thought of anything happening, him being the cause of harm to Sophia, made him sprint so fast that his ears filled with a rushing wind.

There was no time for thoughts. No time for self-recrimination. What was done was done with regards to his detective work… no, he needed to protect this woman. She had only become a target because of him and he needed to kill a killer.

When he had entered the street previously and had seen George pacing, he'd had a rush of panic. Once again that feeling welled up within him as he could not see Officer Brent outside of the door where he'd been told to stand sentinel.

The door was open a little as Stephen approached and, drawing his weapon, he attempted to control his breathing.

He pushed the door and saw Officer Brent lying sprawled on the first three stairs. His mouth open and his eyes unblinking, it was clear that he was dead, his arms clutching his abdomen and blood dripping from the steps.

No doubt Creed had approached under the guise of the caring priest until it was too late for Brent to realise that Creed was in fact the killer. The lad had suffered for his own misjudgement, as well as Stephen's and for that he would forever feel guilty.

Pressing his back to the wall, whilst having his pistol pointing up the stairs, Stephen ascended.

George did not appear. It was all too much to take in. He knew he should call out to offer the attacker opportunity to open conversation. He knew he should bide his time and let the situation develop.

Instead, he rapidly reached the top. In the darkness he could make out that George's door was open, so was his own. He tracked his gun around George's room first… the place was empty. Stephen did not know if this was a good thing or not.

Slowly now he crept to his own room. A mere four feet away from door to door but the gap seemed to open up like an infinitely black hole of potential for life crippling possibilities.

His heart felt set to burst and his breathing was so laboured that any attempt at a stealthy approach was impossible.

Something stirred within the room. A figure almost crouched in the dark with its back against the wall. It was not a crouch though, the legs were spread out. It was sitting. Stephen told the figure to remain where it was or he would open fire. A short pause and then a rasping breath. "Sir… God bless you… It's me, sir… George."

Stephen, not concerned with caution, burst into the room. No lights had been lit and he had not even looked around. He grabbed George, relived that he was still alive.

"George, what happened? Are you okay?"

George smiled. A weak attempt but the faithful old fool was glad of his duty.

"I stopped him, sir… He came up and I had no idea… Practically welcomed him, sir, God bless you, but when I saw his eyes, sir… He was not Father Samuel no more, sir… He was the devil himself. We fought… fell right into this room. I couldn't fire the gun… he had hold it of it and the angle was all wrong. He pushed me back and made for your young lady, sir, God bless you. Hit her, sir. She was up and ready to help an old fool like me, sir, God bless her… but he hit her and knocked her clean out, sir. Damn his eyes, sir, the devil, I tell you…"

Stephen turned his head rapidly and true to the account, Sophia lay upon the bed. He was up and across to her faster than he knew he could move. She was breathing. She had a small cut above her eye and he checked her everywhere else. There was no other damage. His eyes flushed. The pressure behind them made Stephen feel like his head was about to explode.

She had been hurt, she had had a hand raised to her and the God that George blessed would do well to run and hide. If one were to exist, then He too would be feeling the wrath of Detective Howes.

Unequalled tension rose within. A volcano would in fact crumble if it were to challenge Stephen at this moment in time.

He made Sophia comfortable and placed a cover over her. She let out a small moan as he looked once more at her face and edged more towards demonic vengeance rather than erupting rage.

He knew the thoughts that manifested as they had done so on previous occasions, but never in this capacity. He took a cloth that had been laid to dry on the windowsill, a bottle of brandy and tried to make George as comfortable as possible. He too had obtained an abdominal stab wound but obviously being more aware of the priest's intentions, his assault had not been as fatal as poor Officer Brent's.

"He was in a rage, sir… God bless you… he didn't get what he wanted. Did I… did I… did I do good, sir?"

"George, I can never ever thank you enough. Don't worry, my friend. You will be okay. Keep pressure on this and I will get help. George? I will get the man that did this to you and make him pay for all his sins, I promise you that, my friend."

George let out a sob, holding it back and blessing Stephen once again.

A noise was heard behind Stephen. He rose in the gloom and twisted in one motion. The intruder had Stephen's hand clasped around his throat and was being pushed against the wall.

Much more pressure and the intruder's thorax would have been well and truly crushed.

Not a moment too soon, Stephen realised the person who had entered the room was in fact Detective Raffle.

Stephen released him and was forcefully shoved back, more of a defensive move rather than any intention of aggression but Detective Raffle was soon as venomous as ever.

"Howes, you fucking idiot. What are you playing at?"

Stephen apologised, took out his matches and lit candles around the room

"Detective Raffle, I am sorry. I thought you were the Artistic Killer…"

Stephen looked around the room and knew there was no time to waste.

"You remember this lady? The killer came for her and he stabbed George. I need you to get her somewhere safe and get George medical attention, can you do that? I know where he is and trust you with the people I care about most. I shall return as soon as the deed is done but I have to warn you now… the Killer will not survive this night."

Raffle looked from Sophia to George and, with the clear set mind of a man who could keep cool in difficult situations, he told Stephen to go do what he needed to do.

Stephen reassured George and told him to hold on. He thanked Raffle and glanced once more to the woman he knew he loved. He made a silent promise that this time would be the last that he would ever leave her again.

When he reached the street, the rain had started. The glorious clear day had quickly dissipated and the bad weather had come.

CHAPTER 60

From his lodgings, the run passed by in a blur, past the Waterloo Tavern, over the bridge – not even noticing the awful smell of yeast – beyond the house occupied by the Wilberforces and on to the opposite side of the road to the City Hotel. As he scarpered across the road, blind to the passing traffic, the court house to his left and postal office to his right, his footing had never been surer and his will had never been stronger.

He ran past Parliament Street, where a lifetime ago or so it seemed, he had entered a police station with a fully functioning team. A happy and well-oiled place… now it seemed like a ship drifting at sea, whose captain had been cut down and the crew, each in their own way, had been dragged to the depths.

Further and faster, he pressed on, beholding the church in all its gothic presence. The Queen's Dock to the right seemed eerily abandoned. It appeared the crowds of the streets had unknowingly cleared to allow the forthcoming duel.

He slowed and noticed just how bad the rain had become. He passed the tall, solid doors of the Empress where he had planned the heist with Raffle that gave the chance meeting of himself and Sophia.

She had been hurt and would wake afraid, but Raffle was a good man… he would help her.

His soul wanted peace, if there was indeed such a thing.

As the rain pelted his clothing, if Hell were to exist, then Stephen was about to send another evil monster to the pits of it.

The rain hammering the cobbles, bouncing back towards the heavens with the force it landed upon the streets, could not have given Stephen a more dramatic entrance than if a bolt of lightning were to crash as he swung open the large doors to the church.

His stomach knotted as he dreaded to think of how the Artistic Killer had been no more than two hundred metres from where he sat day by day, scouring file after file, detail after detail, gruesome death after gruesome death, looking for something of a hint, when he only needed a short stroll to save him the entirety of his efforts.

He imagined the once 'Creed Winters', but currently 'Father Samuel', pridefully helping the poor during the day and creating his 'Art' in the small hours of the night with that smile of all consuming self-righteousness that came so easy to most serial killers.

It was a form of camouflage to be able to manage that smile, like predators in the wild they would imitate potential victims in their movements and mannerisms.

That is exactly how killers blend so well and people in hindsight say, "I would never have believed him capable of such a thing."

The first kill of most serial killers would be through impulse. A final breaking point that resulted in something they could release from themselves and soon after that they would realise that in that moment, in some cool, controlled depth of their mind, they were in control.

The next kill would be prepared, well-managed and planned. The ability to relish in his or her own creation. Savouring it. An absorption into details which often resulted in some souvenir kept to remind them of that perfect and final moment.

To Stephen, Creed was no different to this.

His first kill was born of an outburst of potential excitement.

The souvenir had been the remains of Craven's wife that travelled back with him in the machine.

Born into this world in the blood of his first victim, already tainted with madness and genius, he was set to become the cloud of thunder to this time sheet's sunny day on such a grand scale that the potential for the sun never to be seen again was vast.

Stephen knew the odds had been stacked against him. From the moment he had taken the task of finding Creed with the intent to kill him, Creed's superior intellect had made him slicker, more careful and mindful of exactly how not to be captured.

But hiding in plain sight, present at the discoveries of his 'Art' for the majority of the time, by request of the police force itself.

This was in case the Lord had a hand to play in the damnation of those he had called back to his kingdom.

Everyone cried for Jesus to save them as the very demon that ended their life, heard the silent pleas for help knowing the devil was in his own details.

It was a new level of evil genius. An all new high and envy of serial killers that would one day be known to wander this world.

Whilst Winters continued to breathe, Stephen felt responsible and when true nature calls, guilt must take a very hushed back seat.

As the rain dripped off him, he entered the shelter of the church, gravity taking its own natural course on the water seemingly soaking into the wanton murderous bones of Stephen, and stopped to take in the area he had just encroached.

The ceilings were vast, the space between floor and roof giving the scene a chill that seemed colder than a dead man's heart with a grimness to match.

A dead space filled only with silence and a dated architecture.

All that could be heard were the drips from Stephen's coat as the door had already closed, encapsulating him into the inevitable, further towards the podium, but then his ears tuned into something else. A quiet humming that was barely audible. He knew the song. It was timeless.

Beethoven's 1810 Für Elise.

Once one of his favourites but he had a feeling after tonight it would no longer remain so.

The church was very poorly lit by a few candles at the front of the nave.

Rows of pews from front to back and a central aisle took up the floor space. The common stone walls with stained glass windows could have been one of thousands of churches up and down the country, but tonight in this one, was a murderer.

The silhouette of a man caught his attention.

Seated in the front row, he could only see the outline, but the dramatic setting laid out told Stephen that Creed had been waiting for him.

It was the backdrop he had expected from the self-obsessed Artistic Killer.

Here Creed was seated in his confines, a painting awaiting the painter to begin.

As the rain cleared from Stephen's face a little, his nose soon became aware of a smell he did not want to be smelling.

Gunpowder.

Lots and lots of gunpowder.

"Good evening, detective. I see you received and understood my correspondence?"

The humming of Beethoven had stopped and Father Samuel's words bounced from ceiling to wall and then to ear drum, breaking the soothing melody, his voice quiet, almost to the point of shyness, but direct as to leave no doubt that he should be listened to. Demanding yet meek.

Stephen knew he had to act whilst he had the chance. The pretend priest was sure of mind, so Stephen had to be sure of foot. Not wanting to startle Creed into acting impulsively and igniting the gunpowder, which could have been anywhere, Stephen began to walk carefully forward.

"A telegram would have been significantly less brutal, Creed."

"Please, detective. 'Creed Winters' was a lifetime ago, or a long time from now, whichever way you wish to perceive it, let's stick to our present titles. You being a detective and myself a priest. It seems more fitting for my… artistic view. A pew on the fifth row will suffice, I don't want you making me drop my candle and spoiling my canvas. This place is not it, but if my hand is forced, it certainly can be."

Stephen had to admire either Creed's guess or his acute senses, as the fifth row of pews was exactly how far he had reached whilst attempting not to cause too much noise while moving forward, which was made almost impossible as something was crunching beneath his feet.

The opening of his mouth was involuntary as he looked down and, in the thin glow of the candlelight, he saw what it was that was making a noise as he stepped along the cold church floor.

It was not extremely apparent where the gunpowder was hidden, as it clearly was not hidden at all. The term 'scattered' would suit its description more suitably. The walkway, from door to pew, was heavy in the dark grey flammable powder.

It had been a smart move on Creed's behalf.

Stephen could not shoot at Creed or even ruckus with him in the house of the Lord, as one single ignition and the explosion would cause tidal waves to crash the shores of China.

Stephen would have to remain as cool as he could muster for now. Even with the possibility of a fatal explosion beneath his boots, he still had Creed's demise in his heart.

"I doubt, Detective Howes, that a telegram would have had you hotfooting here so feverishly. You see, I need your mind fogged by fury. The very last thing I would want or need is for you to formulate a plan."

Creed began to chuckle, a noise that Stephen was sure that only the devil could match in its sinister nature and meaning.

"I have a feeling, Father, that tonight will be the end of one or both of us."

"Indeed, Mr Howes. I too have that feeling." This thought seemed to almost upset Creed as his voice wavered as he continued. All the while unmoving, like a statue carved of death and bones. "Does this not terrify the very core of you, detective? To learn that you may be the only one to remain on this planet that knows how the plot twists in how this world plays out? How people blindly believe that salvation awaits us in the distant future by the second coming of Christ, when, in actual fact, we cease to breed and simply fade out. Like coagulated blood left in the night only to dry and be washed away by the day's rain. We shall simply no longer 'be'. The animals once again ruling the earth and possible evolution taking its millions of years to act and create 'the destroyers' once again."

"Knowing I finished you, Creed, will be enough to help me rest easy."

"FATHER SAMUEL!" Creed yelled.

The outburst made Stephen jump. His body already charged with energy and adrenaline, the raised voice was as unexpected as the reaction from Creed over something so trivial.

"My name… is Father Samuel." His 'self-calming' breath was extremely audible and visual at this distance in the cold air. The fresh breeze of the outdoor rain now a million miles away, Creed's fogged breath hung in the candlelight, dancing to the high roof.

"What are we doing here, 'Father Samuel'? What is our next move?"

Stephen sat down. He realised the madman wanted to rant about his accomplishments and, for the time being, Stephen could do nothing but listen. His attempts to sneak up on Creed had failed and another attempt might encourage him to do something irrational.

"Soon, Stephen, I will pass through that door over there to our right. It leads to the church bell tower. You will witness my 'palette' as you follow and then… then we reach the end of the road. Our place of deciding who will live and who will die. If I reach my end then the world will be rendered dull without my creations. If you die, I will create art with everything and anyone you have grown close to during your time on this Earth. You can drift into the vacuum of death knowing that you were responsible for the torture and demise of many others. If that is not incentive enough for you to stop me, I will never understand what is."

"If I did not know better, I would have to assume you want me to stop you?"

"Perhaps. I have not truly decided yet. It will be God's choice."

Creed bowed his head as though in prayer. Up until then he had not moved an inch.

The church fell into silence.
As hushed as a domino.

CHAPTER 61

"Do you know the moment, Detective Howes, at which your life takes a different course to its original intent? The exact pinpointed split from saint to sinner? I certainly do…

I remember it quite clearly.

I have lived a great many years over you, the inhuman acts that mankind shifts onto one another are far greater in mass compared to what I have done, but my inspiration didn't come from inhumanity.

My reasoning came from beauty.

You will have, no doubt, seen the archives in our time? The libraries dedicated to ensure education continued.

During the times I was not engrossed in the science of trying to give us all a second chance with Professor Wilkinson, as though we, as a collective, thought we deserved a second chance at all, I would visit the archives and admire art.

Many many forms of art, but more directly the reputable members of the ages.

I enjoyed the more colourful painters. Being underground, I think the masses of our times would often find it to appreciate the 'sky' based artwork.

Of course, we were told we could surface once the death squads had cleared the ways but to walk once more upon the world with a tainted sky seemed a nightmare in itself from which I was unable to wake and see that it had all been a figment in the recesses of my mind.

The smog that covered the ceiling of our planet had lost all beauty and so I think that is why I preferred the artists' interpretation… the moment they were created, they were well and truly untainted.

Van Gogh was always the true artist of sky-based canvas.

The spirals mimicking the ever-rolling illumination. More than a photograph could ever capture.

Myself and Craven were confident we were close to the completion of our goal. The realisation that all this madness could soon be over excited us beyond belief.

We had been working non-stop for months, maybe more and eventually fatigue got the better of us.

One night, we decided to reconvene at a later time. I retired to my dwellings but could hardly sleep. I visited the archives and whilst looking through the paintings, knowing I could very well visit the moment they were actually painted, I noticed something.

After that, everything was different.

If the malevolent force had been lying dormant in me for years and chose then to make itself present, I did not know.

If it be fatigue and the creation that would change the world combined, I had no idea, but when the screen brought up Van Gogh's 'Olive Grove', the room filled with an angelic light, the white walls were whiter than ever and seemed to hum for me, and me alone.

Looking closer at the viewing monitor, I no longer viewed six trees and a blue yet cloud-filled sky.

No, now I saw people.

Held aloft, weary and limp. A true envisage from Dante's Inferno itself.

The closest was the most prevalent. Obvious in fact. A woman hanging by her arms viewed from behind with her head bowed forward. I asked someone close by and they could not see what I could.

I spent the next hour looking through painting after painting and within each and every one I noticed something different. Gruesome yet fantastically magnificent. I began to laugh and was asked to leave the archive but I was unable to stop myself.

I rushed to ask Craven if he had ever beheld something so astonishing but whilst making my way to his dwelling, I encountered his wife.

The tree I saw in Van Gogh's painting seemed to be 'her'. I have no idea how or why, but as she stood to greet me as pleasantly as ever, my mind wandered almost to her being one with my own personal creation. I wanted her to become a work of art.

From here on out, you will no doubt be aware of what took place.

I acted impulsively and her demise was the result.

Craven was quite rightly furious but all of this I had foreseen.

She had been murdered.

There were no two ways around that. I had purposely set the machine to present her as never before. The machine fizzed and whirled and right there, before she transformed, she was the woman in the painting, her arms held high whilst she struck the capsule which entombed her, her head bent forward as if she had given up when she knew what was to become of her.

After I had finished, I left the capsule door open and set the controls for this time.

Of course, we fought and I ended up inside the capsule. It was all part of my plan. Hoping for the same result, the widowed professor hit the switch and I arrived here not a moment later."

Stephen knew he could but only listen. Even if an army had burst through the door, there was nothing could be done to stop Creed letting out all he wanted others to hear whilst he held that candle in his hands above the floor of gunpowder.

Stephen decided to engage in the conversation.

"Why now? Why here? Why this time?"

"Excellent question, Detective Howes. One I was quite hoping you would enquire to. The reason to the 'why now'… it seems so trivial but at the time of my decision I was so engrossed in my hatred of an idea that I decided to take action…

A few nights before we were close to completion in our work, myself and Professor Wilkinson had been invited to sit with the high command of Britain Delta and dine.

We talked about things that may be possible with time travel and indeed the correct course of action to take once we had been successful. Whilst having dessert, an officer made a comment that made me grip my wine glass so hard, it shattered in my very hand.

Like the Neanderthal he represented, he blurted out, 'We'll be able to go back and find out who Jack the Ripper was…'

Of all the possibilities that presented themselves, of all the chances that could be taken, I realised that the race we were so determined to save were nothing short of halfwits.

On the forefront of this man's mind was not to set right all the ways that had damned us so willingly, to take the opportunity to advise people of our past in other courses of action but to find the identity of a hooded figure who killed four or five prostitutes.

It was simply incredulous.

I excused myself and left… perhaps this was a deciding factor also. Who can tell these things? What's done is done.

I set the machine to 1880, before Jack the Ripper's murders, and studying the possible suspects that had been hypothesised over the years within the vast amount of books written on the subject, I eliminated each and every possibility to the best of my ability.

There was a mention of an American, but he was not to enter England for a few years.

The four I killed did not die in any grotesque manner of course. I did not want to rouse suspicion.

This is quite easily done when one is a stranger in a city but with the suspects gone, I am to guess the murders simply never had chance to take place."

Stephen thought to point out that what was mentioned in jest during a dinner party, hardly seemed reason enough to travel to a different time and murder people who may or may not have been or become a psychopathic killer, however he suspected that Creed's mind was not as rational as it was intellectual.

"Can I ask you something, Detective Howes?"

Stephen felt to ask if there was any choice in the matter but simply answered, "Yes."

"Are you a religious man?"

"No."

"May I ask why not?"

"Because I have seen enough to realise that if someone out there loved all his creatures and creations, he would not treat them in such a way to cause this much pain and sorrow. Please don't flatter yourself, Father Samuel, I arrived at this conclusion well before we ever crossed paths."

Creed did not answer. He only looked up at the crucified figure of Jesus upon the far wall. The hands held to the cross by nails, a crown of thorns on his head.

"It seems we disagree once more. Actually on many things I imagine, but on the divine I think we share very different opinions. Do you know what I think? I think we are all gods…

Each and every one of us. I listen to the confessions of the wretches that scatter these streets and as pitiful as they are, they are one and all gods in themselves.

What are we told of God?

We were created in his image?

We are all our own image, are we not?

Therefore, we are god-like in the physical sense.

What else?

That God is all knowing?

If we know nothing more, then what else is there to know?

When we discover something as minuscule or grand as it may seem, then we know more and thus knowing more than we ever did. If we do not know 'something', then how could it be anything?

We are told he is infinite. When you watch someone die up close, as I am sure you have, then is that not their own infinity carrying on forever more? The life they know, with its dreams and aspirations and pitiful meaninglessness, comes to a halt but spreads infinity.

It's my belief that God is in each and every one of us. We die and there is no more universe. What is more great and powerful than this?"

Stephen decided to answer, not with intentional bluntness. "And is that what you are, Father Samuel? A 'god killer'? A man who is divine, as long as he exists and ends existence for others?"

"Hmm, you know, Detective Howes, I am unsure myself."

Creed seemed to ponder on every word that Stephen said and perhaps conflicted, not knowing a definitive answer, he spoke softly, "If tonight my journey ends and all fades to black then I guess I shall have my answer."

"Can I ask you a question?" As no objection was to be heard, Stephen continued, "You know how damned this future is? You know we are all set to simply evaporate. It's quite evident you are mad, but why not try and create or invent something that could save us all. Something that will stop us making the same mistake?"

"Forgive my rudeness, detective, but on a grand scale, your dense mentality never ceases to amaze me. Create something more for this world? Any form of advancement in technology would simply rush these fools into self-obliteration sooner rather than later. The sooner you yourself realise that we are heading for damnation and nothing else, the sooner you will feel more free to actually live. Try not to rush as you follow. I still have the candle, remember? I shall see you shortly."

And with not another word, his black-clad frame arose and walked almost ghost-like towards the previously mentioned exit to his right and closed the door behind him.

After everything, the two men shared little words.

There was nothing more that needed to be spoken.

Stephen had been ashamed in his lack of progress in getting closer to killing Creed.

In fact, it was only when the killer had finally decided to give himself away that Stephen had known where to find him.

Not only had he not located the killer on his own merit, but on many occasion, he had stood mere feet away from him.

Each time, Creed had taken care to not let his face be shown, but Stephen had heard of the 'detective's undoing'. These words were spoken to him one night, a long time from now, and under the influence of alcohol. “In your most askew moment on an unsolvable case, the time will come when you realise the key had been directly under your nose the whole time…”

It seemed odd that he would remember the words of his old mentor, Melton Johnson, as that was the beginning of his very first case, as a detective, when he had decided to give up the life of the location squad, or ‘death squad’ as Creed had referred to them.

Melton had been all wise and all knowing. He had taught many a lesson to Stephen, but it seemed not enough, as to date, the Artistic Killer had gotten away with many a murder.

Stephen contemplated firing on Creed as he walked away but he knew there was no bluff to his words. The gunpowder was Creed’s insurance.

Stephen made his way cautiously to the very same door and turned a handle that seemed to have the weight of the world upon its latch.

CHAPTER 62

The room he entered was simply a corridor. A smell that had not being noticeable until he closed the door behind him made Stephen raise his sleeve to his nose.

He knew the smell but didn't know the location. Dead things gave a very distinct aroma. From animals to people, it was always the same.

It had a universal ability to remain a nauseating odour.

He opened a second door and what he observed caused Detective Stephen Howes to stagger back.

The room was littered, scattered and drenched in gore.

Limbs, torsos, clothing and blood scattered in all directions.

Creed Winters had mentioned his 'palette' only moments before but Stephen had had no idea that this was what he'd meant.

The head of a man lay on its side feet away from Stephen. It was clear he had the well-worn features of a lower class drunk before the beheading had taken place.

The arm and upper body of a lady lay strewn upon a table and on the far wall hung a leg, mutilated and severed above the thigh.

Blood was high and low, slippery on the floor and coagulated on the ceiling. Stone walks with blood and very little light gave a red shimmer. The room seemed to reverberate. Torture and suffering had been carried out here.

Stephen had to walk through destruction that looked like a grenade had torn its way through a crowd.

He did not focus on anything, apart from the only other exit. His boots stuck fast with each step and made a wet squelching noise as he lifted them. Bile rose in his throat at the smell but still he moved forward.

As he stepped a little to the side to swing open the oak door to get out of this circle of hell, he was snapped out of his shock-induced haze to see he had stepped on a hand, too small to be an adult's but now no longer attached to anything at all.

Had this been a practice room for Creed Winters?

He was aware that somethings cannot be 'unseen' but they can be avenged. He closed the door behind him and climbed the large stone steps to the top of the church tower.

CHAPTER 63

The rain had made the last few steps slippery, the hatch had recently been opened and Stephen had no idea what waited for him on the other side. He wanted to be out in the rain to clean the previous room off himself. He felt clogged and sticky even though he had touched very little in there.

He had the hammer pulled back on his pistol and swung the hatch open rapidly. With a heavy thud, it clattered behind him. The wind stung his eyes and he turned to see Creed bracing himself in a corner of the tower, standing on top of the waist-high wall.

After everything that had happened from the beginning of his adventure, this was the first time Stephen had seen Creed Winters whole.

He was certainly not a weak man. For an older gentleman, he had the physicality to overpower people yet the demeanour to render them defenceless with kind words.

A perfect killer.

It seemed that now the only victim he was intent on killing, was himself. A rope around his neck stretched across the floor and had been tied to another column in the tower. With no bargaining chip to stop him from killing his target, Stephen raised his gun.

In the howling wind, Creed spoke loud enough for Stephen to hear. "And so it ends, detective. What an artist the world is losing now."

Creed leant back and in that moment, Stephen fired his pistol.

The bullet missed Creed.

But, by pure chance, it did hit the rope a foot above from Creed's neck.

Creed plummeted over the edge.

Everything slowed down to a speed that allowed the raindrops to be admired.

Stephen, as quickly off the mark as a gazelle, raced to the edge to see the rope pull tight then snap where the bullet had weakened it. Creed bounced from the diagonally slated roof and onto the grass with a heavy wet thud. For moments he remained motionless. Rain covering him as the earth should have done a long time ago.

Stephen looked through squinted eyes to see that Creed had landed in a small graveyard.

Not wanting to re-enter the killing room below, Stephen took hold of the sturdy rope and began to climb down the side of the church. When he manoeuvred over the ledge, he instantly regretted the idea, but he had gone too far now to turn back.

When he reached the slated roof, he slid to the edge and made a single storey jump onto the grass, landing merely feet away from the body of Creed Winters.

Standing tall, he took two steps and pushed the body over using his foot and, to his amazement, Creed lived.

There would be no telling how long for, but rasping breath left his body and choking, water-filled breathing attempts were made to continue the cycle of the circulatory system.

Creed cursed barely coherent words. Blood ran from his nose but was diluted by rain before it hit the ground. Steam rose from his body and vengeance shot from his eyes. As he began to choke a little in the last moments of his life, Stephen pulled his gun and angled it at Creed's forehead.

"Professor, these are the last words you will hear so I won't waste them. For all your dramatic fair, for your time travel, your theories and your need to achieve greatness, your death still comes like that of a dog in the street. Pathetic and final."

The shot in the night rang out in time with the lightning.

CHAPTER 64

When Raffle arrived, Stephen stood over Creed's corpse, soaked to the bone. He'd not moved since putting a bullet between the eyes of the demonic Creed Winters.

Nothing particular passed through his mind, only the savouring of the end of the man who had the power to take everything from him.

Raffle took the gun from Stephen and this finally brought him from his trance-like state.

"Howes? Is this the Killer?"

Stephen nodded.

"I don't feel like answering questions too much to a higher power, so how about we clean this up, eh?" Raffle almost had to shout over the rain to be heard. But he saw that Stephen was fully functional once more.

Together they picked the up the body and Stephen led the way back inside the church, giving a stern warning to not drop any flame on the floor to Raffle and, at the scent of what he dreaded to be gunpowder, Raffle instantly knew why.

Creed was dropped heavily at the base of the cross of the crucified Jesus. Stephen located the barrel that had been used to distribute the gunpowder and knew what had to be done.

He told Raffle the plan and although sceptical, he agreed.

Stephen told him about the room at the back of the church and that no one should have to witness the horrors that lay within.

They ran a line of gunpowder out past the arch of the main entrance and tried to keep it running sheltered for as long as possible. When they reached the end of the supply, it was clear that enough distance was between them and the impending destruction.

Before Stephen lit the matches, Raffle stopped him.

"What happens after this?"

Stephen thought for a while before he answered. "I'm going to collect Sophia and leave this place. I have money to set us up far away. I think after all of this, we both deserve a clean break. Unless you have any objections, detective?"

With a sly grin, Detective Raffle shouted over the white noise rain. "Just light the match and make sure you write to me once in a while."

EPILOGUE

Raffle walked into the office sweating from the July sun. The walks into work had certainly seemed a lot more enjoyable recently and he was not sure if it was all weather related. He was about to be a grandfather and his promotion to Chief Inspector meant he no longer had to steal to increase his monthly income.

He walked past the desk of Detective Napier, pushing his feet off the desk. "Dave, you're back on thin ice. Don't push it, eh?"

The manic laugh from Napier was audible throughout the office and although most wouldn't admit it, they were glad to see the detective back and in high spirits.

The newly-appointed Detective Matchett stood to attention out of habit from his army days as he tidied his desk, the one that had previously been manned by the talented Detective Stephen Howes.

Raffle gave an, "At ease, soldier," as he did almost every morning.

There was no standing salute from Ford as his stitches still hurt, although he was safely on the way to recovery.

Flint's desk remained clear and O'Connell followed Chief Inspector Raffle into his office at the rear of the building with some trivial matter. Before he could get into full flow, Raffle stopped O'Connell in his tracks and asked him if it could wait.

Upon Raffle's desk sat a letter addressed directly to him. He recognised the handwriting and wanted time to read it through before updating his squad.

He used his letter opener inscribed, 'In memory of Chief Inspector Rudyard, a leader of men,' and took the letter from the envelope.

Dear Chief Inspector Raffle,

The news of your promotion reached me several days before I penned this letter and I cannot tell you how happy I am for you.

I hope everyone else is fine and if you chose to tell them about this letter, then I hope you will pass on my fondest regards to them all.

Leaving in a hurry, as we did, left me with a great deal of sadness. In all my years, I have never known such a good group of men. Even Flint, with his treacherous ways, was still a good man. I know he will have had his reasons, as do we all.

I do hope to keep in touch as frequently as possible but I wanted to tell you as many details as far as I feel I can divulge to you. I feel after all we have been though, that much is deserved.

I was hired to kill Creed Winters and I was not part of a special branch.

This deception was essential to help in the assistance of catching the now popular yet 'still at large' Artistic Killer. And I do hope you do not hold this against me.

I am sure you are relieved to hear of no further crimes committed by the Killer as I am sure the explosion at the church will have taken up too much of your time as a detective…

Myself and Sophia married last month. The wedding was small but we decided that since we had nobody close with regards family and were only new to St Louis, we were happy to just have each other.

She has taken rather well to the high life, as I was certain she would, and has taken to taunting these Americans to no end. It appears they truly do not appreciate a good joke when they hear one.

Soon enough, I will write again and will attach a return address.

My best to you and your family, and please thank your wife for taking care of Sophia… she too passes her best wishes.

Regards

Stephen LaFarge

(Not my choice)

Raffle placed the letter into his desk drawer and decided he would not share the news just yet.

He sat back and smiled, safe in the knowledge that his friend had made a brand new start.

He took out a bottle of brandy and in the rarest of occasions poured himself a small amount before toasting the deceptive detective… Stephen Howes.

•

George pulled his chair to the table, making a scraping noise to the obvious annoyance of Mrs Prichard.

She scowled as she dropped his plate in front of him.

He knew she had an exterior that radiated annoyance at the smallest of issues, but since he had returned from the hospital, she had cared for him more than any woman would if she was constantly that annoyed.

She sat with George and together they ate in companiable silence.

After a while she asked him if he had had any luck with finding a job.

He said he had not and wondered if she had concerns because of the rent.

"You don't need to worry about that, you silly old goat. I just don't want you laying around all day. Mr Howes has paid you up for more then you should ever need. I have been meaning to ask you about that anyway… when will you clean out his room? You can't wait for ever for him to return."

George had not told his landlady about the letter he had received from Stephen. He had thanked George more than he ever thought necessary and told him if he ever wanted to travel then he should meet him and his new wife in St Louis.

George appreciated the offer, but knew Hull was his home. He was glad to see Stephen safe and well and had decided that very day he would clean out Stephen's old abode.

Whilst going through the drinking cupboard, George checked Mrs Pritchard was not lurking behind him and took several quick slugs of brandy.

He continued further into the cupboard and was shocked by a bright blue glow from beneath some clothing.

Taking out a cube, he felt it pulsing beneath his fingers. He sat on the bed and drank some more.

Whilst pressing the buttons and amusing himself with the funny little noises the box made, he pressed them in a combination that made a little tune he liked. When he heard a click and the lights became brighter, in his state of intoxication George threw the box to the floor a yard or two from him.

The noise from the cube grew louder. The lights got brighter and when it sounded like the intensity could not reach any louder, they simultaneously stopped.

A tiny ghost appeared above the cube which terrified George to the core. He ran from the room screaming in terror.

It was not a ghost at all. The small figure above the cube was that of Craven Wilkinson. Or rather a hologram of Craven Wilkinson but, of course, George had no way of knowing this. The image shimmered and spoke.

"Stephen, if you are hearing this then I am to assume your mission was a success and Creed has suffered at your hands. For this, I cannot tell you how grateful I am. You will be rewarded beyond your needs but I have some very bad news to deliver. If you are not sitting, I suggest you do so now.

I… I have no way to put this easily so I will come out and say it. There is no way to return you to our time.

I know I said I could make it happen, and the guilt is overwhelming, but not as overwhelming as it would have been if I had let that madman run wild. I knew this from the outset. The rabbit I sent back in our demonstrations was indeed sent back but the one I retrieved was its brother.

I had to do this to convince you, and I would not be able to live with myself if I did not resolve my guilt by knowing that where you are now offers far more possibilities.

A life with money and future knowledge gives you more opportunity than you would ever have here, in this dammed and desolate future.

I did not lie about the 'separate sheets' time scenario. Nothing you do will affect how I live this future but my advice to you, if you can bring yourself to take it, would be this, live your life well. We are here for the smallest amount of time, whichever time we reside in… have children and teach them to love, but, most of all, live it well."

The hologram faded and was no more, the lights on the cube extinguished and somewhere else on the planet Stephen Howes was indeed living well.

ACKNOWLEDGEMENTS

Hull is a marmite kind of place… it gets a bad reputation but I grew up there, predominantly on the east side and to see the changes it's gone through has been drastic. Some not always for the best. Its heritage used to be on the cobbles and from the ground up, now it's spraypainted on the walls and you are told to 'look up' at the building to try and catch a glimpse.

The pubs we would drink in were naturally decorated in what's now known as 'vintage'.

I don't think it was because it was behind the times, just because something fits and it's useful, why upgrade?

Anyway, the reason for featuring so much of it in the book (don't worry, if you're not from around there, it won't spoil it) was to try and capture some of that history, some of its old atmosphere so it can be fondly remembered and not leave a bad taste… like marmite.

This book has been a long time coming, about seven years in fact. Maybe more.

I've been through massive life changes since it started and travelled to some strange places to collate and incorporate stories.

Step by step and piece by piece, it's all come together into something I hope you enjoyed.

From sitting in a darkened room, listening to the classical music mentioned, I typed away until finally something that resembled a story made its way into what you hold in your hands

But it's been a labour of love… getting ideas while spending a lost weekend or two in Amsterdam, from people I met there, or moulding actual events and making them sound almost fictional.

Some characters are based on a person or various people closer to home. A book could be written on the writing of this book in itself.

I'd like to thank all the people that listened to me talk about this book with excitement, even all those years ago when it just seemed an idea more than a physical possibility.

I'd like to thank Big Jon for enduring the pub crawl of all the bars mentioned in the book, whilst dressed in 1890's finery… it took courage, valour and hollow legs.

I'd like to thank Mick for introducing me to my publishers, and I'd like to thank my publishers for the encouragement and patience of having to sift through my unconfirmed dyslexia.

I'd like to thank the future TV company that reads the book and says, "This WOULD make a great series, let's contact the writer because we DO need more books set in the North of England."

I would like to thank everyone who ever played a part in this coming together, too many to mention because even as things changed and adapted throughout the years, you played a part, no matter how small or large.

But I'd like to place special thanks to all of my family, especially my dad for his continued support in the only way he knows how.

And finally, I want to dedicate this to Darcie… if this book is my darkness, then you are my light.